THE PLAZA OF ILLUSION

THE PLAZA OF ILLUSION

MARSHALL APPOH

THE PLAZA OF ILLUSION

For my children, Okore and Densua

Thanks to all my friends for their encouragement. And special thanks to Jeremy Baty, Steve Redwood, David Burton, Nuria Izquierdo, and Sean Moores for their guidance and support.

Contents

Chapter 1
(*Trying to leave*)

Osam was six when he lost both parents in a tragic traffic accident. His father's younger brother, uncle Kojo, whom he loved very much, ploughed his living on his cocoa plantation in one of the jungles in Ghana. Kojo thought Osam, a bright boy, would be better off staying in Accra, as he could get the best education in the capital, so he stayed with his aunt, Ekua Mensah, and her husband, Mr Duodu.
Aunt Ekua was a housewife while Mr Duodu taught at Osam's local primary school. They always saw Osam as getting in their way, and he was made to feel like a stranger in his own home.

The couple had two boys; Kofi and Kwame. The former was of the same age group as Osam, while the latter was two years younger. Even though he attended the same school as they did, Osam never got on with his two cousins. They had countless squabbles and fights. Unfortunately for Osam, he almost always lost as the two brothers sometimes ganged up on him. And there were many occasions when he got a good hiding from them while their parents looked the other way. Their only advice to Osam was for him to learn to stand up for himself. But he couldn't hit his cousins back, as he knew that, despite what their parents said, they would make him pay for it later when they got wind of it.
Osam's aunt called him a thief and treated him like a servant. Anytime money went missing at home, he was blamed for it, though he wondered where his cousins got the extra money to spend at school. He had to do all the dirty work while his two cousins went out to play with their friends or watched TV

nearby in one of the neighbours' compound. Mr Kay always brought his big black and white television out into his compound for the numerous local kids to watch their favourite programmes like *Osofo Dadzie*, a Sunday night drama, and the *Hawaii Five-0* series. Some nights, he even offered their favourite sweet, *Black and White,* to those kids who behaved well.

There were times when Osam felt so tired after the day's hard work at school that at home all he wanted to do was have an early night. But he had to wait for his cousins to return home with his small, old, thin mat they sat on to watch TV before he could lay it down in the mosquito-infested sitting room, which was where he had to sleep. Unlike him, his cousins slept in a comfortable bed with a mattress in their parents' bedroom.

Uncle Kojo, who seldom visited him, always thought it was a kind of revenge on his sister's part, as she had never got on well with Osam's late father.

Kojo lived on his plantations near Sefwi, in the Western Region. These farmers made a lot of money though they spent little on themselves. The farmland was near a forest reserve so they habitually received visits from elephants and other wild forest animals. The lands there were mostly cocoa plantations. Even though Uncle Kojo was well-off, his village had neither electricity nor telecommunications. He used to say he could only ring when he went to the nearest town, Meko, about ten kilometres away. This town had all the amenities, including a post office which housed a single telephone from which the people rang. It also had a rural bank, shops and, of course, electricity. Kojo said he used a generator on his farmhouse only from nightfall to midnight as fuel was expensive in that part of the country. Using the generator, he claimed, also helped to ward off wild animals from his farmhouse.

Luckily for Osam, while his two cousins failed, he passed with distinction the much-coveted Common Entrance Examination, and gained admission to his first choice school, the prestigious Achimota Secondary. Unfortunately for him, his aunt claimed it was too expensive and instead sent him to live with his grandparents in Cape Coast where he gained admission to the equally reputable Adisadel College. That was the last he saw of his aunt's family and home, as he opted to stay with his grandparents in Cape Coast instead of returning home to Accra during school holidays.

Even though Osam felt the hurt and pain of these vengeful acts, he also saw the positive side as it helped him to work even harder academically. He also learned to depend on himself-early in life, and that helped him to develop drive and self-belief. After all, where were his two cousins now? Because they were indulged too much, they became spoilt and later became drug addicts. To make matters worse, they never stopped terrorising their parents until their premature deaths from cocaine overdose.

At the weekends, Osam helped his grandmother with her iced-water and bread sales. They were considered feminine jobs, so people laughed as he went from house to house, unwilling and uncomfortable, shouting the famous sales line, *Paanoo hyew!* (*Hot bread!*)
He did his best to avoid meeting schoolmates during his rounds.
Some of his classmates couldn't understand why he didn't tell his grandparents that he was now at secondary school, and thus selling bread was a demeaning thing to do, particularly for a 14-year-old boy. He hated doing it, but he had no choice.

Osam returned to Accra after he had passed with distinction the WAEC GCE O Level examination. He decided to do Physics, Mathematics, Chemistry and the General paper at A level.

Two years later, he passed these exams at PRESEC, one of the prestigious all-boys full boarding schools located in Legon, a suburb of Accra. That is where he met Richard. They were in the same Science course class and hall of residence.
Osam had arrived late for his first Chemistry practical class. The lab was full, except for an empty stool at the middle front table. Richard was the only person occupying that long table, so Osam joined him. This was the beginning of a long acquaintance and friendship.

Osam's grades were good enough for entrance into one of the three state universities, but he turned down the chance to accomplish his childhood dream of becoming an engineer. Instead, he worked on plans to travel to Western Europe or the US during his compulsory one-year pre-university National Service programme. He felt he would be better off there, rather than struggling through the tough university system only to end up in a low-paid job in Accra.

At the end of their compulsory national service programme, Richard proceeded to study at a university in Lagos, in Nigeria. Although his parents lived in the Ghanaian capital, his father was Nigerian-born, and for Richard, it was an opportunity to return to his homeland. He and Osam would not see each other again for almost a year.

Osam got a job as a part-time amateur actor at one of the theatre groups in Accra. He had never acted on stage before, but he became interested after watching the group's performance with a friend at the Accra Arts Centre. Although he was good at it, he didn't allow that to distract him from his ultimate goal of leaving the country.

One such attempt had taken him in a car across the borders of Togo, Benin, Nigeria, Cameroon, Gabon, Morocco and finally to the borders of Melilla, only to be repatriated to Morocco by the Spanish immigration authorities. The visa stamped in his passport turned out to be fake. Somehow, he was able to retrace his way back to Accra - but not without a perilous struggle for twenty-seven days.

Almost a year later, not having learned his lesson well, Osam decided to undertake another risky adventure to Spain. He was the type who refused to play the "what if" game of life with the cards of fear, insecurity, doubt or weakness.

Osam was introduced to one Mr Hamburger by Steve, a friend of Richard's. Steve claimed to know Mr Hamburger well and also knew of many people he had assisted to go to the West. Steve said that he wasn't particularly interested in travelling to the West so hadn't asked for help. Osam knew it was a lie as he was a fellow struggler. Almost every Ghanaian young man would jump at that opportunity if it came along.

Mr Hamburger was in his late forties, and from the same Akan ethnic group as Osam. He told Osam the costs involved in travelling to various places in Western Europe. The cheapest was Spain. For 3000 US dollars, he could take him to Spain. From there he assured him it was easy to move on to England, Germany or France - whichever he preferred.

Osam had lost all his money in the previous failed attempt, so he decided to discuss his *latest* plan with Mona, his current girlfriend, at their weekly hole-and-corner rendezvous. Osam wanted her to request help from her rich parents to finance his latest adventure into Europe.

Mona's father was a Supreme Court Judge, and her mother the Manager of Barclays Bank head office in the centre of Accra.

Osam was never one to be considered *faithful* when it came to romantic relationships. His part-time job as an actor on television and stage for two years had brought him into contact with lots of adoring ladies, and he sure took advantage of them whenever he got the opportunity. He always played safe and kept his heart out of it.

Mona was a third-year law student at the University of Ghana in Accra. She was his fifth-*serious* girlfriend in less than two years. She was 'the one', he had told his friends when she fell for him after one of his brilliant theatre performances at the Accra Arts Centre. She lived in the up-market residential Airport area of Accra. She fitted his idea of the *ideal* woman: tall, fair in complexion, and of course, with a big, round, wriggly bottom.

Osam could not contain his joy as the old *bone shaker* vehicle made its way towards the exclusive area of Accra. Only three classes of people lived here: diplomats, some of Accra's rich and famous, and the domestic workers.

He got off at his usual stop and waited for Mona. Her parents were so strict that he had visited their home just once when they had been away at a funeral. Therefore, he met her at this quiet bus stop about four hundred metres from her parents' two-storey mansion home.
Osam put on his best smile as she appeared in the distance. Even from about two hundred metres, the full glorious black beauty figure of Mona was evident to see. Some of the vehicles tooted their horns as they sped past her voluptuous, curvaceous shape. She had warned him against meeting her there as someone in a passing vehicle might spot them. So, with his back towards the busy road, he waited patiently, taking a quick glance once in a while in her direction. When she was a hop, skip and jump away, he walked to the safety of their favourite, abandoned small shed, away from any prying eyes.

'You've been through this before, Osam,' Mona said as he whispered in her left ear. She had trimmed her already short hair and looked like a typical young Ashanti girl who had just undergone her rite of passage.

'I know. But this time, it's for real, Mona—'

'How do you know? You had the same belief just a few months ago and see what happened—'

'Because…because I can feel it. Look, this man has helped many people. I'm just coming from meeting him to thrash things out. You know I don't trust these *connection men*, but I got positive vibes from this guy.'

'I still think it's too soon to make such an important decision. Why don't you let the dust settle on your last adventure?'

'No, no, no! That's history now. We've got to look forward, Mona. Adversities are opportunities in disguise. Life's for living, not hurting,' Osam replied passionately.

Mona laid her right hand on his lap. 'I admire this enthusiasm and positive mental attitude of yours. That's why I love you so much. But, I think you're too trusting and naive sometimes.'

'What?'

'Osam, they nearly killed you out there. And you nearly died during your jungle trek home. You were beyond recognition. You still have the emotional scars. Are you telling me all of that hasn't served as an object lesson for you?'

'What utter nonsense, Mona! Thanks for the lecture and for bringing up something that you promised never to mention.'

'Osam, you had to hide for weeks from the constant glare and gape of people until you recovered bodily.'

'Stop it, Mona!'

'And in any case, I doubt if my parents will fork out that kind of money to help someone they don't even know. I need to introduce you to them first.'

'Well, you've been saying this for almost a year now, but—'

'Cuz it's not the right time, Osam.'

'Look, tell them I promise to work hard, pay them back every penny, and let you join me in Spain, Germany or England - wherever I find myself.'

'Listen to you; you don't even know where you're going.' She looked away, shaking her head.

'Why, do you doubt me, or what?'

'No. Far from that, Osam. I believe in you. No one's made me feel so special - not even my parents. But the truth of the matter is, they won't fork out that kind of money to someone they don't even know.'

'But I'm your boyfriend!'

'I know, but they don't know that, do they?'

'There you go again with your negative mental attitude. Whose side are you on anyway?'

'I'm not—'

'Yeah, it's like you're unhappy for me—'

'That's not true, Osam, and you know that!' Mona pleaded. She was in tears.

'I've loved and cherished you. And now that I need a bit of support you've suddenly turned into a brick wall. Don't even bother, girl! I'll get the help from somewhere else.' He sprang to his feet and shot off.

'Come back, Osam. Please, come back!' she pleaded.

He skipped across the busy road and walked towards the airport.

It happened like an arrow from a bow, and would be the last time they saw each other.

Osam sent a telegram to his uncle, telling him about his plans to travel abroad, and asking for help. He agreed.

Chapter 2
(Hamburger's home)

Osam knew he was travelling with three other people, but had only expected to meet them on the morning of the trip. At their last meeting, where Osam paid Mr Hamburger the full 3000 dollars, he was told to carry only one small piece of luggage for the trip. This was to make the immigration authorities in Europe less suspicious that he was there to stay indefinitely. Osam was only going as a tourist for a week's holiday.

He arrived bang on time at Mr Hamburger's house in spite of the heavy traffic resulting from the late June morning sub-tropical downpour. Some of the poorer roads in Accra deteriorated when it rained. Not only were there long transportation queues as a result, but the vehicles travelled slowly in the rain-filled and sometimes pot-holed roads. Osam could recall countless occasions when he was splashed with muddy water while walking along the road on a rainy day.

He was the first to arrive at Mr Hamburger's fortified house in East Legon, one of the exclusive areas on the outskirts of Accra. It was his first visit, as their two previous meetings had taken place at different exclusive bars in Accra's city centre.

He rang the gate bell.

'Who is it?' came the already familiar croaky voice of Mr Hamburger.

'It's me, Osam, sir,' he replied in a shaky voice, nervous at his first time speaking through such a device.

'Wait a moment, Osam.' He heard a clicking at the other end.

In less than a minute, he heard approaching footsteps from behind the five-metre-high fortified wall and black cast iron metal gate, with protruding metal spikes at the top.

'You're punctual, Osam,' Mr Hamburger said as he opened the gate.

'You said 9 O'clock. I don't play with people's time. I always arrive in time for an appointment, sir.'

His host was bald and was about a metre and fifty centimetres tall. His large potbelly augmented his huge stocky frame. Osam followed him through the gate and was motioned inside. He entered a large house with an equally large, lawned front garden, which was about 30m long by 10m wide. The marbled house and the sliding feel of the terrazzo floor, as he walked towards the entrance door, spelt luxury and grandeur. The high perimeter walls were all painted white. As they walked towards the house, he noticed for the first time in three meetings how short Mr Hamburger was.

Osam was ushered into a large mirrored living room that was divided into two parts. It was impossible to see the other part due to the huge oak-like, highly polished furniture that served as a room divider. It was impressive, however, to see yourself on all three walls. Osam perceived he lived alone as there was no indication of other people at home. As he took in with measured envy the magnificence of the sitting room, he could hear Barry White's *Satin Soul* playing in the background. He wasn't a fan but pretended to like it by nodding to the unobtrusive soul beat.

'If you work hard when you get to Europe, you could even build something better than this,' Mr Hamburger said, as he motioned him to have a seat.

'You think so?' Osam said with a broad grin.

'I wouldn't say so if I thought otherwise.'

'So, how many years do you think it would take one to build a large mansion like this?' Osam asked, excited.

'It depends on you, depends on what you want in life. There are some people who, when they get to Europe, are so happy with how easy they get money that all they do is enjoy themselves. Others save up and send money home to undertake projects or, better still, return home and start up their own business like I did. I've noticed from our three meetings how *European-minded* you are. You've got a focused attitude and are serious regarding time. These are important ingredients for success.'

'It's amazing you said that because all my friends call me *Obroni,* because of my attitude towards time. I've never come to terms with the Ghanaian psyche. I've never accepted the popular *European time* and *Ghanaian time* expression.'

'It's always a flimsy excuse to give whenever you're late for an appointment or meeting, isn't it?

Osam nodded. 'I think so. It's like, society sees it as *normal* to be late. One of my friends always says: *It's what is achieved within a particular space of time that matters.'*

'But, I think this concept is gradually changing as a result of Western influences. It's like the notion of the superiority of the white man. It'll take a long time to unlearn that belief, just as it took a long time for it to take root in people's consciousness,' Mr Hamburger lectured on.

'Maybe you're right,' Osam responded. He dared not disagree nor argue with someone who would soon help him out of his misery. The man seemed to have a smooth tongue, perhaps to compensate for his lack of height.

'Is it true that white women love Ghanaian men because they are very good in bed?' Osam asked, changing the subject. They both laughed.

'Black power, huh?' Mr Hamburger said. He walked to the refrigerator in the right-hand corner of the first hall, took out a bottle of Coke, and offered it to Osam.

'Thanks,' the latter said as he took the icy-cold drink. He wondered what he had said that merited such a reward. Ghanaians usually offered the customary glass of water to strangers in their homes. Only close friends and important people deserved something extra like soft drinks, juice or alcoholic beverages.

'Feel at home, Osam. I'm just dashing to the toilet.'

'OK, sir,' he responded in his usual formal way.

He had been brought up the old Ghanaian way. One had to talk and respond formally with one's hands clasped behind one's back. It was considered impolite to look an older person straight in the eye when you were spoken to. The custom was to look downwards. *Respect your elders and you will go places*, his strict aunt used to say. It was a shame that she couldn't, or perhaps deliberately didn't, impart the same knowledge to her children.

While he was alone, Osam stood and examined himself in the mirrored walls. He was still vain, 184 metres tall and 78kgs in weight. He wished he was more muscular. That would improve his physique to guarantee a manlier look. He always admired his fair-complexioned skin as that was one of the attractions for Ghanaian females. They had still not relinquished their preference for fair skin. His long but curly black hair was deliberately lightly combed to try to give himself the rough look he always lacked. He suffered so much in Morocco because he had looked too gentle. Even at almost six metres from the nearest mirror, he could see the rough marks on his lips from years of constant lip biting.

The gate bell rang just as Mr Hamburger returned from the toilet with a black plastic comb.

'Please comb your hair properly.'

'Oh, I thought I did—'

'You don't want to give foreign immigration officers any excuse to suspect you. Don't worry, comb it here,' Mr Hamburger said, observing Osam's uneasiness at doing it in the sitting room.

He left Osam but returned momentarily with three young men. They had arrived half-an-hour late. Osam could not comprehend that someone from a poor Ghanaian society would part with as much as $3000 and still be late for their trip to a *better* life.

Osam didn't think Mr Hamburger was in the least bothered by the fact that the others arrived late, as they were all laughing when they entered the living room.

'I hear the traffic is very bad today,' Mr Hamburger said as if apologising for the others' late arrival.

'Are you family?' Osam asked.

'No, we just happened to board the same Trotro,' one of them replied.

Mr Hamburger briefly introduced them and then said they were leaving immediately.

Chapter 3
(*The journey*)

He drove them in his Mercedes to Lome. They navigated in silence during the 168km trip from Accra. All Osam did was bite his lips and intermittently remove the skin caught between the tips of both sets of incisors. This was always a sign of stress or anxiety, a habit that he had tried to abandon.

At 1.05 pm, they arrived at the Ghanaian town of Aflao, which bordered Lome on the Togolese side of the frontier.
Mr Hamburger parked his car in the large public car park at the checkpoint and led them past the long queue towards the entrance.
He seemed to be well connected at both checkpoints as they eased through immigration. Osam and his travelling companions just had to stand by as Mr Hamburger cockily walked up to the front of the queue and handed the immigration officers a brown envelope in front of everyone. The same thing happened on the Togolese side.
When they entered Lome, the capital of Francophone Togo, Mr Hamburger handed them over to a man waiting a couple of metres from the Togo checkpoint. He was introduced as Muru, a Togolese national, very tall for a muscular man, with a big scar across his right cheek. This giant would strike fear in anyone, Osam thought. There was a brief exchange of words between Mr Hamburger and Muru a few metres away from the travelling quartet. Then Mr Hamburger told them Muru was taking over from him and would see to their onward trip to Morocco. There, they would be handed over to one Hossam, who would in turn, take them to Spain. When in Spain, they would be met at the airport by Mr Bawah, a

Spaniard of Ghanaian origin, who would help them to settle in.

'Any questions?' Mr Hamburger asked, looking at each of them in turn.

'No…' Osam said, slowly shaking his head.

'What do we say at the various immigration points?' one of them asked. Osam didn't remember his name, nor those of the other pair.

'Don't worry, Muru will give you all the necessary details,' Mr Hamburger replied with a nod and a thumbs up sign. 'OK, all the best, and please send me a postcard when you get to Spain, he said, shaking their hands in turn. Muru was the lucky one - he got a hug.

Muru drove the four men in his ageing Mustang along the extended seaside highway of Lome to his house on the outskirts of the city. At the border, he had only spoken Pidgin English with Mr Hamburger, but now surprisingly spoke to them in fluent English. All five occupants remained silent as he sped on purposefully.

Muru's house was a two-storey building only a few hundred metres from the beach. The houses in the area were spread out, the neighbourhood quiet and exclusive. Muru said he built the house with the help of people he had helped travel to Western Europe. This was encouraging to Osam and his newly-made friends. They even promised to send him some money to thank him for his help when they got to Spain.

When they entered the house, Muru showed them the packed fridge tucked in one corner of the living room and told them to help themselves while he got their visas and tickets ready for their trip that evening.

While Muru was away, the four got to know each other better. They were in it together, so they had to create a strong bond.

24

Jeff was from the Ga ethnic group of the Greater Accra region. He was born in Osu, the area where the Royal Engineers stayed at the height of British colonialism. He and Osam got on quite well. He was a Pharmacy graduate from the University of Ghana in Accra.

The other two young men, Mark and John, were from the same Akan tribe as Osam. Mark, who had a quirky sense of humour, called himself a *hustler* as he was unemployed and a *struggler* while John said he was a clerk in one of the commercial banks. Osam lied and claimed to work with his father in the import and export business in the port city of Tema, about 25km from Accra.

It was an exciting moment for the quartet. Things were going even quicker than they had expected. All but Osam were going to be on a plane for the first time in their lives and had already begun making plans for when they got there.

Mark, the *hustler*, wanted to stay in Spain for two years and then return home with his savings to set up his own construction business. In Osam's opinion, he was too fidgety and looked like a crook. In spite of each person's secret reservations about the others, all four young men agreed to stick together during the trip and even when they got to Spain.

Muru returned two hours later and distributed their passports, now stamped with Moroccan visas. A one-way plane ticket to Morocco was also tucked in the visa page of their passports. The departure was at 7 p.m that night, almost three hours away.

He gave them a few drills on airport comportment that were over in minutes. The quartet had hardly taken in the drill when Muru was up and going again, this time to the Lomé-Tokoin Airport to prepare the way for their trip.

Before leaving for the airport, Muru reminded them that Mr Hossam would meet them at the airport in Morocco. He would, in turn, see to the final part of their journey to Spain.

At the airport, they didn't have to check in themselves. Muru did all that. He seemed to have had everything sorted when he was there earlier.

He wore a softly tailored black suit and behaved as if he owned the place. He must have been well connected, the way he swaggered through the checkpoints. The quartet was also waved through at the various immigration checkpoints with Muru. He stuck with them all the way to the boarding gate.

Due to *technical* problems they had to wait an hour before finally boarding the aircraft. Muru gave each a big handshake, wished them well, and walked back towards where he had come from.

For some reason, they were given separate seats. This made them uncomfortable. The plane was only a third full, so, thirty minutes into the flight, they joined up along the four middle seats of the Boeing 767. Osam wasn't worried this time - his first adventure to Morocco had been different.

Five hours later their plane touched down at Tangier Ibn Battouta Airport after a brief transit at Rabat Sale Airport in the Moroccan capital. Most of the passengers who started the journey with them had got off there.

The airport looked busy, unlike the one they had left in Lome. The clashing sound-mix of the differing languages filled the warm night air.

As they stood in the long queue at the immigration checkpoint, an immigration officer approached and asked for their passports. Their hearts thumped, and they feared the worst. The middle-aged man in uniform studied their passports in turn, then handed them back, advising them in English to remain in the queue.

'What did the cunt want?' the *hustler* snapped in Twi, as the man returned to his original position.

'Shut it!' Osam hissed.

They went through immigration without further hassle and proceeded towards the waiting crowd at the other end of the airport as if they knew their way. A lanky, middle-aged man approached as they passed through the welcoming crowd.

'Hello, my brothers,' he said, smiling as he offered his right hand.

'Hello,' they all responded in unison.

'My name is Hossam. I'm sure Mr Tuffour and Mr Muru spoke about me,' he continued as he shook their hands, his eyes smiling in turn. Only then did Osam realise that Mr Hamburger's *real* name was Mr Tuffour.

'How did you spot us?" the *hustler* asked. He was getting on Osam's already jittery nerves, breaking all the comportment drills they had gone through at Muru's house.

'Your name sounds like mine, Osam. You be Muslim?' the man said after Osam told him his name. He had ignored the *hustler's* question, which gladdened Osam.

'No. I am a Christian, but I think it's a Muslim name,' Osam said, just to make their new guardian happy, and also to win favour in his eyes. It didn't seem to have the desired effect as Hossam continued walking without saying another word.

Their relief, however, could not be quantified. Hossam hurriedly led them out of the airport into the open air of the North African Arab country. There was a car waiting in the airport car park. Just like Mr Hamburger's, it was a Mercedes 100. Osam's previous experience in Morocco hadn't been a good one. It was better this time.

Mr Hossam's diminutive structure was further accentuated by the long, pink fez he wore on his shaven head. The effect of the scorching, North African sun was apparent on his thin, wrinkled and sullen face, which made his age difficult to gauge. He didn't seem a pleasant man.

'You very late - very,' Hossam said as he negotiated a corner out of the car park.

'The flight was delayed by one hour, sir,' Osam said, firmly re-affirming his self-proclaimed leadership role.

Hossam briefed them as they drove on an outlying road towards what Osam assumed was his house.

'You're leaving soon. There's been a change of plans, so you're going by boat.'

He said Spain had, unbeknown to Mr Hamburger, recently tightened its visa requirements in Morocco. So the quickest and easiest way was by boat to Ceuta. Hossam assured them it wasn't very far and that Mr Bawah would be waiting to receive them when they got to their destination.

Osam had not seen this coming. 'But Mr Bawah is waiting for us at the airport in Spain,' he protested.

'Don't worry, he'll be waiting for you,' Hossam insisted.

'Well, if you say so.' Osam continued.

'Hey, you talk too much. Just do as you're told or you'll go back where you came from! Do you understand me?' Hossam shouted, slapping the steering wheel.

It didn't make sense to Osam, but he kept quiet. He was constantly getting hit with dirty looks from Hossam. He knew Hossam was hiding evil intentions. For the first time since the trip began in Accra that rainy morning, doubt crept into his mind as his first Moroccan experience came flooding back. He looked at his Seiko watch. It was 2.30 a.m. Apart from the *hustler*, who was impassively humming a familiar gospel tune under his breath, one could cut through the growing unease and tension. Osam wondered if they were thinking the same as him.

They drove in silence in the darkness for a while until the car came to a halt near what appeared to be a cliff. Osam could smell the moist ocean breeze in the otherwise warm dry air.

They followed Mr Hossam away from his car, hearing ocean waves in the near distance as he led them along a steep, eroded path until they approached a small sandy shore, where the waves now bellowed. It was deserted.

Then they heard voices calling as they walked along the wet sand. Even in the darkness, they could make out a small boat about 5m by 3m being tossed about by the choppy Mediterranean Sea. As they got nearer, they realised it was filled with people.

When Mr Hossam said they were going by boat, Osam had thought it would be a *real*, big boat - the ones he'd seen anchored along Tema Harbour.

'It's cold. If we had known this, we would have brought along sweaters or something,' Osam said.

Somebody screamed at them to hurry on board. Amidst the prevailing confusion, all four looked towards Hossam in tongue-tied desperation. All they got was a nod of approval. Before they had time to say a word they were already at sea. They were partly soaked as they were helped into the boat.

'Don't forget to write to Mr Tuffour,' Mr Hossam screamed.

'I'll write him his obituary,' the *hustler* whispered. Osam looked at him. The *hustler* hadn't spoken for quite a while. One could detect the fear vividly splashed on his companion's thin face.

There were five women. They, except for one, were grouped together in the middle of the wooden boat as if to show solidarity. One of them was breastfeeding a few-months-old baby. Osam couldn't tell in the darkness whether the poor baby was a boy or girl.

Next to the lactating lady sat a younger lady, her arms crossed upon her knees pressed together. She wore a short skirt and a rather light shirt. Her bulging abdomen clearly indicated she was in the family way.

The rest of the passengers were men, sixteen young men - including Osam and his friends. The rough hair like dreadlocks of some indicated they hadn't touched water for days, if not weeks. All the passengers were wearing thick jumpers and jackets.

One, who seemed to be their leader, dished out do and don't instructions from the rear of the wooden dinghy. He told the quartet and their new companions they would paddle in groups of four for half-an-hour. Anyone who broke this rule would be chucked overboard, he said in English, but with a noticeable Arabic accent. That was when Osam realised the boat had no outboard motor. How could they possibly paddle all the way to Spain? He had no idea of the distance but still wondered. Around him, he heard whispers in Arabic and strange sub-Saharan languages. His knowledge of African languages was limited but he presumed they must be North and West African dialects.

The leader turned to Osam and his friends and angrily ordered them to throw overboard the hand luggage they were still clinging on to, so as not to cause the already overloaded boat to sink. They instinctively did as they were told. Osam realised immediately that his passport was still in his little bag, floating away.

He was terrified. He had neither been in a boat before nor was he a good swimmer, although he had been born along the coast. The leader was not only mean, but too huge to mess around with. His long, shaggy, North African hair and flaming eyes made him look like a pirate. Who knew what evil lurked behind those piercing eyes, Osam thought. The creature fitted the stereotypical action film, *bad guy*. He wondered if he was part of the organised *gang*; in which case they had nothing to fear as he would know what he was doing. The waves endlessly hitting the sides of the already unstable boat added to his prevailing nervous state. He constantly stared at the opaque, moving, watery mounds around the boat

30

and wondered what lay beneath. He could literally and effortlessly touch the sea water. Osam looked back to see how far they were from land. To his surprise, the first group of four were doing just fine as he could see from the fading lights on land that they had already travelled far and fast.

He had heard as a youngster that the deepest part of the ocean was about twenty-four km. What if they were in that section? To make matters worse, they weren't properly dressed for the biting cold. If only that fool of a leader had been patient enough to allow him to wear the blue jumper he had in his little hand luggage! He was already shivering in his thin, white, short-sleeved shirt. He looked around in the darkness of the horizon and spotted some lights emerging from what appeared to be two large vessels. He wondered whether even at that distance they could be spotted. They might be rescued by a sympathetic crew and sent to Spain. He hoped so.

About half an hour into the trip one of the ladies alarmed them when she detected water seeping into the boat from underneath her left foot. She was seated close to the port of the cramped boat. She wore two jumpers, so the leader instructed her to take one off and use it to block the leak. She began weeping and shivering with fear as she did as she was told. The baby began to cry too. The leader instructed Osam to leave his position at the stern to take over from the woman stopping the water inflow. The command came as a welcome relief for Osam as he was sitting precariously on the edge. People were constantly manoeuvring for a better position. It didn't mean he was out of danger, but at least it put him away from danger. He tried to apply as much pressure as he could on the opening in a desperate bid to impress the leader, but it went unnoticed. Moreover, one of the paddling men kept complaining that Osam was getting in his way.

'Next group! Next group!!' shouted the leader. He pointed at Osam and his three friends. 'What are you waiting for? Come on, get on with it!' he continued, still chewing on whatever he had in his thick-lipped mouth.

'What about—'

'What about what? Just leave that. Hey, you, take over from him!' he said in his rather high-toned voice, pointing at the poor, shivering chap sitting next to Osam.

Osam and his friends jumped to their feet to get into position.

Paddling a boat for the first time in his life didn't turn out to be an easy or welcome experience. Osam suddenly remembered Osibisa's song. He began to sing it aloud. His Ghanaian companions joined in. The song was out of sync with their rowing, but that didn't deter them.

We are going
Heaven knows where we are going
We will know we're there
We will get there
Heaven knows how we will get there
We know we will
It will be hard we know
And the road will be muddy and rough
But we'll get there
Heaven knows how we will get there
We know we will
We are going
Heaven knows where we are going
We will know we're there.

In spite of their strenuous efforts, they didn't seem to be making much progress against the growing waves. It was windier now. At one stage, the boat seemed stationary and spun out of control, which drew chuckles from the boat's occupants. As the quartet struggled vainly to steady the boat, the leader, who was sat at the bow, looked unimpressed with the efforts of Osam and his friends.

'Shut your mouths, lazy buffoons!' the leader screamed in uncontrolled fury. 'I'm sure you haven't worked hard all of your life. Do you want us to die here or what?' he continued angrily, this time smacking Osam in the face.

Osam momentarily lost his orientation in the pitch darkness. He felt a whirring in his eardrum as he gradually recovered, a sudden dead hush on the boat now.

'Any lazy person will be thrown overboard, do you all understand?' the leader continued.

Without warning, Osam instinctively charged at the leader. He had had enough of this man. His three friends came to his aid as he struggled feebly against the leader, who was bent on casting him overboard into the rough sea. After many struggles, the fighting pair were separated. In spite of the leader's meanness so far, he seemed to have considerable support among the group. Soon an argument erupted between the two factions, followed by a free-for-all exchange of blows. The women, now acting as peacemakers, screamed in unintelligible languages in a bid to get the warring men to stop. There was an uncontrollable mutiny on the boat, which was now stationary, except for its swings hither and thither against the heightening waves.

In the erupting mayhem, undue weight was transferred to the starboard, and the next thing Osam remembered was freezing seawater, and people screaming in the dark for help.

Osam clutched onto the slippery underside of the boat. He could barely feel his legs, or see around him. Then he saw someone floating and holding onto the boat at the far end.

'Float, Osam, float!' he screamed. It was John.

'I can't. I don't know how,' Osam screamed back in tears. He was being tossed back and forth. He was scared to breathe. Water was entering his nose, and his eyes were burning.

Then a big wave hit Osam's side of the capsized boat. He momentarily lost his grip, but desperately clutched to get it back. His arms were starting to tire. He saw two people disappearing under the wave that followed. There were screams all around, some of them unintelligible. The waves swept people away from the safety of the boat as others, including the leader, tried their utmost to reach the safety of the capsized boat.

'My arms are hurting, John,' Osam screamed.

'OK, hold my hand, hold my hand!' John had his left arm stretched out to Osam.

'I can't. You're too far away. I'm scared!'

'OK, hold on tight. I'm coming to you. Where are Jeff and Mark?'

Osam looked around. He was alone on that side of the boat. He saw people fighting the waves as they were being dragged farther away from safety. 'I haven't seen them,' he turned and yelled back to John. He wasn't there either. 'John? John? Where are you?' John! Jeff! Mark! John!' he screamed.

He was alone now, as far as he could see. It was as if the seabed was dragging him deeper into the dark. He knew he was going to die. He recalled the last time he and his friends went swimming in the sea at Labadi beach. He could not resist the temptation. On the way, they met a man who cautioned them against getting into the water. The rip current was severe that afternoon. They ignored his advice and Osam nearly drowned. One of his friends, on realising Osam's predicament, got back into the water and rescued him.

Osam held on tight, although his arms were frail. He counted to three and attempted to haul himself onto the capsized boat. He slipped and fell back into the gaping water, disappearing beneath the surface. He closed his eyes, for fear of seeing something below. When he resurfaced, he began beating on the water in order to reach the drifting boat. He needed to vomit. He had consumed too much sea water. He kept paddling away with his arms until he neared it. He reached for it but pushed it away instead. He tried to maintain his composure and resumed splashing about and screaming. This time he reached it, touched and grasped it, and gasped for air.

Osam moved his cold hands along the lower side of the upturned boat. His hand brushed over an uneven surface. He repeated the action and realised that it was definitely a dent. Then he recalled the part of the boat that was leaking. He couldn't see clearly, so he decided to wait till first light to investigate it further. He hoped he'd still be alive by then.

He waited for what appeared to be forever as darkness gradually gave way to daylight. The wave's intensity had equally responded to the approaching day's bidding. With each dragging moment, he could see his surroundings better. There was no soul around – not even a ship on the horizon. He looked up to the sky. He hoped a passing plane might just spot him, and call for help. He was scared, starving, and his energy level was really low. Maybe his time wasn't up yet, he thought. He pulled himself together and began planning his next move. He made up his mind.
He looked for the dent. It was about the size of a rugby ball. And yes, there was a little hole right in the middle of it.

He used it to aid him to get on the top of the capsized boat. It was easier than he had anticipated. Once there, and having achieved his objective, he decided it was time to catch some sleep. He spread out and wrapped his whole being as tightly as he could over the dry bottom surface of the boat. When he had got his balance right, his eyes fell shut. The rising sun was providing much-needed warmth. The boat was still unstable, but he knew he was much better off where he presently was.

Chapter 4

Osam opened his eyes to an unfamiliar environment. The smell of chemicals hung in the air. As he gradually regained full consciousness, he realised he was on drips. He was lying in a comfortable bed. He felt woozy as he hated the sight and feel of needles. He had hardly finished organising his thoughts when a nurse walked in holding a file in one hand and a pen in the other. She half-grinned at Osam and said something unintelligible. He smiled back uncomprehendingly. She took some notes and left the room. He recognised the word *gracias* on a notice attached to the back of the closed door of the little room and realised he was in Spain. He lay on his comfortable bed and tried to remember what had led him to his new environment. Try as he did, he could not recall anything beyond his survival efforts in the deep dark Atlantic Ocean.

His thinking was abruptly interrupted when the door opened, and a lady in a dark, smart suit strolled towards the bed. She pulled up a chair and sat beside Osam's bed as the hinged door closed behind her. She was about 1.80 metres tall, of medium build, and very beautiful with dark-blue eyes complementing her long, dark curly hair. She sensually pulled her hair back across her broad feminine shoulders as she stared steadily at Osam.

'Hello!' she said with a sweet smile, revealing two dimples on her smooth tanned cheeks.

'Hello!' Osam replied with a smile, making sure he revealed his white, well-aligned teeth.

'My name is Susana. My friends call me Suzy! You can call me Suzy!' she continued in her strange English accent.

'My name is Osam,' he said, biting his lips.

'Hello Osam,' came the reply, as he stared at this beautiful creature sitting so close. 'You are a very lucky man, Osam! You were rescued by a fishing boat two days ago and brought here.'

'Two days ago!' he said in surprise.

'Yes. We have recovered twenty bodies so far. How many were on board?'

'Twenty-one, including a baby,' he said, as it dawned on him that he had indeed been a very lucky man. He felt delighted to be alive and well but also sickened because he had lost his friends. He felt guilty for his actions that had led to the boat capsizing. He wondered whether the blood of the dead was on his hands. Tears filled his eyes as he wondered at the countless number of people who may have perished in the same way. Their families were too far away to realise what had happened to their loved ones. They would forever talk about them living in the land of the white man, and hope to see them one day.

Strangely, his first thought was of the *hustler,* who had displayed genuine concern for his friends out there in the deep. Osam could vividly remember his worried expression. He was the true hero after all.

'You from *Gana*, no?

'Yes. How did you know?' he asked in surprise.

'My husband is from *Gana*, so I can tell when I see a *Ganese*."

Osam felt like she was lying, hoping that would soften him and thus she would get the information she wanted, but he quickly dismissed this thought. They chatted in English for a short while until he began to feel dizzy.

'Well, thank you Osam. I will come to see you again tomorrow morning,' she said, and with that, she quickly exited the room.

He thought long and hard about what had ensued. Who knew, perhaps he had a chance after all. She might take pity on him and let him stay or help him to escape. He had always thought himself a winner and gone through life thinking that he was *born to win*. What a perfect example to back that belief - meeting an immigration or police officer who happened to be married to a fellow Ghanaian. He began to feel better about the whole situation.

He was on his own until a nurse appeared with some food. She slowly inclined his bed until he was almost upright, brought the special serving table containing the food to his lap, and left without saying a word. He had always had the impression that Spaniards were nice and friendly, but the ones he had encountered so far had not displayed those great qualities.

He gulped down every bit of the paella. It wasn't as nice as the Jollof rice that he was accustomed to, but he was too hungry to even think about what he was eating.

During the night, he hatched a plan of escape from the place. It dawned on him he might be repatriated when they came for him in the morning. He had heard rumour upon rumour of people being repatriated to the countries they came from - in which case he would be sent to Morocco. How would he find his way back to Accra in his present state? Once bitten, twice shy, he thought. He wouldn't want to be the Spanish immigration authority's next repatriation victim. His main problems were that he not only felt unwell, but all he had on was white hospital clothing. There was no way he could escape wearing that.

His mind went to work overtime. He got out of bed to go to the toilet and thus investigate the hospital in an effort to develop his escape plan. He turned the doorknob. It was locked. He tried again and again and again, each time with increased force but all to no avail. He hadn't heard the nurse locking it when she left. He noticed a window adjacent to the bed. He walked up to it, slowly drew the curtain, and peeped through the middle. Not only was the window well secured at the back with iron bars, but he also saw moving military vehicles. He presumed then that he was at a military hospital. There was no way of escape. Even in his weak and vulnerable state, Osam would rather sleep on the streets in Spain than be repatriated in shame to Ghana. How would he face Mona? How would he repay his uncle? He felt the need to disappear for good. In mounting desperation, he returned to his comfortable bed, covered himself completely with the bed sheets, and tried to do what he always did best - hope for the best.

Mid-afternoon the following day, Susana returned. This time, she was wearing a green Khaki-looking uniform. Osam was already seated on the edge of his bed waiting for the inevitable. She smiled and pushed her hair away from her unlined face with her left hand as if she could read Osam's admiration.

He thought her masculine-looking uniform did well to mask her natural feminine beauty. However, he could clearly see the shape of her curvaceous physique.

Soon a nurse came to give Osam his second injection. He hoped it wasn't the same kind he had received that mid-morning as he would struggle to stay awake. He felt angry because no one had even bothered to tell him what was wrong with him, or the events that had led him to the hospital.

When he came round, Osam realised he was being taken, in silence, in a police vehicle, to a waiting aircraft. He wondered what had happened as he was now properly attired. Osam had on a white long-sleeved shirt, a pair of black trousers and black synthetic leather shoes to match. If it weren't for the handcuffs and police, he could easily have passed for a successful businessman.

It was early evening. The clock in the vehicle said 6:21. The rapidly moving windscreen wipers were helpless against the small balls of ice ricocheting against the glass. For the second time in his life, Osam was witnessing a hailstorm. The last time was while his family were visiting Cape Coast. He recalled vividly his grandfather reaching out his arm, from where they were sheltering, into the falling rain to grasp some falling hail, and then putting them on Osam's tongue. They melted rapidly. He was 8 years old.

There was no rain here, only stones. Even the elements seemed to be against him.

The police officer who had persistently stared at him through the driver's mirror while he drove them to the relatively small airport shoved what appeared to be a note in his back pocket, as he was led out of the car by his fellow armed police officers. He felt distraught that they wouldn't let him stay even though he had cooperated fully with the authorities. All he got for his sincerity was a nice pair of clothes and a good pair of handcuffs. He hoped it would be the first and last time he ever had to wear them.

As he settled into his seat, he wondered what was going through the minds of the few other staring occupants. Only as he was being uncuffed did Osam realise how he was visibly shaking. Luckily, he was the only occupant on that row. Was it out of fear or shame?

From his window seat on the twin-engine aircraft, Osam could see in the distance the outskirts of the city he was leaving. He still couldn't tell if it was Tenerife or Las Palmas. The engulfing, hilly and desert-like landscape contrasted with the green tropical landscape he was used to. He hadn't even bothered to ask to which country he was being repatriated.

His fears soon dissipated when the pilot announced the flight was Accra-bound. He felt a mixture of relief and desperation. Relief that the flight was Accra-bound and desperation because for the second time in three months, he was being repatriated. He couldn't bring himself to face the humiliation of deportation, let alone face up to his Uncle. No one at the hospital had even bothered to tell him what was wrong with him, or the measures he should take. Osam felt like committing suicide and mused on the best way to do so during the flight. Life had become like chewing gum - it kept him going but wasn't nourishing him.

They had hardly travelled half an hour when the pilot made a long announcement in Spanish, which was unintelligible to Osam. Not that it bothered him as he was still in deep thought regarding his suicide plans. Well, until he heard the translation in English and the simultaneous U-turn of the aircraft. One of the engines, the pilot had said, was leaking oil, so he was returning to have the problem rectified. He assured all the now panic-stricken passengers not to feel alarmed as his move was only precautionary.

There was a sudden, creeping hush in the aircraft as the stewards and stewardesses calmly walked down the aisle comforting shoulders or gently squeezing arms. In some ways, Osam was glad they were returning to Spain. Who knew, he might be able to escape into the city.

'What time is it?' Osam asked as they touched down, gesturing at his wrist towards the white, ginger-haired lady sitting in the middle seat of the middle aisle.

'8:31 pm,' came the reply.

'You sound American.'

'Yes, I'm American…I'm from San Francisco.'

'Oh, one of my friends lives out there,' Osam lied.

'Cool, nice to meet you,' she said, offering her small right hand. Osam unstrapped his seat belt and stretched across the aisle to shake it.

She moved over to join him as the plane came to a temporary halt and then proceeded to its assigned slot.

'Where are you from?' she asked, her eyes fixed on Osam's.

'Sorry, I'm Osam, Osam Mensah. What's your name, please?' he replied, deliberately evading her question.

'Chelsea.'

'Nice name. There's a football team in London called Chelsea. You know that, don't you?'

'Sorry, I'm not into football. So, where are you from, Osam?'

'Ghana,' he replied, staring at her thin, baby face.

'So, what's going to happen to us?' Osam said, realising that a couple of passengers had their eyes glued on them.

'We wait till they provide us with more information. This is Spain. It won't surprise me if we sit here until *mañana*.'

'What does *mayana* mean?'

'Mañana means tomorrow.'

'You seem to be fluent in Spanish.'

'I've been living here in Malaga for almost two years.'

'Really, what do you do?'

'I'm a teacher. I teach English at an institute in the city.'

'A teacher? Wow, you look young for a teacher.'

'Thanks, but my appearance is deceptive. I'm thirty years old.'

'You're kidding!'

'Yep.'

'So, what did you do to get into this?' she asked in an undertone.

'I entered the country illegally four days ago,' Osam replied. 'We came by boat, but I was the only survivor out of twenty-one people.'

'Don't tell me you were part of the *balseros* who were washed ashore to Algeciras! It was on Andalusia TV.'

'Is that what they're called in this country?'

'Yes, it's used to refer to illegal immigrants who cross into southern Spain from Morocco on boats called *pateras*.'

'It is a common occurrence then?'

'Oh yeah, it's been going on for a long time.'

'To tell you the truth, I don't know where I got rescued. All I know is that I woke up in a hospital bed, got interviewed by a policewoman yesterday, and got driven to this airport this evening. Maybe you can help me, Chelsea. I don't really want to go back to Ghana now. Life is very hard back home,' Osam leaned over and whispered to his newly-met confidante.

'I wish I could help you, but I'm also a foreigner like you.'

Those sweet words sank into the very marrow of his bones, but they were no consolation. 'Yes, you're a foreigner, but an American. I wish I were in your shoes.'

'Maybe you'd be better off back home, Osam. The only thing black people do in Spain is selling on the streets. They're controlled by their Mafia masters. They always get into trouble with the police because it's an illegal activity, and most of them have illegal status too. You see the way people kept staring at you when you got on the plane? Africans are looked down upon in this country. They still think Africa is a jungle or something. There's a lot of ignorance here.'

Then there was an announcement on the PA system.

'Stay with me,' she said as she got up and crossed to the other aisle.

Osam followed; somewhat doubting now as to whether she was a true friend after all.

'What was the announcement about?' he asked Chelsea.

'There's a bus here for us. They'll give us more information with regards to the flight when we get to the terminal.'

They left the aircraft into the warm, humid night air and boarded the bus which was parked only a few metres from the steps leading up to the aircraft.

The bus stopped at the entrance to the terminal. They were met by a nicely dressed lady from Iberia Airlines who led them to an air-conditioned seating area. She informed them it was only a minor fault which would soon be fixed to enable them to fly within two hours. Osam stuck to Chelsea as he had been told. He knew she was doing her best to help him.

Then the lady walked towards Osam and Chelsea.

'You're Osam Mensah, no?'

'Yes, I am please,' he responded politely, his hands behind his back, hoping to win her favour.

'Es este chaval, por favor,' (*This kid, please*) she said as two uniformed policemen appeared behind Osam.

He tried to escape from their clutches but tripped over one of the seats. He was bundled onto the shiny floor. 'Please help me! I don't want to go back...please, have mercy!' he cried in anguish.

The two cops hoisted him off the floor, crossed and stretched his arms behind his back, and whisked him to a small room only a few metres away from where the others were seated. He looked pleadingly at the curious onlookers hoping to arouse pity from some of them. He realised how unwelcome he really was in Spain.

He was told to sit on the only chair in the room as the door banged behind him. He obeyed, put his head in both hands, and stared at the door. He could hear incomprehensible voices on the other side, then one of the policemen re-entered.

'Tienes dinero?'

'I don't understand Spanish – English, English,' Osam said.

'Money, money! You have money? Me give, you go, OK?' he said, looking into Osam's eyes. Osam knew what he wanted. Unfortunately, he didn't have it.

'No money. Me don't have money. Me very poor from Africa. No money!' Osam pleaded in broken English.

The man turned, opened the door and slammed it behind him.

The whole scenario reminded him of his three-day ordeal at Gurugu Mountain. The Spanish immigration officials didn't allow Osam and his fellow economic migrants entry into Melilla because they either had false visas or couldn't pay their way in. He still recalled the numerous stranded black African migrants who had set up camp at the refuge in the woods, and the professional traffickers who would get you across by boat once you had enough cash. On that occasion too, he didn't have the money. He had witnessed gruesome scenes that were typical of desperate and hopeless people. Life-changing Melilla was only a stone's throw away. Numerous people braved climbing over the razor-wire fence or swimming the dark waters to reach the land of hope and glory, often in vain.

Osam was lured into the fellow migrants' gang but was beaten up when they found he had no money to contribute towards food. He was lucky to have escaped with only a knife wound to his back for fighting back. Violence, hunger, disease, fear and cold were the prevailing state of affairs on Gurugu Mountain.

He still remembered vividly the night when the leader of a gang raped him in his tent in the Moroccan forest. The painful and first-time experience seemed to go on forever until Osam felt a sharp burrow of teeth on his shoulder as the perpetrator ejaculated into his bowels. It was a nasty and dirty experience which he hadn't told anyone – not even Richard. Although he was among his own then, it was a war of survival out there. They were either on the run or hiding in the shade of the mountain from merciless Moroccan police officers.

After a while, he began to feel the effect of holding urine in his bladder for so long, fearing it would burst if he didn't visit the bathroom immediately. He got off his chair and walked to the door wondering what to say to attract the attention of the men who had dumped him there.

'Please, I need to go to the bathroom,' Osam said to whoever was on the other side of the door. After a long silence, he repeated the line. It was still greeted with utter silence. He was getting irritated. He turned the door handle with both hands as a way of attracting attention. On his second attempt, the door moved towards him. He was flabbergasted. He tried again and pulled the door. He held it in place with his right foot and ducked his head out. There was nobody about. Ahead of him, he could no longer see his fellow passengers.

He allowed the door to shut quietly behind him with the aid of his left foot, and stayed put for a while. There was no noticeable human movement.

Then to his right Osam saw an approaching policeman. He couldn't make out if it was one of the two who had dealt with him earlier. He put his hands into his pockets, looked away, and began to walk leisurely away from the door.

The cop glanced at him and walked on. Osam continued his journey away from his initial objective and soon found himself outside. His mind raced. He had to act quickly. A bus stopped in front of him.

'¡Levanta tus manos! ¡Levanta tus manos!'(*Raise your arms! Raise your arms!*)

He was scared out of his wits when he heard the sudden shout behind him. He slowly turned round, petrified with fear. Three Spanish cops had their pistols aimed at him from only five metres away. Two were the cops who had dumped him in the room, the other the one he'd just seen.

The bus drove off.

'Levanta tus manos!' (*Arms in the air!*), they shouted again in unison.

'I don't speak Spanish,' Osam cried. 'English, Spanish no, English yes,' he continued calmly. The cops cautiously approached him. Osam stood there waiting for the inevitable. The place was gradually filling up with curious babbling people. Never in his life had he faced such shame, let alone three pointed guns. He really was having pain in Spain.

Two of the cops put their guns in their holsters and wrestled him to the pavement as the third maintained his aim on Osam. As he lay on the uneven pavement, he felt a sharp pain in his neck as one cop pressed his knees firmly against his neck and head. Osam tried to scream but found himself gasping and gulping for air.

'¡Vale, vale Antonio! Vale, le estás asfixiando.' (*OK, OK Antonio! OK, you're asphyxiating him*)

His hands were handcuffed behind him. He was dragged off the ground, and hurried back into the airport, led through a crowd of curious passengers and ultimately into a waiting aircraft.

He was un-cuffed as soon as they sat him in his assigned seat and strapped him into place with his seatbelt. He was back among his fellow passengers, and he was the last to take his seat. He didn't have the courage to look at the rest of the twitchy passengers, let alone seek out Chelsea. He realised he hadn't even inquired where she was heading. An unenthusiastic smile slowly filled his strained face.

The aircraft made a transit stop at Léopold Sédar Senghor International Airport in Dakar. How he wished he could get off the plane and start a new life there! At least no one at home would know he was in Senegal, and not Spain. As an ECOWAS citizen, he could enter the country without any visa. But he still required his travel documentation. He had lost his passport when he escaped the jaws of death at sea. All he had on him were his deportation documents from the Spanish immigration authorities, which he hadn't even bothered to look at. Then he remembered. He dug his right hand into the back pocket of his dark trousers and pulled out the note. It turned out to be a 5000 peseta note. He had never before seen a peseta coin or note, let alone known its value.

Then it dawned on him that he could have bought his freedom at Malaga airport if he had known that he had this money. How close!

Sadly, he folded it twice and hid it in his right sock. He didn't want any police or immigration officer laying his or her hand on it. It could be worth a meal, he thought. He had heard of people being heckled by Ghanaian immigration officers when they were deported home. He hadn't received such treatment when he was repatriated from Libya on his first attempted escapade and hoped he wouldn't have to go through anything different this time. He promised himself to stay calm in the event that they recognised him and heckled him for that. After all, he didn't want to divert undue attention towards himself.

As Osam came back to reality, he saw Chelsea waving at him before exiting the aircraft. He waved back.

Chapter 5
(*Back to square one*)

Fortunately, Osam's fear was unfounded as the immigration officers at the Kotoka International Airport were rather pleasant towards him. Some of them easily recognised who he was and waved him through. He went through immigration smoothly and soon found himself breathing the hot, humid air of Accra again.

It was late Saturday evening, and the sun was almost nestling on the western sub-tropical horizon. Even though he had been away for only six days, things looked different. He presumed it might be the fact that he had gone through three airports in that time. Or, perhaps, he was just happy to be home.

Once outside, one of the many racketeers wouldn't leave him alone. He kept following him until Osam finally gave up and changed his pesetas.

It turned out to be worth about fifty times what he had expected. A hundred pesetas were being exchanged for 1000 cedis. So he had 50,000 cedis, which was a decent amount of money. That would last him for about two weeks even after getting himself some respectable second-hand clothes. He desperately had to find a place to lodge, though.

Osam didn't want to waste his little cash, so rather than taking the usual taxi he decided to walk to the airport junction and take a trotro to his best friend's house. He changed his mind, however, midway through his short journey and made the 18km trip on foot instead.

Richard lived in Nungua, a suburb of Accra. He could not go back to his former rented single-room accommodation in Labadi, in the east of the capital, although all his stuff was

51

there. Many people in his neighbourhood expected him to be in Europe. He would rather get somebody to go for his stuff, as he could not face them.

It turned out to be not only a surprise reunion, but also a happy one. They had seen each other briefly just before Osam set off on his abortive trip, as Richard had just returned home for his long vacation. Osam told him what he had gone through during the past six days.

'Why didn't you seek political asylum?'

'I'm glad I didn't. I met this American girl who told me how inhumanely blacks are treated.'

'You don't believe an American, do you? You think a white person is pleased to see you in his or her country?'

'They put you in detention centres, which are more or less prisons. Until your case is decided, you remain holed up there. Haven't you heard that in the news? These same white people whom our forefathers welcomed into our land, only for them to colonise us, are now putting us in prison for our troubles. They came to our land during their time of need but refuse us entry during our time of need. Strange world, isn't it?' Osam said, pacing up and down frantically now in Richard's room.

'Well, maybe you're right...but I'll settle for that.'

'How can one struggle to get there only to end up in prison? I'm an economic migrant, not a criminal.'

'Well, at least you're lucky to be alive. Many people weren't as lucky as you, Osam. Can you imagine how many wives, husbands, girlfriends and boyfriends are still waiting to hear from their loved ones supposedly living abroad?'

'And how many people are stranded in other African countries?' Osam agreed.

'As the popular Ghanaian adage goes, *if you have life, you have everything.*'

'Oh yes, I forgot to tell you. I could have escaped if I had had money on me.'

'How?'

'One of the policemen asked me for cash.'

'He didn't!'

'Yep, he did. They're all the same. Why do you think people manage to get visas when they pay large sums of money?'

'It's because they have insiders at the various embassies that also profit from it,' Richard agreed.

'Yeah, man!'

Osam made up his mind there and then. He was going to go to Cape Coast, away from prying eyes, to look for a job. He had had enough of this travelling business which was getting him nowhere. He had his grandparents there with whom he could stay until he found a job and his own place. But first, he had to find and deal with Mr Hamburger. He would go to Hell, if that was what it took, to get his money back.

'I would advise against that,' Richard said sympathetically.

'What? You mean I should allow myself to be duped like that? You know how much money I have lost?'

'Yes, you told me, Osam.'

'Over $3000! That's a lot of money! And this is besides what I have had to go through.'

'All I'm saying is that these people are dangerous crooks. They are involved in illegal activity and would do what they have to do to save their necks if you know what I mean.'

'But…what am I gonna do now? I've got no money! Nowhere to lay my head…'

'You know you're always welcome to stay here. I can tell my parents that it's only gonna be temporary.'

'I know…and thanks,' he said, staring at the wall in front of him.

'Look, with your acting experience, it should be easy to find a good job. You will repay your debt to your uncle in no time.'

'Dream on, Richard! I can't even go back to my acting. The

leader warned me not to disappear anymore, or I wasn't welcome back.' Osam chuckled, rolling his eyes.

'I'm sure Mona's parents can easily help you find a job.'

'She's history.'

'Really? I thought you liked her.'

'Long story. I'll fill you in when I'm in the right frame of mind.'

They both sat silently on Richard's single bed in his tiny room, adjacent to his parents' room. All those living there were renting as well. There were about ten families squashed together in two combined two-bedroom houses. There was a large compound where people did their cooking and other domestic activities. Behind the house were two cesspit toilets and two bathrooms, one for females, and the other for males. There were no showers; residents used buckets of water.

'Why don't you come to Tamale with me?' Richard asked Osam.

Richard encouraged him to enrol at his university in Nigeria. There were opportunities there, he claimed, for students to go abroad and work during the summer. There was a publishing house in Sweden that assisted poor students by inviting them from all over the world to operate as salesmen during the summer holidays. It was a lucrative job as all the invited students returned with enough money to finance their education.

He told Osam that he had applied for the current summer's programme, but, unfortunately,- wasn't invited. He was thus going to Tamale, in the Northern part of Ghana, to work as a salesman for an Accra-based publishing house that gave opportunities to students to put their business studies into practice in the field. Participating students also received a good commission. This was an opportunity, he suggested, for them to work together. If Osam could raise enough money, he could apply to study at the University. They could thus apply together for next summer's sales programme in Sweden.

Osam was easily convinced. Not that he had much choice.

This conversation marked the beginning of his genuine friendship with Richard. However, although he liked Richard, there was always something fishy about him that Osam couldn't identify. When they were students at six form level, he had been nicknamed the *schemer* for his ability to turn dire situations to his advantage. He needed that Richard in these moments.

Chapter 6
(Another attempt)

Richard and Osam returned together from Tamale with enough money from their work of almost three months to enable Osam to join Richard in Nigeria, studying business administration like his friend.

They both missed out on the Sweden sales invitation the following year. Richard was lucky enough to get his invitation the year after and promised to work hard to get his best friend to receive an invitation too. Osam returned to work in Tamale for the third year running.

Richard had a very good summer of book sales the first time in Sweden, and although he still hadn't completed his business degree programme, he proceeded from there to England to continue his studies.

A year later, Osam completed his BA in Business Administration - the first person to have a degree in his family. This made him very proud indeed.
Still, he couldn't find a job when he returned to Ghana, as was commonplace for young graduates, so decided to re-join the student sales programme during that year-long vacation.

During the programme, this time in Accra, Osam communicated with Richard, who re-sent him the application forms from Stockholm for the second time. He duly and quickly filled in the form according to Richard's instructions and returned it to him. As it was routine for high performers of the programme to recommend other students, Richard assured Osam that he would present his application in person to Mr Johansson. He was the man who decided who would or would not be invited to the three-month summer sales programme in Sweden, and Richard claimed he had a good relationship with him.

Osam thus put all his hopes on Richard, and the gods.

Almost five years on, and after several failed attempts, Osam was on his way to the land of the white person. He wished his parents were alive to witness his arduous but rapid progression in life. He knew they would be proud of him, as going to Western Europe, for any Ghanaian, was more than a dream come true.

It was also to prove to his ex-girlfriend, Georgina, the only girl he truly loved, that he was *somebody*. He had never been the same since Georgina broke his heart about five years ago, and he looked forward to the day when he would make her regret her actions.

When Osam had returned to Accra, after his first failed attempt to leave the country, he discovered that a *Bogga* from Germany had snatched his girlfriend. He had only been away for two weeks. And to add insult to injury, she left the theatre group as well. Osam was very much in love with her, and his losing her nearly crushed his soul. He never forgave the *Bogga* for *luring* her with his money. And even though she was still with the man, Osam still felt he had something to prove to her – even if only as payback for breaking his heart.

He refused to accept the fact that love was a lottery - sometimes you won, other times you lost.

Chapter 7
(*The moment of truth!*)

When his name was called, Osam wiped his palms on his new suit and stood, taking a moment to let his wobbly knees settle before approaching the Consulate's shiny mahogany desk. The seated and casually-dressed Consulate General, who was overseeing the task herself, handed him his passport. It still looked new, considering the number of times it had been handled and mishandled by West African immigration officers.

'Congratulations!' came the familiar and well-rehearsed line she had said to all those who had gone before him.

'Thank you, madam,' Osam responded, as she handed him the tiny dark booklet.

'Enjoy your trip,' she added.

'I will, thank you,' he whispered, touching his nose briefly with both thumb and index finger.

As he walked off with his passport to join his silently watching fellow invitees, Osam suppressed a great urge to have a look at his visa. Because of his previous acting career, he was held in high esteem by those who knew him – some of whom were among those present. He dared not express his euphoria in public. He just smiled and raised his eyebrows in acknowledgement to whoever caught his eye.

It was Osam's fourth and final application attempt.

He had been devastated when he was rejected the previous year. He had been assured by Richard that he would be invited to take part in the sales programme. Osam was so sure it was done and dusted that he even told his friends about his impending invitation months before the invitees' names were sent to the University campus. To make matters worse, he could only have a fifth and final attempt as he would be 24 then, the cut-off age for applications. He had sensed of late that Richard was also developing the well-known 'culture of silence' syndrome; when the communication flow between emigrants and their loved ones back home gradually faded. So he had to succeed this time around or he would be damned. Fortunately, it had ended well.

He stood between Mac and Andrew, his passport still clutched in his right hand, as they waited for their turn in the office, which was filled with twelve young men and two young women - all patiently waiting in expectation for their moment of glory.

'When is your visa effective?' came Mac's familiar voice.

'Oh, I haven't even looked at it,' he replied with his usual nonchalance.

As if he was doing Mac a favour, Osam leafed through his passport with gusto until he got to the fresh eighth page. Then he knew for the first time in his life that he really was going to Europe - the land of milk and honey.

Oh, how he yearned to be alone, away from his colleagues, just to scream with delight! It was indeed a dream come true.

Chapter 8
(*The trip to Sweden*)

'Sweden, here we come!' whispered Osam to his two friends as their Nigerian Airways aircraft lifted off the tarmac at Mutala Mohammed International Airport. Although they were Ghanaians, they were flying from Lagos because his two friends, Mac and Andrew, had found a better deal from a travel agency in Lagos which routinely offered flight ticket loans to students who were invited to the summer sales programme in Sweden. The agency financed the trip at a lower interest on condition that the loan was repaid during the first two months of working in Sweden. It was a good deal for both parties, so most student invitees signed up for it.

As Osam didn't want to travel alone to the land of the *White Person*, he was forced to return to Nigeria with his friends to buy his return ticket from the same agency. Unlike Mac and Andrew, he had received an unexpected loan from Richard, which had to be repaid at the end of the programme without any interest. Richard had borrowed the £800 from his savings bank to help his best friend. That surprised Osam, because Richard usually gave freely, but not his money. He promised to repay it before the end of the summer.
Osam and his friends were travelling with little hand luggage as advised by the experienced invitees. Most of the returning sales students had bigger suitcases so there was no need to carry lots of stuff to Europe.

At 6 a.m. their plane landed at the dreaded and infamous Heathrow airport. He had heard rumours of countless people that had struggled to leave Ghana only to be disallowed entry here. Osam and his friends were meant to catch their next flight at Gatwick for the final leg of their long trip.

The sun was already up, but for him it still felt nippy, despite being mid-June.

After a long wait due to the flight being from sub-Saharan Africa, Osam and his friends eventually got through immigration. Rumours had been rife in Accra that planes landing at Heathrow from sub-Saharan Africa always alerted the airport officials.

It was a strangely wonderful experience breathing in the cold, damp European oxygen and taking in the grandeur and opulence of such a great country - even though it was only the airport. This included watching people at the restaurants inside the terminal or at the brightly-lit stores; hearing gate agents telling people to board to get to their destinations; and seeing people standing in long queues at the ticket counter checking in, going through immigration, and others standing in the baggage reclaim area waiting to retrieve their belongings. Everything seemed to be in perfect sync. Unlike in his homeland airport, they were led through long and wide corridors under the constant gaze of airport staff. As his eyes wandered hither and thither at the stunning paraphernalia all around, Osam's mind couldn't fathom what the city of London would actually look like.

The lighted atmosphere of the airport reminded him of some of the film scenes he had seen in cinemas in Accra.

Osam admired his first exterior sights as they left Heathrow on their posh coach to Gatwick Airport for their next flight to Arlanda airport in Stockholm. In the distance, he could see tall buildings and lovely road networks like the ones from television and movies. He also saw the green countryside and woodlands as their coach meandered along the almost deserted English motorway. The forests here were unlike the ones in Ghana, which were larger and denser with bigger tree trunks. He felt exhilarated at having been transported into a different civilisation. It felt wonderful to be in the land of the *white person*.

As he leaned his head against the coach window, his young, trouble-filled life began to replay before him...

Chapter 9
(*Life in Sweden*)

They arrived at Arlanda airport at about 4 p.m. local time. The place was bathed in bright sunshine. He had never envisaged seeing as much sunlight in Northern Europe as in Ghana. It was a complete contrast, however, to what they had witnessed in London during their four-hour stay. All three men had an easy passage through immigration as African students were regularly known to arrive for the summer programme.

Mr Ericsson, their waiting host, drove them to the publishing house. There was a residence there that temporarily housed invited students before they were posted to various stations to begin their sales work. It was a large, open, dormitory-like room with several bunk beds. They met students from Kenya, Tanzania, and Zambia, who had arrived the previous day. They were all in high spirits.

Osam and his two friends were taken to a second-hand clothes storeroom in the basement of the large building, where they helped themselves to some used garments for their work ahead. Osam chose some trousers, shirts, and coats.
'I'm afraid you'll need some jumpers as well. The weather is unpredictable here', said Mr Ericsson, his left shoulder leaning against the doorway.
'All right, sir.'
'It's your first year, I presume?'
'Yes, it is,' Osam answered.
'Well, as you already know, this is northern Europe, and the weather here is apt to change without any warning, so it's important to have some reserve clothes on your travels.'

'Many thanks for your advice. I'll always wrap up warm,' Osam said as he added a couple of jumpers to his *Obroni waawu* pile. It reminded him of Katamanto, a market in Accra city centre where he had bought the second-hand clothes he was wearing. They didn't come cheap anymore.

After dinner, they went for a stroll in the city centre. Osam felt strange, surrounded by a sea of white people. Their Nordic features only confirmed his view of Scandinavians as tall, blue-eyed and blond-haired. This contrasted sharply with the people he had seen at Heathrow Airport. Some of the immigration officers there were blacks or people of Asian origin.

There was hardly any litter on the streets and tidy pavements. There were litter bins all over the place. He even found a bin for dog excrement! Everything looked well organised. The buildings, though not *sky-scrapperesque*, were glassy and mostly transparent.

Osam was so used to walking on the edge of unpaved roads and streets that sometimes he found himself slipping into that habit, only to have his friends drag him back onto the pavement. Then he realised he had to press a button at almost every pedestrian crossing of busy roads and wait for the light to turn green or indicate *walk*. As if to confirm his perception of white people, and for that matter Europeans, he noticed they drove in *new* or sparkling vehicles and wore stylish clothes. Everyone seemed content in the sunshine of magnificent Stockholm. There were more blond-haired people, and the women were pretty but thin. He was surprised to find some women wearing only tights in the middle of town! He couldn't resist moving his eyes from one bottom to the next - though he was disappointed they didn't wriggle enough. They seemed more sexually attractive in the pornographic magazines he used to buy than in real life. They were too thin for Osam's liking.

Almost three hours later, they arrived back at their dormitory-like room to find new arrivals. They were three fellow black Africans studying in England, as well as Zak, a Liberian studying in Accra. The *anglicised* Africans looked well dressed and conducted themselves with such elegance, Osam thought. As time went on he found himself speaking less as he realised his English wasn't as polished as he had previously thought. He had been the most fluent until the anglicised Africans arrived. Osam and his five friends sat on their bunk beds and listened to the conversation. They spoke little and felt inferior to their fellow black brothers. They respected them because they lived and studied in England and also spoke English with a fine accent like the native speakers. He thought the anglicised three, as he had begun referring to them in his mind, sensed that as well and seemed to enjoy it.

'Time for bed for me,' said Joseph, the man from Gambia.

'But it's still early,' Osam said, biting his lips.

'Do you know what time it is?' came the reply.

'Blimey!' he hissed as he realised it was 11:17 p.m.

'This is Europe, man. Here the sun sets later in the summer than in Africa,' Joseph said nonchalantly as he slid under the thin white bed cover.

Osam could not believe the sun could stay up that late. Perhaps the white person was *special* after all. The strange thing about it all was that even though it was well past his bedtime, he didn't feel sleepy!

Zak and Osam chatted in muted tones almost all night. They got on so well that they decided to team up for the work ahead.

It was normal for students to be posted in pairs by the publishing house to their various destinations. Since Richard phoned him the day before he left Ghana to say that he wasn't turning up for the summer programme, Osam had wondered who he would be paired with. Mac and Andrew had already planned to work together.

One of the things that brought Zak and Osam together was the fact they both loved reggae music. Zak already knew of him due to his part-time acting career, though Osam didn't know Zak. It didn't surprise him then when Zak suggested they work together.

The following morning, each student received a loan of 100 Swedish kronor from the publishing house before being sent to their respective territories. Osam and Zak were posted to Kristianstad, a big town near Malmo, in the south. Mac and Andrew were posted to Gothenburg, the second largest city. Osam didn't even bother to inquire where the anglicised Africans were posted. He had already had enough of them.

Osam and Zak travelled the 551.3 km to Kristianstad by train. It was the first experience for both of them on a western train. Osam easily took to the mixture of large pine forestry and lovely, green Swedish countryside, as the train snaked its way through.

He was looking forward to working hard to repay his uncle's loan. He still hadn't been able to contact him since his financial help on his aborted trip to Las Palmas. He hadn't mustered up enough courage to tell him that things hadn't worked out and the $3000 loan had only gone down the drain. In fact, Osam had been playing hide and seek with his uncle. He had heard on several occasions that uncle Kojo wasn't in the least bothered about the money and was dying to see him, but Osam couldn't face him.

Mr Johann, the area representative, met them at the train station and drove them to what was to become their home for the next couple of months.

He was in his late fifties, tall, balding, grey-haired and clean-shaven. For a man who was used to receiving and working with African students, Mr Johann struck him as frosty. Osam and Zak did their best to engage him in conversation during the drive, but he seemed intent on maintaining his dignified silence. It wouldn't take the two long to realise it was natural Swedish behaviour to open up only after they got to know you.

He had rented a cheap house for Osam and Zak in Vinör, a small village on the outskirts of Kristianstad. The two-storey detached building, situated at the very periphery of the village, was large, incomplete and deserted. It looked like a haunted house. The large compound of the fenced-in brick house was overgrown with weed. It had eight dusty bedrooms, each containing a well-made bed. This was because it had been used the previous summer by other students. Students used to stay in the same accommodation. They realised that the bed in the only bedroom downstairs was unmade. Osam and Zak felt the place was eerie. There were cobwebs everywhere.

They ultimately found two habitable rooms on the first floor which they used as their bedrooms. There were lights only in the kitchen, which was on the ground floor, and in a bathroom that was located at the far end of the house. The only access to the bathroom was a remote, long staircase located in the unusually over-sized lounge. So they needed a flashlight to find their way to it during the night. It really fitted a ghost house location. It was as though it hadn't been occupied for a long while, and neither of the two new occupants looked forward to their first night in a place which seemed to have been silently crying out for occupation forever.

'You look tired, so I'll give you more time to rest until tomorrow. How does 9 o'clock sound?'

'Yeah, fine by me. What do you reckon, Zak?'

'O-O-OK,' he stammered.

'Good, you have a good night, and we'll get you mopeds tomorrow.'

'Goodbye, sir,' came the chorus.

'In Swedish, it's *hej do*!' he said as he drove off.

'How about ta-ta-taking a look r-r-round the village?' Zak said.

'Yeah, go on. Let's announce ourselves to our new neighbours,' Osam replied, his left arm around his partner's broad shoulders.

'I c-c-c-c-c-can't wait to begin, man.'

'Yeah, me too,' Osam responded with a broad smile. 'Do you plan to return home? It's easier to get a European or American visa from here once you make enough money.'

'I don't know; it depends on how well I fare. A-actually because I-I-I've to pay for the moped this year, m-my plan has always been to try to break even this summer, and the-the-the-then move on next year.'

'I'm definitely not returning. I'm joining a friend in England.'

'I can only dream of being in your situation for someone with your sales experience, and the awards that go with it, I—'

'Actually, it's only one award, but continue…sorry for cutting in.'

'Yes, I hope y-you'd o-o-offer me some h-help along the way.'

'Hey, we're partners, aren't we?' Osam reassured him. He had made it a point not to mention Zak's stammering, which seemed to be getting worse. Osam thought he spoke as incoherently as his illegible handwriting. And deep down in his heart, he feared for him.

It was late afternoon, but the Nordic sun was still up. They strolled along the only main street in the small village of around a hundred detached houses. The street and side streets were deserted, apart from a couple of adolescents riding bikes, who seemed to take a keen interest in them. The kids rode together and followed their two alien neighbours at a measured distance.

'Hej, do you speak English?' Zak asked, turning to face them. They got no response, except for the children stopping their bikes as their neighbours paused.

'English, English. We, English!' Osam urged, pointing to themselves.

They smiled and *bubbled* to each other. Osam and Zak smiled back. They were turning to continue their exploration when a police vehicle turned into their street from one of the many side streets. The slow-moving vehicle drove past and turned right at the second side street.

Osam and Zak walked on until they reached a street that joined to the main road which led to the town centre of Kristianstad. Beyond the nice line of houses lay forests and cultivated farmlands. They had no clue what type of cereals danced beautifully and blithely to the mid-June wind.

They retraced their steps back to their isolated home to begin their arduous task of agreeing and demarcating their respective territories. Some students had paid severely for straying into other students' territories and were never invited back.

Chapter 10
(*First day at work*)

Osam and Zak opted to begin their work in the countryside, as past sales reports indicated they were the best and warmest customers. It was a good way to start, and less intimidating for newcomers like them.

Osam put on his best smile as he approached the first farm house on his blue, second-hand moped. His heart was pounding, in spite of having done this many times before - albeit in a different environment.

Osam parked his moped close to a new silver Volvo right in the middle of the large compound.

Following strictly the drills he had received from Mr Johann, he made his way towards the front door. He went up the five wooden stairs that led to it and firmly knocked. He retreated a step, put his book-filled leather black bag on the step in front of him and stood, hands clasped in front of him, chest out.

He waited for about thirty seconds. When there was no response, he leaned forward and knocked again. He did this again after about a minute, but there was still no response.

He retraced his way to his moped and proceeded to the next house about five hundred metres away.

He encountered the same fate.

Osam had called on thirty-three homes within six hours but not made a sale. All he received were unwelcoming and barking dogs that perhaps were seeing a black man for the first time. Some people were clearly at home but refused to open their doors.

He tried to put on a brave face each time he returned to his moped, but deep down in his heart, he felt dejected and gutted. He hoped Zak was encountering better fortunes in his territory.

He carried his heavy bag to his moped, put it on the small carrier at the back, hopped onto the seat, and started the engine.

As he rode on the untarred road, he soon heard a screeching from the back of the moped. When the sound persisted, he stopped and got off to inspect it. He had a flat back tyre. Studying the wheel, he perceived that it might have been punctured earlier in the day. He wondered what to do. He had only learned to ride the moped that morning, unlike Zak. He had done a few rounds in the village with Mr Johansson in his car right behind. He had had a bad day at work and had been juggling with the idea of returning home before this mishap. He was exhausted. He was about thirty kilometres from home, and it was 4:16 p.m.

Osam arrived home at 10 p.m. The Nordic sun was still up in its glory. Not Osam. He had had to push his moped and its load all the way home. Zilch sales, and a broken body!

There was no sign of Zak in the house. Nor was his moped in their chosen parking area in the kitchen. All Osam wanted to do was get in the shower and go straight to bed - ready to fight another day. He didn't want to think about how he would pay for a new tyre.

As he slipped into sleep, he heard the front door slam shut. He quietly turned to face the wall.

He heard a knock on his door. It opened. Then it closed again.

Osam and Zak worked six days a week and rested on Saturdays. The rest day was always a big respite for them as they were completely exhausted. Sometimes they slept all day, but it still wasn't enough. Saturday evenings were the worst as they had to prepare for another gruelling week ahead.

Less than two weeks into his work, Osam's hands and arms were aching from carrying his thick, fully-laden leather bag for long hours.
Osam had already dismissed his preconceived idea that selling in Sweden was like a stroll in the park and that the West was *heaven* - a place where all things glittered like gold.

They had no idea what was going on in the outside world. They had neither television nor radio in the house. It was as if they were in another world; a beautiful world of contrasting and endless possibilities.
The richest students on campus were those lucky enough to travel to Sweden to work in the summer. Some of them always complained it was hard work. Yet no one believed them as they returned when invited the following summer. If it was that bad, why didn't they stop returning?
But never in his dreams had Osam envisaged such hard work. He had always been a good salesman in Ghana. In fact, he had won the highest sales award in the previous summer programme there. But this had taken him into a whole new league, and he wasn't prepared for it. A normal daily schedule involved working up to 14 hours and travelling up to 100km on his 30km/h moped. He also carried a big leather bag filled with books – some heavy hardcovers. There were incidents when the cumbersome bag which he tied behind his small moped fell off, sometimes damaging the books inside. He had also tumbled off his moped on several occasions from the sudden wind gusts of long vehicles as they passed. With time, he grew to love his bike as it was his only companion in those times of hardship. Most people turned him down, while a few invited him in for a drink, even if they refused to buy the books. Unfortunately, that kind of charity was little comfort to

Osam as what really mattered, as far as he was concerned, were book sales. He always looked forward to diving into the bliss of a warm shower at the end of what was now a catalogue of exhausting days.

That summer turned out to be the worst on record for student vendors, as far as sales were concerned. Only a few students were lucky enough to make any profit. Moreover, Osam and his partner worked in the south where people seemed less generous than those in the north. It was particularly hard for first-time vendors as they had also had to invest in a good moped and return flight tickets. Almost all the profit Osam made went towards reimbursing Richard's loan, and paying for his moped, books, fuel, and food. To survive, Osam and Zak lived on the bare minimum – namely bread, rice, eggs, margarine, canned beans and peas.

Zak wasn't any better as he was less experienced than Osam. The normal thing was to group an experienced student with an inexperienced one so he or she could learn from the other. In their case, however, both were newcomers and struggled to make any sales on their own.

As the programme drew nearer to a close, Osam and Zak grew further apart. They were hardly on speaking terms. Osam had deliberately strayed into Zak's territory on one occasion when he wasn't getting anywhere in his. When Zak realised Osam was playing dirty and complained, Osam claimed it wasn't deliberate. The work had taken its toll on them both, and they took their frustrations out on each other.

All this time, Osam had been planning an escape since he didn't want to return to Ghana with very little money. He wasn't sure either if he would be re-invited for next summer's programme. There was no place for low achievers. Besides, he had invaded someone else's territory. He didn't want to stay illegally in Sweden as he didn't speak Swedish. They were selling in English. It was also too late to apply for a British visa, so he decided - without telling Zak - to enter the UK illegally during his transit in London. In fact, everything had been worked out with Richard in numerous phone calls during the past few weeks.

During one desperate attempt to make a sale in the countryside in the latter days of the programme, Osam came across a lovely isolated house with an enormous well-kept front garden. Even though it was only late August, autumn had already arrived in Sweden, and for the past few days Osam had been experiencing his first European seasonal changes. That day's weather, however, was fine and bright, like those he'd been used to during his first few weeks.

This time, he confidently opened the tiny, wooden gate and entered the garden. He had nothing to lose as he was in his final week. He was hoping to reduce his remaining large stock of books to avoid paying for their return to the depot in Stockholm. He followed the narrow concrete slab path right in the middle of the flower garden.

As he approached the door, he noticed to his right a lady lying on an extended deckchair. She was wearing only her bra and tiny, shiny, sleek knickers. It was the first time in almost three months that he had seen a semi-naked white female.

She raised her upper body with the help of both elbows and stared at the approaching black man. From her expression, Osam thought she realised he was slightly shy, but also enjoying what he saw of her white, voluptuous form. For the first time in Sweden, he was looking at a typically rounded feminine *Ghanaian-like* figure in white skin.

'Hej!' Osam said with an outstretched arm.

'Don't worry, I speak English. Hi! Are you British?'

'Hmm, no, I'm…I'm African. I'm from Ghana in West—'

'You're from where?' she cut in as she leaned forward in a bid to hear him properly.

'I'm from Gha…Gha…Ghana,' Osam replied. He wondered if that would put her off.

'Oh, you're from Ghana!" she replied with a strong emphasis on the *Ghana*. 'The first black Africans to get complete freedom.'

'Wow! That's amazing!'

'I know my history. Accra is the capital, isn't it?' she answered sharply as she heaved herself off the bed.

'Precisely! The first independent black African nation! How did you know that? It's the first time I've met someone here who knows so much about my country.'

'My elder sister did voluntary work there and fell in love with your country! She said Ghanaians are very friendly people. I'm sure she'll be glad to meet you.'

'I see. So, what are you doing exposing yourself to the sun?'

'Sunbathing, of course. I want to darken my skin like yours…well…not exactly, but something close to that.'

'Well, that's interesting.'

He knew that white people loved to sunbathe in order to darken their skin. However, he had never had the chance to see one due to the intensity of the job.

'Our women prefer to be fair, and some even use creams and soaps to try to achieve it."

'And the men?'

'Some men as well.'

'Well, our men want to have darker skins as much as the women. I'm Arna,' she said, looking up into Osam's face.

'I'm Osam. It's a very *African* name, isn't it?' he replied with a degree of uneasiness. He'd never really come to terms with his name. He always wondered why his dad never gave him a *Christian* name. Osam was much more of a mouthful for everyone than, say, Andrew, a name he liked better.

'Yes, but…you're African and a proud one, I hope?

'Oh yes, I am,' he agreed.

Arna looked to be in her mid-twenties. She invited him in after he had introduced himself as an African student selling in Sweden to raise funds for his education in Africa. His eyes stayed glued to her rear as she led him first up the stairs and then into a large, sunlit sitting room. He was already embarrassingly and crudely up and ready.

Osam's favourite part of the female anatomy was the buttocks – particularly big, rounded, wobbly ones - which she truly possessed.

'Tea or coffee?' she asked as she motioned him to make himself comfortable in the well-lit living room.

Osam opted for the latter, despite having never liked coffee since his secondary school days. It made him irritable and gave him insomnia whenever he used it to enable him to stay up at night to study for impending exams. However, he decided to try it as it was the first time he had been offered tea or coffee in Sweden. Strangely enough, the few people who had invited him into their homes offered cold drinks or juices. Why not try it, he thought, as he sat down in her absence.

She appeared from the kitchen carrying two cups. She offered him one.

Taking it by the rim, but then holding the handle, he guzzled his coffee as she sat opposite - his hungry eyes still fixed on her white-skinned body. He quickly gulped what he had in his burning mouth as he sensed the damage he had inflicted on himself. Arna didn't seem to realise as she began talking to him. His mouth and tongue, by this time, were burning like hell.

'Can I use the toilet, please?'

'Of course, it's the first door on the left," she said, pointing towards the semi-dark corridor.

He looked at himself in the tiny bathroom mirror and saw an unusually white tongue, and some peeled inner cheeks and gums. His mouth was on fire. He stooped over the wash basin, opened the cold water tap, and repeatedly scooped water with his right hand into his burning mouth.

When the burning sensation subsided, he dried his mouth with his handkerchief, flushed the toilet, and returned to his seat. He wondered how long he'd been in there.

'So, where's your sister?'

'She lives in London.'

'Oh! I'm going to London soon.'

'Really? When?'

'I...I s...s...still haven't decided. I want to visit some family members who live there before going back to Ghana. I'm gonna confirm my flight this week.'

'And I'm going to London next Wednesday to visit Maria. Sorry, that's my sister's name.'

'You mean...five days from now? Is there an airport here in Kristianstad?'

'Yes, there is, but I'm flying from Stockholm. That's where I live with my parents. This is their summer house, and because I study at the University of Lund, I come here every Friday to spend the weekend.'

'Isn't this a bit large for a summer house?'

'Well, they usually tend to be smaller, but my parents are well-off...as you can clearly see.'

'What about your boyfriend, doesn't he complain that you don't spend weekends with him?'

'Boyfriend? I haven't got a boyfriend.'

'A gorgeous girl like you hasn't got a boyfriend?'

'Swedish men don't like women like me. I'm too fat for them. Look! I need to lose weight.' She turned her back to him, grabbed flesh on her right buttocks, and shook it.

Osam's heart leapt.

'All the men in my country would want to marry someone with such a figure,' Osam said, stealing a glance at the finger marks still showing on her white bottom.

'So, it's true then. Maria said her Ghanaian men colleagues never stopped commenting about her big rear.'

'I like big rears too…well…not very big ones…I mean…yours is perfect. I think a woman has to be feminine and not skinny.'

'I guess your girlfriend is fat then?'

'She's taller than you, but she would die to have your bum! We broke up a couple of months before I came to Sweden.'

She smiled.

'So, where does your sister live in London?'

'Tottenham.'

'That's in East London, isn't it?'

'North.'

'Sorry, North London! How long are you gonna be there?'

'Twelve days.'

She loved to talk and told Osam she was a medical student at the University of Lund, the oldest and most prestigious tertiary institution in Sweden. They also talked extensively about his completed education in Africa and his nearly three-month-long stay in the south of Sweden. He kept back some information, though – like the fact he planned to enter England illegally during his transit there. She was very friendly and asked him to stay for lunch, to which he promptly agreed. She was too beautiful to turn down. It was difficult for Osam to read if she was just being nice, flirting, or genuinely making a pass at him. In the end, Osam thought it didn't make any difference and decided to take his chance. Who knew, he might get *lucky*.

After lunch, she invited Osam for a stroll in the nearby forest which was only a few metres from her home. Its dense green foliage contrasted with the clean, dry paths artificially created in the pine wood. The dead hush of the place gave an eerie but welcoming atmosphere. It was as if even the trees were having a siesta. Osam and Arna walked together, albeit with some distance between them, but there was a slight romantic tension. They walked in silence as if both were wishing the other would say something to break the deafening silence. Osam was too timid.

Conversation flowed easily with time as it became obvious they had a lot in common; they loved Reggae music, she loved the theatre, because her ex-boyfriend was an actor, and their star sign was Taurus. When he realised that they were almost back at her home, Osam stopped, mustered some rustic courage, turned to her, and requested a kiss. He had not kissed - let alone made love to - a white lady before, and wondered what it would be like. It had always been a dream of his to make love to a white lady, to see whether there was any difference between them and their black counterparts.

He reached out and held her left hand. It was warm. He squeezed it gently. Arna threw back her long dark brown hair as they stared into each other's eyes. Everything seemed to halt – except for the dead forest silence.

She smiled shyly and offered Osam a peck on his left cheek instead. Unsatisfied, he insisted. She finally gave in and planted a peck on his lips. Then she quickly turned and walked towards the back entrance door. Osam stood still.

'What you waiting for? Come on.'

He obeyed. He knew she liked him but couldn't work out if he had played his cards well.

Inside, she offered to buy the three most costly books. Later, back at the door, she invited him to visit her again before she left for London. She also gave him her phone number and flight details and Osam promised to let her know his flight details as soon as he confirmed his flight.

What have I got to lose? he silently asked himself.

It had been the best day since his arrival in Sweden. She had fed him well and also bought with hard cash about a week's worth of work.

The sun was still in its majestic splendour, and Osam was loudly whistling his favourite Jimmy Cliff song, I Can See Clearly Now, as he rode back home earlier than usual. He was still feeling the effect of the glass of wine he had drunk at lunch with Arna. He convinced himself that if he had kept at it, he would eventually have got his reward. He was glad to have played the perfect gentleman, though.

He couldn't wait to show off his day's *accomplishment* to Zak. Osam had had a hunch this morning that his partner wasn't going to work and sensed that it was an opportunity to end their on-going *cold war*.

The sun had set, but the evening was still bright when he arrived home around 6 p.m. Zak's bike was leaning against the kitchen wall. He went straight to Zak's bedroom and found him lying on his bed.

'Are you OK, buddy?'

'Yeah, couldn't be better.'

'Can I sit down?'

'Of course you can, man.'

Zak shifted to allow him room on his single bed. Osam sat down. He realised how long it had been since he had last entered Zak's room. It was very tidy.

He told him about his day's experience and his plans to confirm his flight the following day.

'Oh right. W-W-W-W-When are you planning to leave?' Zak asked, with a hint of surprise in his deep voice.

'Ne-ne-next W-Wednesday,' Osam stammered. He had not heard his partner's stammering for a long while.

'What a coincidence. We're leaving this shit on the same day then.'

Osam smiled. 'Oh, you've already booked your flight?' he asked in amazement.

'Y-Y-Y-Y-Yes, I did it this morning as soon as my passport arrived. I didn't go to work today. I had to wait for the p-p-postman's wee-wee-kly dropping.'

'All right, I had guessed that as I was leaving this morning. I didn't know your passport had expired?' Osam replied.

With a broad smile, Zak reached under his pillow and brought out his Liberian passport. As if he had rehearsed it, he opened it straight to a certain page and nonchalantly handed it to Osam.

'You didn't tell me you'd applied for an American visa?'

'N-N-Neither did I d-d-dream in h-h-hell I was gonna be g-g-granted it – p-p-p-particularly with my Swe-dish visa –a-a-about to r-r-run out.'

'Wow! So how many months did they give you?'

'Six months, man, but once I g-get in, I'm go-go-gonna get l-l-lost man – lose myself in the American dream. Wow!' he yelled.

'That's why you didn't even bother going to work.'

'Who c-c-c-cares about this d-d-dirty work? I j-j-just can't wait to g-g-get the hell out of he-here, man.'

Osam didn't know whether to cry or laugh. For the first time, Zak's persistent stammering was getting on his nerves. 'Congrats, man," he said with a wry smile. 'I'm joining Richard in England.'

'Tha-thank God for that, man. I-I-I was a bit wo-worried about y-y-you as soon as my d-d-dream came true thi-this morning.'

'Don't worry, man, I'm fine,' Osam replied. He was rather doubtful about Zak's supposed sympathy for him.

However, Osam didn't tell him about his plans to enter England illegally. He was superstitious when it came to such issues. Since his disappointment at not being invited to Sweden after he had told all his friends about it, he had learned to keep things to himself until he knew the final outcome. He reserved his right to remain silent on this for fear of the potentially serious repercussions. In any case, Zak never bothered to ask.

Zak's revelation had made Osam's plans all the more urgent. The arrival of Friday night did nothing to allay his mounting fear. Try as he did, he couldn't go to sleep. His thoughts drifted to Arna. He had the opportunity either to stay illegally and try his luck with her, or venture into the risky business of slipping into the UK. He knew both options had the potential of landing him back at Mutala International Airport in Lagos. He rolled away from the wall to the edge of the single bed and switched on the bedside lamp. He glanced at his watch, 03:03, and rolled back to his original position, leaving the light on. He needed company. He stared at his parents' black and white photo that he was grasping in his right hand.

Chapter 11

Osam was woken by a loud knock on his door.

It was Zak. 'Wu-Wu-Would you like a-a-anything f-from the su-supermarket?'

Osam hadn't heard that question since their first month together. 'No thanks. I'm going to town later to make some phone calls.'
'OK, s-see you later.'
'See you.'
His small room was bathed in autumnal sunshine. He imagined what might be going through Zak's mind. Whatever it was, he would dearly love to be in Zak's shoes. His heart was hurting so much!
He looked at his wrist watch. It was 10:54.

Later that afternoon, Osam went to the town centre on his moped to ring the travel agency from a public phone box. He had made a decision: he wouldn't return to Ghana – he had never been a quitter! Instead, he would attempt to slip into London and try his luck over there.
Unfortunately for him, he could only confirm his flight for Friday, as the other Gatwick-bound Scandinavian airline flights, including those of Arna and Zak, were fully booked.
On the one hand, he was glad that he wouldn't end up travelling with Zak. On the other hand, he would miss the opportunity to travel with Arna.

He rang Arna and told her of his disappointment. She was equally saddened they couldn't go on the same day at least, if not on the same flight. To make matters worse, the weather had deteriorated so they couldn't see each other that evening, as she said she would have liked to. She therefore gave Osam her contact number and address in North London and told him to keep in touch when he got there.

Chapter 12
(*Leaving Sweden*)

After almost three gruelling months, Osam was leaving Sweden. He had sold his moped cheaply, paid his bills, and was departing with £42.57. That was all he got at the exchange bureau for his 245 Swedish Kronor. He had to succeed in this next attempt to enter the UK clandestinely. There was no way he could survive in Accra with that money. He knew he could go back to his part-time acting career, but nobody expected him back in Ghana so soon. He would also have to contend with being called a *Bogga aye loose.*

To make his situation even more desperate, he didn't have sufficient money to re-route his flight to Accra, instead of Lagos, although a handful of students were returning with even less. Zak had left two days earlier for Accra to garner enough funds for his trip to the US. Osam didn't have a clue how much profit Zak had made.

Osam thought his Swedish experience was better relegated to history. He hoped for something better in England if he was successful sneaking in.

He carried his heavy suitcase and hand luggage to the airport so as not to create any suspicion about his escape plans. The suitcase contained some items of importance to him, but then, in life, sometimes one had to lose in order to gain.

He missed the early bus and thus arrived at Arlanda Airport almost late for his flight. At the check-in, they found out that his visa had expired, so he had to wait a long while as they sorted out his situation with the British immigration authorities, as they effectively had an illegal immigrant on their aircraft transiting Britain to Lagos.

In the end, he was allowed to board and was the last person to do so. The plane was full, and all the angry eyes were fixed on him as he strode along the aisle to his seat.

Then he couldn't find a place in the overhead locker to put his hand luggage.

He was restless throughout the three-hour trip to Gatwick. But he had to be careful not to make it evident.

He had taken dangerous risks in his young life before, but none on this scale, he felt. He had *transit* knowledge of the airport, and even though Richard had told him which train to take to Reading, he was in uncharted waters. Richard wouldn't meet him at the airport as he didn't want to be a part of Osam's risky operation.

Osam's Scandinavian Airways aircraft arrived at his transit point, Gatwick North Terminal, at 10 a.m. He was still filling out his landing card as the plane landed safely.

There was a sudden communiqué about a large armed police presence at the airport due to a bomb threat by the IRA. He listened carefully but didn't have the slightest clue what that meant.

He walked calmly with a group of passengers towards the shuttle train to the South Terminal. When he entered, not only was there no available seat, but it was also filled with armed police officers. He didn't like the look of the bulky, deadly guns they wielded. One of the cops kept looking straight at Osam as he stood biting his lower lip. The situation was oppressive for him. He wondered whether his escape plan was clearly written all over his face. He slowly looked away and rested his tired eyes on one of the windows. It was disconcerting.

His heartbeat raced uncontrollably. His palms began to sweat - despite the cold autumn morning. He resisted the temptation to take out his handkerchief.

He was among the last passengers to get off the shuttle train at the south terminal. He didn't bother to look out for the policeman for fear he might further arouse suspicion.

He was granted a twenty-four-hour visa by the British Immigration authorities. His flight to Lagos from Heathrow was scheduled for one o'clock that afternoon, so he had less than three hours to execute his plan, or sadly catch his onward flight.

Making sure he walked normally, he followed the exit signs inside the well-lit airport until he came to the escalators. His failed Malaga airport escape experience was still vivid. He shunned the escalators and instead opted to use the disabled ramp. He took the sharp bend and standing in the corner was the very same armed policeman who had been studying him on the shuttle train, still wearing the same mean-looking expression on his broad, fat face.

'This route is closed, sir,' boomed the policeman.

'Oh…ehm…what did you say, sir?' Osam stammered, as he struggled to understand.

'Where are you going, sir?'

'Me? Hmmm…' He wasn't sure if he understood him well. Why couldn't he speak slowly and intelligibly? He had gone through the same treatment at the immigration desk.

'The train station is up on the other side of the building. Just follow the signs,' he said, his wary eyes still fixed on Osam.

'Yes sir, thank you, sir,' he said as he turned to escape the man's stare. He understood him this time. With his bag still hanging off his shoulder, he retraced his way up the ramp.

His back felt as heavy as his now leaden legs as he struggled to drag himself away, finally disappearing around the corner.

He went out of the airport as if to board the speed link coach to Heathrow but, instead, still shaking and nervous, bought a rail ticket for Reading.

'You all right?' the ticket lady said from the other side of the glass shield.

'Y-Y-Yes, thank you,' Osam replied forcing a grin.

Luckily, he didn't have to wait long as the next train soon arrived at the platform.

For the first time in his life, he found himself travelling on the reputable British rail. He began remembering how many people he knew who had tried and tried, only to be turned back at the dreaded British airports. For now, at least, he was also an *Englander*. When people asked for him back home in Ghana, they would know he was in London; and one could not quantify the prestige in monetary terms. It really was a moment to savour. He remembered Zak. He wondered what he was up to now.

The trip to Reading--the biggest town in the county of Berkshire--took about an hour and three-quarters. It was uneventful, apart from intermittent stops and an unfriendly inspector who came round shouting *tickets, please*! And a dry *thank you* when you showed it to him.

Osam spent the rest of the trip enjoying the green landscape that defined south-east England's countryside.

Chapter 13
(*Hello Reading!*)

Reading turned out to be a small but busy town. Everyone seemed to know what they were up to, and just getting on with it. He didn't see skyscrapers everywhere as he had thought he would in the west. He had seen very few in Stockholm, and none in Kristianstad, and had thought they would be in abundance in England. Even though it wasn't as clean as Kristianstad or Stockholm, within seconds he saw more black people--and what he thought were Indians--than he had during his whole three-month stay in Sweden.

Reading seemed to be a well-mixed sort of town. He couldn't tell whether he was disappointed or satisfied.

He stood outside the station waiting for Richard. His eyes kept darting from side to side in England's autumn mid-day sun hoping to spot his friend before he was spotted. They used to play that game in Accra. He felt a tap on his shoulder. He turned. It was Richard.

'Next time the drink's on you,' Richard said.

They hugged in their customary brotherly fashion. Richard hadn't changed much except for gaining a few pounds which made him appear a bit shorter than his 1.80 metres. His dark brownish eyes sparkled as he unveiled his trademark sweet smile, revealing his still white, perfectly aligned teeth. There was also a bit of colour in his much darker complexion, and he seemed to walk with a bit of a swagger. His greying hair betrayed his still young age of twenty-five. It was a great reunion, and they had a lot to catch up on as they hadn't seen each other for almost four years.

'Where's your luggage?'

'It should be on its way to Lagos within the hour.'

'So this is all you brought along?'

'I didn't want to raise any suspicion so…'

'Never mind, we'll get you some clothes in an OXFAM shop. Hello? What are you looking at? It's me. What happened to your tongue?' Richard said as he noticed Osam's stare.

'I'm just admiring how good you look now.'

'Oh, you're scaring me now, Osam. Tell me, how was your trip?'

'I'm just lucky to be here, man. I can't believe I'm standing on English soil. I'm so happy, I'm even scared to show it.'

'Well, you're here and you're gonna have to start getting used to it,' Richard said as he waved down a taxi.

On the way, Osam told Richard about his experience with Arna.

'Akwesi, meduru o!' (Akwesi, I've landed!) Osam yelled as they entered Richard's room. They laughed and hugged, and Osam started jumping and dancing uncontrollably. Osam and his best friend were finally reunited.

The next thing he did was to ring Arna using Richard's personal landline telephone. The phone went unanswered so he left a message.

Richard shared a house with his Nigerian landlord and his wife. They were both at work. The terraced house was about a half-hour walk from the station. Richard lived in the attic of the one-storey terraced house about 2km from the town centre. His double bed was right in the middle of the room while the remainder of his belongings, mostly books, were scattered around the four corners. One corner was cleared to accommodate Osam's small hand luggage.

There was an emergency Ghanaian Association meeting that evening, to which he was invited. Richard said its purpose was to assist the few Ghanaians living there. One of the members had suddenly lost her dad in Ghana, so this special meeting was arranged to share her grieving. It was a fine opportunity for Osam to meet his fellow countrymen.

'I've been ringing around for a job for you, but so far I've had no luck on that front. Hopefully, we'll have some good news at the meeting.'

'You mean I start work immediately?'

'Yeah, man. Time and tide wait for no man out here.'

'But I've just arrived. I need time to adjust to my new environment...'

'And how would you pay your bills? Welcome to the land of milk and honey, my friend!' Richard said with a dry grin.

'Why do you keep grinning like that?'

'Like what?'

'Your grinning...it's kind of...strange, lifeless; it doesn't look sincere anymore.'

Richard laughed. 'You mean it?'

'Of course, I do. Why would I lie to you?'

'Well...I don't know why, Osam. I'm sure you'll find lots of that here when you go to the shops. Here you smile for the camera – superficial, know what I mean? You should be careful not to cultivate that, though. And, lest I forget, go softly-softly with the girls here.'

'I'm a good boy now.'

'Good boy, my big toe!'

'They're so thin.'

'That's what men prefer over here.'

'Is your girlfriend like that then?'

'We broke up last month.'

'Was she white?'

'No, she's Caribbean...well, British of Saint Vincent origin.'

'Was she thin as well?'

'You know I've never liked big women like you. But never mind, you'll grow to like them. Some of them are shapely like

Ghanaian women, particularly those from Southern Europe – the type you like.'

'Why did you break up?'

'It's a long story, but you'll soon realise that women here are *less* hard work, as far as chasing them is concerned. They are not like in Ghana, very liberated and more powerful.'

Richard and Osam arrived early at the meeting hall. There was nobody there, so they had to wait outside.

'People always arrive late.'

'You mean over here too?'

'Yep, same old, same old.'

Osam was reunited with some people he had known in Accra. There were about fifty people in the hall. Some were students, others were workers while still others were student-workers.

At the beginning of the rather formal meeting, Osam was presented as a *new arrival*. In traditional Ghanaian style, Osam was asked to stand for all to see him.

'Osam Mensah is Richard's best friend. As usual, please start asking around for a job for him. Also, I've been told that he's single. I mean, a very single man, so ladies, I mean the single ladies…the ball is in your court!' the chairman said.

Everyone burst out laughing. Osam smiled as he sat down. Richard squeezed his knee.

He was particularly impressed with what he saw – everything looked professional and *anglicised,* which reminded him of the insolent student vendors he had met at the publishing house in Stockholm. He began casting his eyes around the meeting hall to see if any of them were among those present. None fitted their physical description. They were all in the same boat now, Osam thought.

At the end of the meeting, Osam had time to talk at length to the people he knew. Some of the others recognised him from his acting.

Osam wondered why many of those who were well-qualified academically still lived in England, instead of returning to work in Ghana. They would walk into the best jobs due to the fact they had their education in the UK.

He got the chance to meet the wives and children of some of those he knew. He also realised that there were lots of beautiful Ghanaian women there alone. Richard told him with time he would encounter lots of single Ghanaian, Caribbean and even White women desperately looking for boyfriends or husbands.

'These are the *MOC* girls,' Richard whispered.

'What's that?'

'Shush! Don't shout. It means Marriage of Convenience girls. If you marry them, you can stay in this country for a long, long time!'

'Yeah?'

'Shhh! I'll tell you more later. Let me introduce you to more people.'

Suddenly, Osam felt like he had been in the UK much longer, and his life in Sweden and Ghana a welcome fading memory. Everyone was very obliging and smiled good-naturedly. Unlike in Ghana where people gave you directions to their homes, phone numbers were exchanged here instead. Everyone had a phone at home. He already had a couple of phone numbers of people he had already known. It was great to have so many phone numbers. Richard's phonebook was almost full.

'There are many Ghanaians here.'

'Not everyone turned up tonight. This is nothing. There are even larger numbers in London,' Richard declared.

'At this rate, there aren't gonna be young people left in Ghana,' Osam joked.
'Yes, I absolutely agree.'
They laughed.

When they returned home, Osam wrote to Uncle Kojo. He explained all that had happened since his last unsuccessful attempt to leave Ghana up until his recent arrival and the current situation in England. He promised to reimburse his uncle as soon as he got a job.

As for Arna, he rang her on numerous occasions on the number she gave him, but he had no response. He guessed it wasn't meant to be.

Chapter 14
(*Life in Reading*)

With each passing day, Reading was becoming strangely familiar to Osam, although everything was still so, so new. Ah well, he thought, life was full of contradictions.

In Accra, he had been made to believe there were so many Ghanaians in England that when he was out and about in town and came across other black people, he assumed they were Ghanaians. He would greet them in English, but they never responded in most cases. The white-skinned folks were the worst, he thought, as not only did they not respond, but also looked at him with suspicion or apathy.

Richard later told him that the Ghanaian custom of greeting people did not work here. Here, you only greeted people you knew. The problem with that was even people you knew always seemed to be in too much of a hurry to talk to you. They were either late to catch the bus, to meet someone or for work. Everyone was either walking quickly or running. Everything seemed to move very fast in this society. There were some people he had not seen since his first Ghanaian meeting. He already felt like he was in a world apart. Life in England was a rat race.

Then he realised that there was no *trotro*--the cheapest form of transport in Ghana--in Reading. Most people caught the bus or walked. There were occasions when he actually saw people in suits hurrying and scurrying to catch the bus. They were supposed to be rich people, weren't they? This was unheard of in Ghana. The bus, *trotro* and walking were meant for the *poor* - even though sometimes one was forced to use them provided no acquaintances were watching.

Almost five weeks after Osam arrived in the UK he was still jobless. He didn't have a National Insurance number, and hence couldn't find a job. Richard was unwilling to allow Osam to use his number, for fear of getting into trouble with the law. He had been on the lookout on Osam's behalf for a fake one to buy, or for a fellow African who was willing to rent out his. However, they were too expensive in both cases when he found one. Besides, he was under pressure to move out. They were getting in each other's way.

No one had warned him about this. Well, Richard did, but Osam never believed him. He had expected to jump straight into a waiting job on his arrival. The plaza of plenty was gradually turning into the plaza of illusion.
The dark mornings and lack of sunshine in the afternoons were affecting his usually bubbly personality. Richard was busy at school and at work. He felt lonely and missed home; life in Ghana was not all doom and gloom all the time. But memories sometimes triggered extremes, yet he knew he couldn't ever relive those good times.
He had no intention of returning to Ghana; at least, not empty-handed as he was in his present state. He thought momentarily about Zak and wondered what he was up to.

Osam usually passed his time alone, either adventuring a tour of the town centre or listening to the local 210 FM station on Richard's cassette player at home. He was forced to watch television and listen to the radio as he was still struggling to understand the local accent. He had always thought he understood and spoke English well until he found himself among native speakers. Richard reassured him that it was normal for new-comers in the UK. It took time for one's hearing to get used to the nuances. Osam was amazed that Richard could tell from people's accents whether they were

Scottish, Welsh, Australian, or from New Zealand. He could even tell from which region an accent originated.

Whenever Osam was in the town centre to window-shop, he always went first to a jeans shop in Friar Street as he fancied one of the white shop assistants. She was tall and plump with a nice dimple whenever she smiled. Though he meant to tell her, he couldn't bring himself to talk to her when they exchanged their usual smiles. All his experience at home came to nought as he froze in her presence. Her male colleague always told Osam right in front of her that she had a soft spot for Osam. She would just smile.

Next, he would proceed to M&S to buy some fruit juices for Richard.

It was busy for a Wednesday mid-morning as he entered through the side entrance, this one being his favourite as these particular doors were automatic.

As Osam kneeled to remove Richard's favourite, he heard a sudden hush. He looked up and saw two cops: a lady and a man. Osam slowly stood up in the fruit isle watching what was going on. The two cops came straight at him and grabbed him.

'You're nicked, mate!' the male cop said as they handcuffed Osam behind his back.

'I have done nothing wrong, sir, madam,' he said, protesting his innocence, his heartbeat racing with dread.

'Explain that when we get to the station, mate,' the lady cop replied, pursing her tiny lips.

'I swear to God! I'm only here to buy some fruit…'

'Sure! That's what you always say, Trevor,' replied the male cop.

'Trevor? But, I'm not called Trevor. My name is Osam, Osam Mensah.'

'What?' the male cop asked with a curt smile.

'My name is Osam Mensah,' Osam insisted. They were almost at Osam's favourite entrance.

'He's got a strong accent, hasn't he?' the lady cop said to her male partner, lifting her shoulders. 'You've got an ID on you?' she continued.

His only ID was an expired student ID card from the University in Nigeria. He dared not show them that lest he got into trouble. Shoppers were now attracted to the scene as he tried to think of what to do. A Ghanaian lady he knew saw Osam but quickly walked on by before he could ask for help. He wondered what she thought of him, or perhaps she didn't want to get involved with the cops. He knew word would spread like wildfire among the Ghanaian community. Osam was an illegal immigrant and he was worried about repatriation if they found out.

'That's not him. Trevor is bald,' came a voice from behind him. They instinctively turned to see who was talking. Osam breathed a sigh of relief. 'I'm head of security,' the man said, flashing a badge. 'And that's not Trevor,' he continued. 'For some strange reason the security guy who called you thought it was. Sorry about that,' he said to the perplexed cops.

'Sorry, mate. Mistaken identity. You're free to go,' the lady cop said, as Osam was freed.

With unmeasurable relief, he stumbled out of the store into the large, busy, pedestrian walkway. He had only one place in mind as he lengthened his strides - home!

Richard couldn't contain his laughter when Osam told him. He had heard at University through another Ghanaian student that a fellow Ghanaian had been arrested for shoplifting.

'You heard it at University? That's amazing!'

'And this afternoon, too. Hey, it's a small Ghanaian community, remember? Walls have ears here.'

'Then tell them I was running errands for you.'

'Won't change anything, Osam.'

'At least try. I flatly denied having had anything to do with any robbery, but it fell on deaf ears.'

Richard was still laughing.

'I think I know who began the rumour. I was scared I would be repatriated, man.'

'If they found out it was true that you were shoplifting, maybe yes.'

'They asked for my ID. The only one I had was the expired one from the University in Nigeria.'

'Did they? That's strange because they hardly ever ask for that kind of stuff. You didn't show it to them, did you?'

'I was just about to when a man appeared from nowhere to say it wasn't me they were looking for. I think God saved me today, Richard.'

This reignited Richard's suppressed laughter. 'So, you believe in God now?'

'I've always believed there is a God. I just don't think He is represented correctly by the various religions. Yeah, He definitely exists.'

'I know many people who had such strong convictions when they arrived in England, but seemed to lose it with time.'

'Please don't put me into that group because I'm not the fanatic or church-going type.'

'Anyway, I honestly think you need to modify both your clothes and way of walking. Sometimes people can tell, just from a glance, whether you're African or not. You need to start behaving like a Black Brit. Because they've suffered a lot of racism, they tend to stand up for their rights and are thus feared by the whites. Their self-confidence is sometimes mistaken for arrogance, but that's one of the ingredients you need, as a Black man, to survive in this racial environment. You need to modify your dress code and the way you walk. Try to dress and walk with a bit of a swagger, you know, moving your shoulders like a black Brit; that way you won't be easily recognised as an African.'

'But I'm proud to be an African!' Osam said.

'And who isn't? But when you're in Rome, you do what the Romans do. It's about survival, my dear friend,' Richard replied with a smile.

Chapter 15

The prolonged boredom from inactivity was steadily getting to Osam, and making him restless. His dream of making money fast and returning home to start up his own business had to be put on ice. He had arrived in England with a well-written recommendation letter from the Ghana Actors Guild. He wanted to try some acting, but Richard warned him off because he was an illegal immigrant. Some Ghanaians even had the audacity to tell him to give himself up as the authorities would definitely catch up with him. There was a lot of scare-mongering. Osam thought they were envious people who, knowing his potential, would rather have him sent home.

Richard, who was a legal immigrant thanks to his student status, got him to register at the nearest doctor's surgery and ultimately found him a cleaning job in the mornings in one of the offices in the town centre. The cleaning supervisor was a good friend of Richard's, and a fellow Ghanaian, so he didn't even ask for the dreaded National Insurance number, as he understood the situation. Richard claimed his friend would tell the employers that Osam had just arrived in England and was awaiting his National Insurance number from the Department of Social Security. With time, he said, they'll forget, and stop asking for it.

Richard had still not completed his MBA programme at the University of Reading, so before he left for lectures, he went to do his two-hour cleaning job. He didn't have a car so he used to wake up at 4.15 a.m. on weekdays in order to make it for the 5.15 a.m. start.

Osam was woken up by Richard the following day. It was raining cats and dogs.

'It's raining. Can't we sleep a bit longer?'

'I beg your pardon? You don't do that here, Osam. Come on, unless you want to lose the job!'

Even though they got up at the same time, Richard was soon ready while Osam was still brushing his teeth. He was never a morning person, so he envisaged tough times ahead.

'You have to learn to do things quickly here, Osam. We're five minutes late already.'

They walked quickly in silence, hands in jacket pockets, the cold autumn morning now only drizzling. Richard didn't have an umbrella. Neither did most people he saw. People walked in the drizzle here - often without raincoats.

In Ghana, people were referred to as 'salt,' as they would quickly run for shelter at the sight of a drizzle.

Despite the fact that he was hardly awake, Osam was nervous and excited to be starting his first job in England. It had taken too long.

They arrived just on time. People were already getting on with their work. Surprisingly for Osam, they were all black Africans – mostly Ghanaians.

'Good morning, Abrantie. This is Osam, my best friend I spoke to you about,' Richard said.

They shook hands, and in typical Ghanaian style, snapped their locked middle fingers simultaneously at the end. Osam wondered whether *Abrantie* was his real name.

'Hello, Osam. Are you the *Obroni*? I heard from some people at the Ghanaian meeting that you speak Twi mixed with English. You're a very lucky man. Anyone who has the honour of being the best friend of this *great* man, Richard is a very lucky man indeed,' the supervisor continued. 'You be careful, though; he can be a real snake in the grass.'

They all laughed.

Osam was taken aback. It looked like word had already gone round about him. It sounded like a joke, but he knew that Abrantie was really having a go at him.

'So, how are you finding England and the cold?' the supervisor continued.

'Tough!' Osam responded, his hands now in his jacket pockets.

'You haven't got into any more trouble since your last brush with the bobbies, have you?'

'No sir,' Osam whispered shyly. He quickly recalled Richard's words that walls had ears.

'And the cold?' Abrantie repeated.

'It's a killer.'

'You ain't seen nothing yet. The real cold will soon begin. Have you seen real snow before?'

'No,' he responded, wondering what in God's name Abrantie was driving at with all the questions. Osam had had enough of him already.

'Have you cooked some *tuo and Nkatie Nkwan* for him?'

'Yes,' said Richard. 'He was surprised to see chicken so cheap over here.'

'And milk as well, I suppose?' said Abrantie.

'Well, we all experienced that, didn't we? The land of milk and honey!'

'As for me, my best meal now is oatmeal mixed with plenty of evaporated milk, and buttered bread!'

'Eeeh, Ghana man, you love cheap stuff!'

'Who doesn't like it cheap? Things like chicken and lamb are *Christmas* foods, and almost untouchable in Ghana. Then you come here and they're just *normal* food.'

'Well, I'll leave you two then,' Richard said to *Abrantie*. 'I'll see you later,' he said to Osam, and quickly disappeared around the corner.

'One of the guys is off so you'll have to cover for him today,' Abrantie said to Osam as he quickly showed him what to do.

His duty that morning was to clean the four toilets on the ground floor of the three-storey office building.

Less than two hours later, Richard came to see how Osam was getting on. He was nowhere near finishing.

'You're making heavy weather of this simple job, Osam. You have to do things quickly; otherwise, you won't last long.'

'Have you finished already?'

'I finished long ago, Osam. In fact, everybody else has finished.'

'But I have to do it properly.'

'Yeah, but you have only two hours to finish doing it properly. Know what I mean?'

'Yeah.'

'OK, you do the toilets and I'll finish the sinks,' Richard said. They went to work.

'Your friend doesn't like me. He's given me the dirtiest job to do.'

'There is no dirtiest job here! And get on with it because time is almost up. Some of the workers will be arriving soon. You are lucky to find a job, and you call it dirty work? Some people do even worse things like washing and cleaning old people. And that includes...'

'Don't tell me their shit as well!'

'You got it, man.'

'What?'

'And what do you think I do when I'm called out to work some nights?'

'I thought that's care work?'

'And what do you think that is, wise guy? You ain't seen nothing yet. This country is about survival. You do things you wouldn't even dream of doing in Ghana. That's why when you send money to people back home and they claim it's insufficient it hurts so much. One only wished they knew what people have to go through just to earn a few pounds an hour!'

They said goodbye to each other outside the office block, as Richard had to go for lectures.
While he walked along the leaf-covered pavement of the now busy road on his way home, Osam thought of his beloved city, Accra. He realised that even in his home country there was an unwritten class system in place.

The *dirty* jobs like cleaning toilets, carrying people's goods at stations, and so on, were normally done by a section of ethnic groups; those from the northern regions of Ghana. People thus began associating them with those fields of work. Osam couldn't help but compare his present situation to theirs, and realised for the first time in his life what it felt like being in that line of business, and being at the bottom of the social hierarchy. Life was rather twisted and sometimes exquisitely beautiful all at once.

After almost two months of waking up late when he didn't have a job, Osam suddenly had to readjust to both waking up very early and the cold chill at that time of the morning. He always looked forward to the weekend when he could make up for lost sleep. There was never a day that he didn't want to stay longer in bed, even though it felt good when he was handed the pay cheque on Friday.

He stayed with Richard in his large rented room until a place of his own was found for him in Oxford Road. It was about four km away from Richard's. He preferred a place away from his fellow Ghanaians so he could do his own thing.

Richard claimed that his landlord had warned him of an imminent rent increase due to Osam's presence. Moreover, he needed his independence back. He had a new girlfriend.

Unlike Richard's, the new area was densely populated with immigrants, mostly from India and Pakistan. This put Osam off when they went to view the advertised vacant room.

As they went up the carpeted wooden stairs to view the room, one of the housemates, an Asian, appeared from his room holding two beer cans. He was singing what sounded like a Peter Tosh song in a high falsetto voice that made the whole experience surreal. Osam looked at his watch. It was 10 a.m. Osam said hello, but the man just stared blankly back.

There was no way he was going to share a house with such a fellow.

What won the argument in the end was the £30 per week rent and its close proximity to the town centre.

His small room was about eight square metres, much smaller than advertised. It was situated on the first floor of a shared, four-bedroom terraced house. His room was so tiny he had to settle for the single bed that just about fit into the room. Even when he slept diagonally, the bed still wasn't long enough for Osam. However, he had to make do with that as it was all he could afford to rent for now.

In Accra, Asians -- particularly Indians and Pakistanis, and Arabs, such as Syrians and Lebanese -- were respected as they owned the grocery shops and big businesses. They were regarded by many to be *slightly better* than Ghanaians because their countries were more developed than Ghana. Also, they had a lighter skin colour. They hardly mixed with local people.

In England, however, Osam was surprised to find they were all classified into the same *coloured* class. They treated each other as equals. He wondered what the consequences would be if people back home knew his newly-discovered reality.

Osam's £100 pay cheque from the morning cleaning was not enough to pay the monthly rent of his tiny room so he had to look for an additional job with longer working hours. There were other expenses like eating, clothing, etc., which needed taking care of. He began to understand why Richard continually told him when he was still in Ghana that living in Europe was tough. He had always given excuses when Osam asked him for help.

He registered with a busy employment agency. They seemed laden with work, so they didn't press him too hard to provide his National Insurance number immediately and offered him a job the very day he registered. It was a five-hour day job in a large railway station coffee shop with a 7 a.m. start. He was to assist with the cleaning.

He arrived twenty minutes early for his job the following Monday. He had explained the situation to Abrantie, who agreed that he could leave early when he finished.

He was introduced to his boss, a Brit of Jamaican origin, called Jarvis. He was slightly taller than Osam, about 1.90 metres, thin, and looked to be in his mid-twenties. He had dreadlocks. Osam liked dreadlocks. He was very glad to be working with a fellow black man. It was just the two of them doing the cleaning in a very busy shop.

'Wots your name, boy?' Jarvis asked.
'Osam.'
He was introduced to three girls who were chatting away in a tiny, smoke-filled room.

'You are African boy too?' Jarvis enquired as they exited the room.

'Yes, sir!' Osam replied, his hand behind his back.

'Why you look away when I talk to you?'

'That's a sign of respect, sir.'

'I know a bloke from Zimbabwe - you from there?'

'No. I'm from Ghana, in West Africa.'

'You got a fag?'

'I beg your pardon?'

'You got a fag? Ciggy?'

'I don't understand, sir?'

'Daft country boy! You got smoke?' he said, with a clear smoking mime.

'Oh, you mean cigarette. Sorry, I don't smoke.'

'How long you've been livin in this country?'

'Ehmm…f-f-five years,' Osam lied. He didn't want to look like a novice in front of him.

'Just follow me!' Jarvis said derisively.

Osam was shown the staff room and then taken straight to the toilets where he was quickly told his job description with a little demonstration of how to do it and told to get on with it. He was to ensure the toilets, corridors and seating places were clean at all times.

'If you wanna survive, you gonna have to work hard here man. No messing around all right, Sam?

'Yes, sir! It's Osam, sir.'

'Well, get on with it, Oh Sam!' Jarvis flatly replied, and with that he disappeared.

Osam found his attitude rude and felt offended.

All Jarvis did on his first day was pop in every now and then, coffee in hand, and criticise him for being too slow.

It was a very disappointing first day as his elation at working with a fellow black man was quickly dashed by his new boss' attitude.

The situation didn't get any better as the week wore on. He learned from Andrea, a Czech lady who worked in the kitchen, that Jarvis' laziness and rudeness had sent many people packing after only a couple of days. Like a lamb, however, Osam bore the criticisms and occasional scolding.

When Osam got home at the end of the fourth day's work, he rang Richard and told him about Jarvis' attitude. Richard admonished him to stand up to him, as that was how a small minority of Caribbean folks and British blacks tended to behave.
'They see Africans as inferior, so they try to dominate you right from the word go,' he said.
'But I thought we were all black people fighting against the same inequality,' Osam sighed.
'In every society, you'll always find exceptions. Not all of them are like that; just as not all white people are racist.'

Osam arrived five minutes late for work the following morning to find Jarvis waiting for him by the door.
'Come in here, Oh Sam, African boy!' he shouted in the already-filled bar.
Osam followed him into the small square staff room.
'You've only been here four days, just four days, and you already coming late, African boy. Is that wot you do in Africa, Oh Sam?'
'Look, I missed the bus, that's why I was late - just five minutes late!' he said as he opened his locker to get out his work overall.
'Hey, African boy, you look me in the eye when you talk to me, you know,' Jarvis insisted.

'Look, have you got a problem with Africans or what?' he said, still concentrating on getting into his work gear. Osam's immediate reaction was to hit out, but he told himself to remain calm.

'Yeah man, I don't like your attitude! This is England. You no more in Africa, man.'

'You still haven't answered my question,' Osam insisted with a forced smile.

'What question, man? You don't mess with me boy, all right? You don't mess with me, man!'

'Look, I don't wanna argue with you over this. We're all black people, and we need to stick together and not fight each other.'

'And who the hell are you to lecture me, you cheeky boy!'

'One moment you call me *boy*, the next you call me *man*...'

'So wot? You wanna play semantics now, huh?' the other replied, moving closer to Osam with every word he uttered. 'I've got a degree in English, you know. What you got, African boy?'

'I'd look for a more respectable job if I were you. And, may I remind you, I've got a first class in Business Administration.'

'Whoops! And you are cleaning floors? He-he-hee!!! I'm sure you're illegal, man. You know you shouldn't be in this country, don't you? I could report you to the cops if you mess with me, you know?'

Osam laughed and made a move towards the door. Jarvis quickly blocked his path. Osam tried to force his way between Jarvis and the door. As he did so, Jarvis held and pressed him up against the door's wooden hinge.

That was the last straw.

Osam kneed him in the groin. Jarvis collapsed to the tiled floor.

Osam said, 'Don't you ever, and I repeat, ever, mess with me or you'll be dead meat, all right?'

'You're fucked, man. I'm gonna report you to the cops, man.' Jarvis said, writhing around in agony and embarrassment on the tiled floor.

'You can tell the Prime Minister!' Osam screamed back, shaking with uncontrolled anger.

Marta rushed from the kitchen to the corridor to witness what was going on. She giggled, her mouth partially covered with her left hand as if to hide it from Jarvis, and disappeared back into the kitchen.

Still fuming, Osam removed his overall, put his jacket back on and, taking a quick glance at Jarvis still on the floor, went past the open kitchen door, and left - but did exchange a nod with Marta.

'Hey, if I just melt away, could that be our secret?' Osam said.

'We never had this conversation,' Marta whispered.

Osam rang Richard's mobile from a phone booth in the town centre and told him what had happened.

'You don't hit someone here, Osam. You could be charged with GBH and be in deep trouble,' Richard said. He was clearly angry.

'What's GBH?' Osam asked, with a hint of guilt.

'Grievous Bodily Harm.'

'You told me to stand up to him. This man was just making my life impossible.'

'Yeah? So, it's my fault now, huh?'

'No, I didn't mean—'

'Listen up, you. You have neither residence nor work permit. You're here illegally, so you have to be very careful in all your actions. If the police get involved, you could be deported straight away even if you were in the right. I'm afraid this is the kind of struggle one goes through here.'

Chapter 16

Richard decided to temporarily dissociate himself from Osam in case Jarvis did report the case to the police, and they came looking for him. Richard saw him as a potential danger to them both, and their future aspirations.

Osam accepted because he didn't have any choice.

By early December, Osam was a lonely man. He went into hiding during the day by walking along the River Thames in Caversham and mixed with pre-Christmas shoppers in Broad Street to window-shop. At night, he slept on the sofa of one of a new friend's houses. Ademola was a Nigerian who had arrived in England only a day before Osam but was already used to life in England as it was his third time. His sometimes erratic behaviour reminded Osam of the *hustler*.

Ademola's girlfriend did night shifts at Reading Hospital. Sleeping over there was, however, on condition that he left the house before 5 o'clock in the morning when she got home. On some nights, Osam slept in a chair at the hospital A&E waiting room. It was easy to blend into the small anxious crowd. He did that for fear of getting nicked; he had to be mobile.

He returned to his own place the following week when his Kenyan friend and flatmate confirmed that there had been no enquiries about him.

He had to find another job fast as it was approaching Christmas. He had also fallen behind with his rent payments. He was not getting by with only the early morning cleaning job. He was surviving on bread and boiled potatoes.

He went back to the job agency that had employed him, but they refused to have anything to do with him anymore, due to what they claimed was *aggressive behaviour without provocation.* Neither did they pay him the money due. They knew he was an illegal immigrant.

A week later Osam found another job as a garden assistant. He was walking past a florist shop one frosty morning when he saw a middle-aged man unloading flower pots from a blue van into the shop. He paused and decided to give the man a hand. The middle-aged man seemed suspicious at first but relaxed when Osam said he was just helping out. When they finished, he begged the man for a job. Osam claimed to be experienced - having worked as a gardener for an English expatriate while he was in Accra. The man gave Osam his business card and told him to report for work the following day.
The remuneration wasn't good, but it was cash-in-hand, which suited him.

He had stopped using Richard's bank account at his request. Ademola helped him open his own current account at Halifax Building Society. In the end, it wasn't as risky as Richard and his friends had told him. The photocopy of the front pages of his valid Ghanaian passport was readily accepted.
Ademola thought that while his fellow Nigerian countrymen were more courageous and adventurous, Ghanaians were too cautious. Osam had been told by some Ghanaians that the immigration authorities knew he was in the country so he would be silly to shoot himself in the foot by exposing his location.
Ademola begged to disagree. Banks and building societies had nothing to do with immigration, he proudly claimed.

Osam's new means of livelihood involved going round companies and rich people's gardens digging out weeds, watering plants, and creating new beds for plants at the garden centre in Tilehurst. It wasn't difficult for an African, except that he couldn't cope with the cold hard ground even though he wore a pair of tough woollen gloves.

In Ghana, people had the misconception about England--and, for that matter, the West in general--being a paradise. This was believed because *Boggas* returning home for holidays had lots of money to spend. Some built big houses and regularly sent money home to help their families; which one struggled to do in Ghana. This led to a mass exodus, at any cost, from Ghana in search of a better life. However, it didn't take long for Osam to realise that premise held no water. One had to work one's socks off, even though that in no way guaranteed success.

He also realised that it was one thing to live legally in England, and another to live illegally. The latter meant you were always watching your back. You always made sure that you gave no hint to the outside world about your illegal immigration status. This meant you always carried an invisible weight on your shoulder for as long as you remained in that state.

Even if you were legal, you had to distinguish whether you were *coloured*. If you were *coloured*, which group did you belong to: Asian or black? If black, you were inexplicably grouped into a sort of hierarchy: Black British, then Afro-Caribbean, and then Africans. So this was the hurdle you had to surpass as an African in Western Europe, particularly in the UK. Racism was so rife that even though as an African you spoke good English, your accent easily gave you away.

Unlike in Ghana, where white people were very much respected, it wasn't generally so when the roles were reversed. While the images seen of the West in Ghana were mostly prosperity, opulence and affluence, the image of Africa in the

West was that of strife, poverty and wars. Some even thought Africa was a country! He was amazed to hear people saying they were going to Africa, instead of, say, Ghana, Nigeria or another country in Africa. If only they knew the diversities that existed from country to country, they wouldn't put them all in the same basket.

So the white man was thus having his cake and eating it!

Osam had already met many people who had held good jobs back home in Ghana, but in England were doing extremely humiliating jobs like cleaning merely to survive. These people, and some of them legal immigrants wouldn't even dream of touching a broom in public in Ghana. These jobs were considered the lowest of the low. In England, however, they were the easiest jobs one could get as a black African. It became a sort of starting point until one was able to move on to a *better* job.

Chapter 17
(*New Year, new opportunities!*)

Christmas 1993 passed by painfully and quietly. Richard was away in Ghana. All his housemates, including his friend, Peter disappeared during this period too. Osam had lied and said that he was going to work during the break. It was eerily silent, and except for meal and bathroom breaks, he would spend all day and night holed up in his room watching television, and feeling sorry for himself. Christmas in Ghana was a very noisy affair: small bombs and firecrackers, people donning their new clothes on Christmas Day for church services and parties, loud traditional carols streaming from radios, tape recorders, and record players. And the wonderful smell of his favourite rice and chicken stew, or Fufu and chicken or mutton soup filling the seasonal Harmattan air. Reading seemed lifeless. But irregular peeps through his thin, worn-out curtain assured him that life was just about dragging on.

Strangely enough, Georgina was an ever-present companion during his Christmas blues. He couldn't stop thinking about her. He thought he had got over her.

He still remembered the first time he saw her as he was being presented as a new member of their theatre club in Accra. Her petite figure was resting on a hard stool, as she was still rehearsing her lines in the script clutched in her little hands. She seemed completely oblivious to Osam's introduction. Osam, who was trembling as he stood with the group's leader in the middle, went straight on and occupied the boss' chair next to hers after the presentation. He quickly realised his mistake and got up.

'Stay, it's fine,' she whispered, her eyes still fixed on the crumpled script.

'But that's the director's—.'

'Evans, I know.' She lifted her head and glanced at him.

'That's OK, Osam, I'll sit on yours,' Evans said calmly.

After the rehearsal, part of the group invited Osam for a drink. He turned them down.

'I'll join you at the next rehearsal on Monday.' They rehearsed on Mondays, Wednesdays and Fridays. In truth, he was completely broke.

'We insist, Osam, please come along,' Georgina said with a shy smile. Her eyes remained locked on his until Osam agreed.

They ended up at her house three hours later, his first time there. Her parents were away for the weekend. And so the adventure continued until Sunday.

Although she wasn't really his type, in terms of her physical appearance, Osam completely fell for her.

She was twenty, two years older than him and studying Law at the University of Ghana, in Legon.

When the Christmas spree was over, Peter, who worked at Gillette, managed to convince the supervisor of the cleaning operatives there to hire Osam. Osam would later discover that Peter and Maxine, almost twenty years his senior, were lovers. Peter was thirty-three and an illegal immigrant like Osam, but he was working using the National Insurance number purchased from a friend who had returned to Kenya a couple of years earlier. He paid almost a thousand pounds for both his bank account and National Insurance number card and had thus taken on the man's identity. Peter was hoping to marry Maxine later that year under his real name in order to acquire the one-year residency right to remain in the UK. After a year, he claimed, he could then apply for the right to remain permanently in the UK.

Osam's job involved cleaning the factory floors, canteen, staff rooms, and toilets during the 6.30 a.m. to 2.15 p.m. shift. The cleaning operatives, as they were called, were made up of four people – Osam being the only male. There were two pretty polish girls, Nina and Martina, both in their early twenties, and Maxine, the supervisor. She was a Brit of Antiguan origin.

Maxine did nothing except read her *Sun* newspaper all day.

Osam pitied her deep down in his heart, as he knew Peter was just using her. With time, however, Osam would learn that preying on Brits by immigrants, or vice versa was a common occurrence in a country where legal immigration was hard to come by.

One thing Maxine didn't do was interfere with Osam and his two female work colleagues' jobs. She gave them leeway in their various duties and only intervened when there was a complaint. The complaints always came from the fussy office workers upstairs, where Nina and Martina worked. Unlike the factory workers who were friendly and down-to-earth, the office workers were disrespectful and chauvinistic. Martina always complained to Maxine about how some office workers deliberately and habitually forced their way into the toilet when it was closed for cleaning. Maxine, however, didn't seem to care much and told the girls to get on with it. Osam thought Maxine was too scared to complain.

Osam didn't have to wake up so early anymore. His new job conflicted with his early morning cleaning job, so he left it when he found a temporary evening cleaning job at a small office in the town centre. His only direct contact with Richard was thus severed.

He replaced Abrantie's pregnant wife who was on maternity leave. It was a 7 p.m to 9 p.m. job. The cleaning bosses had no knowledge of the fact that it was Osam who was actually doing the job. This way her job was protected and Osam could earn extra cash without any NI hassle. When she got paid at the end of the month, Abrantie would withdraw the money and give it to Osam.

He spoke to his boss at the garden centre to allow him to work from 3 pm onwards, but he was flatly refused. He left the job after less than a month. His palms had been getting darker and darker. It got so bad that people kept inquiring what was wrong with them. When he visited the doctor's surgery, he was told to quit the job as it was making the condition worse.

Osam was on a roll. He had a job to go to during the day, and also a two-hour evening job. He felt like he was in another world - a beautiful world of endless possibilities!

He rang Uncle Kojo and told him. He looked forward to repaying his uncle for his generosity though Uncle Kojo told him not to worry. He was glad that things were gradually falling into place for him, after almost four months in England. And though it wasn't Osam's priority, his uncle advised him to send some money home to buy land in Accra to build his own house.

He was working hard and was soon reaping the rewards of his hard labour. He soon realised that in England you could get money to spend if you worked hard - even as a cleaner. He could easily buy certain consumer goods like a hi-fi or car on credit. He could even have a bank loan, as long as he was gainfully employed. There were thus better opportunities here than in Ghana, where only a few people could afford that sort of luxury. He began to understand why *Boggas* had so much money to spend whenever they holidayed in Ghana.

It wasn't easy for Osam, though. He wasn't used to working long hours. He had been crying out for a job, but soon the daily treadmill caught up with him. Not only was it a battle waking up in the cold, dark winter mornings for work, he was also struggling to make it in on time. He always cursed the *poor* alarm clock as soon as it rang at 6 a.m. In Ghana, he would be allowed to be late a few times. He could even fake illness. Not here.

Osam always felt so exhausted from the stress and strains of his jobs at the end of the working week that he not only began to lose the urge to work, he also spent most of the weekend in bed.
Peter invited him for a weekend night out on numerous occasions, but that was the last thing on his mind. He was advised that what he was feeling was normal, as all newcomers went through it until their bodies adjusted to the different European working culture. In Accra, the stress was the result of wondering where his next meal was coming from. Here, it was the result of hard work and being on time. What he could easily get away with in Accra, here he couldn't. In Accra, one could be late for work as a result of the rain, here you had to arrive on time in blizzards or you were out on the street. He began to understand why people didn't have time for him when he first arrived in England.

Osam reluctantly tried coffee, upon Peter's advice. He always felt awake and alert after he had had his Colombian coffee in the mornings, but struggled to sleep at night. This cycle not only made Osam stressed but also lowered his resistance to disease. Soon he felt the pressure building up and found himself striving for balance in such an alien way of life. It was curious; as if time was on fast-forward.

It wasn't long before he was struck down with the flu virus. It was the first time in his life that he had had the flu. Initially, he thought it was malaria until his GP told him otherwise.

Chapter 18
(*Birthday boy!*)

It was early spring. Osam started going clubbing with his friends at the weekends. He wasn't living in fear anymore. He was doing as the *Romans* do.

He used to go out alone as Richard wasn't the going out type. However, he soon realised the importance of hunting in packs and joined Peter and his *gang*, which also included Ademola. It was a black African group, and although they were just acquaintances, they stuck together; after all, they were in the same hustling boat in England.

Most of the Ghanaians he knew were Christians who thought it was wrong to go to places like nightclubs. He wasn't a Christian so didn't understand what all the fuss was about.

Another section of the Ghanaian community also frowned on that habit. They felt that the money was best saved, as England wasn't their homeland. They would rather send the money to help their families back home, invest it in a business venture, or build their own dream homes. Richard had told Osam about a cleaner who owned a fleet of vehicles in Ghana that were used in the road haulage industry. Osam had a hunch that a small section of the Ghanaian community gossiped about him because of his apparently happy-go-lucky attitude and an insatiable taste for European life and nightlife. However much it bothered him, it didn't stop him. He felt none of those talking about him had paid for his trip to the UK. After all, he just couldn't save, save and save. Unlike Ghana, England was a stressful environment, so he had to strike a happy medium between enjoying himself and saving money. The latter was an almost impossible feat as far as he was concerned. He regarded those gossips as people who never minded their own business but spent more time minding others'.

Osam also loved his football, and as he used to do in Accra, he supported his local side, and regularly went to Elm Park to watch his beloved Reading FC fight it out with other national football league teams. They were lying third in the first division league table, with only the top two teams going up automatically to play in the Premiership next season. The next four teams in the table fought it out to gain the right to play in the Promised Land through a playoff.

In Accra, he rarely missed the chance to watch his favourite team, Accra Hearts of Oak fight it out with other clubs in the Ghanaian first division. He particularly remembered the high-tension matches against the arch-rival, Asante Kotoko, when they used to chant their favourite club anthem in four-part harmony at their Accra Sports Stadium home ground:

Arose, arose, arose
Be quiet, and don't be silly
We are the famous Hearts of Oak
We never say die!

Coincidentally, Osam's 26th birthday fell on a Saturday. He invited Richard and Ademola to watch a game of football together at Elms Park, and for a night out later.

In the end, he had to go alone as Richard couldn't make it because he had the flu.

Although they were still friends, he knew their relationship was strained. It hadn't been the same since he moved out, and the Jarvis incident.

As for his housemates, apart from Peter, it was a clear case of every man for himself, and God for us all.

Peter was away in Brighton for the weekend with Maxine, while Ademola was scared of getting caught up with *hooligans*. Despite Osam's reassurances that he had been there on many occasions without any problems, Ademola was petrified - particularly as it involved Cardiff City FC. They were notorious for some of their fans. However, Ademola promised to join Osam for the night out.

Throughout the week, the Reading Post had urged fans to turn up in large numbers to boost Reading's drive for automatic promotion.

Watching football at stadiums wasn't very popular among blacks and Asians due to racism at such venues in the past. In those days, black football players were booed, had bananas thrown at them or had monkey sounds directed at them. Thanks to legislation, these were things of the past, but still few blacks and Asians ventured into the stadiums to watch their idols or teams play. They would rather watch on TV in their homes or pubs. Osam wasn't bothered by that. He always donned his official white and blue home kit and matching scarf whenever he could afford a home game, and went to watch *the men in blue*.

The whole town centre that day was swamped by police officers, some on horseback, to maintain peace and order in the otherwise quiet town.

When Osam entered the stadium, it was a sea of blue and white home fans, except for a couple of hundred Cardiff fans. Unlike his previous visits, the place already had a charged atmosphere as the compact arena ricocheted with sporting and unsporting songs and chants from the rival fans. The place reverberated with the sound of music and dancing from the close to 13,000 seated fans.

On his previous visits to the stadium, Osam had tried to learn some of the songs, but couldn't catch some of the words. This time, he was determined to listen carefully, or request the chant words from someone, instead of foolishly lip-syncing. He found it embarrassing when his lip movements didn't match the lyrics.

As Osam stood taking in the electric atmosphere, he suddenly felt like a fish out of water in the all-white arena as he realised people were staring at him. It wasn't the first time, but he wasn't used to it yet. He nervously fished his way between knees of varying lengths in his desperate bid to locate his seat. Ultimately, he found it just three rows central and above where he had previously been standing. He had bought one of the most expensive seats in order to be as far as possible from the radical fans of both teams. But, though he was central and thus had an almost perfect view of the perfectly-laid pitch, he wasn't too far away from the corner which seated the radical City fans.

On his way to his seat, he passed a fellow black man with long, flowing dreadlocks talking to what appeared to be his white mates. They exchanged the usual *brotherly* nod, even though they didn't know each other. He reminded him of Jarvis.

During the match, which kicked off at the usual 3 p.m., Osam realised that a section of the rival fans--who were separated by about fifty police officers--spent their entire time singing and chanting insults at each other. They seemed not in the least interested in the match in progress.

As the match advanced, so did City's dominance. It soon became a one-sided first half as the *Bluebirds* dominated but without luck in front of Reading's goal. Their fans continued singing songs of support to their players on the pitch. That gave Osam time to learn the words of the songs in his rather subdued area of the stadium.

Early in the second half, the home fans came alive as Reading scored against the run of play. There was jubilation and ecstasy as they all joined in one noisy chorus chanting of their own.
Cardiff City fans, until the goal, had been boisterous in their support, singing:

Cardiff City till I die
I'm Cardiff City till I die
I know, and I'm sure
That I'm Cardiff City till I die!

The Reading fans' jubilant response after the goal put them one nil up was:
You're not singing anymore
You're not singing
You're not singing
You're not singing anymore!
You're not singing anymore!

Suddenly, the Cardiff City fans erupted with:
Come on Cardiff City
Come on Cardiff City
Come on Cardiff City
Oh, Cardiff, we love you!

Then the Reading fans, now getting wound up, responded with:
Qué será, será
Whatever will be, will be
We're going to the Premier League
Qué será, será!

131

So the tit-for-tat chants went on and on and on until the final whistle. The atmosphere was so charged you could almost cut through the mounting tension.

In the end, both teams shared the points as the match ended in a 1-1 draw. But in Osam's view, Cardiff City fans won the chanting contest through their passion and vivacity.

He joined the sea of blue fans walking home along Oxford Road towards the town centre. He attached himself to a small group of ten who were discussing the game. He always did that to make new friends, as well as improve his accent. He knew some fans sometimes had difficulty understanding him, but he didn't care. He just found it a great opportunity to learn to speak like them.

Later that evening, Ademola arrived at Osam's house, as promised, for their Saturday night out. He was leaving the UK the following week, having been granted a three-month American tourist visa. As far as the American Embassy officials were concerned, Ademola was going on a two-week holiday. But he had no intention of returning. And like Osam, he had no future plan of returning to his homeland.

Luckily for Ademola, he also had a one-year UK residence visa so he was a legal immigrant – a position Osam would readily swap at any price. They got on well as Osam spoke some Yoruba, Ademola's native tongue. Ademola's Black English girlfriend nurse was on the night shift that weekend, so he thought he was a free man to be *naughty*.

Even though Osam always considered himself a womaniser back home in Ghana, he found the going tough in England. He had encountered middle-aged women, who were quite easy to pull, but his main problem was the fact that he wasn't prepared to settle for anything less than the *ideal* woman. He had steadily developed a strong affinity for tall, plump, blonde girls. Unfortunately, there weren't lots of them in nightclubs and thus, they were hard to get.

Today was his birthday, so he had decided that he would settle for anything in a skirt. He found himself in the rare situation of not having slept with a woman for almost a year.

Both he and his friend were on the pull that night.

Osam and Ademola stepped out of the front door into the quiet street. It was 9:45 p.m., about the time most people were out and about. Osam and Ademola decided to walk the almost 2 km to the town centre.

Ademola noticed and called Osam's attention to his unlaced brand new leather shoes. He bent down to lace them properly. They were Italian shoes he had bought at Principles for Men during the week as a birthday present for himself.

They continued ahead until they got to the main road that led to the town centre. As they turned right onto Oxford Road, they saw Jarvis and what appeared to be his friends approaching only ten metres away. All five looked like rowdies and troublemakers. They seemed excited about something that one of them had said and were laughing irrepressibly loud.

'Nincompoops!' Ademola whispered. There was no response from Osam, whose adrenaline was now pumping in readiness for a fight or flight situation.

'Hey, Ohsam, bru'ver! Howiz things, man?' Jarvis said as their eyes met just before the two groups did.

'Cool, cool man,' he responded in a nonchalant manner, trying desperately to conceal his inner terror.

'That's mi African bru'ver warrior, man,' Jarvis said to his mates, who acknowledged Osam and Ademola with handshakes.

'So, wot you up to now, man?'

'Just hustling man...just hustling,' trying to imitate Jarvis' accent.

'I left those fuckers, man. They paid shit money, man!'

'All right, man, meeting some friends in town for a night out so will catch you guys later, man.'

'All right man, Respect!''

'Respect!' responded Osam, and with that, they marched on into town.

'You're well-connected, man,' Ademola said, clearly impressed.

'Long story, man,' Osam replied with a smile, still replaying with disbelief in his mind what had just ensued. He had expected a nasty situation, but in the end, it all worked in his favour.

'What a strange world, birthday boy,' he whispered to himself.

They stopped at a nearby pub for a quick pint of lager before proceeding to the nightclub.

It looked empty from the outside, and he wondered whether he had made the right choice in coming to his favourite place.

Deez, a nightclub particularly aimed at the thirty-something and over age group, had recently become popular among youngsters, even though they were always a minority. Its location was excellent, right in the town centre. The music was a mix of predominantly oldies pop and some modern tunes.

'Sorry mates, it's full,' said one of the three smartly dressed bouncers stationed at the entrance.

Osam turned back.

'But you're allowing others to enter,' Ademola said, as they saw three ladies enter.

'Don't worry, Ademola. Let's go somewhere else.'

'Look, this is not fair. This man comes here every weekend, and this is how you treat him?' Ademola continued, raising his voice.

One of the bouncers held the door open and motioned them in. 'Damned white racists!' Ademola murmured as they entered the dimmed atmosphere. 'You have to fight for your rights, Osam. You're here to spend money, so you have every right like them.'

'You've got your papers, I haven't.'

'Then everyone will realise this if you stay quiet and submissive, Osam. The louder you are, the better.'

The place was almost full. Osam glanced at his watch to confirm the time of 10.00 p.m. It only usually got full around midnight. He was quietly happy as Ade was visiting the club for the first time. It was Osam's round for the drinks.

They had hardly moved up the short flight of stairs with their drinks toward his usual standing spot by the edge of the unusual hexagonal dance floor when he noticed a pretty blond-haired lady dancing rather wildly. She was tipsy, flirting, or just calling for attention.

Her long, wavy hair reminded him of Martina, his gorgeous Polish colleague. Though they fancied each other, he still hadn't mustered up enough courage to ask her out. Another problem was the unspoken fact that they were both illegal immigrants and thus any relationship wouldn't benefit either of them, in the short run at least.

He hadn't seen this lady before, in spite of the fact that he was a regular at this club.

She looked up at Osam from the dance floor. Osam held her stare for a moment and then averted his eyes. He had been outstared, and that made him angry.

From the corner of his eye, he could see her smiling at him. He tried to play hard to get but found himself succumbing to her intermittent glances.

She was motioning him to the dance floor with her left index finger. Osam smiled back but didn't respond to her teasing call. In truth, he didn't know how to handle the situation in such a crowded atmosphere. All eyes must be on him. He took a long timid sip at his drink.

She was blond, about 1.80 metres tall, and a slim figure to match. She wore a faded, short, elastic jeans skirt which, unfortunately, didn't match the sexy beige top. The tightness of the skirt, however, showed off her tiny wobbly bottom as she moved. Her good looks matched by her flirty dancing attracted his attention, as well as that of other males.

At the end of the track, she left the dance floor and strutted past Osam. He playfully blocked her with his left arm. She stopped, turned, and in a moment was in his arms.

What am I gonna say to her? he thought anxiously, surprised by her actions. Lack of flirtatious practice had dampened his wooing abilities. 'You're a very good dancer,' he said.

'You think so?' she retorted with a sweet alluring smile. He knew then that she was there for the taking. Her eyes, a bit dazed, betrayed her emotions.

'It's my birthday today. Can I have a dance with you later?' he asked shyly.

'Oh, congratulations! How old are you?'

'Twenty-six. And you?'

'You should know better than to ask about a girl's age, mister!'

'Sorry. What's your name?'

'Arya, and I'm twenty-four.' With that, she turned and left.

He tried to stop her by holding onto her tiny right hand, but she pulled free and walked off. She seemed aloof and untamed.

His eyes followed her sensuous walk back to join a group of girls. Her slightly bowlegged gait appeared to float her along with the thumping beat. She was darkly sensual and mysterious. Osam hoped he hadn't blown it.

'This could be your lucky night, birthday boy,' Ademola said.

Osam had forgotten his friend was there.

'I hope so, man. Tonight, I'm not gonna be picky; I'll settle for any woman - short, tall, thin, fat, single-mum, old, anybody…except a man, of course.'

'Oh! What happened to Mr Choosy?'

'Not tonight,' he replied.

'I'm glad you're seeing sense now. I've always told you that the matured wines are the best on the market.'

Osam laughed loudly, casting a furtive glance at Arya and her friends out of the corner of his eyes. This seemed to augment the interest of one of two plump, middle-aged women who'd been trying to come on to them since he and Ademola had settled in his favourite spot. The bigger lady kept moving her hips from side to side to the current tune while staring at Osam. Almost literally trumpeting, *come and get me*! Once in a while, she would turn around and show off her assets.

He liked the way she moved them in sync with the music. They were perfect. But he didn't want people thinking he was too desperate. He would have responded if they had been there alone, or the lights were dimmer.

'Stop settling for second best all the time.' Osam teased.

'Oh yeah? Well, firstly, there's less or no competition. And secondly, and most importantly, at the end of the day or night, you know your satisfaction is guaranteed. They treat you good both in and out of the divan. No one's gonna steal her from you, know what I mean?'

He nodded his agreement, recalling the countless nights he had left girl-less at the end of the session. It wasn't that he couldn't dance - he was very good at it. He was tall, strongly built, and fair-skinned for an African. But for some strange reason he just couldn't pull the younger ladies. He would either lose out to a Caribbean or another black guy. He always blamed his shyness or African accent for his failures. Ademola, however, thought of him as one who hadn't a clue how to make the most of his physical qualities and natural abilities.

Osam decided not to follow Arya but instead flirt around as he normally did. If she were interested, she would come back to him.

He seemed to do well with his flirting as if all the women were his for the asking.

'That's what happens when it's certain that you're gonna score. All the women seem to be throwing themselves at you.'

'There's an Akan saying that *if you look into a bottle through the opening with both eyes, you'll end up losing them.*'

'Ah, that's a good one!' Ademola laughed. 'So, what are you gonna do now? A young and easy-to-lose girl, or these two fresh mamas who are ready to rock and roll? A bird in the hand…'

'…is worth two in the bush,' Osam finished off. 'I don't know, man. They're gorgeous, aren't they?'

'Single and successful!' Ademola urged enticingly, as he took a long sip at his lager.

'You're getting pissed already!' Osam blurted.

He recalled the many occasions he had had to drag his friend home. One such occasion, Ade threatened to take his trousers off in the streets, but Osam managed to persuade him to wait till he got home. For someone of his skinny size, he could put away an impressive amount of beer. Peter was even worse. Unlike Ade, he never seemed to get roughed up by the previous night's drinking binge.

Half-an-hour later, while he was dancing to a slow R&B tune, he felt the softness of what appeared to be a lady's breast press against his back, followed by a left arm that came to rest on his left shoulder. He took the arm, and knowing who it was, turned to find Arya holding two bottles of Budweiser in her right hand, deftly with the necks crossing each other. She offered him one, which he accepted.

'Thanks. How did you know what to get me?' he asked.

'I saw you drinking your bottle from where I was standing.' She pointed to where her three female friends stood. They half waved so he waved back. They must have been talking about him, he thought. He needed them on his side if he wished to succeed.

'Are you Swedish?'

'Yes, how did you know?'

'Det har skriftligt över hela din framsida' (It's written all over your face)

'Du talar Svenska! Var har du lärt att tala Svenska? (You speak Swedish! Where did you learn to speak Svenska?)

'Jag bodde och arbetade i Kristianstad i ungefär tre månader. (I lived and worked in Kristianstad for about three months.)

'Wow!' she responded with a twinkle in her eyes.

He introduced Ademola, who was now puffing away on his cigarette.

'Ciggy?' Ademola said, offering her one.

'No, thanks. I don't smoke,' she replied. 'Do you smoke?' she continued this time to Osam.

'No, I don't. Why? You are looking for a smoker?'

'No. Don't be silly! I was just asking.' She laughed loudly while running her tiny fingers through her short hair in a provocative manner.

'My friends have boyfriends; otherwise, I would have introduced you to the one of your choice,' she said shyly to Ademola, who was staring at her friends.

As if by providence, the track *Mr Loverman* began playing.

She dragged Osam by the left hand onto the dance floor. They danced provocatively, their bodies in close proximity, gyrating to the slow, smooching reggae tune. Osam's heart raced uncontrollably. He knew he'd scored tonight, as long as he could maintain the *afterglow* until closing time.

He had missed out many times before in England, as well as on Arna.

He glanced up to find Ademola canoodling the woman who had constantly been staring at him before. Doubt seeped into him as his mind brooded on the coincidence regarding both Swedish name sounds. He hoped he hadn't blown his chance for the night.

She rammed the key into the keyhole on the second attempt. Considering the flat's pitch dark foyer, she must have done this several times, Osam thought. He was uptight, never having slept with a white girl before.

A sudden tug at his arm interrupted his thinking, and he found himself in a dark, spacious, star-lit environment. Sparkling, effervescent plastic stars on the dark ceiling produced a starry night sky effect.

He had hardly taken in the dark room when she planted her lips on his. Her tongue went straight into action, exploring the depth underneath his responding tongue. Her cat-like nails ran up and down his muscular back while her right hand ran over the big scar on his upper left back. He held and squeezed her tiny onion-shaped rear flesh first with his right hand and then the left - trying to keep up with her wanton momentum. She was already warm and breathing loudly. An exhilarating shudder swept through him as he felt the softness of her onion cheeks. Her already taut and erect nipples constantly brushed against his own ultra-sensitive nipples. Like a tigress, she jumped and straddled him with her tiny but strong legs. He felt her short, teasing skirt roll up her tiny waist as she cross-locked her legs just below his bottom. He resisted the strong urge to lay her on the bed beside them. He held her tightly in place instead. He shrieked with uncontrolled joy as she sucked hard on his tiny nipples in turn through his shirt. His racing heartbeat synced with the gyration of her unrestrained hips as they swirled in a firm, uneven motion against his already hardened cock. Her sighs and soft groans of ecstasy rippled through the room in a crescendo as his fingers went to work - playfully poking at her already wet bush from behind.

'Now! Now!' she whispered coquettishly. 'Please, I'm ready!' she pleaded as she ripped off his smoke-filled Polo shirt.

Later, as he lay exhausted on his back on her water bed, it began to sink in that he had just made love, for the first time in his life, to a white girl in her own bed. Even though he felt great, he realised it wasn't any different after all to making love to a black girl. It had turned out to be an anti-climactic after-taste. In fact, his last sexual act, which happened to be a one-night-stand with a West Indian girl, had been more intense and vigorous.

He glanced at the twenty-four-year-old White girl lying next to him. Only the regular movement of her flat abdomen indicated she was alive. Unlike Arna, Arya had a tall, slender but rounded figure.

He didn't want it to be only a one-night-stand and hoped she wouldn't slip through his fingers like Arna. His watch read 5:00 a.m. as she snuggled her naked body even closer to his. Her tiny white form was still visible in the darkness. He wanted to revisit it.

Osam was abruptly woken by his digital wristwatch alarm. He gently reached across to the small bedside table and quickly turned it off, so as not to wake Arya. He had forgotten to disable the alarm as he normally did on Fridays. He knew it was 5:30, the hour he woke up on weekdays. He could not recall when he had taken it off during the night.

He turned over onto his right side to see if she had been woken by the alarm, but it seemed to have had no visible effect. She was still curled close to him; this time, her legs now intertwined with his. She looked babyish and innocent in her deep repose, her rapid eye movement indicating she was in a dreamland. Osam wondered what lay beneath the exterior of this beautiful feminine creature lying next to him.

He stayed put for a while, studying the untidy, medium-sized room. The little bed was situated right in the middle of the room. To the right of the bed was the radiator, which looked new, the intermittent clicking indicating the heating was on.

Opposite the bed was a large, dark-brown wardrobe. It looked too large for the room though there was still ample space to move about freely. On top of the wardrobe were two small-sized Carlton suitcases, one black, and the other green.

To his left was a dressing mirror, on top of which were various female accessories and a framed photo of a middle-aged couple, probably in their fifties. Osam presumed they were her parents.

His attention was diverted to the white ceiling, which was sparsely filled with night skyline objects. There were white, effervescent shapes of a moon, and various shapes of the stars. Their effect in the brightening daylight was minimal.

Osam slowly untangled himself from Arya's clutches, and quietly got out of the soft, comfortable bed. He found his Calvin Klein boxers next to the foot of the single bed and put them on. He trod lightly on the soft, light-blue carpeted floor and exited the room.

He returned about half-an-hour later with a serving plate of fried eggs and mushroom, toasted brown bread, sliced tomatoes, and a glass of orange juice. He gently placed it on the bed and touched Arya, who was now facing the other way.

'Wakey-wakey!' he whispered softly into her right, double-pierced earlobe.

'Why are you out of bed?' she said, as she opened her sleepy left eye, and then the right, which was still squashed against the soft, white pillow.

'Breakfast in bed,' he replied with a smile, wondering if his Saturday morning inspiration had backfired.

'Oh, that's very sweet! What time is it?' she said as she lifted her head to study the contents of the serving plate on the bed.

'6:10, would you like me to prepare you some tea or coffee?'

'No, that's fine,' she said, now sitting.

'Actually, I went to have a pee, and when I passed the kitchen afterwards, the breakfast idea came up.'

Osam placed his pillow behind Arya's back to provide a more comfortable rest.

She showed no sign of appreciation, except to tuck into the contents of the plate with the knife and fork In spite of the fact that she had just woken up, Osam couldn't help but admire the natural beauty of the naked female before him. He hoped he had done enough to win her favour, if not her heart. He wondered, however, why out of the whole club last night she had picked him.

'I'll kill you the next time you wake me up that early on a weekend,' she exclaimed as she placed the tray on her side of the bed.

The next time? Osam thought with a smile. 'I'd like to see you again.'

'When?' she asked.

'Hmmm...this afternoon...tomorrow...and...every day after that.'

'Come here, you sweetie.' She motioned him towards the bed with her index finger.

Osam readily obliged.

Chapter 19

Three months later, Osam moved into her one-bedroom flat at her request. They had fallen head over heels for each other. Also, she never felt comfortable whenever she visited him in his tiny room. He opted to move in on a Friday while she was working. He had very little to show. The boot of the black cab was more than enough for his new large suitcase, which he had bought purposely for the move, and his six-month-old black Sony Compact Hi-Fi stereo system.

Arya agreed to change her water bed for a more traditional one. It still retained its position in the bedroom.

Arya had a degree in Business Management from the University of Lund and a good job, compared to his as a cleaner. She worked as a marketing manager for a small firm in the town.

During one of their discussions about life in Sweden, she wanted to know why Osam sometimes called her Arna.

He hadn't realised.

Osam told her about Arna and how they'd met.

'What coincidence, huh? Arya and Arna!'

'Yeah, life, they say, is full of surprises.'

'Is she the girl who gave you the scar on your back, then?'

'No. We never slept together. That's a knife scar. I got it in a fight in Morocco, during my first attempt to travel to Europe.'

'It's a vicious-looking scar,' she said, fondling it.

'Yes, why do you always touch it when we make love?'

'I like it. Makes you look both nasty and harmless at the same time.' She giggled.

'Yeah?' Osam couldn't believe it. He always tried to hide it from people.

'So Arna was your first European love, then.'

'Like I said, I never heard of her again.'

'Would you like to?'

'No, I've got you, and I wouldn't swap you for any...'

'Come on, not even Julia Roberts?'

'Julia Roberts? Well...If you were Julia Roberts, I wouldn't have had the greatest opportunity of meeting you, would I?

She smiled. 'You know, I've lived with you for almost...two months now, and yet I hardly know anything about you, even though you know all about me.'

'Well, you haven't asked, my love. It shows how interested you are in me,' he said with a sarcastic wink.

'Hey, you watch it!' she said with a light slap on his cheek. 'OK, tell me about you, stranger.'

'Me? Long story.'

'I'm all ears, babe. It's Friday night, and we've got all the time in the world.'

'Well, my name's Osam Kweku Mensah—'

'I know.'

'Relax. I've got to start somewhere, haven't I?'

'Yeah. That reminds me, you said your traditional name's *Kweku* because you're born on...Monday, did you say?'

'Wednesday. As I said before, it is a tradition particularly among the Akans in Ghana for you to be named according to which day of the week you were born.'

'What about Monday?'

'Why, were you born on Monday?'

'Me? I don't have a clue, Osam,' she said in a torrent of laughter. 'Continue, please.'

Osam told her his life story - everything.

'Blimey! Well, long it is!' she exclaimed.

'I warned you.'

'Oh my God! I can't believe you survived such a terrible ordeal!'

'That's life…'

'Have you sought help with the rape experience?'

'What help?'

'I mean, psychological help or something…to help you…deal with such…'

'Nooooo. You guys in the west are so weak that you seek help for everything. We have strong backbones!'

'So do you have any mental pictures of your parents?'

'Vaguely…my uncle always said that I physically resembled my mum.'

'Really?'

'Well, so he said, but then he also said I take after my dad in terms of character.'

There was a brief silence.

'Come here!' Arya said, shifting closer to Osam and hugging him. They remained in the embrace for a while.

'I don't think I could have survived that type of hardship or occurrence,' she whispered, as she felt teardrops on her left shoulder.

'That's OK, Osam. I'll take care of you.'

It was the first time he had opened himself up to anyone but he still didn't dare hold her gaze, not ready to see his weaker self through her eyes.

'You're OK?' she asked as he calmed down.

'Yeah, I'm OK, thanks.'

'Is that what you guys go through to get here? Gosh, Africans are all smiles and happy when they appear on television.'

'Well, I don't know about other people's experiences, but I'm sure they might have similar or worse. Thousands use unseaworthy boats to try to reach Spain and Italy, falsely portrayed as a gateway to wealthier parts of Western Europe. Hundreds die in the attempt or get stuck if they get there.'

'How tragic! So how do you guys cope with the disappointments?'

'What disappointments?'

'I mean…when you realise that things ain't what they're supposed to be…I mean, here in the west.'

'Plaza of illusion!'

They both sat absolutely motionless.

'Well, what can you do? You just get on with it. You're here already. You're just relieved to be here. It's tough…really tough. But you can't go back empty-handed. There are people, sometimes a whole family back home, that have invested their all in you. Some aren't able to cope with all that – the new environment, the treatment you receive, the disappointment, the stress to survive and send money home, and the true reality of being unwanted.'

'The world's so unfair, innit?'

'All we ask for is the opportunity to work. Cuz we're hard-working, we borrow loads of money just to get here and…and…do the dirty work that Brits don't wanna do, you know. Look around you, the riches of the West have been and still are scavenged from our effort. They won't admit it, but it's a fact.'

She sat motionlessly.

'Consider this. Can you imagine an illegal immigrant running to the police to report any injustice or aggression towards him? He or she is scared of the police in the first place. I mean, you wouldn't even dream of going to the police, not after escaping from their clutches.'

'Oh yes, so what really happened?'

'Well, another long story. This was just before I got the job at Gillette. Briefly, these Home Office guys rounded us all up in the middle of the night while we had our usual break around 2 a.m.'

'You mean while you were cleaning the supermarket?'

'Yep. It was an all-night job, so we had our hour break at that time. Most people slept during the period.'

'Oh, so you guys were really caught napping then.'

'Uh-huh. We--I mean about three of us who hadn't dozed off--suddenly saw these guys, about eight of them, walk into the canteen and close the door. Even before they introduced themselves and asked for our documentation, we had sussed out who they were.'

'Really? How?'

'It was a known secret among illegal immigrants. You can't imagine the scene, Arya, the overwhelming sense of loss. We were all begging and crying for mercy. Like sheep to the slaughterhouse, we were loaded into this big waiting van, and off we went. The windows were high up near the ceiling of the van so you couldn't see anything. It was similar to a prison van. And we were fifteen: eleven men and four women – all West Africans.'

'So?'

'Well, all of a sudden, the van slowed down and gradually came to a stop. We were told to get out of the vehicle, cuz there was some kind of problem. They didn't tell us what it was. So we did as we were told, and just waited for our fate. It was a very cold October 13, I remember clearly. The only thing they said was that another vehicle was on its way.'

'But why didn't they make you stay in the vehicle as it was cold?'

'I don't know. But they were also out of their two cars which had been escorting us. So we were all standing on the M4 hard shoulder. All at once, I felt some strength in my legs. I took a look at the officers and their batons hanging from their waistline belts. Then, I quickly jumped over the barrier, and legged it in the dark through the surrounding fields.'

'Wow, how brave, Osam!'

149

'I just galloped and galloped and galloped! I didn't even know where I was going. But I knew I was going in the direction of Reading. I got to Reading about three hours later – hungry, cold, and completely rattled.'

'Did you go to—'

'Richard's place? No.'

'Why?'

'It was too dangerous, and he's very touchy about immigration issues. That's why I decided to spend the night with these homeless blokes under the road bridges near the Iceland supermarket.'

'What happened to the others, do you know?'

'I don't know. I didn't ask, and I've never seen them since.'

'So…let me get this clear. Do you mean that people coming from Africa don't know this reality?'

'Some do know…I mean, because they're told. The problem is no one believes it…or should I say…they refuse to believe it. The argument is, if it was that bad, why are you still there?'

'Would you like to go back to Ghana?'

Osam paused. 'Good question!' he said pensively. 'Hmm…for a visit, yes…yes!'

'Why would you rather stay where you don't feel welcome?'

'Another good question. Hmm…There's a statement in Born Fi Dead…'

'What's that?'

'The book I finished reading last week.'

'Ah, you mean the one about the Yardie underworld stuff.'

'Yeah, Laurie Gunst, the writer, makes an assessment of the situation which I concur with completely.

'And that is?'

'That a lot of people are caught up in a Catch-22 situation of being lost in the land of paradise, the unwritten cultural law that says if you don't return from the West with your pockets full, then don't come back at all. It's incomprehensible to return home poor. That scenario is so humiliating it is unthinkable. The best approach is to keep alive the faith. So people doggedly stay on, freezing through one winter after another, until the dream is dead. Even then, only a few relinquish it.'

'Wow, you seem to have it memorised.'

'Yep, cuz in my opinion that encapsulates the way of thinking of someone from a developing country. The illusion continues.'

There was a long pause.

'Hey, why am I telling you all this? I guess I've already blown my chance with you now that you know all about me...including my illegal status.'

'Silly boy!'

'Look at you, you've got everything; your parents are rich, you've got a good job, your own flat...'

'Our flat!'

'OK, our flat.' He grinned.

'And what about my parents being rich?'

'You know there's something I've always wanted to ask you.'

'What?'

'Why among the whole lot at the club that night did you choose a poor African boy like me?'

'It wasn't love at first sight, I assure you. As far as I was concerned it was supposed to be just a one-night stand. Besides, you spoke Svenska – oh my God!' she said as she uncrossed her legs. 'Actually, Julie spotted you first when you entered the club. She would've pounced on you if she was single. She pointed you out to me in the corner of the club, and then I laid my eyes on you, and the rest is history.'

'And my accent?'

'What about it?'

'I mean...it didn't bother you that I was African?'

'Why should that bother me? As far as I'm concerned nationality wasn't… and still isn't… an issue. Is it an issue for you?'

'Me? Absolutely not!'

'You didn't fall in love with me because of my accent, did you? Because I've only lived in England for three years and I do have an accent as well.'

'It's difficult for Africans to get certain jobs because of their accents.'

'Yeah, but business is business, and love is love. I actually love your accent, you know.'

'Yeah?'

'Yes, I do. It's kind of…not English…not Caribbean…and it isn't the typical African accent. It's kind of a mix of all three…know what I mean?

'No.'

'In any case, it didn't matter then and…doesn't matter now.'

'So you still love me despite knowing my difficult past?'

'If anything, you've increased your chances. I love your sincerity.'

'You sure you ain't loving me out of pity?'

'You know you're a great guy, Osam. But it's amazing how sometimes you negate that with cheap, stupid comments like that.'

'I'm sorry. I didn't mean to…'

'Come here.' She motioned Osam into her wide-open arms. 'Marry me.'

Osam greeted that with dumb silence. 'Marry? Why, are you out of your mind?'

'No, it's because I'm madly in love with you. And secondly, you would be legal.'

It was the greatest news possible for an illegal immigrant, as people paid up to £4000 for marriages of convenience.

'I don't want to marry you for the wrong reason, Arya.'

'Silly boy! How dare you doubt my feelings for you?'

'I don't doubt you. No, don't get me wrong. I just think it's too soon – that's all,' Osam said, trying to conceal his euphoria. Here he was being offered legal status on a golden plate.

'Why? We've known each other long enough, haven't we?'

'Yeah, but you're white and I'm black; you have no experience with black people—'

'I do.'

'But you told me when we met that you hadn't.'

'I've had experiences with you, a black man, remember? Look Osam, I don't need experience to love. When you fall in love, you know it. And that's the scary bit. Because, whether you like it or not, you're stuck!'

He felt touched by her sweet words. He knew he loved her too, but wasn't sure if it was strong enough for marriage. Even though marriage would profit him more than her, she was too good and generous to be messed around. For once he was listening not to his fool heart, but his head.

'Moreover,' she said, with her trademark sweet smile, 'as they say, *have a black, never look back*.'

'Yeah, you don't believe that rubbish, do you?' he said, this time with a broad smile.

'How cocky, how cocky, look at you!'

She had hit the epicentre of his masculinity and he really felt good about himself.

He gave her another month to think hard about what she was proposing. He hoped in his heart that, in the end, he wouldn't have played a foolish game.

Chapter 20

Three weeks later, they agreed it was best to just live together as that would still be enough for Osam to regularise his stay in the UK.

They visited a local solicitor who agreed to act on Osam's behalf. Charlie, one of his acquaintances, highly recommended him, having been helped by him in the past.

'The Home Office is serious about marriages of convenience these days,' said the middle-aged white man sitting at the opposite end of the desk.

'What's that?' asked Arya.

'It's the situation where a foreign national marries a UK or European Union citizen so he or she can have legal documentation to remain in the country – the UK, in this case.'

'But we've been living together for some time now,' Osam said.

'How long?'

Arya and Osam looked at each other.

'Well, we've been seeing each other for the past four months or so, but living together for about a month,' Osam replied.

'That's not long enough to apply for a residence permit on the basis of co-habiting. I can go ahead with it if that's what you want but...'

'What would you advise?'

'You either get married as soon as possible at the registry with a couple of friends...all you need are two witnesses though it's better to have a couple of people around so that when the immigration officers have a look at your wedding photos they won't doubt its genuineness. Or, you wait for a couple of months of living together, then I can apply on your behalf on that basis – it's your decision.

'How long does it take for the application to go through in both cases?' Osam asked.

'It depends on the proofs presented to support it. Firstly, you must open a joint bank account and start paying your salaries or wages into it. Secondly, the more money you have in the account, the better it is. So if you can get some friends and family to transfer some loans, that'll help. But don't do the transfers or deposits at the same time. It must be done periodically and in small chunks. Thirdly, have all utilities like water, gas, etc. in both names. Finally, tell your friends, home and abroad, to start sending you letters and postcards with both of your names on the envelope. Come back to me in two months when you've got all this evidence, and I'll put in your application. All things going well, you should get your residency within four months. Immigration officers might also pay you a surprise early morning visit during your application period.'

'The visit's not a problem. I thought it took longer than four months,' Osam gasped.

'It can take longer because applicants don't supply the correct documentation, or their solicitors don't give them the correct advice.'

The lawyer also claimed that since Osam had initially entered the country illegally, he would have to bribe his way at the Home Office to facilitate the process. For £2000, Mr Andrews promised to get the job done within three months.

They chose the co-habiting option.

Osam didn't have the cash to pay the initial deposit of £500, so he took out a loan from his bank while Arya convinced her parents to transfer £2000 into the account every month for the next six months. That money would be returned as soon as Osam's immigration problem was sorted out.

The day Osam went to make the deposit payment, he met Sam, a fellow Ghanaian, who was a trainee solicitor at those very same chambers. He still lived at home so he made the almost 80 km daily trip from Tottenham to Reading by train.
It was encouraging to find a fellow countryman working his way up the legal profession ladder.
Since he arrived in England, Osam always admired people in white-collar jobs; particularly if they were black, like Sam. He always wished he worked in an office as he felt that looked more respectable than his present job as a cleaner. He knew he was doing the cleaning job because that was the only job he could do in his present situation. He considered it as something temporary; knowing that one day he would achieve his aim of getting a real job. Firstly, his illegal immigration status had to be resolved, and secondly, he had to improve himself academically.
He thus registered to do the part-time CIMA course at Reading College. It was a course he had always wanted to do but couldn't afford while in Ghana.
He went to college on Monday, Wednesday and Friday evenings. Due to the demands of the course he had no choice but to leave the evening cleaning job - even though he knew it would adversely affect his already stretched finances.
Luckily for him, Arya offered to pay half of the course fees, which he readily accepted.
Osam did not know what she saw in him. She was blindingly generous.

Chapter 21
(*Four years later*)

Osam wasn't studying anymore. He was awaiting the results of the final part of the CIMA course. He was exempt from certain subjects at the first stage because of his Business Administration degree. He was part-qualified now, as he had successfully gone through the Operational, Management and Strategic levels. He hadn't bothered to look for a white-collar job yet. He and Arya agreed that it would be better if he qualified fully first, and then searched for a job in that field.

Osam was still in the same morning cleaning job. However, he had risen to the position of Supervisor. Maxine, the old Supervisor, who was now Peter's wife, had taken early retirement the previous year. Before she left, she strongly recommended Osam to the Area Manager for her vacant position. Osam was particularly surprised, as not only were the Polish girls employed before him, but he still hadn't provided his National Insurance number.

The girls didn't seem bothered by Osam's promotion. They were persistent work absentees, which always resulted in Osam covering for either, or in some cases both.

Osam thus thought that his promotion was a reward for his hard work or a clear case of positive discrimination.

For the first time in his life, he was in a position of authority, which brought with it a slight raise in his meagre remuneration.

The first thing he tried to do was exercise his newly-acquired authority by employing one of the numerous Ghanaian newcomers in Reading to cover his vacant position.

Unfortunately, Osam's request was turned down by the Area Manager. When he protested, he was told to either accept it or leave. In the end, knowing he was working without a National Insurance number, he gave in.

The results were finally released in May. He had passed.
He had been quietly confident about his chances. He was particularly happy that he had not repeated any part of the course during the four-year part-time study, unlike some of his mates at the college. Osam was now a qualified Chartered Management Accountant, who was living with a girl who had a Master's degree in Management. He had always been good academically, and he prided himself on that. He could at long last look forward to satisfying his dream of working in a white-collar job. He wondered now how he would cope working with white people in an office environment.

But the best was yet to come. Their lawyer rang later that evening to inform them that the Home Office had granted Osam a five-year resident permit. That was the real icing on the cake. He felt like a huge weight had been lifted off his shoulders. The enormous relief he experienced with his new legal status surprised even him. He never really realised he'd been carrying such pressure all this while.

He still hadn't heard from Ademola since he left for the US on *holiday* almost four years before.
Peter and Maxine had moved to Saint Vincent. She had won a six-figure amount on the national lottery, and they felt England wasn't the place for them anymore.
He rang Richard to tell him the good news. He wasn't home. He tried his mobile.
'You're never at home, bad boy!'
'Ha! Look who's talking,' Richard teased.
'Where're you?'

'In the town centre – window shopping.'

'Hmm! Not bad for some, huh?'

'I'm not shopping – just window shopping. Why don't you come out for a pint?'

'I can't. I'll explain why in…'

'Blimey! You've been under the thumb since you moved in with Arya.'

'Why is everyone saying that? Arya said she bumped into some Ghanaian girls recently who made the same insinuation.'

'Did they?'

'Not directly, perhaps. But indirectly…'

'Because we hardly see you, man.'

'Yeah, I know. I'm just too busy; work, school, homelife, etc…you know the life here. Anyway, have I got news for you!'

'What news? Have you got your results?'

'Yes, I received them two days ago…'

'Sorry?'

'I received the results two days…'

'Can you turn down the music in the background? …I can't hear you…'

'Oh, sorry.' Osam put down the receiver on the small bedside table, which also housed the base station, took the remote control from the bed, and reduced the volume of Peter Tosh.

'Can you hear me now?'

'Yes, continue…'

'Yes, as I was saying, I've received my exam results.'

'And…'

'I passed, of course!'

'That doesn't surprise me. Apart from being a bright student, you've always locked yourself in during your holidays to study.'

'Books first, mate!'

'Yessir! And you waited for two days to tell your best friend? Congratulations, anyway!'

'Now wait for the big one: the lawyer just rang to say that my residency has been granted!'

'Wow, that calls for a celebration. How did Arya react?'

'I don't know.'

'What do you mean you don't know?'

'She hasn't arrived from work yet.'

'Right. Well, well, well! Did they give you one year?'

'Five years! Five good years, man!! Arya is Swedish, remember?'

'Right. They took a long time, didn't they?'

'The lawyer told me last year, or the year before, I don't remember, that my name had popped up on their *wanted list.*'

'Wanted list?'

'Remember when I escaped from them when I was cleaning at the supermarket?'

'Hmmm…no. I didn't know that.'

'Oh, I thought I had told you.'

'Nope. And I'm sure there's loads of stuff that you haven't told me. Never mind.'

'Our friendship hasn't always been smooth sailing, and you know that, Richard.'

'Anyway, so when can you apply for permanent residency then?'

'After the fifth year, I think. I'll ask the solicitor when I go for my passport tomorrow.'

'The bloody British huh? If you marry their own, they give you one-year residency and-permanent residency after that.'

'But, hey, who cares? Five years of freedom man! The gods have smiled on me!'

'Yes, I absolutely agree. You're a very lucky boy! You've only been here…how long now—'

'Four years, and a bit…um…almost five years.'

'The gods have always smiled on you, Osam. I mean, for you to meet a girl with such kindness and understanding…a girl whose mum has been involved in helping refugees in her country—'

'But just listen to the jobs I've gone through: gardening, cleaning, bricklaying, fruit picking, selling pirate tapes and CDs…I've done all the dirty jobs.'

'Yeah…it's been tough-going, hasn't it? But, this has always been the life of illegal immigrants, and you know that very well. Anyway, as the Bible says: *the first shall be the last, and the last shall be the first.* I entered this country before you, but you have now more *peso* than I have.'

'Don't be silly, Richard!'

'Look, I only get one-year visas, and this is because I'm studying. They can easily reject my application when it's time for renewal. Only God knows what will happen when I complete my course.'

'Why don't you get hitched to a Brit?'

'The young women don't love me. Perhaps I'm not cool enough. Sometimes I wish I were you. In fact, I wish I had Arya.'

'Silly bugger!'

'Just joking, Osam.'

'And the older ones?'

'You don't expect me to go for second-hand or desperate women, do you? I don't want to be a laughing stock in the Ghanaian community. People admire you for your woman; she's young, pretty, friendly, and a very good person as well. You've got it all made, man.'

'I don't know…ehm…yes, I think so.'

'I must confess that initially I thought you were in it just for the purpose of immigration.'

'Why did you think that?'

'Because she wasn't your type.'

'What do you mean?'

'Come on, Osam, you always go for girls with big bums...'

'Big wobbly bums...'

'Yes, big wobbly bums.'

'You don't always get what you want in life, innit?'

'Of course, I know you're in love with her. Otherwise, you wouldn't be with her for that long...well...unless you're planning to do a runner now that you've got yourself sorted – as many do.'

'Well, thanks for the vote of confidence.'

'You're welcome, sir.'

'So what about doing an MOC?' Osam suggested.

'It's too expensive. They know the score, so the bitches demand too much these days. Moreover, some of them threaten you about informing the police about the deal once they finish spending the money.'

'You're kidding!'

'It's business, Osam...big business. Unless you pay them more money, they'll go to the cops.'

'Are you sure, Richard? There's lots of rumour-mongering in Ghanaian circles, you know.'

'That's a fact, Osam.'

'Well, that's awful then.'

'Yeah, man. Many people have fallen victim to that. There's a new and better connection these days.'

'What's that?'

'Using women or girls from other EU countries. They charge less and are also easier to control.'

'It's amazing how these solicitors always seem to be a step ahead of the authorities. So, are you gonna try that then?'

'Money money money, Osam. You know the system; you can buy your immigration if you have the cash! I'm already working more that I'm legally allowed to...'

'Yeah, everybody does it, Richard.'

'I know, but one has to be careful, particularly now I've only got a couple of months to go.'

'Go for a loan. That's what the banks are there for, innit?'

'Innit? You're talking like them, Osam.'

'You haven't forgotten your kind advice to me to behave like them, innit?'

They both laughed.

'Ah, talking about banks, when I go for the letter from the solicitor tomorrow, I'm going straight to the social security office to apply for my NI number. After more than four years in England, I'm gonna have an NI number. Incredible! Patience, they say, is a virtue. I'm glad I didn't buy or use somebody else's. Can you imagine living with two identities?'

'I'm happy for you. But I've been waiting for you to thank me for my help all these years, Osam.'

'Thanks, Richard, without your help I don't know where I would be. Thanks, man!'

'That's OK. Anyway, coming back to the issue of immigration, I've been thinking about that, but I don't know whether I can afford to pay it.'

'Who knows, if I get a good job soon, I could help.'

'No. I could just vanish in the system if I couldn't repay it. Like some people do.'

'Anyway, jokes apart, I literally felt a burden lifted off me when I received the news.'

'Well, what do you expect? People pay thousands for visa renewals and marriage connections. You're a very lucky man, my friend.'

'No, it isn't just that. It's the feeling that I had been unconsciously carrying this fear of deportation all this while. It's just difficult to explain the emotion.'

'Well—'

'Anyway, how are things with you?' Osam cut in.

'I'm good, thanks. We need to start putting flesh on the bare bones of our home-return project, now that you've become a legal *alien*. You've got no excuse now.'

'Yeah, it's been a long time since we discussed that, hasn't it?'

'No, you seemed very interested in the idea when you first arrived, but lately your interest seems to have wavered, if not waned.'

'Very good point. But first, I need to find a job. I can't return to Ghana empty-handed.'

'Don't worry, soon your heart's desire will be granted.'

'I'm sure of that, man. Anyway, I've got to go now, I still haven't done the cooking and Arya should be home soon.'

'All right, I'll call you at the weekend.' With that, they hung up.

He quickly rushed downstairs to a nearby off-licence to buy a bottle of champagne.

At dinner that evening, Osam waited until after their fruit dessert to spill the beans. He went into their small kitchen and re-appeared holding the champagne in one hand and two champagne glasses crossed at the stem in the other.

'I thought we already celebrated your exam success?'

'Oh, you haven't heard the news? Poor girl, what can I say?'

'What? Tell me, please!'

'Mr Hussein rang to say that the Home Office has granted me a five-year resident visa,' he said as he poured the champagne into her glass. 'After four years, two lawyers…and…how much have we spent in all?'

'At long last, congratulations, Osam! Who cares how much we have spent? You deserve every penny of it. Come here, my boy.' She motioned Osam onto her lap. They embraced and were soon locked in a long passionate kiss.

As the news quickly spread, Osam was treated with much respect among the African--and particularly the Ghanaian-- community in the town for his recent academic achievement.

He still hadn't travelled outside the UK, due to his final stage CIMA examination. His residence application had taken longer than his solicitor had led them to believe. According to Mr Hussein, there had been a rapid increase in *Marriage of Convenience* cases, so the Home Office was vigilant about residence applications.

Arya worked as the Marketing Manager for a multinational company in London. They had been planning to go to Sweden on holiday for the past four years, only for their hopes to be dashed by the long wait.

In fact, at one stage they even decided to get married in order to speed up the process, but the solicitor told them to be patient and advised against it.

Osam was thus looking forward to visiting Arya's parents soon in Stockholm. He had met them only twice when they visited Reading. They had genuinely welcomed Osam with open arms into their little girl's life, and family.

Chapter 22

(Search for the dream job)

Osam was focused and dedicated as he applied for all Management Accountant and related positions in the local newspapers. Also, he sent out his updated Curriculum Vitae to the large companies based in and around Reading. He couldn't wait to find himself in a straight tie sitting among office colleagues.

Unfortunately, he kept getting rebuffed. The companies thanked him for his application and wished him well in the future. Strangely, the reply messages were almost identical though they came from different companies, and Osam soon became familiar with their style.

After weeks of trying without even a single invitation for an interview, Osam diverted his attention to the employment agencies. Their standard responses of 'We will keep your CV on our database' weren't what he expected, but were a glimmer of hope nevertheless. But behind his bravado exterior, his recent victories were starting to leave a rather sour taste in his mouth.

Almost three months of trying without any success elapsed. He still had not found his *dream* job. He was getting down and desperate. So was Arya, who couldn't understand why a qualified Management Accountant couldn't even get an interview.

Osam sought advice from Charlie, one of his acquaintances. He worked for an insurance company in Swindon, a town only a few kilometres from Reading. He drove a BMW convertible and was known for his eccentric and flamboyant lifestyle.

He offered Osam a job as an insurance broker. Osam turned it down because he didn't want to go near any profession that involved selling or cold-calling. His disastrous experience in Sweden had left deep scars.

'You Ghanaians are undoubtedly intelligent but slow. You'll never get a job with this kind of CV. It's too bland,' Charlie said in his fake Caribbean accent.
'You think so?'
'Yeah, man! Why did you wait to finish the course before looking for a job in that field?'
'Arya and I thought it was better that I concentrate on finishing it.'
'Oh yeah, how're you two getting on? You still living together?'
'Yep! Still going strong.'
'I saw her with Richard in the checkout queue at Sainsbury's last Saturday afternoon. Unfortunately, I was in a hurry and couldn't speak to them. Please, give her my best regards.'
'Oh, they haven't told me anything yet.'
'Careful, brother, with this Richard guy – he's crafty.'
Osam smiled.
'Right, now back to the matter of the moment. Ehmm…where was I?'
'About not looking for a—'
'Yeah, yeah, as I was saying, you have no experience. All you have is theoretical knowledge, you know. If you had been in a related job, this would have been a great opportunity to

present to them what you've got, and perhaps move on within the organisation. You know what I mean?'

'Yes, but the problem is that I was illegal until last year,' Osam said submissively, biting his lips.

'Yeah, but being illegal doesn't mean that you can't work in offices. After all, employers don't ask to see your passport, do they? All they want is your NI number, that's all. If they ask to see your work permit because of your obvious African accent, tell them you're British, even though you spent most of your life in Africa....'

'I'm scared to go into that...'

'Silly boy! That's your best chance. If you say that with confidence, no one will ask for any proof. If you don't use your head in this country, you'll rot, my friend.'

'And the NI number?'

'What about it?'

'I don't have an NI number yet. I've only the temporary one they gave me when I applied for it after I was granted the five-year residence.'

'You're kidding me! No National Insurance number? How have you managed to stay in your job *all these years*?' Charlie replied.

'Well, they stopped asking for it after a while.'

'Why haven't you used someone else's number to work with? It's very easy to get one these days, you know. Or, you could have bought a fake one, man.'

'Yeah, but then you have to assume another person's name and—'

'That's what I did when I came here, you know. Loads of people do it. Later on, I got mine with my real name on it.'

'And how did you cope with the change?'

'Yep, you find people calling you with a different name every now and then, but you learn to live with it. Many times I had to explain why I had that many names. Your job is to teach people to unlearn using your old name, it's that simple. Some people still address me with my old name.'

'Incredible.'

'But don't worry about that now - you're legal. But, I must salute your guts, man. I don't blame you. Many Africans struggle because they don't get the right advice when they get to this country. I also had to go through that myself. It's always good to see a fellow African who strives to get higher in the job market. There are so many languishing down the bottom of the ladder with an inferiority complex.'

'So, what do you suggest I do?' Osam said, getting tired of Charlie's lecturing.

'Look, you've done well with your CIMA qualification, and I congratulate you on your achievement. But you're not just a black man, you're an African. You have to prove yourself more than a white British. You know what I mean? Possessing a CIMA qualification doesn't guarantee you a job - particularly being an African. I'm sorry, but that's the situation in this country. People say I'm pessimistic, but I don't think I am. Look, when I came to this country, I already had my MBA from Nigeria. But it took me a very long time before I found an administration job. I knew I was better qualified, but I had no choice but to begin at the bottom of the ladder. I've had to work my way through this problem into the kind of man I am today. One of the lessons this country has taught me, as an African who wants to succeed, is to learn the art of conformity.'

He narrated his shocking personal experiences, which resulted in him having to marry a white British girl to give him some *respect* in the society. Charlie told him to consider why some great black men had white companions. 'Once you're black, you're forever black in the eyes of the white man - no matter your achievements in life,' he said repeatedly.

Osam listened attentively to what he was saying, hardly moving.

Charlie helped Osam create a new CV, which he claimed would produce results. There was no mention of the cleaning job he had done for the past four years. Neither did he indicate he had been doing brickwork and laundry jobs at weekends while he did the CIMA course. Instead, it was full of fictitious companies he had worked for in various administrative positions during the previous four years. The contacts for these companies were all Charlie and his friends. He also advised Osam to register with the employment agencies in the town and to send his CVs to companies outside Reading.

His opportunity knocked three months later. Osam got a job interview through a local agency as an accounts assistant at a small courier company based in Bracknell town centre. If he got the job, he would have to make a daily 20 km trip by train or bus, despite the remuneration being less than his current job.

Even though he was over-qualified for the position, he was astonished that he still had to go through a lengthy interview. To his surprise, the interviewer confessed to only having five GCSEs. His keyboard speed was also tested. Osam was convinced he wouldn't get the job because the interviewer thought he was only using the place as a stepping stone. However, Osam drummed it in again and again that he would be there to stay.
Yet he knew the young man was right. For him, it would just be a good start until he gained enough confidence to find a better job.
Later at home, when Osam asked Arya's advice about taking the job, she seemed indifferent.

The following morning, Osam received a phone call. He had been chosen. He was completely over the moon. He thought he had finally turned the page in his life's current chapter. His annual remuneration of £8,800 was about £900 less than what he got for his cleaning supervisor job. Not that he cared, as his days as a cleaning supervisor would soon be a thing of the past. Moreover, he would now be wearing a shirt and tie to work.

That evening, he and Arya went to Debenhams in the town centre to buy some new work clothes. Osam also bought an Italian brown leather bag. He felt a bit awkward as he tried on his clothes in front of the bathroom mirror. Apart from the interview, he had never worn a tie before.

The following morning Osam felt very ill-at-ease as he walked to catch the bus to his new job. He had the strange sensation that all eyes were on him. It was as if every face he looked at was already glued to his. Moreover, the shirt collar tickled his neck. He felt unsophisticated.

Osam trembled with fear as he went through the smaller front entrance meant for the office workers. He felt like a fish out of water - being the only black person there. He also realised that he was *over-dressed*; he could easily have passed for the company boss who introduced him in a small office.

'This is Ohsam, Ohsam Mensa,' the boss said.

'That doesn't sound British? Where are you from?' said the younger of the two women who until now had been typing.

'I-I-I'm from Ghana.'

'Guyana. That's a lovely country. My husband and I were there on holiday two years ago.'

'N-not Guyana, Ghana,' Osam replied with a sheepish grin.

'Gana. Is that in the Caribbean as well?' the second lady asked.

'No, it's in Africa, West Africa, to be precise. It is located on West Africa's Gulf of Guinea; bordering the North Atlantic

Ocean between the Francophone countries of Cote d'Ivoire and Togo.'

'Right.'

'Sorry...' said Ken, cutting in. 'Kerry, would you show Ohsam what to do!' he said and left the small office.

Osam shared his office with three white workers: Kerry and Monica, his fellow accounts assistants who were in their fifties; and John, the Accountant who was forty-nine, although his pronounced balding made him appear older.

Osam's little desk, which was situated at the far end corner of the small office, was old and empty except for a dusty computer and a large writing pad which had the previous year's calendar on it. The six cupboards were filled with thick accounts ledger books. The remainder of the books were haphazardly scattered above the cupboards and in every spare space on the old, green carpet. There was very little room to manoeuvre in the well-lit office as if they had been squashed into it. The air inside this windowless office was warm and stale. Osam was drenched in sweat due to the sweltering heat and regularly popped outside clandestinely to dry off.

But that didn't bother Osam, as it was better than sitting in his old, small and poorly-ventilated cleaning supervisor office surrounded by mopping materials and a thick scent of cleaning detergents. The only source of breeze in his previous office was through the door, which always remained open.

Later that evening, Osam told Arya about his day.

'We all have butterflies when we start a new job. Don't worry, you'll get over it.'

'They're all white. It's really strange being the only black guy around.'

'I thought it was the same in your previous job.'

'Well...but I had Eastern European girls working with me.'

'What about that? They're not as black as you, are they, Osam?'

'Yeah, but we're all in the same soup. They're discriminated against just like us.'

'You've got this thing about discrimination…you better get it out of your system or else you'll get nowhere professionally. You've worked so hard to get to where you are now.'

'You'll never understand what it is to be black.'

'Then spend your energy wallowing in someone else's perception of you.'

Despite Osam's high qualification, he spent most of the time photocopying, and occasionally inputting data, if he was lucky. To improve his chances of spending more time on the computer, he bought himself a second-hand personal computer to work on his typing speed. Instead of the television, he spent two hours each weekday evening--and four hours during the weekends--practising on his typing instructor programme. He was typing at twenty words per minute when he began. A month later, it had increased to forty-five, then fifty after three months.

Unfortunately, they still wouldn't give him the chance to prove himself, even though he was better qualified than his boss. On one occasion, he took his CIMA certificate to work and showed it to the company boss when the opportunity arrived. He just smiled and walked off.

Despite that, Osam still enjoyed the stolen glances from some of his African *brethren* while on his way to work. Unlike his previous job, this was nine-to-five, and he got paid overtime. He knew that no condition was permanent, and patiently and anxiously waited for his chance.

The last straw came when he was told to assist the courier drivers in loading their vehicles until someone else was hired. He had also gradually become the unofficial Teaboy. He began to understand where he stood as far as working with them was concerned. But he was a proud man and still went to work smartly dressed as before, despite being told by Ken to wear casual clothes.

He never told Arya about what he was going through at work, even though she laid into him sometimes for his dirty office clothes. He preferred to suffer in silence.

After almost six months in the job, Arya got him to apply for a vacant assistant accountant position advertised on her company's notice board. She even got the application forms for him to fill in.

Osam was pleasantly surprised when he was offered an interview. He knew he had the right qualification, but lacked the necessary experience he claimed in his revised curriculum vitae.

The interview turned out to be the easiest he had gone through in his life. The interviewer seemed satisfied when Osam explained that he had opted to work in a low employment position to gain experience. He seemed particularly impressed with Ken's recommendations. Osam presumed that either Ken was happy to see him go, or he genuinely respected Osam, despite seeming to treat him with contempt.

He got the job.

He always attributed the ease with which he got it to his connection with Arya, although she always denied playing an active part.

He was given a three-month probationary period to prove himself.

Chapter 23

Osam travelled to work in London with Arya on his first day. He found it strange that they were going to be working in the same place. They would be seeing each other almost all the time, which he thought wouldn't be good for their relationship. Osam needed her, however, as he had little knowledge of London. The last time he was there was about three months before when Martina and Nina, his Polish work colleagues, invited him to a friend's party in Wood Green, north London. He had told Arya that he was visiting an old Ghanaian friend in Shepherds Bush. But the truth, when it ultimately came out, nearly led to the breakdown of their relationship.

It was normal for people to travel from Reading to London to work. He was ready for the almost 90 km daily return trip on the M4 and M25 motorways to work in central London.
He wore his new dark-brown Debenhams suit and a pair of black shoes. His light brown silk tie perfectly matched his cuff-linked white and brown striped shirt. He had dressed to impress, and though he was poor, he looked like a young London City executive. It was a far cry from his first day at his previous job. And that was good enough for him.

He wondered what they thought of him as the department head introduced him to the team, claiming Osam's immediate boss was running late. The department was made up of seven men and four women – all white. Though they all seemed polite towards him and wished him well, he felt uncomfortable. He would have to learn to deal with it if he was to succeed in the job. He was invited to a birthday party for that Friday evening in the Social Club, which he accepted because he didn't want to turn anyone down so soon, and he and Arya had nothing planned for the weekend.

After the formal introduction, James, the Financial Director, invited him to his office for a chat. He had already met him as he was present during both interviews. He seemed a pleasant, straight-forward person.

'Close the door, please. Want some coffee?' James asked as they entered his opulent office.

'No thanks,' Osam replied as he looked around. 'You have a lovely office, sir,' he continued. He had learned during his sales training to show interest in people by saying positive things about something they had. It did work wonders sometimes.

'Please don't address me as '*sir*', Osam. I hope I've got the pronunciation right this time,' he said, referring to his numerous attempts during the interview. 'I'll show you your office in a minute. I've just been told the facilities management guys are still connecting the office equipment. Your job requires that you have your own office. Sorry about the delay.'

'No problem,' Osam said, his hands firmly behind his back.

'As you've already seen, it's a small but vibrant team. There is always pressure as we are always working to deadlines. If you aren't sure of anything, please ask anybody in the team for assistance. Better that way than getting things done incorrectly. Julie will give you some quick training after lunch.' He stopped when his phone rang. 'Excuse me,' he said as he picked it up. 'James speaking...all right thanks. Come with me, please. Your office is now ready,' he said as he hung up the receiver in its shiny, silver base.

It was a fair-sized, square-shaped, blue-carpeted office. The medium-sized desk was situated almost in the centre. There was just enough space from the wall for the wheel-based executive chair to move from the slot beneath the desk. The strong wood and varnish smell from the light-brown desk indicated it was either new or recently polished. The desk looked bare apart from the 17-inch monitor which rested on the left-hand corner. The credenza near his desk to the right looked older. There was a large painting on the beige wall to the left of the desk. The high, transparent, glass window by the door provided a perfect view. Even though he had his own office, there was no hiding from the prying eyes of people walking past. And it was a busy corridor.

This was to be his workplace for how long he didn't know. He looked up to see if anyone was watching him as he reviewed it.

'Hi, my name's Julie,' a woman said, stepping through his open door and extending her hand. 'I'm sure you remember me. I have just been told you've been invited to my birthday do later this afternoon.'

He shifted uncomfortably in his seat and wondered what she thought of him. 'Hi, the name is Osam,' he responded, ill at ease.

'I know. I was at the club the night you met Arya,' she responded in a hushed whisper, running her little fingers through her short brown hair.

'Oh, right. Silly me! Please forgive me for not recognising you.'

'No, don't be silly. It's rather unfortunate that we haven't met since. But don't you worry, I know a lot about you already,' she continued.

'Good stuff, I suppose.' He stared into her blue eyes as if ordered to detect flaws.

'Hmmm…girly, girly stuff, if you know what I mean? Anyway, I'm in the office next door if you need any assistance. I will see you this afternoon in my office for some quick training. And, ah, don't forget the *do*, please.' She left, not even bothering to wait for his response.

Osam thought her confidence and positive demeanour were typical of a powerful, successful woman.

He closed the door softly until he heard the click of the catch and walked slowly towards his chair. Then he realised his left shoelace was undone. He crouched down close to his office door and did it. He wondered how long she had been watching him during his silent self-evaluation.

He rushed back to his seat as his phone rang.

'Hello, Osam speaking, how may I help?'

'Hello, Osam speaking, how may I help?' came the imitative voice.

'Hey, it's good to hear from you. I've been wondering when you would ring to ask how I'm getting on.'

'I know. I just wanted to give you some space to settle down.'

'How did you know my number, anyway? And, by the way, you're the first person to ring me, congratulations!'

'I got it off Jon, the man who installed it in your office this morning.'

'Did I sound OK on the phone?'

'Yep, you sounded fine, babe.'

'What about my greeting?'

'You mean, *Hello, Osam speaking, how may*—'

'There you go again…'

'No, it's cool; sounds very professional actually,' she chuckled.

'Seriously, what do you think?'

'Osam, I said it's fine. I would tell you if it wasn't, OK?' She sounded tired of his usual insecurity.

'So, how's the day gone for you, honey?' he said, trying to make amends.

'Very busy! It's been one of those days, Osam. I just can't get myself motivated. Ah, Julie and I have just been talking about you.'

'Talking about me? What have you been saying…?'

'Nothing improper, she said she left your office a while ago. She's always thought of you as a real hunk. I think she's still got a soft spot for you.'

'Oh yeah? What more?'

'Stop behaving like a child, Osam. Actually, she thought you're shy, but I told her you're coy, not shy.'

'Boy, that's a bit cheeky, isn't it?'

'You're coming down to the restaurant for lunch, aren't you?'

'Yes, but I'm afraid you'll have to come fetch me. I don't know my way around.'

'I'll be down in a minute. I tell you what? You could come with Julie. I'll tell her to fetch…'

'Not again, honey, it's my first day, and I don't really know her—'

'OK, Osam, see you in a minute.'

'Are you upset?'

'No, not at all. See you, honey.' She hung up.

His phone rang again as soon as he replaced the handset.

'Hello, this is Osam, how may I help you?'

'Hi Osam, Julie here. You are joining us for lunch, aren't you?'

'Yeah, Arya's coming down for me in a minute.'

'All right then, see you later.'

'See you later, Julie.'

That evening as they lay in each other's arms on the sitting room sofa watching their favourite EastEnders on TV, Osam replayed in his mind his first day at work behind a proper office desk. He now understood why Arya always complained of fatigue at the end of the working week. He had been thrown into the deep end from day one. He had realised the vast difference between accountancy theory and practice. He had put undue pressure on himself by claiming to know more than he did. He had no choice but to force himself to learn things on his own – and quickly. He already felt drained after only one day. He wondered if he would ever get used to his new routine over the coming days or weeks or years. He was clear about one thing, though: he had ultimately achieved his aim of working in a white-collar job. Not that his previous job as an accounts assistant wasn't significant. People who knew him thought he was a man of great responsibility in his previous job. This time, he was working in a *real* responsible position at a multinational company in London, and that made a great difference. His present achievement was beyond his wildest dreams, and he was bent on making it work, despite the added stress that came with it. It was challenging, but rewarding at the same time.

'Thanks, Arya!'

'What for?'

'I wouldn't be here if it wasn't for you.'

'Don't be silly, Osam!'

'I'm serious, Arya, I want you to know that I really appreciate all you've done for me.'

'I hope you'll survive, because it's a busy department, as you've already noticed.'

'Yep. I made it through today without any bruises, so that's as good as it gets for now! It hasn't been easy getting there, but it's gonna be even harder to get me out. I really appreciate all the effort you've put into our relationship. The travelling, the stressful work environment...'

Arya burst out laughing. 'Don't worry babe, you'll get used to it after a while. It's only a job, at the end of the day.'

He was tempted to tell her about the toughness of his first day but suppressed the thought.

'Osam?'

'Yes, honey?'

184

'Can you please make me a cup of tea?'

'Of course,' he said. He was reluctant to disengage from their romantic comfort but obliged all the same. He had some washing up to do but was playing lazy that evening. So far, Arya hadn't complained like she used to; perhaps realising that Osam might be tired, too.

He returned a couple of minutes later with two cups of tea.

'You know we've always talked about getting into the property business.'

'Yeah. Careful, it's hot!' Osam responded as he handed Arya her cup.

'How would you like living in the countryside?' she said as she took it.

'You mean on a farm?'

'No, I mean in a village on the outskirts of Reading – Tilehurst, Caversham, Thatcham...'

'You're not happy here?' Osam said, sipping his hot tea.

'No, I like it here. Except it is too central, I think. I miss the quiet and peace of the countryside. It's better to return home from work to some kind of tranquillity.' She was referring to her parents' country home in beautiful Sandön, one of the villages on the outskirts of Stockholm.

'Well, I just feel the countryside is too conservative and all-white if you know what I mean?'

'Yeah, you're right...'

'But if you need a change, we could sell this flat and move into one of the nearby villages.'

'You sure you wouldn't mind? I'm sure we can afford it now that you're in a good job. We can even look at the possibility of renting out this place.'

'You don't think it's too soon to get into the property business?'

'Why? Do you think so?' Arya asked, typically answering a question with a question - usually wrong-footing Osam in the process.

'Well, I only began today…'

'Yeah, but that shouldn't stop us looking around, should it?'

'You're right. I'll get the Reading Evening post tomorrow,' Osam said.

'No, it's better on Thursdays. There's a property section in that. Fancy an early night?'

'You bet I do!' Osam responded with a twinkle in his eyes.

'But, no boom-boom tonight, huh?'

'Oh no! Please!! It's been a long time,' Osam pleaded.

'Not tonight, Osam; I've had a stressful day. Tomorrow night, and that's a promise.'

'Yeah sure, I've heard that anthem before, Miss.'

Chapter 24
(Caversham, Reading)

Two months later, Osam and Arya sold their flat, which had been their home for almost four years, and bought a four-bedroom house in Caversham, about three km from the town centre, as the properties in the small villages were way beyond their means.

It was a Victorian-style house with almost two hundred square metres of land across both front and back gardens. The Thames was only a hundred metres away while the area was popular with joggers. It was relatively cheap as it was in need of extensive renovation.

They also bought a BMW. Arya drove a company Audi, so Osam used the BMW for his runs. There were only a small number of ethnic minorities living locally, so he thought he had to show off a bit so as to gain the *deserved* respect in his new, almost all-white community.

They had no plans yet to start a family, as Arya still wished to return to her home country in the near future, something that brought occasional tension into their relationship. Osam hadn't had a great time in Sweden and had no plans to move there, at least not yet. He felt more at home in the UK.

Richard and Charlie helped during their arduous weekend move, particularly proud of his achievements academically, and now buying--albeit with Arya--such a beautiful house.

Mid-Saturday morning of the first weekend, with their things still all over the place in their new home, the phone rang.
'Osam, phone's ringing.'

'Ain't getting out of bed, Arya. Why should I always be the one who picks up the phone? And the phone's on your side of the bed anyway.'

'All right, all right, I'll get it.'

It was Maria, her mum. They chatted in Swedish for a long while and then she hung up softly.

'Is everything all right? You sounded...'

'My dad's been diagnosed with lung cancer.'

'No!' Osam said, rolling over to her side of the bed. 'Is it—'

'According to my mum, lung cancer usually remains undetected until a patient develops symptoms, and by that time, it is pretty well advanced.'

'Has it metastasized?'

'They don't know yet,' she replied with resignation.

'Oh, dear! So, what's gonna happen now?'

'Well, my mum said he had been complaining since last week of shortness of breath and dull chest pain, in addition to his usual coughing fits. Then, during the week, he began coughing up blood, which prompted the medical check-up. They aren't sure yet if it has already spread. However, the test result later last week means he has to be operated on Monday afternoon.'

'You mean in two days?'

'Yep.'

'Gosh! How old is Sven?'

'Sixty.'

'How long has he been smoking?'

'Strangely enough, he started late in life. He began when he was thirty-one. He was influenced by my mum, who used to be a chain smoker and only quit five years ago. He found it cool when mum smoked while sipping her black coffee after meals. However, she quit on her fiftieth birthday, as a result of the no-smoking campaign adverts on Swedish television.'

'So, where's he now, at home?'

'No, he's been in hospital since yesterday,' she said as she fought back an ocean of tears. Sadness was written all over her thin, beautiful face.

Osam drew closer together and hugged her. She put her arms around him. His heart was also breaking, but he knew he had to detach himself from the present if he really wanted to help her.

This left an indelible mark on their otherwise flourishing relationship. Both Osam and Arya were devastated. Arya particularly, as her dad wouldn't quit smoking even after being diagnosed. He claimed that there was no point as he was going to die anyway.

Osam had grown to love them as his own parents, and they him as their son. He had lacked parental love as a growing boy in Accra and always instinctively yearned for the type of attention and care which Arya's parents naturally provided. Arya was an only child, and so they regarded him as their son. Sven had even proposed handing over the business to both of them when he retired. He ran a large travel agency in Stockholm. She was very close to her family, particularly her dad. It was to be a critical moment in their almost five-year relationship.

Understandably, Arya wished to return immediately to be by her family's side. She felt they--particularly her mum--needed her most at this critical time.

They couldn't find anyone they trusted to look after the house, as Richard was busy at work, so they decided that Arya would go to Stockholm alone. Moreover, Osam was still relatively new in his job.

On Monday morning, while Osam went to work, Arya rang her boss from home to inform him of the news. He was very understanding and granted her a two-week unpaid holiday.

They were in constant touch with each other. Osam felt strange and lonely without her at work and on his return home. At lunch with Julie, Arya's dad dominated their conversation.

He hated cooking after a dragging day's work, and thus went straight to the nearby chip shop for his good old English fish and chips. Arya had helped cut back his fish and chips consumption. She claimed it was unhealthy food. Osam always ate it behind her back, though, in order not to upset her.

Later that Thursday evening, while he was in the middle of watching EastEnders, his mobile phone rang. It was Arya.

'Hey, how was the operation?'

'It went well, according to the surgeon.'

'Oh, that's fantastic! My mind's been unsettled all day because of it. What a relief!'

'Now the bad news. He's dying. The cancerous cells have spread extensively to other parts of his body, so there's no hope for him. He's been given a few months to live.'

Osam nearly choked on the popcorn remains still in his mouth. For a moment, he didn't know how to react. He had never felt that empty in his life. It reminded him of his stoned reaction when uncle Kojo, Auntie Ekua, and her husband took him into his parents' bedroom and dropped the bombshell.

'Oh no! Surely they can do something, Arya.'

'Well, they would like to try radiation, which is used for patients who have a disseminated type of cancer...'

'What's that?'

'That's the medical term for cancer that is widely spread since surgery simply can't get at and remove all the malignant cells.'

'And...'

'Yeah, we're gonna go ahead with it as there is still hope -- albeit little -- of destroying any cancer cells that remained after the surgery.'

'And when is that gonna start, and how are they taking the whole thing?'

'My mum's obviously shattered, but my dad's good.'

'Do you want me there? I don't mind taking a few days off. I told James about it at work today and he asked if I wished to do so.'

'No, we're all right for now. I'm coming back next week. What about you, are you OK?'

'OK? Well, my father-in-law is very ill, my girlfriend's away, and you think I'd be OK? What have we done to deserve this? Everything's been on a roll for us for some time now and...and now this shattering news!'

'Don't worry, honey, we'll cope. We always have coped. Anyway, you get yourself some sleep and I'll call you at work tomorrow, OK?'

'Julie sends her regards.'

'Thanks, tell her I'll call her at work tomorrow.'

'All right, goodnight, babe.'

'Goodnight, honey.'

He rang Richard. They were meant to go to an emergency Ghanaian meeting and, later on, a pub crawl if the news from Stockholm turned out to be positive.

He hadn't been to any meeting since his recent altercations with two members. Osam particularly enjoyed the meeting as they were planning the annual Christmas party. But, as in life, the meeting didn't close without a little return of agitation. A section of the attendees got upset when Osam complained about the poor punctuality of some members. It didn't go down well as he hardly attended meetings anyway. Some took the opportunity to tell him face to face of their dislike for him. And being a proud man, he made sure he replied in kind.

Some disliked, and rightly so, the fact that when Osam spoke Twi, he mixed it with English - a bad practice he cultivated while in Accra. He thought speaking that way gave him gravitas in a Ghanaian society where the English language was important. He was particularly upset when they accused him of behaving as if he was superior to them, or that he was a white man in a black skin.

After the tense meeting, they decided to go to a pub in the town centre instead to drink away their sorrows. Like Osam, Richard felt devastated about the news from Stockholm.

Chapter 25

Arya returned a week later in a very melancholic state to confirm his fears.

She was moving back to Stockholm.

Sven's condition had worsened. He was due to begin the radiation therapy the following week at the private hospital. Her parents wanted her to take over the family business while he underwent radiation. Moreover, as the rightful heir to the business, she needed to know how it operated.
Arya offered her resignation with immediate effect.

Things were happening too fast for Osam and he felt powerless and helpless. He was taken completely by surprise, and could hardly believe Arya was serious when she told him she was moving back to her home country.
There was so much anger: she blamed him for not doing enough in their present situation while he blamed her for taking decisions without due consideration of his feelings. Their recent love-making seemed to have lost something of the earlier passion. He suspected that she was using her current tragedy as an excuse to leave him.

Ten days later they agreed to use her time away in Stockholm as a trial separation. The tension between them had ultimately snapped. They had rapidly grown apart during the trying weeks, so it was the easiest and best option under the circumstances. Luckily for Osam, it wasn't a large mortgage so he could afford to live alone.

He was in two minds as to what to do in the situation. He was a proud man and, apart from Richard, kept things to himself. He had a job and didn't want to move to Stockholm, even though he still loved her so much.

Chapter 26

They both cried at the airport at her departure. He returned home and realised how much he couldn't live without her. With the passage of time, things turned from bad to worse for Osam. He couldn't cope with his present dual stress of living without Arya and the mounting workload. He lost the drive and single-mindedness that had been his trademark. He felt lethargic and empty and soon lost the will to live.

It didn't take long before he began to take *too* many days off. Then reliable news filtered through from work that the company was going under. Their only hope was a takeover bid on the table from one of their competitors. Fortunately, the takeover bid went through three days later.
Unfortunately, it resulted in him losing his job. His boss assured him that it wasn't for his times off work. Osam didn't believe him. He was the only one who lost his job in the department.

As if that wasn't enough, his uncle rang to tell him of the death of Auntie Ekua and her husband the day before. They'd died in a motor accident while on their way from Accra to Cape Coast. Osam was devastated. His parents had died in a similar manner. Even though Osam still disliked his aunt for what she had done to him, she was his aunt, and he had lately been sending her some money through Uncle Kojo. He knew deep down in his heart that his life would not be the same if he had not gone through his childhood experience.

That news seemed to be the last straw that broke the camel's back, as Osam fell into a state of acute anxiety. He was struggling to survive his triple heartbreak. He was hardly sleeping, felt lethargic, and on rare occasions noticed sweaty palms and severe chest pains. He soon found repose and comfort in the bottle.

Richard did his best to provide support, but it wasn't enough due to his own daily work. On several occasions, both Richard and Arya--who was in constant touch from Stockholm--encouraged Osam to seek psychological help, but Osam's pride and stubbornness got the best of him. Rising from the ashes had always been his forte. This time, however, he seemed to be irreversibly broken, eager to disappear for good. It made no difference whether or not he was alive. He was operating on autopilot now; booze had stealthily become his best companion.

A month later, Arya was in London at a trade fair. She paid Osam a surprise visit to find him in a sorry state. He had been out on his own the previous night and was lying in his own vomit in their unlocked house.

'Oh my God, what's happened to you, Osam?' she shouted.

'I'm just tired. That's all,' he snapped.

'Just tired? Look at you. You look awful, Osam! Have you—'

'What do you care anyway?' he said, biting his lips.

'What do I care? I care enough to come all the way from Sweden to pay you a visit, Osam. And stop biting those bloody lips!' She had always hated that habit.

'And who asked you to come, anyway?'

'I beg your pardon? You have a cheek, haven't you? This is my house too, silly bugger! I can do whatever I want. It's amazing how that selfish, little boy inside you still doesn't want to grow up. I'm really sick and tired of your self-pity. You have to learn to accept responsibility for your own actions. Where's the Osam I met and fell in love with?'

'There you go again.'

'I'm sorry, Osam, but someone has to say it. You've got to learn to take control of your life. It´s about time you wised up.'

'Another one of my long list of defects, I suppose. Look, I strive hard for perfection but fall humanly short sometimes. I try, Arya, I try!' he muttered.

'For goodness sake, Osam, enough of that! Look, if you don't want my help, just spit it out, and I'll be on my way, all right?' she said, taking her little hand luggage and turning towards their front door. She stopped in her tracks. Osam was sobbing. She walked back to him and cuddled him warmly. They were in a flood of tears together.

'My life is a mess, Arya. My life's worth nothing without you!' With that, he began shaking convulsively.

Arya was scared and rang for an ambulance. He came around when Arya poured cold water on him.

As they waited, Arya did her best to clean him, as well as assuring him that he would be OK and that she would be at his side all the way.

The ambulance arrived fifteen minutes later and took him to the hospital. She accompanied him, his big hands in her tiny ones. He barely registered the weight she had lost, and couldn't summon the energy to rebuke her for reducing what remained of her wobbly bum.

Trembling and sweating, Osam was taken to the Accidents and Emergency department of the Royal Berkshire Hospital in Reading. As he lay on his bed, he complained of chest pains and difficulty breathing and was later diagnosed with moderate anxiety attack.

He was prescribed some medication and encouraged to do meditation or yoga exercise routines which would help relieve some of the edginess.

As they were walking towards the town centre to buy his prescription, a speeding BMW pulled up. It was Charlie. Osam and Arya hadn't seen him for months. Even though it was a busy road, he put on the emergency lights and got out of the car to greet them.

'Hey Osam, how're you doing?'

'I'm not too bad.'

They shook hands and embraced warmly. He also shook hands with Arya.

'I like your *black man's wife*, Charlie,' Arya said.

'Black man's wife?' Osam said. 'You've lost me...'

'His BMW, Osam!'

'Ah right. I didn't know that. Well, it actually is, you know.' They all laughed.

'How're you guys? Long-time no see!' Charlie continued.

'Well, you're too busy to even visit your friends, aren't you?'

'I'm sorry, man. You know how life is here. Where're you going?'

'The town centre.'

'Sorry that I haven't been able to visit you. I've just been too busy.' Charlie shrugged.

'Don't worry, man. How's things anyway?'

'Could be worse. Where're you coming from?'

'I had an attack this morning, so I was sent to the A&E in an ambulance.'

'Oh dear. You take it easy, man. So, what did the quacks say?'

'Not much really. He gave me a prescription, that's why I'm going to the town centre.' He showed him the prescription form.

'I'd go easy on that if I were you.'

'Why?'

'You're lucky they didn't send you to Fair Mile.'

'What's that?'

'It's near Oxford. It's where the crazy people are sent.'

'And why did you say—'

'Once they see that you're black, they send you there straight away.'

'No!'

'Take it from me, man. This has been going on for a long time now. It's a potential scandal, man.'

'I guess I'll fit right in! In fact, I may never get out because the doctors may not be able to tell the difference between the crazy ones and me.'

'Don't be silly, Osam!' Arya snapped.

'Really,' Charlie cut in, 'I'm not joking. My ex-wife told me about this. You know she's a psychiatric nurse, don't you?'

'Did I hear ex-wife?'

'We separated, man. I thought you knew.'

'Really?'

'Yeah…about a month ago. So I don't live at that address anymore.'

'You sold that nice house?'

'No, she kicked me out! Anyway, got to run now. I'll give you a ring later today, all right? The number hasn't changed, has it?'

'Not the mobile, but the landline has. Don't forget we live in Caversham now.'

'Sorry, but I don't ring mobiles – too expensive.'

Osam gave him his new landline number.

'See you later, guys.' With that, he sped off.

They continued their short trip to the town centre.

'You're very quiet.'

'You already know my opinion about this so-called friend of yours, Osam,' she snapped.

He held his peace. Yikes! She had been chatting away to him nicely, he thought.

Later that afternoon, Charlie rang as promised. It was the first time he'd actually kept his promise, as far as Osam could remember.

'I'm sorry for cutting short the conversation. I didn't want to embarrass Arya.'

'No, why?'

'Is she there?'

'No, she's gone to Sainsbury's.'

'I didn't want to say some sensitive things in front of her, know what I mean?'

'Don't worry, she's cool. So, tell me what's been going on in your life. Where do you live now?'

'At Tilehurst. I've rented a two-bedroom house there.'

'What led to the break-up then?'

'It's been on the cards for some time now, you know.' He told Osam his story.

'Really?'

'Oh yeah. We just came to an agreement that I'd move out of the house as soon as I was granted my British passport.'

'Agreement!'

'She agreed not to interfere with my application if I promised to move out. Normally she's a bit heavy going, but she understood me on this.'

'So, what's gonna happen to your little girl?'

'Well, she's gonna stay with Linda. The women here get everything when you separate. All your hard work comes to nothing, man.'

'Oh dear. How do you feel, man?'

'What can I do? Nothing. I've seen worse, man. I missed the burials of my parents because I couldn't leave this country. It took me nine years before I was able to return to Nigeria to visit their graves. That's life – you just have to take it on the chin.'

'Wow!'

'Look, I know people with more serious stories than mine. Thankfully, I've still got a job, and my British passport, so I'll have to get on with it. What about you guys, I thought you'd separated? You back together again?'

'How did you know we broke up?'

'It's a small town, Osam…even though you've been trying to hide it from me.'

'No, no, no! She's only here for a visit – well, she came to London for a conference.'

'Well, she must still be in love with you.'

'I don't know about that, Charlie. Rivers do run dry, you know.'

'Depends what type of river – love or lust.'

Osam paused.

'Well, she's allowed you to shag her, hasn't she?'

'No way!'

'You're still in love with her?' He asked after a little pause.

Osam sighed. 'I don't know, Charlie. It's a clear case of can't live with her, can't live without her.'

'I think you still do, Osam, so fight for her.'

'She hurt me. She left me.'

Osam told Charlie what had led to the breakup.

'Can I let you in on a secret? It's about Richard and Arya.'

'Arya and Richard? You mean my friend, Richard? What is it?'

'Well…it's a secret spreading in your Ghanaian community. You must know it.'

'I ain't in the loop, and you know that.'

They both laughed.

He told Osam.

Osam didn't believe him. In fact, he had never believed this guy. He heard the front door shut softly and changed the subject.

They talked on. Charlie told Osam about the new insurance broker company he had established recently in the town centre. He had left his old job to go it alone. He offered Osam the chance to work with him when he got well. Charlie also advised Osam to try to get a British passport as quickly as possible, meaning get hitched to a British girl.

Osam kept getting nailed by his weaknesses and faults. From periodic stares and avoidances, it was as if his enemies could somehow read him like an open book. They seemed to be everywhere he turned to for *safety*. He had nowhere else to hide. Then a new day had dawned and his downcast world transformed into hazy sunshine! Arya was his new day. He was glad to have her around.
Despite the fact that he hadn't attended a Ghanaian meeting for a long while, a couple of Ghanaians he knew visited him at home during these hard times, for which he was very grateful.

Arya returned to Stockholm a day after Maria rang to say that Sven's condition had suddenly deteriorated.
Sadly, Sven lost his fight that same week.
Osam was again lonely, sick and jobless.

Chapter 27

Three months had passed since Osam returned from Sven's funeral in Stockholm. Not only was he over his acute anxiety attack, but he was almost back to his old vibrant self. His return to the place where it all began hadn't been a sweet one, but his re-entry into England had been an effortless one. Unfortunately, he was still struggling to find a decent job. He was barely able to pay for the BMW and the mortgage. Arya advised him to sell the car and count their losses, but he couldn't bring himself to, as it would become obvious that he was struggling on his own. In the end, he went back to doing some office cleaning in the mornings and evenings.

He applied to many companies for Management Accounting or related job positions as well as Accounts Administration posts. However, the responses were either that he was too qualified or had too little experience. He thus barely survived on the little money he received for part-time account jobs through the local agencies. He wasn't a permanent UK resident yet so he couldn't sign on. He relied on his two credit cards, which got him into serious debt.

He started doing night shifts stacking crates of bread and loading them into dispatch vehicles at a bakery in Woodley through a job agency. It didn't pay much, but at least he was able to write and submit more job applications.

As things got worse, Arya offered Osam the opportunity to work with her in Sweden but he turned it down. There were so many things going on in their personal lives that he wasn't sure if moving there wouldn't have a negative effect.

Moreover, apart from the language issue, he would have nobody to rely on if he had personal problems.

Upon her insistence, however, he had no choice but to agree to sell the car.

On the very day he was to advertise it in the Reading Post, he was invited for an interview the following week in London. It was for the position of Assistant Accountant in a large engineering firm. Even though he had little hope of landing the job, he told Arya about it, hoping that would give him enough reason to keep the car for a little longer.

He got the job at the second interview. Although he had known he stood a chance when he was invited back, he still couldn't believe his luck when they rang to tell him the good news. As usual, he rang Arya and told her. She was happy for him. When they hung up, he rang to inform Richard as well.

It had taken ages, but Osam was glad to have finally turned the corner. He would have preferred a job in Reading, but all the best offers seemed to come from London. He wondered if he wouldn't be better off living in London, instead of commuting. He dismissed the idea outright. It was a good place to work, but too expensive to live. Besides, they hadn't decided what to do with their house.

It didn't take Osam long to get into the routine and rigours of his new job. He enjoyed it, particularly because he did more than the position entailed. Unlike his previous job, he was actually doing the work of a Management Accountant, thus practising what he had studied. He didn't have his own office, though. It was an open–plan office where the important people were separated only by screens. Osam had a screen too.

There were also three black British ladies in his department, so his wasn't the only black face there. Not only was the pay very good, but he also got on well with Andrew, his 42-year-old boss. Andrew did a two-year voluntary work placement in Togo before going on to study at Oxford University, and he had also visited Ghana during his stay in the Francophone country. He loved to practise the little French he still remembered with Osam every now and then. He even showed him some of his *highlife* music collection he'd brought from Ghana. He was a bubbly character and seemed to be liked by everyone in the department.

The same, however, could not be said of George, the brash, uncouth head of the Treasury Department. He was short, bald, and fat like a pig. Except for his pot-belly, he could easily pass for a rugby hooker. To Osam, he wore the face of a hooligan and didn't appear to have many friends.

Osam and George never liked each other. Vicky, one of the secretaries in his department, surmised that George was a racist who had also never got on with Osam's predecessor, British of Indian origin. Fortunately, or unfortunately for Osam, George was also a good friend of Andrew's; however, it did not appear to affect their professional relationship.

Charlie encouraged Osam to go out more. He thought it would help him rediscover his old, lost self, and thus win his life back.

Even though it was almost six months since he and Arya had broken up, he never stopped thinking about her. He still loved her, and yet he never told her about his enduring feelings during their now irregular phone calls. He could not summon the strength to overcome his pride.

Going out again was strange as he had quit doing so when he used to be with Arya. He went out alone, except when Richard, or sometimes Charlie, was available. He turned his attention again to football. He had not had the time to follow Reading FC's progress in the league, since their unsuccessful playoff final with Bolton at Wembley Stadium almost five years ago. Life was beginning to look normal again.

Chapter 28
(*Six Months Later*)

Osam returned home from Mallorca at 7 p.m, dropped his small luggage on the floor, and in utter desperation and exasperation headed straight for the bedroom. He switched off his mobile phone and connected it to the cable still plugged into the wall socket.

He sat on his bed contemplating in detail the enormity of his final decision.

With tears streaming down his cheeks, he whispered softly to himself: 'She isn't worth the march down the aisle.'

But it was still a never-ending nightmare!

Later, he had a warm bath and retired to bed after a double shot of whisky. The phone rang as he lay there prostrate. He was in no mood to talk to anyone.

'Hi, sweetheart!'

It was the distinct, sweet voice of Amelia on the answering machine. She confessed. *Everything...*

It was all just an accident...or was it?

'Excuse me!' she said, covering her mouth with her right hand.

'Not to worry,' Osam replied, even though he could see the damage to his white Calvin Klein shirt. He dared not show his anger. After all, this was supposed to be a first-rate party. Everyone was supposed to be nice or *pretend* to be nice, at least, until the alcohol took its toll.

As he turned to look at the culprit, he found himself not just looking but *staring*. What a beauty!

'Did I stumble into you?' he inquired sluggishly, already feeling the effect of the rum.

'No, I did. And the guilty one is Amelia - Amelia Spencer,' she continued.

'Osam Mensah,' he replied, trying hard to control his sway.

'Oh, you're the Assistant Accountant, aren't you? I spoke to you last week about advertising.'

'Oh yeah!' he replied, pretending to remember her and hiding his nervousness. One thing was for sure: her black hair and broad feminine shoulders reminded him of Suzy, the Spanish Guardia Civil, who interviewed him during his aborted trip to Las Palmas. She also seemed to have a great taste for fashion, walking with grace in her Burberry clothes and handbag.

As they shook hands, he felt her responding warmly to his stare – his face at this point almost agape. He was captivated. Her smile was warm and natural. Her dimpled cheeks as she smiled amplified her beauty. Even though she wasn't blonde, he'd always liked women with dimples. She looked almost too pretty for her high status.

Osam was awakened by the sound of the shower in the adjacent room. He realised he was in an alien environment, strange and isolated lying naked in bed. It was right in the centre of this massive room, which reminded him of his first night at Arya's. Looking around, it seemed to be the only object in the unusually large bedroom. Before he could finish taking the room in, she appeared in the doorway, clinging to her bath towel as she realised he was awake. It was tight against her moist skin, revealing her curves as she walked towards the bed. He could see the uppermost part of her large breasts.

She was about 1.80 metres tall, slightly built and with curly black hair which fell over those broad but feminine shoulders. For the first time, he could see how well-endowed she was in the pelvic region too.

'Good morning!' came her tender whisper.

'Morning,' he replied drowsily, oblivious momentarily of his nudity.

'Make yourself comfortable,' she said as she left the room.

He lay still, silently trying to recollect what had happened the previous night.

As Osam and Amelia conversed at the breakfast table, they realised they had much in common. They both worked for corporate organisations. They were both thirty, single and successful in their respective fields. He was a corporate Assistant Accountant, she an Advertising Consultant. Above all, they decided to see each other again.

She offered to give him a lift home, which he courteously turned down. She had done enough already. His shirt was washed and ironed. She seemed the domestic type, which suited him. Being African, he was fed up with the degree of equality between men and women in Western society.

He wanted the previous night's experience to be more than a one-night stand. He wanted to have a British passport as quickly as possible. He was rapidly moving up the corporate ladder and needed a woman of her class by his side to give him more clout.

He proposed to her on their thirtieth day and their twentieth rendezvous, and she said the big 'yes'. She watched in rapture as he caressed the diamond ring down to the base of her ring finger.

They agreed to get married as quickly as possible. They just could not live apart. Osam didn't want this one to slip through his fingers. His recent monthly mobile phone bill had tripled – not that it made any dent in his healthy bank account.

Amelia and her mates arranged to have the hen night in Mallorca. Low temperatures and persistent rain hadn't made May in England a cheery one.

The choice of Spain as the destination came as no surprise. Her mum, Carmen, was born in Valencia. However, even though Amelia had wild Latina tendencies, she felt more English than her mum wished her to be. Almost everything her mum told her about Spain was negative, so she didn't want to have anything to do with that country. She had read that men were still macho and dominant while women were still homely, even in these modern times. What an opportunity to satisfy her mum's desire by visiting her land of birth!

Her late grandparents were Republicans who fled to England during the height of the Spanish Civil War. They never returned, not even for a visit, as they lost some of their family during the war, and also lost contact as the years went by.

It was just after midnight and the nightclub was heaving. The sounds of English and German lingos filled the air, giving credence to the idea of Mallorca as an Anglo-Germanic holiday spot.

Amelia and her three friends, Nikki, Ann and Jules, had been on a pub crawl since midday.

Barely standing, tipsy in front of the busy cocktail bar, waiting for her drinks, she constantly felt the bulge of a man pressing against her bum cheeks. She felt uncomfortable at first but started to enjoy it, for some strange reason, as the bulge got harder and larger. She turned around clutching the four glasses.

'Puedo ayudarte?'

Instead of responding she found herself staring at the front of his Knickerbockers shorts. 'Beg your pardon?' she said in her usual posh accent as she came to her senses. 'No, I don't need help, thanks.'

'Eres muy guapa,' he continued.

She didn't quite catch what he had just said! 'Que...es...ehm...*whopper*?' Stuttering through the few words she had learned before embarking on the trip. She just wanted to confirm she had heard him right.

'No, I...mean you...very *beautiful*...in Spanish is *guapa!*'

She felt feminine, wanted.

She looked over his shoulder to the seats where her party had been sitting, only to find them empty. From the corner of her left eye, she saw her friends dancing away with male partners. As the man motioned her to dance, she excused herself while she put the drinks on their table.

They danced to various tunes. The music changed, as if by providence, to slow salsa. They found themselves responding to the soft Latin tune. His large coarse hands never strayed from her bum, gently squeezing as they danced closely and smoothly.

He squeezed tighter, and she felt a quick rush of bitter-sweet exhilaration surge through her awakened body. She was at his mercy! Never did she think she would have a soft spot for controlling men, but she appeared to be enjoying the new experience of being possessed and dominated.

She was in deep thought as the soft curtains of her third-floor hotel suite danced in the cool morning breeze. Well, she had been desperate for a shag last night and would have fallen for anyone, even in a skirt!

A soft knock on her door interrupted her thoughts. She reluctantly got out of bed and, still naked, languidly walked towards the door, stealing another look at the young, handsome, Mediterranean beefcake in her bed. She didn't even know his name.

She opened the door to Osam, who was in his usual smart casual wear. The weight of the bouquet he held in his left hand was apparent as he thrust it towards her as if relieved to be ridding himself of it.

'Surprise, surprise!!' he exclaimed, his face awash with immeasurable delight.

Amelia stood as if glued to the wooden floor. She was too stunned to move. This wasn't part of the script - not yet at least.

Osam entered just as the young man, oblivious to the noise, stretched and yawned lazily on the bed, revealing his strong muscular body.

'What's this? What's going on here?' Osam asked incredulously.

'It's not what you think…Ehmm…I had too much to drink last night—'

'I beg your pardon? Are you listening to yourself?'

He left the room in disgust and headed straight for the airport, praying to God that what he had just witnessed would turn out to be just a bad dream…

At the airport, his first instinct was to ring Arya and tell her what had happened. On second thought, however, he dismissed that idea. He just needed some time on his own. The last thing he wanted to see or talk to was another woman.

The phone rang again – interrupting the replay of the events in his mind.

'Talk to me, Os...please, talk to me...'

The mention of Os - Amelia's sweet nickname for him, struck the softest spot in his heart. He still loved her - deep down in his heart, he knew that. She would always be his Spanish Guardia Civil girl.
'I'm really, really sorry! I still love you, if you would have me back...yes, I know I don't deserve it...I know...but please forgive me Os. I know you're there, so please pick up the phone so we can talk about it...please!' She wept as she spoke, then waited for a long while, and then hung up.

Seconds later the phone rang again. He wanted to pick it up this time. It could be Richard. But he felt unable to walk to the handset. He lay still waiting for the answering machine to take over.
'Os, it's me again...forgot to say that we're returning to London tomorrow afternoon. I'll come straight over to your place...hope you'll be home....I love you...so much...more than you think...see you tomorrow evening...darling...' Then she hung up for the second time.

He felt woozy; maybe his heart really was broken forever and he no longer felt the need to try and mend it, just for it to be broken again. He felt lost.
He stumbled over the bed, picked up the cordless phone receiver from its base, and returned to bed. He rang Richard to tell him what had happened. After all, they had planned the surprise trip to Mallorca together. He left a message as his call went unanswered.

He felt no better the following morning as he lay in bed in his two-bedroom flat. He picked up the cordless phone and rang Richard. He still hadn't returned his call which was unusual. They had been there for each other in recent months. His phone went unanswered again, so he left a message to call him back urgently. He tried his mobile phone, but that also went unanswered. He was too angry to leave another message.

Richard had never been shy to express his doubts about their relationship. He always felt that it was too soon for Osam to get into a serious relationship after the sudden, traumatic end to the previous one. Richard and Arya got on so well and he felt Osam should have moved to Sweden with her. Sometimes Osam hated Richard for *always* sticking with Arya whenever he had to settle a dispute between them.

Amelia's parents, who were openly racist, had also been against the relationship from the start. She had told Osam on many occasions about how her parents had warned her that Osam only wanted her so he could stay permanently in the country. Osam always assured her that he wouldn't be in his job if he were an illegal immigrant. He thought they must be rejoicing now it was all over, being a clear case of *I told you so.* He always found it difficult to comprehend how Amelia's mother, Carmen, could be racist when her Republican parents had also been forced to escape to live in England.

His phone rang as soon as he hung up. He thought it was Richard returning his call, but it turned out to be Arya. It was always a welcome relief to hear from her.

He told her about Amelia.

Both knew they still had a soft spot in their hearts for each other. The problem was they were too headstrong to admit it. She always wanted him to be happy and was even due to arrive the following week for the Saturday wedding.

She was saddened by his present situation and suggested he take a break to visit Ghana since he hadn't been home for almost seven years. *You have no excuse now!* she used to say since he was granted his five-year leave to remain in the UK. He promised to think hard about her suggestion and ring her back in a few days. With that, he hung up.

He reflected on their conversation in his jumbled mind as he lay on his bed. He enjoyed his life in England so much that going home wasn't a present priority.

Unlike him, Richard went home once a year even though he was still studying. He had even managed to build himself a *mansion* where he stayed whenever he was in Accra.

Osam was in constant touch with his Uncle, who never stopped telling him to come home one day and marry a *real* woman. He still had this archaic idea that Osam would lose his *soul* marrying a white girl.

He also claimed his health was failing and thus wanted to see him before he went to the land of the gods.

Like Osam, his Uncle was a very proud man and wanted to show him off to all who had eyes to see. Maybe it was time to visit.

The phone rang again. He was getting pissed off now. He snatched up the handset.

'Who is it'?'

'What do you mean who is it?' came Richard's refreshing voice. With clear relief, he narrated in detail what had happened, as Richard listened in incredulous silence.

'I'm on my way; should be with you in about thirty minutes.'

Osam was quietly happy because he really needed someone by his side, even though he had turned down Arya's offer.

He heard a knock on the door at 11:05 a.m. He realised he hadn't eaten since his arrival yesterday from Mallorca.

Richard entered without saying a word and headed straight to his favourite reclining armchair. 'So, what are we gonna do now?' he asked as he sat.

Osam had always admired Richard's emphatic and positive approach to problem-solving, like, '*what are we gonna do*?' One that always stuck with him was his preferred reference to '*situations*' instead of '*problems*'. He was a beautiful man with a kind heart.

'Well, like I told you before, I think that's it.'

'Don't you think it's too soon?'

'Richard, she even had the audacity to tell me everything – I mean, everything and in great detail.'

'Yeah, that's nerves, man. Wow! Perhaps she just felt she had nothing to lose opening up her heart to you that way. After all, you are her future hubby.'

'Richard, I have put so much into this relationship in spite of all the obstacles. For Amelia to treat me this way, particularly when the wedding is only a week away! Only a week, Richard, only a week!'

With that, he began sobbing. Richard walked up to him and embraced him. Osam was the bigger, stronger and the richer, but Richard was always the one who anchored him emotionally.

'I don't think I can trust any white girl again. In the end, they still think they're superior to us.'

'You don't think you're generalising a bit here?' Richard said with sympathy.

'Generalising? Where's Amelia? Where's Arya now?'

There was a moment's stunned silence.

'I think it's more complicated than that, Osam. Perhaps you need to take time and sort yourself out. You've become a success story in the Ghanaian community in Reading. But it looks as if this success has also placed you on a kind of uncontrollable roller coaster. Success is a journey, not a destination. It's one thing to be successful, and another to get above yourself, because other people, your own people, don't happen to have your social status. I'm not saying that's what you think -- don't get me wrong -- but, unfortunately, that's the impression people seem to gather. Perhaps you don't realise, but it's like you're trying hard, unconsciously maybe, to alienate everyone else from your life...I don't know. Despite everything, this is not our country. Never forget your humble beginnings, and all the struggles you went through before landing here. Don't lose the focus.'

Osam sat unmoving, holding his head in both hands.
'I was really surprised when you told me you were going to get married. It's only been a few months since you came out of a series of difficulties in your life. Moreover, you hardly knew this Amelia girl. You've been in this sudden *rush* to get married while neglecting your friends at the same time. It's as if you've got to prove something or...I don't know. As for me, it's like I'm only needed when the bad times come knocking. Sometimes I ask myself whatever happened to the young, handsome, womanising Osam that I've always known. Anyway, have you had breakfast?' Richard asked, trying to change the subject.
'No,' came the reply, as if from a little child. It was the closest to the bone comment Richard had ever made to his friend.
'Now, you sit down while I prepare for us some real Ghanaian Omelette.'
He knew Osam couldn't refuse that offer as it was one of his favourite Ghanaian dishes; fresh fried eggs mixed with thinly sliced fresh onions and tomatoes. He usually ate it with buttered bread and hot cocoa drink called Milo.

Osam didn't have Milo at home, so they had to make do with green tea.

'I have been doing some thinking since last night. I would like to take a break to go to Ghana in August.'

'That's less than three months away! Well, that's amazing. I thought you never ever wanted to return…'

'Not only that, but I've also been thinking about your business proposition,' Osam said as they munched.

That seemed to surprise Richard, probably because he had been trying, without success, for almost a year to convince his friend that they return to Accra to set up their own business. It was the new tendency among Ghanaians living abroad. And from all the reports so far, most of them seemed to be doing quite well. Richard was moving back to Accra in December to start up his own business. He had been encouraged through symposiums organised by the Ghanaian High Commission in London. It urged Ghanaians living abroad to return home to help in the nation-building. Osam knew it would be too soon for him as December was only five months away, but he could use it as a path-finding trip. They could both use their expertise in business studies to do something for themselves. Richard had just completed his MBA at Reading University.

'I think you're in a difficult time now to be thinking about that. Besides, I'm leaving in five months' time,' Richard said, quietly happy to hear that from his beloved friend.

'That's why I want to go and see the present conditions and make my own judgement. The problem is I don't know what to expect. I have lost contact with all my *friends* because I've never really communicated with them while I have been here. I would like to make you a proposition. What if I pay for your flight?'

'The problem is I can't afford to go to Ghana before December.'

'I'll foot your return ticket, don't worry…that is if you would like to go.'

'You need my help, Osam. If you want me to accompany you home, I will. You can even stay in my house if you like. Let me think about it, OK?'

'Well, the sooner, the better, so that I can look for a valid reason to tell my boss.'

'I'll let you know by tomorrow, I promise.'

Chapter 29

Amelia was history...well, almost history. Two months had passed. The marriage plans were cancelled and they agreed to break up. Though Osam had moved on from his broken heart blues, he still had not got over her. Richard was an ever-present support for him during that difficult period. Fortunately, he didn't suffer any severe mental anxiety as he had when he broke up with Arya. Perhaps he had finally learnt detachment.

Arya planned to take some time off work to visit Reading while Osam was away in Ghana. Though their romance was now a thing of the past, they had gradually grown to be good friends. She had even told Osam that she was seeing someone though it wasn't a serious relationship yet.

The only thing Osam wasn't coping properly with was the pressure involved with his job. His boss was away on a two-week holiday, so he had had to take over his responsibilities during this period. He already knew he had bitten off more than he could chew (with his regular job) as he sometimes had to work at weekends in order to catch up. He was undoubtedly excited about his fast-approaching holiday. One thing he wasn't looking forward to, though, was the executive meeting the following day. He had been invited to take the place of his boss. He didn't know what to expect as not only would it be his first such meeting, but he would also be rubbing shoulders with important departmental heads.

Also, on the agenda was the protracted hostile takeover bid for a rival company. Osam's company had been trying to take over one of their competitors. To make matters worse, BB, their main competitor, had not only entered the race but now looked the clear favourite. Osam had managed to get insider information which he hoped could help them in this acrimonious takeover. Whether it would be accepted or not was another matter.

He arrived three minutes late to the meeting as he was stopped by the police in Reading for a *routine* check-up. He was enraged as he knew it was simply because he was a Black man driving a top of the range BMW. It wasn't the first time it had happened to him or any black person, and wouldn't be the last.

He entered apologetically and took his seat next to George, right in the middle of the quadrant-shaped seating. All sixteen pairs of eyes momentarily fixed on him as he brought the early Friday morning executive meeting to a temporary halt.

He was more of a spectator in what he thought was a wishy-washy meeting until it came to the final point of the agenda that concerned the Finance Department.

George said, 'I would suggest we gracefully pull out before we lose out to BB. I think that would not only save our blushes but also keep our reputation intact.' Then he tossed down the report he had been holding and leaned back in his chair.

Bill, the chief executive, agreed. 'I would go with that suggestion. We can't afford to endlessly spend so much time and money only to lose out and have our good reputation tainted in full gaze of the business community.'

'Can I come in here—'

'The financial market is very unstable now so it might be a blessing in disguise.' He turned to Osam. 'Did you wish to say something, Osam?' he asked, all eyes in the room now fixed on Osam. George appeared to have won the first ever duel between them. He grinned.

Osam cleared his throat. 'Excuse me,' he murmured apologetically. 'I have been in constant touch during the week with Julie Monk, the Management Accountant of BB. We used to be colleagues at my previous job. She has agreed to pass on to me some critical financial information she thinks might help us in the takeover bid.'

'Yeah, right! What sort of information?' George asked, scratching his bald head and rolling his eyes.

'May I?' Osam asked Bill.

There was a brief silence. Bill nodded. Without more ado, Osam got up, walked over to Bill and handed him a sealed, white envelope. Everyone waited.

'This is fantastic news!' Bill declared after he finished reading. 'Why is she doing this?'

'She's leaving the company in a fortnight. She's found another job in the city.'

There was a rush to see what Bill had on his desk.

When George saw it, he huffed. 'No. We can't do that. That's commercial espionage and unethical'.

'I can take it from here, George,' Bill said. 'And when did you suddenly become Mr Ethics? Good work, Osam. How soon can you have that?' he asked, turning his attention to Osam.

'On one condition, though.'

'How much is she asking for?'

'No, it's not about money.'

'What then?'

'She wants the source to be kept anonymous.'

'Tell her she has my word. When can we have it?'

'As soon as you want it, sir,' Osam said.

'How about Monday morning?'

'It will be on your desk then, sir.'

'Well, in the absence of any other matters, I pronounce this meeting closed,' Bill said with finality. He had a plane to catch to Paris that afternoon.

There were congratulations all around from the other members, including George.

Osam had had the last laugh after all.

The following Monday Andrew came into Osam's office to tell him that he was leaving the organisation as his family were relocating to Barcelona. He had been offered a job in one of the foreign banks there while on holiday. Andrew thus encouraged him to apply for his position.

Osam was taken aback.

'No, I can't do that,' he said as he bit his lips.

'Why? I'm leaving and you've shown that you're capable of assuming this role. Come to think of it, Bill spoke well of you in his office this morning.'

'Did he?'

'Absolutely! Anyway, you have a think about it.' He left to answer his incessantly ringing phone.

Osam reflected on their conversation all morning.

That afternoon he went to the toilet for his daily five minutes meditation exercise, still well-dressed, sitting on the loo seat. He was soon interrupted.

'I handed in my resignation this morning,' Andrew revealed, in his deep baritone voice.

'Did you get the job in Barcelona?' the croaky voice of George asked.

'You bet!'

'Wow, living in the sunny world of Spain!' George said as they emptied their bladders into the urinal.

'It's not always warm there, I was told. I've also got to learn Spanish - though it's not a priority.'

'What about Catalan, do you have to learn that too?'

'Not for now, I guess.'

'So, are they gonna advertise your position?'

'I don't know yet. I'm meeting Bill later this afternoon. I told Osam this morning to apply if ever the job was advertised.'

'The African! I've had enough of them. First, we allow them in, and then they compete with us for the few jobs there are.'

'He's a good chap, you know. He did a good job while I was away,' Andrew said as they washed their hands.

'That black bastard! He deliberately made me look like a fool at Friday's meeting,' George said with his peculiar vehemence. Osam wondered whether George had considered that someone might be in one of the four cubicles. 'I don't know what you see in that busy-for-nothing bloke,' George continued.

Osam realised then that his loo door wasn't closed properly. He thought he had locked it, but noticed that the catch was damaged.

'You two don't seem to get on, why?'

'He's a proud black son of a bitch. He thinks he's like one of us but…once black, always black! I still hold onto the wise old saying, *no dogs, no Irish and no Blacks*! No wonder Amelia came to that realisation early enough and left him! I can't believe…'

His sentence faded as Osam flushed the toilet. He opened his loo door and exited into the open area. He had heard enough of George's rubbish.

There was a tense hush as Osam, taking his time, and making them squirm, washed his hands, wiped them on the toilet towel, and walked past the two dumbfounded figures without saying a word.

Osam entered his office holding a cup of white coffee from the nearest coffee machine.

He wondered what more would have been said had he stayed put a bit longer. Would Andrew have gone along with

George's apparent hatred for him? What had he done to deserve such blatant racial resentment?

It didn't take long for Osam to make up his mind. He was going to follow Andrew's suggestion.

Chapter 30
(*The visit home*)

'Where did the time go?' Osam asked himself as he dropped onto his living room sofa. Seven weeks ago when he bought his ticket from the local travel agency, he had thought he had ample time to prepare for his trip to Ghana. After procrastinations upon procrastinations, he realised he only had three days to prepare for his fifteen-day trip.

He was picking up Arya from Heathrow Airport late in the evening. They had finally decided to sell their house and split the profit. Osam already had too much on his plate at work to take care of such a big property alone. It had only been on the market for a week, but the response, so far, had been positive. She seemed happy when they last chatted on the phone. She had settled into the family business after a few early hitches. But it was doing well now, and she was glad and looking forward to returning to England after almost six months away to supervise the house sale while Osam was away. Deep down in his heart he suspected that Arya was only coming to make sure that Osam didn't abscond with her part of the profit once the house was sold.

As was the norm, some Ghanaians had already brought money and presents to be passed on to their respective families in Accra. Unlike Richard, only a few people ventured to relay things through him.
Osam was particularly glad that Richard not only agreed to travel with him but also promised to provide him lodging in his *mansion*. He still needed his support. Osam thought Richard had never forgiven him for constantly turning him

down whenever he suggested they should return home and start up a business together. He was going to see things for himself now.

Richard perhaps thought of him as a gifted man who always thought above his station. He had helped Osam get to England, yet the latter was much better off, so life might seem rather unfair.

He wondered with mixed feelings what to expect after so many tales about the dramatic, positive turnaround of the Ghanaian economy. His silly, exaggerated fears sometimes caused Richard to wonder whether Osam realised he was returning to his own home country.

Osam was particularly looking forward to seeing his Uncle again. He had told him to be at the airport for his arrival. He was the only member of his small family that he held in high esteem. Uncle Kojo was a very conservative man, so Osam had had his hair trimmed at *Stylus*, a unisex hair salon for black people on Oxford Road. He would be very proud to show him his CIMA certificate.

He had been running on empty for a couple of weeks, and couldn't wait to leave Britain's shores for the first time.

However, he worried how his old-time acting and non-acting friends would receive him since he had not kept in touch with them all these years. And none of them knew he was returning home.

Chapter 31
(Home at last!)

At 20:13 hours GMT, Kotoka International Airport welcomed a frequent, much-loved visitor to the shores of the Gulf of Guinea. Many families and friends had gathered to welcome their own on the British Airways aircraft which was now taxiing to a standstill.

Among the one hundred and twenty passengers were Richard and his twitchy friend, Osam, enjoying the slow taxiing of the aircraft to its assigned slot in the rather small airport. Unlike Heathrow, there were only a few aircraft.

Osam sat in his seat and quietly enjoyed his mind's playback of the beautiful aerial sight of Accra. The cluster of lights below dancing in the humid Atlantic coastal atmosphere brought back welcome memories. It seemed a long time though it was but eight years since he left.

Osam descended the flight of steps and stepped onto the tarmac. He bent and touched his first piece of land as they walked towards the airport entrance. He received smiles and grins from some of his fellow passengers.

They went through immigration smoothly to his surprise. Gone were the days when one was hustled into parting with some cash. Soon they were pushing their loaded trolleys out of the airport into the thick, humid night air of Accra. He felt a rush of exhilaration run through him.

They had opted to travel in August when the temperatures were mild and sometimes dropped down to as low as 18 degrees Celsius at night. While the waiting public outside had jumpers and jackets on against the prevailing low temperatures, the *just arrived* or the *Boggas* were wearing shirts or T-shirts. In spite of that, Osam still felt the heat and high humidity.

Osam spotted Uncle Kojo in the throng. They both deviated towards where he was waiting. Richard's cousins joined them as he warmly shook hands with Osam's uncle.

Despite his apparent *Westernised* senses, he could still smell the newness of Uncle Kojo's textile cloth with eagle patterns as they tenderly hugged each other. For a Ghanaian at home, he had been brave to wear only the traditional cloth. Osam perceived he had bought it just for the occasion.

'*Akwaaba*, my son!' he said. He always addressed him as *son*.

'Thank you,' Osam replied, beaming a broad smile.

Apart from the expanded shine on the crest of his head and more grey in what was left of his hair, Uncle Kojo didn't seem to have changed much. A second look, however, revealed that he appeared thinner and his chunky six-foot frame had begun to stoop. He had been unwell for some time and had always urged Osam to return home so he could see him before his *death*.

'How are you feeling, Uncle Kojo?'

'I'm fine, my son. The gods are still protecting me.'

'What about the rest of the family?' Osam continued - not wanting to press further regarding his health. He would ask later.

'Everyone is fine, my son. They're looking forward to seeing you. You look good, but rather thin, Kweku. People coming from the white man's land all look fat and good,' Uncle Kojo said, calling him by his traditional name as they left the airport with Richard's two-man welcoming party in his recently sent second-hand Toyota pickup. Richard also had a

BMW, which he used for his rounds whenever he was in Ghana.

It had been a long time since he was addressed by the name, *Kweku.*

Though Richard's welcoming party was his cousins, Osam was meeting them for the first time. They lived in and looked after his seven-bedroom *mansion.*

'You people still hold onto this *archaic* mentality,' Osam said with a false grin in response to his uncle's comment about his thin figure.

'And when did you learn to speak to elders like that!' Uncle Kojo replied.

As Osam turned to his uncle in the back seat, he noticed the other occupants grinning uncomfortably at Uncle Kojo's remark. Osam shifted in his front seat.

In Ghanaian tradition, being fat was associated with good living. Some even took traditional medicines which were supposed to make them put on more weight. Hence Osam, living in the white man's land, which is the land of plenty, was expected to be fatter than he looked. He was now 84 kg, 4 kilogrammes heavier than when he had left for Western Europe.

He smiled at his Uncle's remark and quickly returned to staring straight ahead as Richard negotiated a curve out of the airport's car park.

In Ghanaian society, the older generation, or elders, are much revered as they are considered wise, experienced and knowledgeable. So, one has to be careful when he or she speaks to them.

No matter how old Osam was, Uncle Kojo was still his uncle, and, therefore, had the right to say whatever he wished without opposition. Even if one wanted to challenge an elder, it had to be done with tact and caution in order not to offend.

'Is the white girl not feeding you well? We hear these European girls don't know how to cook so they just feed on uncooked leaves.'

'I'm fine, Uncle Kojo,' Osam replied with an emphatic tone and resumed biting his lips.

'Uncle, Osam is much fitter than I am. In England, we call him *Obroni* because he behaves like white people by running along the road to exercise his body,' Richard said in defence of his friend.

'Really? Osam has always been a white man in black skin. He's the book man of our family. He speaks English like the white man and has a university degree,' Uncle Kojo replied with an element of pride.

He was a typical countryman who still believed that the white man was superior to the black man. So the fact that his nephew was being compared to the white man made him very proud indeed. Osam wondered how he would feel if he knew the surprise he had in wait for him. He was quietly enjoying what was ensuing and hoped that Richard's cousins were listening attentively.

He was disappointed that Richard didn't go on to proclaim that he was even better qualified, worked with white people, had lived with a white girl, and spoke better English than before. Osam wished that during his short stay it would be obvious for all who came into contact with him to see and know who he really was.

They arrived at Richard's *mansion* about forty-five minutes later. It looked even better than the video had depicted. He was proud of his beautiful house, and rightly so.

It was built on a double plot of land, so most was converted into a flower garden. It was situated on Spintex Road, the latest chic housing development area in Accra. In fact, its pomp reminded Osam of Mr Hamburger's mansion.

He thought Richard's was a mansion, but some of the newly constructed houses nearby were breathtakingly opulent. Richard told him that's what those living in the West were doing these days, investing in such elaborate properties where they stayed when holidaying in Accra.

The first thing Osam wanted to do, after they had unpacked, was eat some *real* Ghanaian food. He missed his favourite *Banku* and *okra* stew. Richard had some Cedis at home, so all five of them drove to a nearby bar called *The Point.*

It was already bubbling with well-dressed people as they drove into the semi-lit large compound. Almost all the seats were occupied by happy diners either tucking into their meals or chatting.

Within seconds, they were led to their centre table by a smart waitress. Osam couldn't stop watching people eating with their hands.

Ghanaians easily detect a *Bogga*. Both of them wore just T-shirts and jeans yet they were easily identified as Londoners without uttering a word. Osam would later realise that their way of dressing and comportment gave them away. A handful had families or friends living there and asked questions with regards to the general conditions in the UK. Osam gladly answered.

Osam devoured the best *banku and okra soup* dish he had had in years. Although the soup was thick, it wasn't sticky and slimy. It still wasn't difficult to swallow the soft banku.

He had eaten it and other Ghanaian dishes in Reading when marking special Ghanaian occasions, like the March 6 Independence Day, but this one was special – the real deal. All the right natural ingredients were perfectly mixed!

There's no place like home.

After downing two bottles of Guinness, he was slightly tipsy when they returned home, so went straight to bed.

Uncle Kojo was already awake when Osam arose the following morning around 8 am. The African sun was already in its glory, sending magnificent and refreshing rays down onto its own.

The two of them had a long chat in Richard's back garden. Uncle Kojo narrated a lot of things that had happened in their small family in his absence. He was told about the deaths as well as the births. He advised Osam to visit Cape Coast as his grandparents were anxious to see him too.

Uncle wished to return to his village that same day as he had to see his local doctor in the neighbouring big town in two days. Most importantly, his young wife was expecting their child. His youngest conquest and fourth wife was a 20-year-old girl called Lydia. He divorced his third wife the previous year--with whom he had a boy--to marry her. He thus had three boys from his three previous marriages. His present wife was the daughter of one of his plantation farm workers.

As a relatively rich man in a rural area, he could afford to have as many wives as he wished, or would be offered girls by their parents for marriage. He said he had already asked for the hand of the daughter of the richest man in the village for Osam. She was a student at the University of Ghana and very intelligent, but she was also submissive like a dog. Uncle Kojo claimed Osam would jump on her the first time he laid his eyes on her.

Later, Osam and Richard drove to the dealership in Richard's car to pick up the BMW Osam had purchased for Uncle Kojo. They went through the familiar roads he had previously walked, and even went past the area in the airport residential area where Georgina and Mona, his ex-girlfriends, used to live. He wondered whether she was still with the *Bogga* or lived there again with her parents. Whatever she was up to,

Osam had every intention of tracking her down to show her what he'd become.

They stopped at a Forex bureau. Osam exchanged £500 while Richard changed £200. The exchange rate was 8000 cedis to a pound. £500 was almost equivalent to two months' salary for a Regional Director of Education. It was a lot of money by Ghanaian standards. Osam had £6000 cash on him; he intended to use half to purchase the second hand BMW for Uncle Kojo. He had also brought along his visa card, in case of emergency.

As a *Bogga*, he also had an obligation to his family and friends, particularly as he'd been away so long. One had to be financially prepared as once friends and family knew you were back in their midst, there was literally a *queue* for a share of your treasure.

As they waited for their money from their respective cashiers, a man entered from an office behind the cashiers' enclosure. He looked familiar, yet Osam couldn't put a name to the face.

'I think I know that man from somewhere, but I can't remember where,' Osam said to Richard, who was now counting his cedis. Osam didn't even bother to count his wad of two thousand denomination cedi notes. He pulled out a small quantity from the middle of a wad and, without counting them, handed them to the pretty young lady who had just served him.

'Oh, thank you!' she said in typical Ghanaian style, her eyes lit up with sheer joy.

'You're welcome.'

'Eh! Abrantie John!' Richard interrupted when he took a look at the man.

Osam remembered him now. He suddenly recalled their first encounter. It wasn't a good one. He hoped this would be.

He had left the UK two years ago to return home to start up his own business. He had been fed up with the tough life over there. He had put on considerable weight and had also shaved his hair. He looked meaner now than the last time Osam saw him – the day he quit his early morning cleaning job.

Later, he had heard that *Abrantie* had moved to Shepherd's Bush in London.

'Hey, Richard! Hey, *Obroni*! Akwaaba ooo!' he shouted in the typical Ghanaian manner as he entered the customer section to embrace them in turn, Richard first.

'When did you arrive in town?'

'Last night,' they said in unison.

'Hey, what is *Obroni* doing in our beautiful country?'

'What do you mean?' Osam asked with a frown.

'You said you would never return to Ghana, didn't you?'

'Not for good.'

'Don't worry; the beautiful Ghanaian ladies will treat you like a king. Once they know you've just arrived from England, they'll fall for you! Man, you're now a *Bogga*! Be careful, though, as some of these women are notorious thieves. Many men on holidays from the West have easily fallen for their dirty tricks,' he said to Osam, their right hands still clasped in typical Ghanaian handshake.

He invited them into his small office where they spoke at length. Richard and Osam told Abrantie John about their intentions to return home soon to start up a business. He encouraged them to do so as the market was ripe. He also revealed to them the latest profitable business of commercial farming. He said because land was expensive these days in Ghana, only the rich could afford to go into that business. Moreover, he had no formal business training so he was hesitant to enter into such a venture. He told them he owned the Forex Bureau and was luckily doing well with his other import and export company. He later showed them his new

Mercedes convertible which had been delivered the previous day. Osam was dumbfounded. He had known John when he struggled in England two years ago, now he seemed to be living like a king.

'Look, you are the people the country needs, not us. You guys have all these university degrees behind you and yet you're still living in the white man's land and helping it to get better, even though they treat you badly.' Osam and Richard smiled faintly. Abrantie gave an awkward laugh, drew closer to them and gave them a warm hug in turn.

'You know,' said Osam. 'When I told my boss about my holiday in my home country he asked what I was still doing in the UK with all my degrees and experience. That really surprised me, you know why? Because, when I arrived in England, it was the same question I used to ask whenever I saw a fellow, well-educated Ghanaian and African. I always said that I would be out of England if I possessed their degrees. But then, you get it and it's like a contagious disease; you lose the urge to return home for good the longer you stay. It's as if you're being kept there by an external force or something. You know what I mean?' Osam was biting his lower lip.

'You see!' John said.

'One of my lecturers also said something along those lines during my graduation. He asked if I planned to return home to apply what I had learned,' Richard said, nodding.

'So when did you suddenly become so political?' Osam asked John. He had never expected those words would come from him. He used to be just a simple, illegal immigrant cleaner in Reading.

'Politics? Who wants to be a politician in this country? One day you're a hero, the next they want to kill you. Business is where the enjoyment is. I know a lot of Africans rotting away in the UK when our continent badly needs them, you know?'

They both knew there was truth and sense in what he was saying.

'They suffer in the cold winter after winter, but they still remain there,' he continued.

'Man, I still remember my first winter,' Osam chipped in.

'No Ghana man or woman will ever forget their first winter,' Richard declared.

'I opened the front door to go for my morning cleaning, and everything before me was white,' Osam continued.

'It was quite an exciting moment for me; I had been looking forward to it,' Richard jumped in.

'You're kidding me!' replied Abrantie.

'Yes, I really was. I wanted to confirm what I had seen in all the films on television. You won't believe it, but I even have photos of the footprints of people indelibly displayed on the fallen snow.'

'Ah, there you go. I never knew we had a snow watcher in our midst then,' Abrantie joked.

'People brave all that, and when they send money home, it's hardly appreciated,' Osam said.

'You can say that again. I know someone who returned home to nothing. His brother had spent all the money he had been sending to build a house for him,' Abrantie agreed.

'Oh no!' Osam exclaimed slowly shaking his head and smiling wryly.

'He even sent him photos of the house…but unfortunately, it was somebody else's house!'

'That's awful!' Osam muttered under his breath.

'I hear that happens all the time. That's why I made sure I returned home yearly to see for myself the work on my house,' said Richard.

'The man hasn't returned home since.'

'I don't blame him!' agreed Osam.

Richard nodded.

'I'm sure many people want to send money home, but the question is who to trust.'

'The worst ones are the family members. They think you owe them a favour. You do your best, but it's never good enough,' Abrantie stated firmly.

They talked on for a long while. He told them among other things the situation in the country. He invited them for lunch at his home, but they told him they had other matters to attend to as they had only arrived the previous night.

The three of them agreed to meet up for a drink, where John promised to introduce them to what he called *real women* to make their stay in Accra worthwhile.

While Richard was driving to the BMW dealer showroom at Osu, Osam wondered whether there was any truth in Abrantie's claims that young Ghanaian ladies still fell easily for *Boggas* like him. He knew it was so in the past, but he thought things might have changed with the passage of time.

They arrived back at Richard's mansion four hours later due to heavy traffic on Accra's congested roads. Osam struggled to drive as it was completely different to the only one he knew - the British way of driving on the left. He had never driven when he was in Ghana as he got his driving licence during his second year in England. He also couldn't compete with the local aggressive driving display. The guilty ones were the taxi and *trotro* drivers who sometimes stopped without any indication whatsoever to pick up wayside passengers scattered along the busy roads. What surprised Osam was that motorists just sat patiently waiting in their vehicles.

The surprise in Uncle Kojo's eyes was indescribable, his tears evidence of his inner feelings.

'I never doubted I'd live to see this day, Kweku Mensah.'

'This is for the faith you have always had, and continue to have, in me,' Osam said as he presented the car keys to him. Richard and his cousins clapped their hands in delight. Osam joined in.

'With this, Opanin Kojo will become the king of the jungle,' his uncle joked as he settled himself cautiously into the driver's seat.

'It's only a second-hand car, uncle.'

'Yes, and it's a BMW! Everything outside and inside looks new to me.'

'Yeah, it's been re-sprayed, but it is five years old.'

Osam and Richard watched him as he practised driving his new *high-tech* car. Uncle Kojo owned a Peugeot 504 estate car. He happily claimed this would be the only BMW in the whole district.

Uncle Kojo left early the following day in his new car.

They still had a lot to discuss. He hadn't even touched on what he claimed was critical for Osam to know. He looked forward to seeing Osam again in five days when he planned to visit him in his village. It had taken hours to convince Osam to make the trip. Osam claimed he was scared of the wild jungle animals that Uncle Kojo said frequently visited them. He even said elephants sometimes walked through and destroyed their planted crops. But all they did, he claimed now, was make large noises and then flee! Osam only agreed after Richard had offered to accompany him.

Chapter 32

In the following days, Osam had time to tour the *new* and now expanded city of Accra. He visited some old friends, his old secondary school, and other places of interest like Kwame Nkrumah Circle, Parliament House, and Accra International Conference Centre.

So far, his strategy had worked with six friends he had managed to visit. He always gave them their presents, in the shape of a white envelope containing 500,000 cedis first, before his apologies followed. It was about two months' salary for some of them even in *good* jobs. In his heart, he knew he was buying his way back to them. But Osam cared less about that as long as he had an audience with them. It worked. It was mutually beneficial for both parties involved.

But he also quickly realised that money was leaving his hands too easily and he needed to calm down. He wasn't there to save his fellow citizens.

He even paid a visit to the Accra Arts Centre on a mid-afternoon. That was where his now-disbanded amateur group used to rehearse during weekday evenings. It was far removed from its heyday when it used to be one of the centres of attraction for tourists. There were fewer shops and people. And the small amateur theatre groups were no longer having their rehearsals outside. The high, enormous wooden entrance door was shut. When he used to live in Accra, the new building was already being built about two kilometres north. One could still hear the sound of the high tide hitting the sandy shore.

Osam walked the same route through the busy craftsmen and women, down to the sandy beach about a hundred metres away from the Arts Centre, like he used to. He always went down there to practise his voice articulation.

The beach looked unexpectedly deserted - except for two young lovers soaking in the breezy, romantic atmosphere. As he stood on the sandy beach, he remembered how during his regular voice exercise, some of the beach walkers would stop to wonder whether he was losing it, as he screamed at the incoming Atlantic waves. Osam recalled once when he was practising for an annual holiday performance at the Art Centre. He had been roaring as he scanned the 'Hark The Herald Angels Sing' lyrics on his crumpled music sheet, totally oblivious of his cracking baritone voice and sheer intensity until he was interrupted by a random beach walker tripping over her dog when his not so angelic voice frightened her. He had jumped back like a startled rabbit!

He wasn't blessed with a good voice, but that did nothing to stop him joining his school's Christmas choir. Then he realised his poor articulation when he began his amateur acting career. He had had time on his hands then, so he would come to this beach a couple of hours before his three-times-a-week acting rehearsal and work on it.

His articulation improved but not his singing.

It was also his first time on a beach, since his second, fatal, aborted trip to Spain. He quickly cast the memory of it where it belonged - his subconscious; he had since moved on.

To his right, he could clearly see the lighthouse tower of Accra, about 2 km away. While almost the same distance away to his left, he saw the white, fortified Christianborg Castle, the residence of Ghana's head of state, still suffering the bashings of the ocean waves in the humid Accra sun. Its seemingly precarious position along a cliff gave the impression of an impending collapse into the angry and expectant water. Osam had always thought so since he first saw it as a ten-year-old. The water was incessantly crashing up against this castle as he looked. It still appeared unscathed. He stared at the sea. The passage of time felt illusory, yet distinct; the experience of being home and being connected, major events, turning points, people. Osam was finding it hard to define himself.

He retraced his way back and walked on to the next attraction beside the Arts Centre. The Kwame Nkrumah Centre was still standing, people walking in and out. He had always wondered why it was painted white. He still didn't bother to walk in to ask.

Then he remembered something and taking a few steps backwards he looked down the road opposite the Arts Centre and found that the local cinema was still there. He and his friends used to go there all the time. They would come on Saturday nights when he had no theatre performance.

The High Court buildings were to his right. These Colonial-era buildings reminded him of his grandparents, as they were so much in love with the style that they always came to see them whenever they visited Accra. Osam was particularly looking forward to going to Cape Coast, the hometown of his late parents, to visit his grandparents, and the graves of his parents, his aunt and uncle, and his two cousins. The city's Fetu Afahye Festival, which started on the first Saturday in September, was only two weeks away. He would love to see the feverish preparations being made as the day approached.

Next was the central library, where he would sometimes go as a teenager to study or read. People were always queuing outside before it opened in the mornings to get a seat.

He entered the centre and tried to see if he could catch a glimpse of the Baden Powell Memorial Hall on the other side of the high street, but the Bank of Ghana buildings were blocking his view. The Democratic Youth League of Ghana, of which he had been a member, used to receive talks there from important personalities, including government ministers.

The city centre was bustling with life, and although Accra had undergone drastic structural and economic changes, thankfully some things remained the same.

Within the few years he had been away, Accra had expanded and merged into the smaller villages and towns that surrounded it.

Makola Shopping Centre, the then central focal point of shopping in Accra, was now housed in a shopping arcade. Traders there used to hoard goods, and at the start of the first revolution in Ghana had become so powerful that the Revolution leaders decided to dismantle it. There were rumours of *Juju* stuff like snakes and other strange creatures found in stores. It wasn't easy, but the government finally succeeded.

The road systems had drastically improved. There were flyovers interconnecting other roads, some of them new. It was as if he was in Lagos, where flyovers were common when he studied there. During those times, he had admired them with envy, and always wished that someday his beloved Accra could also boast of such man-made hanging and suspended roads. Amazingly, he hadn't had to wait long for that wish to be realised; and that made him proud indeed. Though he saw the *trotro* vehicles and taxis in large numbers, he hardly saw the public buses. Instead, the stations were filled with modern, long-distance coaches. There was a drastic increase in shops and merchandising along the roadsides. The streets were still filled with beggars, petty traders and the usual young street hawkers - all trying to catch potential customers before they got to the main shops and marketplaces. It wasn't new to Osam; the scenes brought back memories of his adolescence.

As a growing 10-year-old boy, he sold magazines and razor blades in the dangerous traffic of Accra's late evening rush hour to supplement the inadequate food at home. He used to dash between vehicles haggling and hustling people in their cars. He had to compete with other children, and that called for alertness and dexterity. These were children who had been abandoned, had parents who were too sick to look after them, or too poor to take care of them. It was a risky business, and Osam often had close knockdown encounters. But in spite of the fact that he was in that business for almost two-and-a-half years, his adoptive family never got wind of it.

Auntie Mensah always served him less food than she did her own children. To compensate for that, he used to drink plenty of water after his meals to *feel* and *stay* full much longer. Sometimes, he used his little profit to buy food at a nearby night market as a *top-up*.

He recalled times when they used to vandalise people's mango trees in their homes when they were ripe. They used to dig up the ground to store the unripe ones, as the earth's natural heat ripened them faster. Sometimes Osam's teeth became so oversensitive after eating so many mangoes that he couldn't bring himself to chew on his favourite yam and stew dinner meal.

Osam was introduced to street hawking by Kofi, a boy next door who attended the same primary school as Osam. He lived with his wicked stepmother who cared little about him – only about her nocturnal job as a prostitute in a hotel.

Osam and Kofi became friends when they were both drafted into the school's football team. They played together as central defenders though Kofi was the more gifted. Besides the school team, Kofi also played for Soccer Missionaries, a local juvenile football team. He introduced Osam to the team manager, but even though Osam was enrolled into the team, his Aunt wouldn't allow it, so sadly he was forced to quit.

The team's coach owned a toiletry shop in the city centre. In order to sell his products quickly, and also help some of the poor boys, he distributed toiletry products he sold in his shop to some of the *trusted* footballers for them to sell for a little profit. Kofi used to collect the Permasharp and Gillette blades from the shop in the mornings on his way to school and sold them when school finished in the late afternoons. Kofi, being a good businessman even at that tender age, in turn, subcontracted some of his stock to Osam.

Osam had no great ambitions then and wondered what future lay before the present numerous and shabbily-dressed juvenile street sellers who came from Accra's well-marked shanty towns. Though some of them were quite young, they already seemed experienced in the art of street hawking. All Osam did as a youngster was to recite the popular line of wanting to be a medical doctor whenever he was asked. Never in his dreams did he imagine he would end up where he presently was. For a moment, he forgot himself and became immersed in the fragility and joyful presence of living in their world. In the midst of despair, hope persists, he thought.

He paused for a while to wonder where Kofi was…

They lost contact when he went to secondary school in Cape Coast. This was the first time that he had thought about him since they said goodbye. He felt greatly touched.

But, despite the noticeable and rapid changes, Osam felt sad that a large section of society, as usual, seemed to have been left behind in the country's rapid economic progress.

Osam also realised that the bars in Accra were full of people - mostly young people who seemed to be doing well in whatever they were up to. Some of them drove the latest versions of top-of-the-range cars. He found almost all consumables that were on sale in England also available in Accra. The place heaved with modern nightclubs and various top-end restaurants which were well patronised by the growing, new, young middle class. Osam liked what he saw.

It wasn't that people didn't want to travel to Europe anymore. Far from that, the craze was still there, perhaps even more than seven years before when he had moved heaven and earth in order to leave the then-decaying system. However, there seemed to be opportunities around for younger people to engage in various forms of business. One of his old friends, now a successful businessman, told him how the information technology boom had created numerous prosperous entrepreneurs. Telecommunication centres had sprung up all over the place. And people were in there either using the internet or making and receiving phone calls from abroad.

Osam was now a *Bogga*, but for the first time since he arrived back in Accra, he really wanted to stay. All his fears of not being able to readjust to the unrushed and undemanding Ghanaian lifestyle were now distant memories.

He recalled the old, wise saying, *there's no place like home*.

Chapter 33
(*The trip to visit Uncle Kojo*)

The rare sight of hustling and bustling in the street, the unending high-pitched noises from the street hawkers, each trying to out-pitch the other, the honking sounds of the neighbouring vehicles in this slow-moving tailback, all added to Osam's persistent distress.

It was sunset in the large market town in the Brong Ahafo region of Ghana. It was Thursday, the *market day*; the busiest. There were the usual frantic bargaining all around which usually signalled it was time to head home.

Well, Osam's journey had just begun. Ahead of him lay a 200 km drive to visit his 60-year-old uncle for the first time in his remote village, Nkwanta, in the Western region of Ghana. His uncle preferred this route, as it appeared to be the quickest way to his village.

He was travelling alone as Richard had had to rush to visit his sick mother in Kodie, his village near Kumasi, the previous day.

Though the sun had almost set, he could still see the opulent green canopy of the virgin-but-vintage forest far beyond waiting to welcome them into its realm.

'*Paanoo hyew!*' (*Hot bread!*) interrupted a young girl shouting the famous sales line.

'Debi, medase,' (*No, thanks!*) he replied in Twi as well, not even bothering to look at her. He was fuming with indignation and rightly so. They were almost four hours behind schedule. He was supposed to be at his destination by now. He had gotten into trouble with the driver and station authorities when he complained about the long delay. They got particularly upset when Osam told them it wasn't like that in England. They warned him not to impose his western views on them, and even threatened to eject him from the vehicle.

He wondered how in such modern times people still hadn't learned to be punctual. The excuse he kept getting was the same old flimsy *African time*.
How could the country progress economically if the basic element of time was not strictly adhered to?

Conditions were far removed from the Western lifestyle he was now used to. Even though it was mid-August and supposed to be mild, the sun was beating down like hell. He had already consumed two litres of bottled water. His multi-function, waterproof wristwatch at one point registered 38 degrees Celsius. His long legs were dripping with sweat underneath his designer blue jeans. Apparently, it had been roasting a month earlier, so he had totally lucked out. In spite of that, he had already darkened a couple of shades.

Osam was wearing a light-brown T-shirt on top of his blue jeans. Around his waist was his bum bag containing his passport (which he wanted to show to his uncle's family and farm workers), his wallet, Motorola mobile phone, condoms and a few male extras like a nail clipper, toothbrush and toothpaste. He and his uncle agreed that they would wait for Osam at his village stop for three hours, up to 8 o'clock, and then return home. Beyond that time, he said, it wasn't safe to be out and about alone in the forest. He assured Osam that it was only a four-hour journey.
He had felt re-assured by the driver's warning before they set off that there would be no toilet breaks or stops due to the late departure. He also said that almost three-quarters of the road was in better shape due to the on-going road works.

Not only was the road uneven and not tarred, but it was also dusty and narrow. Those sitting at the edges of the lorry had to constantly bear the lashings from the surrounding hedges and shrubs.

The vehicle was a *boneshaker*; made up of two parts. The driver's cockpit adjoined the wooden passenger carriage by means of a solid shaft. The front, ceiling, and bottom part of the rectangular-shaped passenger carriage were completely sealed. The wooden floor served as a passenger footrest. The opposite ends, which were open, were joined by long, thin, wooden seats across. There were ten rows of seating in total. The sides and back were sealed up to the passenger seating level, providing ample space to jump out of the carriage from the three ends; being the sides and back which were not covered. Every long seat carried six passengers; so there were sixty in total, including the *mate*, the driver's assistant. His job was to collect the fares and alert the driver when someone wished to alight at their destination. They were a bit squashed in his fourth-row seat as two of the three women had enormous bottoms. Osam had little comfort sitting at the edge of the right window as he felt the dust gust as well.

On the western horizon was the most beautiful sunset Osam had ever seen. He felt as if the diminishing light rays were reaching out and touching him. It suddenly burst into flames, for one moment, but it occurred so rapidly that it was over in a few minutes. Such is life, he thought; over like the flash of a firefly. Then he saw amidst the tall forest trees, with their varying green leaves, the scrumptious pink fluffy clouds against the darkening evening blue sky. Hope flamed in Osam.

The fading lights spelled the end of town and the beginning of the trip to the forest.

As they tunnelled and zoomed along the narrow road, which could easily qualify as a single lane, he could faintly hear the strange wailing of an animal in the murky distance. The dark, verdant feeling surrounding them as they pummelled along the pot-holed, dusty road gave an eerie atmosphere. The truck, however, did provide refuge. Only heaven knew what lay beyond the growing darkness in the forest thickets. Sometimes the road got so narrow he wondered what would happen in the event of an approaching vehicle, or a strange arm suddenly emerging and snatching him into the vast emptiness of the forest. A quick glance at his watch indicated 6.17 p.m. They had lost almost an hour in the traffic jam in town.

As a youngster growing up in Accra, he was told stories about dwarves and spirits taking over the forest at nightfall. He remembered people claiming to have heard drumming and chanting in the forest on sacred days. He recalled Uncle Kojo telling them of a great warrior of his village who never returned home. Tuesday in that village was the day of the dwarves and spirits. It was considered sacred. Hence, there was no farming. Unfortunately, the great man stayed too long on his farm Monday night, and when the spirits came to *purify* the forest they found him in their path and took him away. His body was never found.

Forty-five minutes into the journey Osam was already feeling sleepy from the day's tropical heat. It had been a long day. However, his drowsiness was interrupted when they were told to get off the lorry as they had reached a long hilly stretch of road. According to the driver's mate, around two hundred metres of the road ahead was so bad that drivers did that part of the road without passengers. There was actually an old jack-knifed truck hanging perilously from the edge. The irony was that it happened to be the widest part of the road they had used so far, yet it looked so treacherously eroded from the persistent tropical forest rains that he feared for the young driver, even though he might have navigated it many times.

The sun had baked and cracked the reddish earth on which he was walking. It was as if it was impatiently awaiting the rains for a welcome relief. Both driver and mate assured them that the remaining stretch of road was better as it had been laid recently.

They all did the short walk as they watched--some in absolute horror--the lorry beavering its way up the slippery gully road swinging hither and thither as if outside forces on both sides were blocking it from falling onto its side.

Osam struggled to keep up with the rest of the passengers due to his sleepiness and was already nodding off a couple of minutes into the resumption of their journey.

Rain, as he had learnt at primary school, came down in splashes not drops in this part of the Ghanaian forest. Although the apparently sleeping forest on both sides of the road was now further away, he could still see from that highest point, even in the growing darkness, the charm and appeal of a huge sea of wavy, green foliage. It was indeed a breath-taking sight. The moments of greatest beauty were the ones that made Osam respect the deepest; with appreciation, awe, humility, and wonder. It was humbling.

It reminded Osam of Uncle Kojo's saying that the forest looks like one big tree from a distance, but as one gets closer to it, the trees begin to move apart.

He always used this proverb whenever he wanted to tell the young Osam that there is more to everything than meets the eye in life.

'Kojokrom junction!' shouted a woman from one of the backseats.

Osam awoke from a slumber. A dim light flashed on in the carriage as the truck gradually decelerated and pulled up at a small clearing. He wondered how a woman could disembark alone in such conditions.

It was 9.50p.m.

In the darkness, he could faintly distinguish a small lane amidst the shrubs. There were three spotlights to his right as she alighted, and with the mate's help carried her hefty load and steadily disappeared into the dead of night.

While this was going on, the driver announced that if anyone wanted to have a pee they were free to do so.

As if they had all been waiting for exactly that, there was a welcome rush out of the carriage. They were already three and a half hours into their journey. Even for a novice like him, the thick smell of the burnt, decomposed and fresh leafy wood was apparent in the still, heavy night air. The moist, fallen leaves formed a soft carpet on the hard forest ground. Amidst those were searching sounds of the creatures of the night indicating life still continued unabated.

The women, he noticed, were urinating closer to the truck while the men went further afield.

Osam had not finished when he was frozen by a sudden stampede. Everyone around him started running helter-skelter, some screaming. He instinctively joined the melee and ran as fast as he could in the dark. He was unsuccessfully trying to stop himself from urinating in his pants. After a while, he vaguely heard the mate screaming for them to return to the lorry.

'Get in quickly!' he shrieked.

In the commotion, his now acclimatised eyes exposed how he was heading in the opposite direction. A sudden tumble over a hard object stopped him in his tracks. He lay still for what seemed like ten seconds, quietly bearing the unbearable pain in the lower part of his left knee. About a hundred metres ahead he heard the vehicle starting up, and a few seconds later, hurriedly driving off.

'Please stay, wait for me,' Osam vainly whispered, knowing he had just missed the lorry.

Reverberating around him was the deep sound of men chanting and singing war-like songs. He tried to understand what they were saying but struggled with the Akan accent in this part of the country. In the melee, he thought he heard someone say '*some couldn't escape*,' amidst the dancing throng. He could tell from their burning lamps and torches they were just metres away from where he was. They might have been the spotlights he had seen when the lorry pulled up for the lady to alight at the junction. Was she a phantom as he had surmised in the safety of the lorry? He wanted to ring for help using his mobile phone but was scared its light would give him away. He wished he had changed its light settings. But then, he wouldn't see the keypads in this dark anyway. What if the phone rang? He was doomed in all cases.

He knew, through rumours as a youngster, that it was a tradition in this part of the country to kill people, particularly unwary strangers when a king or chief died. Death in many African traditions was only a transition, a passage from this physical world to the spiritual realm of the gods. For a person's--and, in this case, a king's--status on earth to be recognised in the land of the gods, he needed to be accompanied by people proclaiming his status when he arrived at his new permanent and higher domain. Hence, they needed to have some *heads* for the dead king. The people killed were then buried alongside the king as part of a ritual.

Of course, he hadn't heard about any royal death. In any case, he was in the middle of nowhere and in deep trouble if he was caught up in a similar ritual. He heard himself praying for God's help. That surprised him, as he couldn't remember the last time he had prayed. He believed in God and used to pray as a youngster, but ceased when he reached adolescence.

His eyes having now fully acclimatised to his surroundings, he turned to escape but was again frozen by a startled, wavering, soft, feminine voice from behind.

'Please don't leave me.'

He almost fainted.

'Please take me with you,' the feminine voice continued.

He slowly turned in the darkness to see a sprawled figure about five metres away clutching at the protruding root of a giant tree, barely able to make her out in the darkness.

It appeared to be Linda, the third-year university student in his party of travellers. She was in her early twenties, and even though they only spoke briefly at the station her overpowering beauty failed to mask her bitchiness. Some of the male passengers had whispered about her while they were waiting at the station. Her frequent back and forth dancing strolls in front of the males were clearly symbolic provocative gestures. She was a cutie, and she knew it. It was, as some of them noted, a deliberate Ghanaian feminine tease.

In the dark, he could read from her body language that she was injured or in some sort of discomfort.

He motioned for her to be quiet, his index finger across his lips, realising the pursuers were even closer than before. He beckoned her to follow, then turned and quietly began clawing his way on his knees through the soft undergrowth as fast and noiselessly as he could. The pain had now subsided. He quickened as their chanting voices got closer, making sure he made as little noise as possible as he trampled on the fallen forest leaves. About thirty seconds into his flight he realised, in his rush to flee, he hadn't checked on his partner. He had half-turned when he heard a loud feminine scream.

'Help me! Help me!!'

'No! No!! No!!!' Osam half-screamed in anger at himself as he realised in the pitch blackness that he was alone.

He stayed put for a while, listening to the diminishing struggles of their captive, and the indistinguishable murmurs of the group. A sudden burst of laughter reverberated through the darkness.

The wind picked up and he could smell rain in the dampening air. He guessed they didn't welcome it as he could hear them retreating hurriedly from where he was hiding.

When their hurried retreat was almost inaudible, he resumed his trek in the abyss of darkness. His whole body was shaking with fear. He had no jungle training whatsoever, except for hiking and trekking in a less dense forest in his church's youth society. He learned among other things the basic survival stuff like finding a river and following its flow to the next village, constructing a campfire, and how to leave traces behind so one could be rescued.

He set about looking for a place to spend the night. He wanted a sheltered tree to climb as the mosquitoes were feasting on him. Sleeping up high might also save him from nocturnal wild animals on the hunt. He cared less about the mosquitoes feasting on his blood than he did about their infuriating noise. He wished they would just bite him, suck his blood, and then leave him in peace.

He saw in the nightlight a *climbable* tree. He was almost halfway towards it when he felt sharp, painful bites first on his foot, then rapid movements up both feet and legs. He had stumbled into fire ants. He instinctively let go of the branch he was holding and landed hard on the buttress roots of the big tree. The ants' bites were largely concentrated on the lower part of his body. He tried to sweep them away with his hands as their sharp bites became unbearable.

It began to drizzle. Soon the drizzle turned into rain, and then a storm. He had felt the growing wind but hadn't expected the rain to come so soon. The bloody ants were climbing his thighs. He ran from the tree he was sheltering under and found another not too far off and took off his jeans. He removed his underwear as well when he received bites there too. He felt a sharp stinging at the base of his scrotum. He reached out, got hold of the impudent ant, and squeezed it into oblivion. He shook his jeans violently in the moist air and moved on to what appeared to be a hut. He presumed it to be a farmer's refuge. He bent down to pick up his small phosphorescent Swiss knife which had fallen out of the back jeans pocket. He put his underwear back on but was scared to wear his jeans. He was sure some of the ants would still be stuck on the fabric so he decided to whack it several times against a nearby tree. He stood stock still when he heard something in the nearby bushes.

Silence filled the moist air, except for the sound of the now dwindling rain. The lightning violently flashed in the darkened protective canopy, followed by a thunderous roar. He thought he saw a figure – what appeared to be a figure. He wasn't sure. He was scared stiff. He moved to hide behind his sheltered refuge. Only then did he realise he had been standing on a grave. He jumped so high he struck his head against a tree branch. A few mounds and tombstones here and there indicated he was in a cemetery. With the smell of death instantly haunting the serene atmosphere, he turned and ran. He looked back quickly and saw the strange figure following, about fifty metres away. He could see it clearly, it was real. Or was he dreaming? It was as though it wasn't sprinting but floating. Osam stopped. He waited with great dread for the inevitable.

As it got closer, he saw the shape of two bright, glowing eyes. He could see nothing behind those lights. For a couple of seconds which seemed like an eternity, it hung there, staring into his tired eyes. A piercing chill ran up his whole being. He thought he had come face to face with a big cat. The figure then sprang high into the air above him and gradually vanished into the night sky, his eyes instinctively following its flight.

An owl hooted nearby, breaking the silence prevailing in the damp forest. He hated owls. They were instruments of evil spirits.

He took two deep breaths, gathered enough strength, and started galloping away from the hoots, still holding tightly to his jeans. He tripped on something solid, slipped on wet ground, and then went on a free fall down, down and down until he felt a big crushing splash.

He had fallen into a flowing river. Though it had been raining, the water temperature was still warm, perhaps from the fervent heat of the day on the forest floor.

After being dragged by the water uncontrollably for a time, his midriff crashed into the buttress root of a fallen tree. He grabbed one of its branches. It was slippery, but he held on tightly. He remained still for a moment, and when his vision adjusted to his new surroundings, he dragged himself out of the water. He quickly made for a tree and climbed up.

He stayed put for a long while, taking in the dim sights and chilling sounds of the forest from his new refuge. He ached all over but didn't seem to have any injury. He checked his watch. It was 12.15 a.m. He couldn't see far, yet he heard the constant forest life below. He didn't even try to sleep.

Chapter 34

A loud echo woke him from his deep and peaceful slumber. He waited for a sign of movement from below. There was no perceptible danger. The blackness of the night was gradually disappearing. In the distance, he faintly saw something floating ahead.

He soon realised that it was his pair of jeans which he had lost during the impact on the water. They seemed to have gotten stuck on a small fallen tree branch.

He angrily wondered what he had done to deserve what he was going through. He touched the left side of his forehead. There was some dry blood, but it was only a small cut. He glanced at his watch. It was 4:09 am. He opened his now discoloured bum bag to check the state of its contents -- particularly his mobile phone -- and to his surprise, everything seemed in good condition. He took out the phone and noticed he had just one battery life left. He waited while the phone searched for coverage. After almost a minute without success, he got fed up and proceeded to ring Richard's mobile phone. There was no luck – just the most frustrating scenario for anyone in his dangerous situation: he had the phone but couldn't use it.

He wondered whether someone somewhere wanted him dead. Maybe he had been baited into travel so he could be killed. He had heard cases in the UK of unsuspecting returnees going delirious and mad, or in some cases, killed by witches. One particular incident still fresh in his mind was the case of a young man who fell ill as soon as he got to the UK. After two years of suffering and no cure, he was encouraged to return home for some traditional medication. He died in his sleep the very day he arrived back home. Who knew, maybe someone in Osam's family wanted him dead, or he might have angered the gods in some way. Or perhaps he was paying for his sins that had led to the death of his fellow travellers at sea.

As he sat safe but shivering up the drying tree, he could still see his trousers flaring and dancing on the opposite bank of the river. It was clearer now that they had got stuck on a nearby shrub whose branches were dancing in the flowing torrent. He had to be quick or he'd lose them when they got free of whatever was holding them in place. But he was reluctant to get back on the forest floor and then swim about fifty metres across the rapidly-flowing river to reach them. Besides, the current was stronger as that part of the forest was steeper. Painfully, the best option was to stay put.

After a long while, he sniffed for any sign of danger. When he was satisfied, he carefully descended the tree. As he was doing so, he saw his jeans disappear into the distance. He had lost them, again; this time, he knew, for good.

'Bugger!' he screamed. What was he going to do? All he had on was a moist T-shirt and underwear.

He wished he had put on his boxer shorts. He always wore boxer shorts due to the hot climate, but for some weird reason had opted for normal underwear the morning of his departure. He was furious with himself. Luckily, the long T-shirt partially covered his manhood. There was no object more valuable than a man's life, he thought. At least he still had his sandals and bum bag intact. He opened it and took out his mobile phone to try ringing again, but it was still out of coverage range. His legs and thighs were marked with the bites of the fire ants. He stood for a while to try to estimate where he was. He trekked away from the river, on through the less dense part of the forest until he came to a farm. Mist blanketed the area. As he jumped over a log, he wondered whether he would ever make it to Uncle Kojo's.

He felt hungry when he entered the cash crop farm. They were cassava, yam, plantain and corn plants. He could clearly see the sparsely clouded blue sky as that area of about a thousand square metres was less forest-like. He uprooted a small cassava plant, peeled off the covering with his Swiss knife and chewed on its white, edible and juicy root. It didn't taste great, but he needed to eat something. He had chosen the cassava because yam tubers were slimy while the plantain and corn had no fruits yet. When he finished, he drank the water caught up in the smaller plantain plant leaves. The sight of the farm gave him some much-needed hope as he knew there must be people living nearby.

He was soon proved right as he came to a small farm house at 5.40 a.m. Though he couldn't see the rising sun on the horizon, it was already gradually dissolving the darkness. He heard indistinguishable sounds as he happily approached the small hut. As he got closer, he realised the sound was actually emanating from it. He stopped in the hedge about four metres away to take a breather and organise his jumbled thoughts.

'ooo... oh... ohh... oooH ...OHHHH yes!' came a high-pitched feminine voice in obvious ecstasy; the sound of copulation. There was a momentary silence.

'MM...ah...mm...MMMMM...YES...YES...harder...faster ...faster...faster...faster...Yes! Yes!!Yes!!!'

She went on yelling as the sound of the rapidly moving bed indicated the intercourse was reaching its climax. There was a sudden crescendo of screams of oohs and aahs from both orgasm-spent individuals, then a moment of quiet. Osam waited. Time ticked on. He stared at the concrete hut. Even in his helpless situation, he felt jealous of the lucky guy.

He wondered whether to continue or stay put.

After a long thought, he opted for the latter as he heard their voices. A man appeared. He approached steadily, stopped about two metres short of the bushes, and began to urinate.

Osam wondered if he could be seen, as he could clearly see the man's small, short and circumcised penis. Size, they said, didn't matter, but Osam thought he must be a great lover with that little piece of manhood. He was slightly built and looked to be in his mid-twenties. He was about 1.70 metres tall, and only wore white underwear. He looked weak and shattered from his recent exertions. He shook his penis rather violently when he finished and slotted it back into his underwear.

After a long while, he reappeared, shabbily-dressed this time, and disappeared into the bush nearby with a big shiny machete.

'Don't stay too long. I'll be waiting for you tonight,' he half-shouted as he disappeared into the thicket in the distance.

Osam crawled closer but was stopped in his tracks when a young lady appeared from around the corner wearing a short cloth loosely tied around the top of her breast. It was so short he could see all of her firm thighs up to her bum, which was just partly covered. She stopped, turned her back in his direction, spread her strong legs, and also urinated. He could see her big, well-rounded bottom now, and the big multi-coloured bead that was loosely sprawled around her upper bottom. She wore no underwear. He was turned on by her wriggling action as she walked away and disappeared around the corner.

After a long while--still thinking about his next plan of action--she reappeared dressed. The attire was tight. As if she had overheard his current thinking process, she turned quickly, glanced in his direction, and then proceeded leisurely along the same path the man had taken. For the first time, he saw her clearly.

Osam's jaw dropped in cold shock. It was the same university girl he had travelled with; the very same girl he had tried but failed to save and who was captured and, he thought, killed.

Before he could react, she disappeared. She was wearing a blue dress, not the red one she had on the previous day.

What happened? How did she end up here? He clearly remembered her telling him she was visiting her parents. She had also claimed that her dad was a very rich farmer in one of the towns.

She suddenly reappeared, went into the hut, and after a short while he heard a door shut. He saw her take another pathway just to the right of his position and disappear from his view into some shrubby growth. She carried the same small, brown handbag. He cautiously jumped up and followed her. His limbs were tired from crouching for a long time. He remembered he only had on his underwear. He dashed back to the small hut, checked that no one was coming, opened the unlocked door and tiptoed into the room. It was dark except for weak rays of light from the rising sun coming through the space between the thatched roof and clay walls. There was an old brown pair of shorts lying by a water pot. He grabbed them and a small piece of bread from a tiny stool by the bed and rushed out as he thought he heard someone whistling as they came towards the hut. He hid in a small bush, and after a couple of seconds the thin, young man reappeared. He cursed as he noticed the door of the hut was ajar.

When the young man disappeared inside, Osam made a quick but quiet dash in the same direction Linda had taken a couple of minutes before. Moving with great care, he followed the narrow pathway until it dawned on him that he still had the stolen shorts in his left hand. He put them on, but they were too small, so tight they tore open at the back when he bent to pick up the dropped bread. He munched on the small sweet loaf and quickly pursued the girl until rounding a curve in the now thickening growth, he saw her about twenty metres ahead.

She must have heard him through the noise he made walking through the fallen leaves which carpeted the forest floor because she looked back and saw him. To his surprise, she continued walking. He was sure she didn't recognise him as he could easily pass for a local farmer. Before she reached the next curve, she turned again and looked at him, this time with astonishment - her eyes bulging in disbelief. She was still staring at him with the same uneasy fondness she had when their eyes locked into each other's the first time at the station.

Typically for him, he lusted after her. He had an uncontrollable urge to have his way with her. He didn't want to scare her, though, so he smiled and urged her not to run. She seemed glued to the wet ground. He walked softly towards her and stopped about eight metres away. She looked at him from head to toe, then again, and then at his dirty pair of tight, brown shorts. He felt uneasy about them as his manhood was squeezed uncomfortably to the right side.

'I'm sorry I left you last night. I thought you were right behind me,' he said apologetically. 'I thought they captured you.'

'Yeah, but it's a long story. How are you? What happened to you?' she asked, taking another quick look at his shorts.

'Well, where do I start?' he replied with a long sigh. 'First of all, I was bitten by fire ants, and then I fell into a river.'

'Really?'

'Yes!' Osam replied, getting much closer and showing her the head laceration and the dried blood. As he did so, three giant young men in farm clothes appeared on the pathway. He hoped they hadn't overheard what had been discussed.

They said a casual 'hello' as they passed, to which Linda, with a smile, responded in kind. Osam did too.

Just the sight of those three strong men with their sharpened machetes sent fear waves through him. He wondered whether they were among their pursuers last night. And, if they were, whether they were aware that he knew what they had been up to.

Linda motioned him to move on. He told her he wanted to return to Accra, but first, he needed a good bath and something to eat. She told him she was going for a day visit to her sick dad, who also happened to be the traditional Chief in Meko. If Osam wasn't in a hurry, he could accompany her to her parents' town and return with her to Accra tomorrow. One part of his brain went to work on hearing that name as it rang a bell. The other part told him not to stick with her, for all her beauty and his lust. He knew her beauty carried a fatal attraction, but like a dog, he yielded to his fool heart. He kept falling easily; a great failing. He knew his heart would be broken a thousand times if he didn't manage to remain detached. The fact that she had claimed to be royal also drew her to him. He told her he would reimburse every dime she spent on him when they got back to Accra. Once again she looked at him with an uneasy sense of attraction and told him not to worry.

They reached the junction where they were to wait for a taxi to the main town. There was no one at the stop, which only had a small bench to seat two. He wondered how many people used it, as a taxi in this part of the world, according to his uncle, was expensive. She told him to wait at the junction while she went to get him something to wear from a nearby friend. He wondered why she didn't get it from her *boyfriend*. Perhaps she didn't want Osam to meet him and vice versa. As she left, he wondered how many villagers she had bedded. He took out his mobile phone to check if he had any messages or missed calls; the battery was now flat.

She returned shortly with a pair of brown striped trousers and a white T-shirt.

Hiding in a nearby bush, he unbuckled his bum bag, took off the old dirty clothes and put on the *new* ones. Luckily they fitted him fine. His sandals looked OK, apart from a little dirt and discoloration. All that was left was his body stench.

267

They didn't have to wait long. An old taxi soon came clattering to a halt when Linda signalled with her right hand, it being rude in Ghanaian custom to make signals with the left hand. The left hand was the one used to do filthy things like cleaning yourself when you went to the toilet.

The passengers and the driver seemed to know Linda as they exchanged greetings. They even inquired about her dad's health.

There was only space for one person on the back seat, but there were two passengers in the front passenger seat so Linda suggested to the middle-aged driver that she wouldn't mind sitting on Osam's lap, an offer which he duly accepted.

It took them half an hour to get to Meko, a large village, although the locals referred to it as a town. It seemed busy as he could hear the habitual calls from petty traders in the market to their left. It also had a rural bank and a small post office. Some of the traders were at the station, hoping to be the first to catch the arriving customers. There was also a tiny police station situated right among the numerous shops in the village centre.

They got out at the taxi rank, just beside the town's generator. Osam noticed that there were more taxis arriving at the town than leaving. All the taxis had the bright orange colour scheme on the four fenders – just like the ones he had chartered in Accra.

There was only one passenger seated in the taxi at the front of about ten, all waiting for their turn. He wondered how long the poor chap had been waiting.

There were wooden electricity posts at various points in the village which carried power to the homes and the few commercial buildings. Most of the people were middle-aged and mainly cocoa farmers. They were draped in their traditional clothes in the mid-morning sun. There were only a few women about, either buying or selling a product. They had donned their traditional female long dress, skirt and top set, and wrap wear, and head kerchiefs to match.

People in this part of the country were considered rich, due to the large cocoa farmlands they owned. Within a short time, Osam realised that they didn't need to spend much money on expensive clothes and material possessions. They lived simple lives. Most of their hard-earned money was saved. The wealth was apparent from the concrete edifices in the town. In Ghanaian villages, there were usually more mud homes and fewer concrete homes, normally inhabited by the rich, or people who received help from affluent family members living in the cities or abroad.

From the main station, Osam and Linda went first to one of her female friends who lived in a single concrete-built room. Nana said it was a present from her dad when she had successfully completed secondary school.
Linda left Osam with Nana and assured him she would return as soon as she had seen her parents.
Nana was friendly. Like Linda, she looked to be in her early twenties. Unlike Linda, however, she was slim and ugly.
Osam had a long bath in the little bathroom situated near her little house. He made sure to clean the wound, now starting to heal, he had sustained in the river. Even though he had had a short-cropped haircut before leaving England, it was still long enough to hide the small wound from the prying eyes of villagers.
Later, he had some homemade *yam* and vegetable stew. Afterwards, all he wanted to do was sleep, but Nana was the talkative type and wouldn't stop yapping. He allowed her to do so as he lay on her wooden double bed mattress. She sat across him in a desperate bid, as it were, to get his waning attention.

Linda and Nana had been friends since childhood. Her father worked on one of Linda's dad's cocoa plantations. They both went to the same primary and secondary schools. Unfortunately, despite getting better grades than Linda at the GCE Advanced level exams, Nana didn't go to the University as her parents could not afford to finance it. She was thus a cashier at the only rural bank in the area. She told him Linda claimed he was her boyfriend living in Europe. Osam confirmed that without hesitation.

'Ah!' He remembered he had to recharge his mobile phone. He touched his waist. Then it hit him. He had left his bum bag in the bushes where he changed into the new clothes. He had to go back for it.

'I've got to go back.'

'Go back where?'

'Ehm...Meda. I've just realised that I left my bum belt there. It contains my wallet, mobile phone, daily anti-malaria tablet, and, most importantly, my passport and return ticket to the UK.'

'Oh, dear! How could you have misplaced such important stuff?'

'I'll explain as soon as I return. Can I borrow some money off you?'

She dashed to the small chest of drawers adjacent to the bed and opened her purse. 'I don't have sufficient money on me. Here, that's the exact return fare by taxi.'

He didn't believe her claim that it was the only cash she had. Not that it mattered as he had lots of money stashed away in his wallet.

As they walked towards the station, he remembered to inquire if she knew where Nkwanta was. She showed him the road that led there. It was 15km about away, she said, but in the exact opposite direction to where he was heading.

Chapter 35

The rusty and dusty taxi came to a halt fifteen metres away from where Osam had swapped clothes. The driver claimed he didn't have change. Osam was taken aback as Nana claimed to have given him the exact fare. He happily brushed it aside as a tip. Osam ran quickly to the spot and searched the area, but there was no sign of the bag.

After double-checking to be sure, he retraced his way back to the stop where he and Linda had boarded the taxi. A look at his watch indicated it was 5:04 p.m, which meant he had a few hours of daylight to play with before he returned to Nana's house. Just as he got there, he saw the three young men he had seen earlier that morning, as well as the young man who had been with Linda.

They must have realised he was looking for something as they were whispering and looking in his direction. They didn't look friendly as all three stood akimbo, with those sharp machetes still hanging on their hips. Linda's friend, however, didn't possess a machete.

'ɛnyɛ owura yi na ne nfonin bɔ passport no mu?'(*Isn't this the man whose photo is in the passport?*) Osam heard the one who was with Linda whisper as he approached them.

'Ka wano tum!' (*Shut up!*) one of them whispered back.

'Have any of you seen a bum bag lying about?' Osam asked with seeming calm in English, trying hard to conceal his nervousness. It was a popular strategy he employed to work his way through difficult circumstances. People tended to accord more respect to those who spoke fluent English. The idea was to put them on the defensive.

'Yɛnka brofo wɔ ha!' (*English isn't spoken here!*) came the reply from one of them.

'I beg your pardon?' Osam asked, pretending not to understand the language. It was a calculated risk as the three men might have heard him speaking to Linda in Twi.

'Wo kaasε, wo yε Obroni anaa? Wonkyεn yεn wate? Adeε asa, nka woawu!' (*Do you think you are a white man? You're not superior to any of us standing here, all right? You're lucky it isn't nightfall; you'd be a dead man!*) came the reply from the meanest looking of the three.

That confirmed his earlier fears of them being among the group the night before. His strategy was working in his favour, at least for now.

Just then he realised Linda's friend was wearing what appeared to be his bum bag.

'Can I see that bag please?' Osam asked, pointing at the bum bag.

'Kwasia me nfa ma wo bio!' (*Stupid man, you won't have it back!*) the man retorted.

He knew it was his bag. He attempted two brave steps forward but was stopped in his tracks as the meanest and seeming leader dragged out his shiny machete. The leader displayed his anger in rustic, clear body gestures in a bid to scare Osam. Even from that distance, Osam could feel the heat from his fixed stare.

Then the man began chanting softly in the local dialect. Osam was struggling to comprehend it. The other two joined in. The three began dancing and mumbling the chants as they turned their attention towards Osam. The earlier quietness was quickly converting into a war-like atmosphere.

'Wo wo wo, I don't want any trouble, guys! All I want is my bag back. Look, we can talk business OK? You can have half of the money...all the money, if that's what you want,' Osam said, trying to raise his voice with every syllable. He knew he was in a tricky and intimidating situation as he could see no other soul around.

Three of the four men began approaching him but were abruptly held back by the leader, who now held in his right hand the leather bum bag.

These were real jungle warriors holding pure rustic but effective armoury, and Osam imagined being beaten up, much worse with a machete and never getting his possessions.

To his surprise, he found himself standing his ground. He began to tremble at the knees. To mask it, he began marching on the spot. Even though he was scared stiff, he seemed ready to defend his position. His Judo coach at the University campus always emphasised the element of surprise during combat. '*The first strike strikes fear,*' he used to say. Osam felt the adrenaline rush through his body in preparation for a flight or fight situation.

'Abranteɛ, wo firi he? ɛdeɛn na na wo ne Linda ɛyɛ anɔpa yi? Wo'nim sɛ ɔyɛ obi mpena anaa? (Gentleman, *where are you from, and what were you doing this morning with Linda? Don't you know she's someone's girlfriend?*) the leader said as he casually approached Osam.

Osam could smell the pungent odour coming from the leader as he snarled. His machete was held firmly in his left hand, clearly a southpaw, and the bum bag in the right. His welling anger was clearly highlighted by his wide-eyed gestures as he mockingly approached Osam alone. The others burst out laughing.

Before he could say anything more, Osam, like a Yokozuna, wrestled him to the ground. The leader lost both machete and bag in the process, which Osam quickly grabbed. The others remained where they stood. Realising their apparent lack of reaction, Osam sprinted away with both the bag and machete and vanished into the nearby darkening forest. He looked back to see if he was being pursued, but to his surprise, they were attending to their fallen leader. He continued to run as fast as he could, not caring where he was heading as long as he was far away from them.

It was 5:30 pm and Osam could see only fading remnants of the sun's rays on the forest ground. He stopped when he passed a cocoa farm and ran into a dense thicket. Trying to control his panting hysteria, he checked the contents of the bag clutched in his right hand.

His passport and other contents like his anti-malaria tablets and return ticket looked fine, but his wallet and mobile phone were gone.

'Cannibals! Thieves!!' he hissed angrily under his breath. There had been considerable amounts of pounds and cedis, a couple of bank debit and credit cards, and store cards in the wallet. He was angry with himself for leaving the bag there in the first place.

Also, with the mobile phone, he could have charged the battery somewhere and tried to ring Richard for help. Now he had no access to all the stored numbers, and he hadn't memorised any of them – not even Richard's. They must have found it not long before he got there. He put on his bum bag-- tightly this time--around his waist and followed a nearby clean pathway. He began to replay in his mind what had just ensued as he walked quickly along the path. There was no way he could go back for his wallet and mobile phone. He had played a very dangerous poker bad image game and surprisingly won - well, half won. He was neither a gambler nor a trouble seeker but always stood up for his rights. Now, here he was again, back in the same forest where he had nearly lost his life the previous night. To add more fuel to the already burning fire, he had gotten into a fight with some members of last night's mob. He wondered what lay in store as darkness began blanketing the jungle. A playback of his arduous trek from Morocco to Ghana suddenly filled his weary mind. He wondered what the final outcome would be this time.

He passed a little settlement of two big mud houses and a smaller one. There was a table full of a variety of well-arranged fruits, which Osam presumed were for sale. He stopped, emptied his right pocket and found that he didn't even have any change to spend.

'Agoo!' (*Knock-knock!*) he said, as he entered the small compound.

'Amee!' (*Come in!*) came the response from inside the smaller hut, which he now realised was the kitchen.

As he approached the table, a woman emerged from the hut holding a ladle. She must have been in the middle of cooking. She was middle-aged with uncovered, plaited hair.

'Maadwo.' (Good evening.)

'Maadwo, Owura.' (Good evening, gentleman.)

'Wo tɔn anaa?' (*Are these for sale?*) Osam asked.

'Aane. Wo'nfiri ɛkuraa yi ase?' (*Yes. You aren't from this village, are you?*)

'Daabi; me bɛ sera obi ɛwɔ ha.' (*I'm visiting someone her*e.)

'Woana?' (*Who?*)

She was asking too many questions for a village woman talking to an unknown man from the city.

'Me pa wo a chɛw, me tumi anya nsuo anom?' (*Please, can I have some water to drink?*) he said, changing the subject.

She returned after a moment from the kitchen with some water in a calabash. He took out one of his anti-malaria tablets, put it in his mouth, and emptied the calabash in no time.

The woman smiled in amazement. 'Fa nia wo bɛ tumi.' (*Take as much as you want.*) she said, quickly rushing back to the kitchen as she smelt something burning.

Osam helped himself to some oranges, finely-cut sugar cane, and bananas.

'Medase oo!!' (*Thanks!!*) he said as he rushed out of the compound into the surrounding forest.

The last remnant of the setting sun was apparent. He took off his white T-shirt--which would easily expose him in the darkness--folded it neatly, and shoved it into the front of his brown trousers. He decided to go back to the woman's village to find a dark shirt to wear. There didn't seem to be a man at home. As he turned, he heard someone whistling and approaching. He dashed behind a big tree. A middle-aged man walked past and entered the compound about ten metres from where Osam was hiding. The man took off his shirt, hung it on what appeared to be a nail on a post near the centre of the compound, and entered the kitchen. Instinctively, Osam tiptoed to the post, grabbed the dirty shirt, and a brown cloth beside it, and ran off into the forest. He didn't stop running until the path came to an end when he reached a cassava farm.

It was now dark, except for this large farm, which had no canopies. He decided to look for a place to spend the night. On second thoughts, he decided to go further as he had stolen a shirt from the last farmhouse. He walked through the numerous slender cassava sticks until he came to the beginning of the forest thicket. He uprooted another tuber as he had the previous day. He had suffered no apparent side effect, as he had first feared. He put on the stolen shirt. It looked like typical farm clothes - sweaty, dirty and stinky. It might not have seen the laundry bucket for years. He wished he could have worn it over the white T-shirt, but the foul-smelling shirt had lost its buttons.

He followed a little-used path at the periphery of the farm into the darkness of the thick jungle. It wasn't long before he found a big tree, about ten metres away, where he decided to stay the night. He cautiously cut some plantain leaves from a young banana plant and made another belt to hold the machete in place around his hip, like a gun in its holster. He carried the remaining three leaves to the foot of the tree in case it rained during the night. He recalled how as a boy his grandfather cut plantain leaves for them to use as umbrellas whenever it rained as they went to or from his cocoa farm. They didn't have to worry whenever it rained on the farm as there was a hut where they could shelter. He always loved the family Easter holiday trips to Cape Coast to visit their extended family. They were the only times he received any kind of pampering. That was a long time ago, and the forest was nowhere near where he presently found himself.

Osam changed his mind and searched for another tree instead. He was scared of sleeping on the forest floor, and the tree was too big to climb in case of an emergency. He could only rely on concealment for protection in the present situation.
It didn't take him long to find a tree with big, strong, spreading branches. He cautiously climbed it, sat akimbo on one of the big branches, and leaned his back against the trunk. He used to climb mango trees with his friends when he was little. His newly-found refuge was not comfortable, but at least he was off the ground, about eight metres below.

Nightfall brought dead silence and the creeping, busy nightlife of the tropical forest. Even from above he could smell the peculiar mix of humid earth and fresh and dead forest foliage. It also brought a welcome contemplation. The passage of time he realised was so illusory, yet distinct. Here he was in a strange and unlikely environment, yet he appeared to be getting used to it.
He had been riding nonchalantly on society's dream train of career, money, and security. It felt like grasping at straws. The only thing that defined him was now. It was both humbling

and saddening. Then it dawned on him. He should have mentioned his uncle's name when the lady asked. He cursed himself. He would retrace his way to the farmhouse at first light to inquire.

He rested his head against the tree branch, tearing up as he relaxed, and hoped that the coming night would bring with it good tidings for the following day. A poem he wrote for a competition when he was at secondary school sprang to mind. He didn't win any prize for it, but his classmates liked it.

Contemplation

Sitting under this oaky tree
Gazing across the darkening cloud
Watching the falling day go by
Fainting light spelling end of day

Staring at obscured stars from this oaky tree
Wondering who's up there staring down at me
Blinding flash ripples across the angry clouds
Rain dripping down the oaky tree

Living the night from this oaky tree
Feeling the noiseless chilly wind
Sounds of life about – life still goes on
Looking ahead to the coming day

Watching daybreak from this oaky tree
Rays of hope from the sun emerge
Shining through the young darkening clouds
Oh, day, what in store have you got for me?

It was just past midnight. It had been drizzling incessantly for some time. Fortunately, the tree and the foul-smelling cloth were providing good protection against the light rain. His clothes beneath were almost dry. Most importantly, the rain had helped drive away the mosquitoes, which brought him welcome relief and deep sleep. Unlike the previous night, he had not had any encounters with fire ants. He knew he would be in deep trouble if he got attacked by them up a tree.

His welcome sleep was interrupted by the sudden outbreak of a stampede, followed by large thumps on the forest floor as people seemed to be running helter-skelter. He stayed put in his hideout. Soon, the absolute silence was restored to the virgin forest, except for the punctuated, distinct eerie hoots of an owl that wouldn't leave him in peace. He moved the strip of rag covering him and consulted his watch. It was 2.05 am. He waited. Time ticked on. He stared into the void of darkness.

About fifteen minutes later, he hung the cloth on a nearby branch and carefully climbed down the tree to investigate.

At the bottom, he cautiously crawled towards the direction where he thought the sound had originated. He stopped in his tracks when he saw what appeared to be a not-too-distant mound. He froze on the moist forest floor, struggling to breathe. He opened his mouth to make it easier. He was fairly certain he was walking into a trap, or an ambush, and wished he hadn't descended from his treetop refuge.
He wondered how he could defend himself if he were attacked by a nocturnal predator. Then he remembered he had a machete. He felt for it with his right hand. Like a true friend, it was still by his side. Still crouching, he approached the object cautiously, reached it, waited a couple of seconds, and then slowly reached out and touched it. It felt like a sack. He pressed it firmly and felt the dry beans of what appeared to be cocoa. He stayed put for a while. Then he silently untied one of the bags. He took out a bean, smelled it, and chewed on the familiar bitterness. He had tried if before and knew how it tasted. Even in the darkness, he realised it was a half full sack

of cocoa beans. He found three more sacks lying not too far off.

They were cocoa smugglers. Strangely enough, none of them had suffered any rain lashings, so the Ivorian border must be nearby.

He returned to his safe haven base at the foot of the tree and waited - in case the cocoa carriers or owners returned. His mind went to work.

At 2.40 am, there was still no sign of people returning. His spirit was restless, but his resolve as clear as water. He left his hiding place and again crawled cautiously towards the sacks. He reached them, paused and then slowly reached for the closest one.

One at a time, he dragged the three sacks to his hiding place, making sure he left no trail.

Once they were in place, he left his hiding place and went on the tiny pathway he had used the previous night - his prized asset still hanging by his right hip. He lost his sense of direction when he came to a small junction. He didn't recollect seeing it the previous night.

He chose to go right and continued on that path. After a long walk, he retraced his tracks as he had a strong hunch he was going the wrong way. Even in the still darkness, he was sure he had come across the dead but still standing wooden tree the previous evening during his flight back into the forest.

He had gone past his hiding spot. After what seemed like ages, he saw in the distance lights from what appeared to be a village. It brought him relief as it seemed days since he had seen any nightlight from villages or cars. He continued cautiously until he reached the outskirts.

He waited, wrestling with whether to wear his white T-shirt or not. He should have brought his cover cloth. He took his T-shirt out, put it on, and pressed on. A cock crowed nearby. He continued. It was 3:31 am.

He was almost at the edge of the village when he saw a man coming towards him. Osam began trembling uncontrollably as he approached the tall, muscular man, who could easily pass for a heavyweight boxer.

'Où est Kuku? Pour quoi tu n'es pas à l'heure?' (*Where is Kuku? Why aren't you on time?*) he shouted in anger as he came up to Osam.

'Monsieur, Kuku est malade,' (*Mr Kuku is unwell*) Osam responded with the little French he was surprised he still remembered from school. He had never liked his abrasive Togolese French tutor.

He had to try to act naturally or he was in trouble. He told the man, sometimes in bad French, that he was acting on behalf of Kuku. He told him the carriers of the cocoa sacks, who were doing the operation for the first time, were not prepared to come closer to the village. During the argument that had ensued, they dropped the bags and left.

Without saying a further word, the big man left, heading towards the village in disgust. Osam didn't know what to do. The decision was soon made for him as the man returned with three young men marching in line behind him. They must have been in their late teens.

'Allez!' (*Come on!*) he said angrily as he bit into a kola nut and began to chew.

Osam led them in prolonged silence towards his hiding place. His heartbeat raced as they approached the spot. He still had his machete hanging from his hip, with which he hoped he could defend himself if need be.

The young men loaded the sacks onto their heads as Monsieur took out some folded notes from his pocket and handed it to Osam. Without saying a word, he turned and followed his men into the night. Surprisingly, they went towards the village. Perhaps the border police were in on the smuggling.

Osam couldn't believe his luck as he stood clutching the money in his right hand. He felt that the same gods he had blamed for all his troubles were on his side after all.

Did he hear something? Yes, whispering not too far away. Thinking it might be the smugglers returning to claim their treasure, he crouched quickly, and slowly crawled to his hiding spot opposite the direction from where the sound was emanating. He watched two men who looked like hunters walk towards the village. They were speaking French and holding their guns on their right shoulders.

When they were gone, he quickly took off his white shirt, folded it as neatly as he could, and again shoved it into the front of his trousers. He put on the farmer's shirt. Like a snake, he quietly made his way, with his fruits, out of his spot until he came to a small clearing. He could faintly see the lights from the village. He was a little hazy about what to do next.

He opted to enter the sleepy village through another route so as not to encounter Monsieur. He got to a small hut which appeared to be someone's room. He could clearly hear voices in French emanating from it. He took out his white T-shirt, put it on again, and entered the village. He began whistling softly to himself, pretending to be a resident returning home. His legs were in a high state of sprint-readiness in case of emergency. He realised he was still on the outskirts, and, therefore, went towards the centre. He passed what appeared to be the village's public place of convenience. He was looking for an opportunity to check the cash stashed in his right pocket. He came to a quiet area, under an old street lamp, where he took out his money and counted his prize. They were brand new 10,000 franc notes and came to CFA90,000 in total.

He hadn't handled CFA Francs since he studied in Nigeria. He and his friends had usually travelled by car to school in Nigeria and, therefore, needed some cash in francs both to shop and also bribe their way through the borders of the Francophone countries of Togo and Benin. Even though a Ghanaian required no visas to travel through those countries, bribing at the borders was endemic. You always had the hard choice of paying your way through, getting delayed, or being disallowed entry.

Osam found a couple of armed police officers patrolling in the distance. One of them held a small transistor radio to his left ear. He had to be careful since his passport was not stamped on entry, which meant he could be arrested if they found him. He thanked his stars for the fact that he had brought and found his passport. He knew border police patrols were normal in these areas due to incessant cocoa smuggling from the Ghana side to the neighbouring Ivory Coast side. Uncle told him that the farmers received better value for a bag of cocoa there than they received from the state, so some of them sold part of their produce across the border.

The narrow and dark alleys made him fear for his safety and that of his newly-made fortune. He decided to go to the public toilet to hide there until daybreak.

Chapter 36

A cock crow woke Osam. He couldn't recollect the last time he had heard one. He wondered what the day ahead had in store for him. He checked the time; it was 5:15 am. He wanted to leave the village as early as he could to avoid any obvious problem resulting from the cocoa sale. He might already be a wanted man. He left the public place of convenience where he had been hiding. It had two doors at both ends of the rectangular building. He had stood in one of the many toilet chambers, and only squatted down, as if he was defecating, whenever he heard someone enter. The toilet's single dim light bulb was still on. He looked for a place to wash his face and foul-smelling armpits, feeling sick from staying so long there.

Then a short, stout man walked to all the occupied chambers and asked them to vacate immediately. He spoke with so much authority that Osam followed the other scurrying men. He was the toilet cleaner.

He decided to take a walk around the small village to acclimatise to his new environment. He wasn't going to hide away.

It was about 30,000 sq metres with the thatched houses haphazardly built. The buildings looked old and unplanned except for the lorry station, which was concrete. The surrounding forest gave the village an eerie calmness in the early morning light. It was obvious from the various lined stalls that it was a vibrant, border market village.

In the compound of a nearby house, he heard a billy goat bleating as it chased other goats. Ahead he saw a dominant cock chasing away an intruding cockerel. A sudden splash of

285

water from one of the neighbouring houses abruptly stopped the dominant cock in its tracks. The sights and sounds of a waking West African village were different to the vigorous and vivacious dawn of the European one he was used to. It did bring back vivid memories of his time in Cape Coast.

Osam arrived at the lorry station that was already beginning to fill up with queuing travellers. The prevailing mixed sounds indicated that French and English were the lingua franca even in this part of the world. There was also a taxi rank on the right-hand side. Osam wondered where those dirty taxis headed to. There was a sign indicating the growing queue was for Kumasi. It was a welcome relief. He could finally head back to Accra. Uncle Kojo would understand if he explained what had happened. Moreover, he could ring Arya when he reached Kumasi to tell her to transfer some money to him, and also cancel the missing credit cards.

'A quelle heure part le camion pour Kumasi? (*What time does the lorry leave for Kumasi?*) he asked a young lady standing at the end of the queue.

'A six heures trente,' (*At 6.30pm.*) she replied, staring at Osam from head to toe.

'Et quel est le prix?' (*And what's the fare?*)

'Vingt mille francs.' (*Twenty thousand francs.*)

'Y-a-t-il un téléphone au village?' (*And is there a telephone in this village?*) he continued.

'Non!' (*No!*) she replied in the typical impolite Francophone tone.

'Merci, mademoiselle. Une minute,' (*Thanks, lady. Back in a minute.*) he said, signalling with his hand to the lady to reserve his position in the queue while he was away. He was feeling hungry already so joined another queue to buy some cooked rice. It didn't look hygienic, but it smelt good. It seemed a popular spot, as in no time the queue grew longer and longer.

'Si?' (*Yes?*) came the question when it got to Osam's turn.

'Mille, s'il vous plait.' (*A thousand, please.*)

'Mille de quoi?' (*Thousand of what?*) she replied impatiently.

'Du riz, s'il vous plait, et deux æufs à la coque.' (*Of rice, please, and two boiled eggs.*)

'Deux milles céfa,' (*Two thousand céfa.*) she said when she had finished with Osam's request.

He already had a ten thousand franc note ready in his hand which he handed over and took the plate of rice.

'Fausse monnaie!' (*Counterfeit money!*), came the angry reply as she studied in detail the note in her hand. She threw it back at Osam and took back the plate of rice - whispering what appeared to be an insult.

It all happened too quickly for him to react. He left the queue in total embarrassment and retired to a quiet spot away from everyone. It dawned on him that he wasn't out of the woods yet. If all the notes were counterfeits, then he couldn't travel to Kumasi as planned and was thus in trouble. He took out another note at random, and away from prying eyes went to another lady selling fried doughnuts. He had the same response. They all seemed to be experts in detecting fake currency. He took out the remaining notes and handed them to the lady for her expert examination, and the prognosis wasn't good for Osam. He knew then that he couldn't travel to Kumasi.

'Son of a bitch!' he screamed, oblivious of the watching doughnut seller. 'What am I going to do now?' he said, almost in tears.

He had an idea. He found a young girl selling peanuts in a corner away from the doughnut lady. He walked up to her and bought some. He handed her one of the notes, this time, a slightly crumpled one. But, to his disappointment, she claimed she didn't have change. Her suspicious look clearly indicated it was more than that. He moved on in disgust until he found another young girl selling boiled corn. She didn't have change either.

He was hungry and running out of time and ideas.

Then he realised he couldn't have travelled even if he had money. He also had to contend with the fact that his passport was not stamped on entry into the Ivory Coast. There was no way he could cross the border unless, perhaps, he paid his way.

As the day wore on, he saw numerous French police officers parading the small market village. They were renowned for their regular demand to see passports or travel documents. He would be detained if he was stopped. He decided to look for a Ghanaian village where he could try to change the money. Who knew, the gods might smile on him.

He retraced the way he had come in during the night. He was almost on the path that led out of the village when he heard wrangling voices.

He instinctively halted when he heard cocoa mentioned. He peeped through the shrubs providing him cover to see Monsieur and a middle-aged man involved in a heated argument. As it raged on, Osam deduced that Monsieur was insisting he had paid the money to Kuku's *assistant*.

'Que fais-tu là-bas?' (*What are you doing over there?*) came a deep voice from behind him.

He froze in terror.

'Je suis en train de faire pipi,' (*I'm having a pee.*) he replied, almost choking on his words as he turned to find a gun-wielding Ivorian police officer metres away.

'Merde! Dégagez d'ici! (*Shit! Bugger off!*) the officer angrily pointed towards the village.

'D'accord, d'accord! Merci!' (*All right, all right! Thanks!*) Osam responded as he did up his fly and proceeded down the path.

He turned right at the next junction, and vanished around the corner away from the village and walked casually towards the Ghanaian side of the border. His back felt as heavy as lead as he continued, expecting someone to stop him from behind. He doubled his strides until he disappeared around a corner along the path. Osam looked back and then around him and started running like a rattled hare. He was trembling as he crossed the no man's land. He stopped under a big tree to take a breather.

Deep down in his heart Osam knew his only hope of getting back to Kumasi was for him to return to the village. He didn't even know its name.

It was past mid-day now. In the end, he finally decided to do so, and left his hiding place with trepidation and headed back. Before he left, he hid his prized machete behind a tree.

He went past a market lady who was clearly returning home early. Her big, aluminium selling tray looked empty.

'Maakye oo.' (*Good morning.*) she said in Twi as she passed.

'Maakye.' (*Good morning.*) Osam responded lukewarmly.

Moments later he saw something lying crumpled ahead on the path. Thinking it was a snake, he approached with care and dread, but it was a lady's cloth money belt usually worn by Ghanaian market women to stash their cash.

He picked it up, and to his surprise, it contained money – loads of mixed CFA and cedi notes and coins. He was convinced it belonged to the lady who had just passed.

His first instinct was to take the money and run. On second thought, however, he paused and thought about the poor woman going home without her hard earned cash.

Eventually, he decided to take the 20,000 francs he needed for his fare to Kumasi and return the rest to her. She seemed to have had a profitable day at her stall.

He added a couple of crumpled fake notes and scurried after her until after about five minutes, he saw her ahead. She was humming as she scurried along the path.

'Woayera wo sika anaa?' (*Have you lost your money?*) he shouted. Osam could read the horror on her fat face as she felt around her broad waist.

'Awurade eii! Me da wo ase owura. Onyame nhyira wo!!' (*Oh, my God! Thank you, gentleman. God bless you!!*) she said hysterically as he handed her the money belt. She instantly began scrutinising it.

He left her and scuttled back towards the village. It was almost 4 o'clock now and he was dying of hunger and thirst. Though he still felt guilty about his actions, he half-praised himself for returning the money, albeit 20,000 francs less. He always prided himself on his sincerity and good principles. No wonder his friends referred to him as a softie when he was a youngster because he always wanted to do the right thing, as was taught him at Sunday school. He heard shuffling in the thicket to his left but didn't even bother to look back. The next rumbling echoing sound of an elephant only served to accelerate his trot into a sprint. He had never run so fast since his escapade on the M4.

Panting heavily, Osam ran to the wooden ticket cubicle at the station.

All the tickets for the only trip of the week to Kumasi were sold out.

'Please, help me; I need to be in Kumasi tomorrow,' Osam pleaded, straining to hold his breath.

'I can't do anything for you, my friend; all the tickets have been sold.'

'But it's only 4:30 pm! And I've been here all day – you haven't seen me?'

He shook his head while looking the other way.

'Oh dear, what am I going to do now,' he said in desperation. His encounter with the elephants reminded him that perhaps his adventure in the forest had ended.

The place was almost deserted but for the ticket seller and the driver who was chatting to his young mate. Osam turned and walked dejectedly towards a nearby deserted shed. He stopped half-way and walked back to the ticket seller.

'Please, do something to help me. I really must be in Kumasi tomorrow to attend to an emergency.'

'Ghana man, if you no stop shouting at me, I go call police.' (*Ghanaian man, if you don't stop shouting at me, I'll call the police.*)

'No no no, I'm sorry, sir. I'm just desperate…'

'Look, I told you I can't help you. There's the driver; why don't you talk to him, foolish man?'

'Where you dey go, mai broder?' (*Where are you going, my brother?*) came the question from the driver's direction. The pigeon English had an unmistakably Asante accent.

'Kumasi, sir, I'm attending a funeral tomorrow,' Osam lied in a pleading voice to the approaching driver.

'Twenty tausind céfa!' (*Twenty thousand céfa!*) he said with his right hand outstretched. Osam couldn't believe his luck. He quickly tucked his right hand into his back pocket and handed the woman's folded note to the driver.

'Get in,' he half-shouted at Osam.

'Ibi full, boss,' (*It's full, boss.*) came the mate's voice.

'Find a place for him,' the driver shouted back as he walked towards the vehicle.

Osam jumped onto the *bone shaker*. It looked like those were the only type of vehicles that could conquer the terrain in this part of the world.

He knew he would either have to stoop or crouch throughout the whole trip until someone got off along the way. Not that he cared. They set off on time. He was almost dozing off.

It looked very much like the one he had taken for his fateful trip. The passenger wagon wasn't high enough for his almost six-foot frame. The driver's mate asked him to squeeze himself through the knees of the front passengers and sit on the wooden floor of the wagon, to the annoyance of some. Well, he had paid and had a right to the space just like them, he thought.

It wasn't long before he realised what a long trip it was going to be for him seated in that position. He was always being tossed to and fro and against the hard wooden floor as the lorry hit pothole upon pothole. He soon felt sick. He loosened his bum bag buckle a bit.

He usually crouched through the pothole periods and then sat back when the road felt less uneven, only to be knocked back down hard by another pothole. He felt embarrassed as some of the passengers began to giggle. Others looked at him in pity. *How dare they!* he thought.

Even in a state of helplessness, he never forgot his silly empty pride.

An hour or so into the journey, the lorry stopped at an old roadside restaurant for a short break. The smell of food that lingered in the still, warm, humid air sent Osam's salivary glands into action. He hadn't eaten properly for almost a day and felt weak.

'Please, would you mind buying me some doughnuts?' said one of the passengers as they alighted from the vehicle.

Who the hell did he think he was! Osam thought.

Then he realised that the man was holding two wooden crutches.

'Yeah, no problem. How many would you like?'

'Three, please. I can't walk properly, that's why I've asked you for the favour.' He handed Osam a new CFA10000 Franc note.

'Do they still take CFA here?' he asked, wondering if it was more counterfeit money. He had suddenly developed a fear of new CFA notes.

'Yes, we're still in CFA territory. The drivers normally use this longer route to avoid the main border town as some passengers don't have passports.'

What priceless information and a welcome relief for him. He had been worried sick. He felt like hugging and kissing the man but contained his elation.

As Osam walked off, he dwelt on the fact that he could have added a few counterfeits to the money he had given the driver if he had had time to think. It was too late now.

He needed to take his anti-malaria tablet, but not on an empty stomach. He tried using his money to buy some food, but it was to no avail. They identified fake money with so much ease it was beyond belief. So he devised a plan. He had to survive.

Still in the queue, he scrutinised both notes which looked identical to him. When it got to his turn, he bought the doughnuts for the man, whom he hadn't even bothered to ask for his name. He then bought himself some food and bottled water. Unfortunately, he overspent and was handed back only insignificant coins. He told the female rice seller to reduce the quantity of the rice he had bought from her earlier, but she refused. She claimed it was already soiled with oil from the stew spread on top of the rice. He reluctantly left the queue and put the coins in his back pocket. When he finished his meal, he waited with baited breath until there was a queue to enter the lorry.

With empty confidence, he handed the man his doughnuts and, making sure the man saw everything, took out a new 10000 note from his pocket, folded it and pushed it into the man's breast pocket.

'The doughnuts were cheap, so I took care of it.'

'That's very kind of you, sir. Thanks, for—'

'Hey, are you going to sit down or keep blocking our way?' came an unfriendly voice from a passenger behind Osam.

'I'm sorry,' he said as the man tucked into one of his doughnuts, not even bothering to check the note in his pocket.

Osam resumed his crouching position. He noticed that one of the middle-aged women sitting behind the man kept staring at him. Was it disgust at what he had done, or admiration? The lorry pulled out of the small roadside parking back onto the narrow, dusty and pothole-infested road.

Osam's eyes darted at the nearly dark carriage interior, settling unintentionally on the staring woman. She was still staring at him. Osam smiled apprehensively and slowly looked away to the outside.

He was woken by a loud noise.

In the darkness, waking passengers were inquiring what had happened. The light came on,- followed by a gradual deceleration. The vehicle had suffered a puncture. Incredibly, there was neither hysteria nor screaming. They remained strangely calm as it steadily came to a halt by a shed by the side of the road.

'Everybody out!' shouted the mate.

Osam hoped it wasn't a re-run.

All the passengers got out and scattered around the margins of the dusty road. Some of them even sat in the side bushes.

'Are we still in Ivory Coast?' Osam asked the mate as he helped him and the driver remove the warm and damaged left rear wheel.

'No, we're in Ghana now. This is *Nkwanta*.'

Osam was dumbstruck; he couldn't believe what he'd just heard. He came out of his stooping position and walked towards the shed which was already occupied by three of the passengers. Stuck in the ground was a small signpost with *Nkwanta* inscribed on it. Even in the darkness, he could faintly see that the plywood was held across in place by a large crooked nail, which made it almost impossible to read the inscription due to the fading white paint.

There was a tiny lane leading from the thicket. He saw the back of a thatched house a few metres away. He cautiously followed the lane until he came to the hut. A man came out as Osam approached the entrance. He was holding a sharp machete in his left hand and a small hoe in his right.

'Please, is this *Nkwanta*?' Osam asked, his hands clasped behind his back.

'Yes, it is. Can I help you?' the man asked.

'Do you know a man called Kojo Mensah?'

'Opanin Kojo Mensah. Yes, I know him. His village isn't far from here. I don't suppose you're his nephew from the land of the white man, are you?' he said, sizing him up.

'Yes, I am. My name is Osam, Osam Mensah, his nephew,' he responded with a broad grin.

'The whole family and the farm workers were here two nights ago waiting for your arrival.'

'Could you take me to his village please?' Osam asked enthusiastically.

'I wish I could, my son. Unfortunately, I'm going to check my traps which are in the opposite direction," he replied, studying Osam. 'Here, I'll show you where he lives – it's easy. Just follow this path until you come to another farmhouse. Your uncle's is the next after that. You ask anybody you see over there, and they'll take you to his village. You can't lose your way.'

'Thank you, sir,' Osam said as the man quickly walked where Osam had come from.

He was in two minds. The decision was made for him when he looked back and faintly caught a glimpse of the rear lights of the vehicle gradually disappearing around a curve into the still night. Strangely enough, he had heard no one calling out for him.

A quick glance at his watch indicated it was exactly 7:10 p.m. Osam hesitated, and then reluctantly followed the path into the eerie forest night.

Chapter 37

It was frighteningly quiet as if everything had come to a sudden halt. Even the leaves of the nearby shrubs showed no sign of noticeable movement. He was terrified.

He quickly wiped that from his mind and instead thought about his present condition, while hardening his heart to any future inevitability.

He continued down the steep, declining, shrubby path with the thick forest a couple of metres away. Thankfully, he at least didn't have to walk through the jungle.

He was dying for a pee but was scared to do so. He just wanted to find any sign of light ahead, but it wasn't forthcoming. He felt movements along his long legs, followed by sharp bites between his toes, then ankles.

'Bugger!' he hissed, as he realised he had stumbled through more fire ants.

He ran back and then stopped when it dawned on him that he was running in the wrong direction. He painfully began to rid himself of the ants. Some got onto his hands as he took off his sandals. He had to get back on track, he thought. Getting back to the man's house was out of the question. What if he wasn't a real person? Without thinking further, he hopped back into the ants' way. They had indeed occupied a large chunk of the tiny path.

The result wasn't as bad as he had feared.

As he rid himself of the remnants, he walked on. He was experiencing too many coincidences for his liking.

He kept looking anxiously at his watch. He had been walking for almost twenty minutes. He began to doubt if he was getting anywhere as the forest was getting thicker and thicker. He wanted to retrace his way back to the junction, but then he would have the ants to contend with again. And what if the ants now occupied a larger section of the path? He was convinced he would come to a farm settlement as this path had to lead somewhere.

And so it did.

After about three more minutes walking, he saw a faint light in the distance. Could it be Uncle Kojo's farmhouse? The path gradually turned right and into what, in the dark, appeared to be a cassava farm. Never had he felt so good and safe since his return home. It was a farmhouse!

Some dogs barked as he got closer to the burning lamp in the middle of the compound. He pressed on. He wasn't scared anymore. He was among people who knew Uncle Kojo.

There were two dogs; one seemed to be all-white while the other had irregular black and white patterns. Fortunately for him, they continued barking but timidly backed away from him as he cautiously approached the larger of the two huts. He thanked his stars. Rural dogs tended to be used for hunting, and would normally attack a stranger - particularly in the dark.

He didn't have to worry long as the door opened even before he reached it. A man came out of the hut holding a large, unlit torch. It wasn't Uncle Kojo, but Osam didn't care. He had met someone, at least.

'Good evening, sir,' the man said in Twi.

'My name is Osam Mensah, the nephew of Kojo Mensah. I have come from Accra to see him.'

'Kojo Mensah?' the man inquired incredulously against the persistent background barking.

Osam could see him clearly now as his eyes acclimatised to his new environment. He was middle-aged and of medium build. He was about 1.90 metres tall and wore only a tiny pair of shorts. Perhaps that's why, Osam thought, he came out confidently even without his flashlight switched on.

'Aaah, *Opanin* Kojo Mensah!' the man said. 'He lives on the other side of the road,' he continued. Osam wondered what that meant exactly.

'Wait while I put on a shirt to take you.' And with that, he disappeared into the hut.

Even though rural folks were renowned for their kindness and help, it still surprised Osam that the man never seemed bothered that his sleep had been interrupted by a complete stranger. He could hear unintelligible whispers within the dark hut, probably talking to his wife. What if...? His thoughts were interrupted when the man re-appeared wearing a white shirt and a bigger pair of shorts.

They took a different route and walked in complete silence.

Maybe the forest abhorred noise in the darkness of the night. For some strange reason, Osam found himself walking in front. His granddad used to do the same thing to him as a youngster. The man had his dry cell flashlight on so they could see some distance ahead of the path as they made their way through a large cassava farm, thicker forest, then across a dusty road onto another path. The man moved to the front to lead Osam. He began walking faster, and Osam struggled to keep up. He was adeptly manoeuvring the tiny, busy path. They continued on this small path in the thickening forest until Osam heard the familiar sound of fallen, dry cocoa leaves. He particularly enjoyed the comforting feel of the leaf-carpeted forest floor. His grandfather used to take him to his large cocoa farm whenever he was in Cape Coast. He could even make out some of the cocoa pods on the trees as they walked through the plantation. He wondered how long some of those trees had been standing.

Uncle Kojo's status became apparent when they arrived at his farmhouse, for not only did they trek through a larger farm for a very long time, his settlement was still bigger.

It had a larger compound, and the houses were joined in an L-shape. Osam could see about eight doors. There were three large burning kerosene lamps; one in the middle of the compound, and the other two at the opposite ends. All three lamps were attached to a wooden post. They entered the compound through one of the corners, so he presumed the other would be another route in or out of the farmhouse.

'Agooooooo!' said the man, whose identity he hadn't even thought to ask, as they entered the compound to loud barking from a chained dog near one of the doors. It must be a wild dog for it to remain in chains, even at night, Osam thought. His heart was now pounding with glee. He knew he had finally arrived at his destination.
'Ameeeeeee!' came a reply.
'It's Opanin Kwame,' the man said. 'You have a visitor from Accra,' he continued, this time in English, as they waited in the centre of the compound.
There were movements in the various rooms, and then, as if by calculation, the inhabitants came out one at a time, Uncle Kojo first. Osam breathed a huge sigh of relief. Other worries suddenly paled into insignificance.
The journey from Accra was supposed to have taken about 11 hours, but almost three gruelling days later here he finally was – home at last!

There was a rush from everyone to embrace Osam as the sound of *Akwaaba* filled the humid night air. Osam wondered what they would think of him in his present state. He suppressed the urge to tell them his story there and then.

'Kuku, put your elder brother's bags in his room!' Uncle Kojo commanded as Osam shook hands with his hosts.

'I don't have luggage; I lost it on my way here,' Osam replied, still contemplating the just mentioned name, *Kuku*. He hoped his cousin was not at the centre of the cocoa fiasco.

'Oh no! Where did this happen, my son?'

'Don't worry, Uncle Kojo. I'm glad to be home.'

Uncle was the last--being the family head--to welcome him, and with a big hug, too. Someone brought out some chairs for them. The older people, of whom there were about ten, including Osam and Opanin Kwame, sat down. The younger generation stood and watched in awe. He was sure they were wondering who the hell he thought he was, interrupting their nice sleep and seemingly getting away with it.

As was the custom, water was passed around, even at that time of night.

'Kuku, get your elder brother some bottled water from his room,' Uncle Kojo ordered. Even though he knew it was well-water, he turned down the bottled water and drank the same as everyone else. He had been cautioned by his GP to drink only bottled water as he had been away from Ghana too long, but tradition was tradition.

As custom demanded, both parties had to tell the other their mission.

Opanin Kwame was the first, being the host.

'Well, we had a good day, thanks to the gods. I couldn't sleep properly because my nephew hadn't arrived as he promised. Then I heard the dogs barking, followed by the knock,' Uncle Kojo finished off his introductory speech.

To Osam's surprise, Uncle Kwame began with customary efficiency, way back from what had happened in the evening before he went to bed right to the sound of the dogs during Osam's arrival at Uncle Kojo's farmhouse. Normally, one had to be brief in such circumstances, but Opanin Kwame went on and on and on. Perhaps, Osam thought, he was basking in the glory of being the one who found the *lost one.*

Uncle Kojo was rather brief. He just said who Osam was, where he had come from in Europe, and that he had been expecting him, but gave up when he didn't arrive. He finished by thanking Opanin Kwame for what he had done. He promised him they would pay him a visit the following day to formally introduce Osam to him and his family, as custom demanded.

When Opanin Kwame left, Uncle Kojo poured libation to the ancestors for granting Osam a safe journey from Accra to Nkwanta.

Osam needed a bath, badly, and told his uncle. He had one before retiring to bed; a large bucketful of warm water in the toilet annexe.

Chapter 38

Osam was woken by the sound of a moving car. He had had the best rest in three days. He remained on the soft mattress. The bed was situated on the right-hand side of the square room. It was the first thing visible when the door was opened. The door was shut, but there was still enough light to see the room.

He had two soft pillows even though he was alone in bed. Uncle Kojo told him last night that the room had been specially prepared three days earlier for his coming, and they had decided to leave the room vacant for another week in case he turned up.

Apart from the wooden bed, the white sheets all looked new. The walls were painted with white emulsion paint. White was a sign of purity in the Ghanaian tradition, so he wondered what his Uncle had in mind during the refurbishment. On the wall opposite the double bed hung a large picture of Jesus.

Osam could hear voices from without. Despite the standing fan blowing only a few metres away, he could still feel the sun's heat. A look at his watch indicated it was eleven o'clock. He rolled to the edge of the bed and sat upright. He was only wearing his underwear. He hadn't gone to bed in pyjamas since he arrived in Accra.

He went through his usual routine of stretching and pushing his chest forward and outward until he heard a 'crack'. He had learned that from his uncle. In Reading, he only did that when Arya wasn't around.

He slid back into his clothes, neatly folded by the side of the bed. He opened the door and stepped into the large, open, sun-drenched compound. It was empty, so he had the chance to properly take the place in. He could clearly see now how dirty his clothes were.

The L-shaped building was concrete. There was a tiny pathway between where the buildings converged. It was as if the builders realised too late that they had to leave some space to allow passage from that end. Just like his room, the exterior was painted white, and covered with shiny aluminium roofing. About ten metres of the land around the compound and the main building was well-weeded.

The place looked deserted except for the chained black dog which began barking when it saw him. As Osam studied the tall, besieging, dense trees--all seeming to be quietly fighting for supremacy--he heard the slamming of a car door from around the direction of the little entrance. He went towards the tiny pathway between the two buildings to investigate.

Uncle Kojo emerged from his BMW parked in what looked more like a shed than a garage. Even from a distance, the battering from the rough and uneven road was clear for all to see. Perhaps it was the wrong type of present after all, he thought. The shed, which was situated at the edge of the weeded area, gave protection from the rain, though, as it was completely roofed with aluminium sheets. Not far from the garage was another small shed which housed a rusty electricity generator. It was the powerhouse of the farmhouse. Uncle Kojo's old Peugeot was parked a few metres away from this small shed. Sadly, it had been relegated and left to the mercies of the natural elements. There was a dusty road leading from the garage into the forest. Osam presumed it was the link to the *main* road.

'Hello, my son. Did you sleep well?' Uncle Kojo said with a broad smile.

'Yes, I did. Thanks. How are you?'

'I'm fine, my son. Oh dear, you look rough. Are you OK, Osam?' he asked, his eyes popping as he saw him for the first time in broad daylight.

'I'll explain later, Uncle Kojo.'

'You must be starving. Let me first show you the place of convenience. We don't have your type of modern lavatory system here yet, so please pardon me for that.'

'Don't worry, Uncle,' he replied.

It was situated in a thicket fifty metres away on the other side of the compound away from the main buildings. It was the concrete part of the forest peripheral. Even though the smell wasn't apparent from the compound, it stank like hell when he approached. There were two entrances. He presumed the other must be for the ladies, even though there was no sign.

The room was tiny - just big enough to fit an average person. It was well protected from rain or the sunshine, with a normal toilet seat on a smooth, cemented, elevated section. One sat on it as with normal WC toilets, except you had to wait to hear the sound of your defecation as it dropped for a couple of seconds after its release. Osam wasn't alone for long, as he soon heard someone using the adjacent toilet. Only a wall separated the two. He felt a bit awkward.

'Don't worry, Osam, it's me. Passengers not travelling to Sefwi, the final destination, but to the surrounding villages, usually prefer to get off and wait in Meko when it's as late as when you arrived. I should have told you that. I'm sure some of the passengers thought you were brave to alight there all alone. In fact, Kuku and I waited till 10 p.m. I had planned to go to Meko this morning to ring you to determine why you failed to turn up. I hear the road has been completely surfaced now.'

The mention of *Meko* brought back memories of Linda. His leaving was unceremonious, and he would love to go back to see her. More so, as he owed her friend some money.

'I wish I had known that, Uncle Kojo. My journey began three days ago.'

'Really, sometimes it does take that long from Accra, you know?'

'Well, I got into a bit of a problem…'

'What problem? Did you have an accident or something?'

'Well, it's a long story, Uncle. I'll tell you when we finish.'

'Is that why you lost your bag? When I saw you in those clothes, I knew there was something untoward. I hope you're all right, son?'

'Don't get alarmed. I'm fine.'

That seemed to calm Uncle Kojo. There was an unusually long pause.

'Have you visited Cape Coast yet to see your grandparents?'

'Not yet. I'll definitely do that before I return to England,' Osam replied.

'The last time I saw them, they told me they had been planning a visit here before they joined our ancestors.'

'Ah, right.'

Uncle Kojo was in the mood to chat. Osam wasn't. He couldn't stand the stench from both fresh and decaying human faeces. More so, he would have preferred to defecate in complete privacy.

Uncle Kojo sat in silence as Osam narrated his experiences. For once, he never interrupted.

'I thought you said it wasn't serious. This is a serious matter, Kweku Mensah.'

'I've had some close shaves this past couple of days, Uncle. But, I'm here now, and that's what matters.'

306

'But…I thought I told you about the local festival celebration this week.'

'Did you?'

'I think I did, Osam. I also said that it's a normal practice, as part of the celebration, for the young men of the village to go to the forest. My secret plan was for you to join them when you arrived.'

'So you mean no one of importance has died?'

'Of course not! Only animals are killed. No human gets killed for that, my son. Where did you get those twisted ideas from? It's a ritual to thank our ancestors and gods for the year's bumper harvest. The ritual killings stopped ages ago.'

'When I was in my youth, some people went to prison for doing that, didn't they?'

'Osam…Osam…Osam. Listen, that only happened because those evil people decided to do that, and they faced the long arm of the law, my son.'

Osam could not believe what he was hearing. It appeared all the troubles he'd been through the last few days and nights had all been of his own making.

'I can't believe you still came despite all the troubles you've been through.'

'Well, I gave you my word, didn't I?'

'I feel responsible and guilty.'

'No, it isn't your fault. It's just that everything seemed so real at that time of the night.'

'So your passport and return ticket are OK?'

'Yes, they are. I badly need some new clothes, though.'

'We'll go to Meko. As for the money, you don't have to worry.'

Osam didn't tell him about Linda and his trip to Meko. 'Yes, I will need a big loan as all my money's been stolen. I promise to send you my payment as soon as I return to the UK.'

'Don't worry, my son.'

'Ah, I also need to ring to cancel the bank cards when we get to…'

'…Meko.'

'Yes. Meko.'

He removed the folded stash of notes from his pocket and dropped it down the toilet hole.

Two days later, the baby was still unborn. It was mid-afternoon of the second day and he was due to leave early the following morning. He had had a wonderful time. He had been enjoying the star treatment he received from the village folks whenever his proud uncle paraded him before them. Even the chief of the village had requested to meet him. He hadn't felt that pampered and flattered in all his life.

His only complaint was the fact that they kept giving him too much food, and when he told them he was full, they didn't understand. They seemed offended that Osam didn't like the food – which wasn't the case.

Whenever one passed a settlement, tradition demanded that the person stopped and partook of whatever they were eating. These people were surrounded by food, and lots of it, so when they cooked, they always had a surplus for any passers-by. In the end, by the time Osam returned to Uncle Kojo's village, he was too full to eat the special food that had been prepared for him. Seafood was a delicacy in that part of the land. Uncle Kojo had spent a fortune to get the best for his home-coming nephew.

Almost all his fears turned out to be unfounded. Apart from a few monkeys and snakes, he hadn't encountered any of the big cats or elephants that were supposed to be there in abundance in this part of the jungle. He had so many imaginary and augmented fears that he actually began living it even before he travelled, and later during the trip. He thought his unfounded fear had preoccupied him to the extent of provoking his nightmarish experiences. He recalled once lambasting Arya for saying that she was scared to travel to Africa. Now here he was, an African, behaving as if he was in an alien environment.

It was still scary, particularly at night. He could clearly hear nocturnal animals in the forest - several metres away from the farmhouse. One particular animal would wail almost all night although Uncle Kojo reassured him it was harmless.
His time there had thus been a period of education: reprogramming and reconditioning - a necessity to combat his acquired chronic fear.

Uncle Kojo had bottled water ready for Osam when he arrived. However, his stomach upset persisted. Although he liked them, he hadn't grown used to the hot, spicy, Ghanaian meals. He missed his good old fish and chips.

That afternoon, Uncle Kojo showed him all his lands. They were very large farms indeed. Unfortunately, they weren't registered as yet at the Land Registry, since they had been bought directly from the village chief, who then instructed boundaries be created to divide one farm from the other. In all, he calculated there were about fifteen hectares of land. They were mostly cocoa plantations and a few cash crops like cassava, plantain, yam and maize, for their daily consumption. He had five workers employed to work alongside Osam's three cousins. They all lived in the farmhouse.
Uncle Kojo had a boy from each of his last three marriages.
Kuku, Kwabena and Kwesi were 25, 22 and 17 years old, respectively. They had never liked school, so had worked all their lives on the farm. Uncle Kojo said he had plans to buy plots of land for Kuku and Kwabena when they started *behaving* like adults.

Osam learned later that both of them were known womanisers in the area. Like father, like son.

Later that afternoon, Osam and Uncle Kojo went for a quiet walk in the forest.
It reminded him of his romantic walk with Arna at her parents' country house.
This setting, however, was different; everything was bigger, denser, darker, fresher, and frighteningly mysterious.
While his uncle seemed to be at ease and in tune with his domain, Osam was completely out of step and ill at ease.
They belonged to different worlds.

Not too long into the relaxing walk, they came to a small shed with a bench big enough to accommodate three people.
'Let's sit, my son. I'm an old man now you know,' Uncle Kojo said.
'You? Old man?' Osam laughed.
'Thank you, my son, for honouring your old man with this *aeroplane*.'
'It's a car, Uncle Kojo.'
'Yes. But everyone is talking about it. You have to teach me before you leave as I still don't understand some of the complex things the book says. You know I only have a middle school education. Anyway, Kweku, all the lands that I have shown you belong to you.'
'Sorry? What are you talking about, Uncle Kojo?'
'You heard me. That's why I wanted you to come and see for yourself what you've got waiting for you,' he continued.
'And my cousins?' he asked in disbelief.
'Your dad bought these lands when they became available many years ago. They weren't worth much then because people weren't interested in coming to live here. The government later stepped in to stop any further sales to protect the remainder of the forest. Kwabena Otobaw Mensah didn't

310

have enough money, but he was wise enough to invest it here. He knew that his little brother loved farming so he bought them so I could farm on them as long as I wanted. Through that, I have been able to acquire lands of my own, though not as large as these, in a village about 10km away. I´m sure you now understand why I always moved heaven and Earth to help you whenever you needed it.'

'And you declined to accept the loan payment,' Osam murmured.

'Exactly. But we also had an unwritten agreement; that I will hand them over to his children before my death. I'm sixty-one years old now, and in life, you never know what might happen tomorrow or even the next minute. The problem is that none of the lands you see here is registered at the Land Registry Office. But thank God, he has blessed the family with an intelligent and knowledgeable person - which is you, their one and only child. I advise you to do the registrations of the lands before you go back to England.'

'But—'

'Let me finish, Osam. These days, people like you are buying lands and growing oranges, pineapples and other fruits, and selling them abroad. You will be amazed to find young people riding in big cars. They don't even have a third of the land you've got and yet they are doing so well. Why do you think I insisted on you coming all the way here to visit me? So you can see how we survive in the bush? I could have told you that, and I'm sure I've told you that many times before, with a little bit of exaggeration, as you well know by now. I wanted you to see for yourself and hopefully, appreciate what you've got. I've always wondered, why doesn't my son leave the land of the white man and return home to work on what is rightfully his? You're a king, Osam. You're a very rich man. You can sell them and I promise you, you'll make a lot of money, but I'm sure someone as intelligent as you will think twice before doing so. But then, as I said, it's yours. So you

311

can do whatever you want. I can only advise. As for my children, I have enough money saved for them. Kuku and Kwabena said they wanted their own bona fide lands, so I'm in the process of buying them theirs. Afterwards, they are adults and can choose to do what they want with it. They know that all the land belongs to you, even though I haven't told them the secret yet. I just felt it was best that you knew first, before anybody else. I want you to think hard about it before making any decision as to what you want to do with them. If you can give me an answer before you leave tomorrow, I can start the process of registering the land.'

Osam sat in silence as his uncle related what seemed a well-rehearsed narration. He was tearful as his dad's name came up. He couldn't remember the last time someone mentioned it. He had very little recollection of his father, whose life as a primary school principal meant that he saw very little of him as a boy. All he had of him was a black and white photo of both parents, which he'd always kept in his wallet since moving to England. His late aunt had given it to him before he left for secondary school in Cape Coast. She said it was the only photo she had of them. And they had always been faithful companions since. His new life without them wouldn't be the same, he knew. Leaving the forest without them in his wallet was akin to deserting them in an alien land. That hurt him indeed.

'Let's walk on, my son,' Uncle Kojo said, his thin right arm on Osam's broad shoulders.

They walked in silence for a while, as if both were wishing the other would say something to break it.

'This then brings me to the second and, I think, most important reason why I've been urging you for the past two months to return home. I know you've always been asking what was wrong with me. But I never told you the truth because I've always known deep down in my heart and soul that I'll see you before…'

'Before what, Uncle?' He sensed he wouldn't like what was coming.

'I'm dying, Kweku. The doctors say I don't have much time to live.'

'What?' Osam said as if hit in the face. 'Pardon me, but you shouldn't be using such language.' He chose his words carefully so as not to offend his revered Uncle.

'I know this will come as a big surprise to you. That's why I wanted to tell you in person and in private.'

'But—'

'Let me finish. For almost a year now, I haven't felt well. The doctors just couldn't identify what was wrong. In the end, they did, three months ago, when I went to Korle-Bu Teaching Hospital, in Accra, for a test. Unfortunately, it came too late as I was diagnosed with cancer of the colon. I wish you had been there with me because I didn't understand all the difficult medical terms they used. The doctor told me I'd feel better if they operated on me. To cut a long story short, my son... they told me a few days after the operation that the vital organs in my body were infected, so I had little time to live.'

'Oh God, not again! Not again, please!!' He remembered what had happened to Sven, Arya's dad. He was reliving that experience all over again. He hadn't even told Uncle Kojo about that sudden death. 'You can't have cancer! I thought it was a white man's disease,' he said, as tears dripped down his cheeks. They stopped by a young mahogany tree. 'Have you told the family?'

'No, no, no. I'm the head of the family. When the head dies or is perceived to be dying, the rest of the family dies. It's been a tough few months for me, but I have always had to be strong. Strong men die singing, not crying, my son. That's why the family needs you now. You are my nephew, and custom

313

demands that you succeed me when I'm gone. There isn't anyone adequate enough left to do so in the family apart from you.'

'But I hardly know the family, Uncle. My life has changed. It isn't here anymore. My life is in England. I've worked so hard to reach where I am now. I just can't let go of everything.'

Uncle Kojo was shaking his head as Osam was speaking. 'Oh my son, you can't turn away from your responsibilities to the remainder of the Mensah family. A timid person is not only a weak person but a danger to himself and his setting. Your cousins and the rest of the family look up to you and adore you. You can't let them down, my son. It doesn't mean you have to live here – far from that. But tradition is tradition. White people have theirs, and we have ours. The gods and ancestors won't take it lightly if you shun it, Kweku Mensah. They won't,' he ended sternly.

Osam sat still for a while, chewing over the impact of those words. 'Have you sought a second opinion?'

'Yes, I had it confirmed at a private clinic in Cantonment when I was in Accra last month. Don't forget we have first class doctors here too, you know.'

Osam held his head in both hands, staring at the leafy earth in front of him.

'Anyway, how's your wife?'

'We're not actually married – we only live together.'

'Isn't it taboo over there too?' Kojo asked incredulously.

'No, it's absolutely normal, actually. But Uncle, people did the same in Accra when I used to live in Ghana.'

'Yes, but those people are living in sin!'

'In fact, I think there're more people living together like us than married people in the UK. They're more relaxed about this kind of thing.'

'Do you plan to marry her? Is she a good woman? Are the women like ours?'

'Women are women, Uncle, wherever they are. Of course, there are physical and cultural differences, but in the end, just like all men, they're the same.'

'Ultimately, you'll have to come home to marry properly, as tradition demands, Osam. You're the head of the family now.'

Osam greeted that with a broad smile. It was the third time his Uncle had touched on that topic, and he wouldn't dare say anything to the contrary.

They walked on in silent contemplation until they came to a river. As usual, Uncle Kojo had something to say about it. Osam was particularly interested as he was convinced it was the river into which he had fallen. The higher water level hadn't receded yet. He felt an eerie sensation in the still, heavy, evening air. He glanced around the immense but confining forest. They were alone.

A crow flew away from the river bank onto a barren tree branch nearby.

'Let's go back, Osam. It's getting dark.'

He readily concurred.

As they walked towards the village, Osam wondered if this would be his last encounter with his dear Uncle. He had a lot of thinking to do – and within a limited time too.

Chapter 39
(*Back in Accra*)

'So, how was your trip to the forest?' Richard asked as they left the station in his car, looking quizzically at Osam's small head scar.

'Long story! It was…intriguing stuff, but sad towards the end.'

'Yeah?'

'Oh, I was swamped with love.'

'Did the poor village girls survive your powerful advances?'

Osam chuckled. 'Well, at least, it only took me twelve hours or so to return, instead of the three days it took me to get there.'

He narrated his eventful trip to Richard as they drove through the traffic-jammed streets of Accra, and his decision.

'I can't believe you believe that stuff, Osam. I don't think a white person would ever go to that extent.' There was a hint of anger in his voice.

'Hey, you didn't go with me cuz you were scared too, your mum's illness was just an excuse, Richard.'

'Well, who wouldn't be scared to go to such a place, the way your uncle had described it?'

'Come to think of it, everybody ran for safety during the night of the stampede. Even the driver drove off without checking to see if all the passengers were accounted for.'

'As far as I can recall, that practice stopped many years ago.'

'Yeah, Uncle Kojo cleared that up, but that assertion would have vanished into thin air if you were in my shoes in that circumstance, Richard. Anyway, I need a really good bath, a pedicure, and a manicure. Ah, and I need to ring Arya about cancelling the stolen cards and all. But first, I need to buy a cheap mobile phone.'

They drove in silence

Osam had finally made his decision.
He would ring his uncle the following day, as promised, and tell him to go ahead with the land registration. In Ghana, money talks, he had said; one could pay for things to be done quickly. He had promised Osam to get it done before he returned to England if he gave the go-ahead.
He also told Richard about his difficult decision to return home and not only convert some of the lands into commercial farms but to also assume the arduous responsibility as head of the Mensah family. He knew his uncle would be over the moon.
'You have changed a lot, Osam.'
'Why do you say that?'
'I don't know…but ever since your problems with Amelia you have become a different person. You are calmer, less boastful…'
'Everything was topsy-turvy in my life then. All those problems made me realise how much I needed people in my life, instead of driving them away as I have always done.'
'But are you sure you're prepared for that kind of job? I mean, you didn't really have a great time visiting there, did you?'
'I can't let the family down. They really need me now. What happens when my uncle dies? The little family left will be fractured into insignificance. That's all I've got, Richard…well, I've got a friend like you who has always stood by me, but if you know what I mean…'
'I do, Osam. Don't forget we've been friends for a long, long time. And I think you'll not only make a good family head, but we'll make a good and successful team as well. This is our country, man. You're a qualified Chartered Management

Accountant, I've got my MBA. How do we expect things to get better if all we do is criticise how bad and corrupt our country is, and yet continue living in somebody else's, and contribute to their growth and development? Things are not easy in Ghana, we all know that. But we are young, and others are making it big time, man. If we don't strike while the iron is hot, as the saying goes, by the time we decide to return home there will be complete saturation.'

'People keep saying they'll come back home to settle, but only a few people actually do.'

'I always say this: the more people wait, the more they get stuck there. It's almost impossible to get the so-called *requisite* money. It always goes back into the system.'

'They're not fools, are they?'

'As for you, you'd better start letting go of those *Obroni* tendencies, otherwise you won't survive even in your own country.'

Osam needed no preaching now as he knew the wisdom of what Richard said. In Europe, he always had to struggle or fight for respect. In Ghana, it came naturally. People respected you for your hard work and sweat. He would also be among his own kind, and thus wouldn't have to constantly fight racism anymore.

That evening Osam and Richard met Abrantie John at Afrikiko, a popular bar in Accra. As usual, he arrived late but was accompanied by three pretty girls as promised.

Osam couldn't believe his eyes as they fell on the prettiest of the girls. She had soft brown skin and almond eyes. His heart skipped a beat, and then suddenly increased in tempo.

It was the same girl he had travelled with when he went to visit his uncle. She was even wearing the same red, tight and provocative dress. What a small world, he thought as the four approached their table. Their eyes met, and they smiled.

Mercy, the thinnest, was introduced as John's *girlfriend*. While the medium build, average height girl, was Eve.

Though John was married, it wasn't uncommon for Ghanaian men to cheat on their wives - particularly if they were rich. Uncle Kojo always had a saying, *when you have a farm, you need a garden as well*; the farm being the wife and the garden, the mistress. He claimed that the garden would always provide the basic cooking needs like vegetables.

The three girls were friends and fellow students at the University of Ghana.

John's hard job of matchmaking was made easier when he realised that Osam and Linda appeared to know each other and were already chatting away. Richard thus had to settle for Eve whether he liked it or not, as it became apparent there was no way Osam would let go of his prized, well-endowed asset.

Osam said, 'So, when did you return?'

'Return? From where?'

'From your village, I mean…whatchamacallit…'

'Meko.'

'Meko! Yes, when did you return?'

'I've always been here. I haven't been to Meko lately. And how did you know I was from there anyway?'

'I thought from your smile that you recognised me when you saw me.'

'Oh, I didn't know we'd met.' She laughed derisively. 'You'll have to remind me.'

'Ghanaian girls! Always playing hard to get,' Osam said with a wry smile.

'Believe me, I don't remember meeting you,' she said with a beautiful smile.

'So you mean you don't remember the forest in Sefwi?'

'Forest in Sefwi...forest in Sefwi...you haven't met my twin sister, have you?'

'Twin sister? Yeah sure, don't give me that crap!'

'Yeah, I've got an identical twin. You can ask my friends.'

Osam turned to Eve and Mercy, who nodded.

'But how can both of you have the same name? This is weird.'

'We don't have the same name.'

'But...you were introduced as Linda.'

'Minda, not Linda. Linda's my twin sister. So, you've met her then? She visited our parents last week. She was going to go for two days but decided to stay for a couple more. She's coming back to Accra next week. And what was a *Bogga* like you doing over there?'

'We travelled in the same vehicle. I visited my uncle at Nkwanta.'

'Oh, I've never ever seen you there.'

'It was my first time—'

'This man is whiter than *Obroni*. He's too posh to live in such a forest - in fact, any forest.' He winked at Osam.

They all burst out laughing. Osam didn't find it funny.

'Oh yeah?' Minda responded, her eyes glued to Osam's.

'In England we all called him *Obroni*,' Abrantie said.

'Wow. Is that where you got this head wound?'

'Yes, actually. I knocked my head against a low branch. Anyway, back to the point. It was my first visit to Nkwanta.'

'I know Nkwanta. What's your uncle's name?'

'Opanin Kojo Mensah.'

'You're joking! That's my dad's best friend. I'm sure you met him, Nana...'

'I didn't stay long.'

'So, what do you think about my sister?'

'She's very nice, just like you.'

'Did you like her?'

'I like you.'

'Did you like my sister?' she pressed.

'No, we just happened to be travelling together. So, once again, I like you.'

She smiled. She must have heard that from men many times.

All six got stuck in a conversation about the three friends' European experiences and didn't notice as darkness blanketed the serene place.

Abrantie John had another surprise for them.

Around midnight, they drove to a top-end nightclub in Tema.

It was located by the sea, and from the large balcony, the seawater was a gorgeous turquoise-marine against the well-lit shore. It was one of those rare cold nights with a full moon. The full moon itself was big and yellow against the night sky; even nature indicated the greater intensity of living there. Osam's mind flashed back to his experience in the deep seas of Morocco. It just would not let him go.

'Let's get in. It's cold out here,' said Minda, clutching Osam's left arm, interrupting his mind's playback.

Richard, Abrantie John and the other two girls were about to enter the club.

It was small and packed to the brim. The latest highlife music was blasting away as clubbers danced feverishly to its rhythm. They didn't have to pay for anything as they were Abrantie John's guests. He owned the club.

John and Mercy chatted while the pairs who had just been introduced busily got to know each other.

They drank and danced. Osam had his first chance to actually touch and squeeze her lovely extra-large bum. They drank, danced and kissed again and again until they wanted more of each other.

Osam was so hot that he asked for Richard's car keys so he could make love to Minda in the semi-dark, exclusive club car park. She refused. She claimed she had already allowed Osam to go beyond the customary boundary by allowing him to touch and kiss her in public.

'You aren't in England, you know. Count yourself lucky I've allowed you to touch my expensive *asset*. You should know better!' she said matter-of-factly.

They woke up just after mid-day in each other's arms. He couldn't remember what had ensued the night before. He felt spent and lifeless. One thing was for sure: they were naked, so it was easy to read between the lines. The smell and proof of copulation were clearly evident.

He wondered how he had fared. He hadn't made love to a black girl since he met Arya, so he was curious.

Richard and Osam later drove the girls to their hall of residence at Legon.

Minda was all over him during the drive as they sat alone in the back seat.

They promised to pick them up at 9 pm that night. When they drove off, he couldn't take his eyes off her soft wriggling pelvic region as she walked girlishly and teasingly with Eve towards the campus entrance.

'Blimey! You're shagging something, man!' said Richard, who couldn't resist the temptation to look.

'I can't believe I bonked that arse! Shit!'

'You really gave it to her, man!' Richard continued.

'Why?'

'Come on, she was screaming and crying out for more, man.'

'Oh shut it!'

'You couldn't have been that drunk, Osam. We didn't sleep all night. You guys went on and on and on, I was even embarrassed. I was already tired after only one round - even though I could tell from Eve's fidgets that she wanted more.'

'Yeah, go tell that to the Marines!' Osam responded.

'I'm sure she's doubly happy now!'

'Why?'

'Well…a great shag…and money.'

'Well, you told me that was the new deal, didn't you?

'How much did you give her?'

'500,000 cedis.'

'500,000! That's about fifty pounds! Too much, Osam; she'll think you're loaded, which is the impression others have, as you well know by now. I thought you were broke.'

'I took out a loan from my uncle, so I'm OK. She even claimed it was too much and turned it down until I insisted she took it.'

'Of course, how do you expect her to behave? She had to play it that way, man.'

'How much money did you give Eve?'

'I'm *Bogga aye loose,* so I only gave her 150,000 cedis, and she was very happy. For a student, that's a lot of money.'

'She asked me this morning if I had a girlfriend.'

'Accra girls! I bet she's looking for a man. What did you tell her?'

'That I'm single of course!'

'She wouldn't mind even if you were married. You don't think she's single, do you? I'm sure she thinks you aren't telling her the truth.'

'I'm just wondering what's gonna happen when I meet Linda again. Minda and I have hit it off straight away.'

'Who's Linda?'

'Her twin sister. The girl I met when I went to Nkwanta.'

'Ah right. Wow, what a coincidence. Maybe you could pass her over to me. Is she as pretty as Minda?'

'There're identical!'

Richard beamed.

Osam and Minda saw each other during the remainder of his holidays in Accra. He wondered whether she was with him because of his money, or the fact that he lived in England. But then, who wouldn't behave that way, he thought. No one goes for the worst in life. Georgina had left him for someone better. Though Minda revealed more about herself and her family during their time together, Osam still hadn't re-met her twin sister, even though she was back in Accra.

Either Minda didn't want any competition, or Linda had something to hide. Nor was there any mention of her boyfriend; that is, if one ever existed. He wasn't in the least bothered as long as she was readily available whenever he wanted her.

Chapter 40
(*Paying Georgina a visit*)

It was mid-morning on Wednesday. They were flying back to England in two days.

Osam knocked on Richard's door. He had told Richard before retiring to bed the previous night that he would be visiting Georgina today.

'Yes, come in.'

Osam opened the door and entered the pleasant environment. Richard was lying on his king-sized bed, his arms and legs splayed out.

'Wow, you're dressed to kill. The key's on the coffee table in the lounge,' he said sleepily.

'I'm going by taxi.'

'Why would you waste money when you have a car available?'

'I don't want her to misinterpret my visit. Moreover, I don't think I can cope with the wild driving here.'

'I thought you wanted to make a point.'

'Yeah, but... I think I'd rather go in a taxi.'

'Suit yourself. Remember, we're supposed to go to Cape Coast today, and we're meeting the girls tonight as well,' Richard said as Osam turned towards the door.

'I'll be back in a couple of hours. It's only a social call, remember.'

Osam walked the 700 metres of gravel road to the junction. He hired a taxi to the airport residential area. Even though he really wanted to see her, he hadn't had time to go looking until now.

He wondered how Georgina would receive him when they saw each other again; not that he still had any feelings for her. He didn't want to create that impression; hence, his deliberate waiting to see her until just a few days before his departure to England.

He paid his fare and got out of the old taxi at his chosen stop. It was the very place where he used to meet up with Mona. He briefly inspected it as the taxi drove off. Everything remained the same. Even the small bench they used to sit on was still there.

He took a quick glance as he walked past Mona's house and continued his almost 1km journey on foot. The street looked deserted yet familiar.

The place had undergone significant change externally, but its fascinating and uniform social mix still persisted. He saw the numerous embassy flags still flapping away in the late morning sun. He had made countless trips here while dating Georgina, and later Mona.

He walked up to the recognisable light-brown, metal gate of the two-storey building, and rang the gate bell. For the first time, he was panicky. There was a long pause. He took two long deep breaths.

'Who be that?' (*Who's that?*) came a loud, Pidgin English response from behind the opaque, heavy metal gate.

'It's me, Osam,' he responded with a mixture of confidence and anticipation.

'Who?'

'Osam Mensah.'

There was a short silence, except for approaching footsteps on the familiar gravelled compound towards the gate. He waited. He was going over his memorised one-liners.

The little door of the main gate swung open. It wasn't Muri, the garden boy.

'Who you dey look for, sah?' the shabbily-dressed man said, taking a quick head-to-toe look at Osam, who was specially dressed for the occasion.

'Hello, I would like to see Georgina Thompson, please,' he responded with a curt smile.

'There's no Georgina *Tomson* here, sah,' the middle-aged man said, taking a second look at Osam's clothes; perhaps deducing now that Osam was a *Bogga*.

'OK, can I speak to Mr and Mrs Thompson, please?'

'Rong adres, *sah*…dey no coll dem so, *sah*… '

'Who's there, Adamu? What does he want?' It was the voice of a man with what sounded like a German accent.

'Mr & Mrs Thompson, sir.'

Osam looked through the small entrance and saw a ginger-haired white man in a blue bathrobe on that familiar terrace. That used to be their favourite sitting place. As a lover of flowers, Georgina adored sitting on the terrace to admire the numerous flowers of the large, front garden.

'They don't live here anymore, please go away! Adamu, have you finished watering the garden?' the man shouted at the poor middle-aged man, who smiled apologetically at Osam, and quickly shut the door of the gate.

'Do you please know their forwarding address?' Osam asked. He got no response, even though he heard footsteps. 'Please, I've just arrived from London with a very important message for them,' Osam continued, making sure he sharpened his accent to sound more English. But all he got back was the same rude and deliberate silence.

He crossed the road, hoping against hope to see the white man. But the wall and gate were too high to see within – even from that distance.

He was angry and disappointed. What had he done to deserve that churlish behaviour from a white man in his own country?

It was supposed to have been one of the highlights of his return trip, but his moment of sweet revenge had indeed ended in complete failure.

He paused briefly when he got to Mona's house on the way back. He tried to peer through the metal gate. He heard an approaching woofing on the other side. Some things hadn't changed. Osam moved on.

Richard was ready and waiting when Osam arrived in his taxi. He paid the driver and sprinted towards Richard's gate. Osam was still determined to go ahead with his planned trip. There was no excuse for him not to visit his family's hometown. Richard was particularly excited about the trip since he had never visited what used to be the old coastal and colonial capital city of the then Gold Coast, which was later renamed Ghana when it gained independence from Britain.

He allowed Osam to do the driving as he was the returning prodigal son. The festival was already in full swing in the city - doubling their journey time.

For Osam, it was almost seven years since he had last visited his family home, to say goodbye to them before leaving for Sweden.

Richard was anxious to see the city, so they decided first to have a quick drive through the centre before going to Osam's family home.

They proceeded from there to visit the infamous Cape Coast Castle. This was one of the final stops of some of the transatlantic slaves before they were shipped to the then New World. It was both sad and emotional; particularly for someone returning from the land of the white man. Though Osam had been here on many occasions, its powerful impact endured. They wept when they came out of the famous *door of no return*. Once the slaves entered that chamber, their fate was sealed.

For him, it was as if black people were created to be *disadvantaged*. Things hadn't changed much even after colonisation. The status quo remained, and the struggle for emancipation continued unabated.

From there, they went straight to Osam's grandparents on the city outskirts. Osam made Richard park his car in a semi-tarred street, three minutes' walk from the family house. Everything looked the same. The crowded old houses were still standing, as was the open stinky gutter in the middle of the alleyway that led to their home.

The house itself was old and big with a large, cemented compound. There were eight single room doors making up the U-shaped earthy structure. Apart from his grandparents' room, which happened to be the first one in line on the left-hand side, all the zinc roofs were archaic and rusty - resulting from many years of lashing by the winds blowing from the ocean, only three hundred metres away. The large entrance was open and without a gate, which was typical of the surrounding houses.

The old, dripping water tap in the middle of the compound was flanked by an even older, sealed and disused water well. Osam still remembered playfully running around the well with his late cousins during the whole family's rare trips there for holidays. There was no tap then, but the well faithfully served the whole house. Everything about the place looked strangely familiar to Osam.

There were no adults, only nine adolescents playing in the compound.

'Bugger!' Osam whispered, but loud enough for the children to hear. They didn't need to understand the expression as his body language said it all.

They were a couple of hours late! Their surprise hadn't worked, after all. Osam's grandparents had left that very morning to visit Uncle Kojo at Nkwanta. Osam knew they had had no idea that he was back in Ghana. It looked as if he wasn't going to see them before he returned to England as they were going to be away for the next two weeks.

Osam and Richard inspected the house for fifteen minutes with the few family members who were at home. They even had a look at the little wood at the back of the house where as kids they used to play hide-and-seek in the evenings and looked for snails at night during the rainy season.

A middle-aged lady whom Osam knew entered the large compound.

'Eh, Osam! When did you arrive?' she half-shouted, re-arranging her head scarf as she approached. She curtsied as she offered them her right hand in turn, a typical courteous traditional greeting. She was a part of Osam's extended family.

'Well, here, I'd say roughly twenty minutes ago, but from England about twenty days ago, but I've been staying in Accra.'

'Oh, so you missed your grandparents.'

'Yes, I've just been told.'

'How long are you going to stay?'

'You mean in Ghana before I return to England?'

'No, I mean here in Cape Coast?'

'Well, we had planned to stay the whole day, but as they're not here, I think we'll return.'

'They've never stopped talking about you. Will you come back to see them before you return to England?'

'No, I'm going back soon.'

She had returned from the market to pick up some more plantain to replenish her diminishing stock.

Osam reached into his small carrier bag and brought out some high-value notes tied together with a cotton cord. 'Can I leave this with you for them?'

'Yes, I'll give it to them when they return. How much is that, please?'

'Two million cedis. Please count them to confirm.'

'No, I believe you, Osam,' she said, smiling non-stop now. All the children rushed closer on seeing the money change hands.

'This is for you,' Osam said as he handed her a wad of notes.

'Oh, thank you o!' she replied in typical Ghanaian style as she tucked it beneath the old textile wrapped around her waist.

'And this is for all these and other kids of this house,' Osam said, handing her another wad of notes.

'Oh, they thank you, o! Hey, children, say thank you to Uncle.'

'Thank you!' came the sweet chorus.

Osam and Richard retraced their steps to the parked car. Some of the kids followed and waved them off, Richard driving this time around.

They stopped at the cemetery. Richard waited in the car as Osam went to pay his respects to his late family.

It was brief but poignant and heart-rending. But it was also an act of liberation.

Chapter 41
(*The return to England*)

Highlife music was playing at full blast in Richard's living room. Osam was sad because he was leaving.

But it was also a moment of great joy. Abena, Osam's new cousin, was born just after he had left Nkwanta. Uncle Kojo wanted it as a goodbye surprise, so he had waited to reveal the news until he arrived yesterday.

Richard's home was filled with his and Osam's close family members. Osam paid for his uncle and his two cousins to stay in a guest house only a ten minutes' drive away.

'Your grandparents will be very grateful for their present. And so will your late father and mother.'

'It's amazing and heartbreaking the way I missed out on seeing them.'

'They'll be disappointed, too. But that's life, my son; there's a reason for every occurrence. I'm sure you'll see your grandparents the next time you come home.'

'Which may be sooner than you think,' Osam chipped in.

'Hallelujah!' Uncle Kojo exclaimed as he handed the land registration documents to Osam. 'A wife will be waiting for you by the time you arrive.'

They all laughed.

Minda and Osam had spent their last night together – and so had Richard and Eve. Both girls had left early together for the city centre to get some presents for their respective departing partners.

Osam had returned to Ghana with a fear of alienation, but he was leaving in a blaze of glory. Most of his friends, including those he hadn't seen, were at the airport to see him and Richard off.

Osam's luggage was much lighter than on his arrival. His friends and cousins had snapped up his clothes. He wasn't alone, as Richard had also suffered a similar fate, but he was used to it. He understood the unwritten rule that the clothes you brought to these shores remained here; the unprivileged also had to share in the spoils of your labour.

Minda and Eve were already at the airport when Osam and Richard and their entourage arrived. The two girls weren't alone this time. Linda was also present, wearing the same red dress as Minda. Osam waved at them as the three girls approached. He couldn't make out any distinctive difference between the twins.

'Hey, *Atta Kakra* and *Panin*! How are you, my children? I was talking to your dad a few days ago and he told me you had visited them recently,' Uncle Kojo yelled as they joined the three girls.

One thing was plain to Osam though; the two girls were not as noisy in public as they were in bed.

'Yes, uncle, we're fine.'

Osam exchanged smiles with them behind Uncle Kojo's back.
'This is my son, and we've come to see him off. He's returning to England. Let me introduce you—'
'We're here because of him,' they said simultaneously, resulting in a fit of laughter for the momentary coincidence.
'Oh, you've already met?'
'Yes, Uncle. I travelled with Linda on the same truck when I visited you. Remember I told you I met a nice lady—'
'Oooh yes, I remember now. But that was all you said. Their dad is our town's chief, and he's my friend,' he said with a

336

satisfied smile. 'She's going to be your future wife!' Uncle Kojo whispered into Osam's right ear.

Osam grinned amiably.

Osam's two cousins began chatting with Linda and Minda as Osam and Richard left their respective families and friends to check-in.

He was in pensive mood. He still hadn't had the chance to talk to Linda about what really happened on his fateful trip to Nkwanta. It was still an unresolved puzzle.

'You've hardly said anything to her,' Richard said as they approached the check-in desk.

'Who?'

'Minda's sister.'

'I don't want to give my uncle the wrong idea. It's kind of strange meeting her again, though.'

'Why, you like her too?'

'No, no, it's not that. What about you, are you still interested?'

'Sure, I wouldn't mind preparing the ground for the next time I'm around.' He rubbed his hands in glee.

'The problem is I don't know which of the two my uncle said was going to be my future wife.'

As they returned from the check-in desk, Osam looked towards their small party among the multitude waiting outside in Accra's late evening cool humid breeze. It was time to say goodbye. Osam had never thought the day would come when he would be the one in the privileged position of being waved goodbye to by several hands simultaneously.

Chapter 42

It had been a long eight-hour return flight, yet Osam was looking forward to unveiling to Arya his decision to return home to Ghana for good. He had bought some souvenirs like *Kente* cloths, scarves and dresses, traditional earrings, necklaces, and bracelets for her. He had bought nothing for himself due to his intention to return to Ghana.

As their British Airways plane taxied along the tarmac, he had vivid memories of his first landing here with his friends on their way to Sweden. He had never envisaged his life would turn out this way. He hoped Mac and Andrew were all right, wherever they were. The last time he saw them was when he waved goodbye to them from his platform as both groups waited for their trains to take them to their respective territories. They had been in great spirits with high hopes.

'Time to go, Osam,' Richard interrupted.

'Yeah, sure.'

'As I told you before we left, there's nothing to worry about. You're legal now,' he whispered as they joined the queue in the gangway. Osam had been anxious that he might not be able to re-enter, even with his legal status.

He studied his fellow passengers on the fully-laden aircraft, most of whom had their landing cards in their passports, to see if he could read any signs of trepidation, particularly for those landing here for the first time. He sincerely hoped no one would be sent back.

The contrast couldn't have been clearer; even though it was still late August, the autumnal rains had already begun in earnest in England. The country was cold, grey, damp and windy. That's the way he spelt England.

Osam was missing home already. He had lost the desire of living again in England. He wasn't looking forward to going back to work the following day.

Arya was waiting at the arrival lounge of Heathrow Airport's terminal four as they emerged from the immigration clearance lobby. She was still feeling sleepy; they had landed at 5:30 am. Osam thought she looked both beautiful and *un-African* as he caught a glimpse of her amidst the waiting crowd of mainly blacks. Her bright eyes lit up her face. She seemed to float as she ran with abandon towards him and threw herself into his arms.

Osam had hardly come to terms with the surprise welcome when for the first time in about a year Arya planted her lips on his and they kissed passionately. He couldn't believe the ease and naturalness of it. Richard, standing five metres away, looked on in suppressed astonishment. Osam saw her smiling at Richard as she disentangled herself from his embrace.

'Come on, give us a hug.' She stretched out her arms and embraced Richard too. 'So, how was it?'

'What, the kiss?' Osam replied jokingly.

'No, silly boy; I mean the trip,' she said with a smile.

'Fantastic! Absolutely fantastic!!'

'I can see cuz you look much darker now. I'm sure you've been sunbathing with the exotic Ghanaian girls.'

'Don't be silly!'

'Go on then, tell me. How were your uncle and the rest of the family, your friends? I'm excited to know. Ah, and the lost bank cards have been sorted out.'

'Oh, that's a great relief! Thanks. Long story, will tell you when we get home.'

They dropped Richard at his flat and continued to their house.

Arya had booked a table for just the two of them at La Italiana, a very popular Italian restaurant in Reading. But it was to be a waste as they went straight for each other as soon as they entered the flat.

It was as if they had been looking forward to making love so much that it was all over in minutes, rather than what they were used to when they lived together, which seemed like a long time ago.

As they lay in each other's arms in consummated exhaustion, he wondered whether this meant they were back together again.

The following day, Osam rang Richard from work to tell him what had happened between him and Arya.

'Have you told her what happened?' he asked in a flat voice.

'Happened where?'

'I mean in Ghana.'

Osam lied. 'Yes, except about Linda, of course.'

'Well, that's obvious. What about your decision to return home?'

'Not yet. I didn't have the stomach to tell her so soon.'

'I'm afraid you'll have to tell her sooner rather than later. Don't forget we've got less than three months to go.'

'Yeah, you're right. I haven't even thought about that,' he replied, as he resumed biting his lower lip.

'I don't want you to feel pressurised or anything. At the end of the day, it's your life and you have the final word,' Richard said, with a hint of despair in his flat voice, as if he was getting tired of Osam's indecisiveness.

'Will you let me take care of this? It's between Arya and me. I´ll let her know when the time is right, OK?'

'All right…all right…didn't mean to interfere—'

Osam hung up.

Later that afternoon, Osam became worried when Bill, the executive director of the organisation, rang him for a word in his office upstairs. He wondered if it had anything to do with the conversation he had overheard in the loo before he left for Ghana. Surprisingly, neither Andrew, who was leaving the organisation in three days nor he, had said a word about the incident.

He passed Andrew's office, hoping to tell him about it – in case he had anything to say before he saw Bill. His office was empty. He thought he must be busy saying goodbyes to the staff.

Bill's secretary was on the phone when he entered her large office. She stopped talking, covered the mouthpiece, and motioned him into Bill's office.

His heart was pounding as he entered the large, elegant office. He nearly choked on his chewing gum when he saw Andrew and George standing there. He had forgotten to spit it out.

They looked up as he entered noiselessly and hesitantly. As if Osam had interrupted a gossip session, George immediately left without saying a word.

'Hello Osam,' said Bill, with a mild smile on his thin lips. Andrew stood in a relaxed mood and winked.

True to his supposition, it did have something to do with that conversation. Osam was offered the job of Management Accountant on a strong recommendation from Andrew. The executive board were just waiting for his '*yes*' before they could make it official.

'Yes,' he found himself saying, still mystified.

'Congratulations, Osam,' Bill said, with a broader smile this time as they shook hands.

'Well done, Osam. You deserve it,' Andrew finally said with another wink of his left eye.

'In the next couple of days, you should receive a formal contract to that effect. Andrew will be working with you in the few days he has left. He said you didn't need much training, which was a big plus in our final decision. One issue that isn't resolved yet is the fact that you aren't a permanent UK resident.'

'I'll apply for it in the next couple of days, sir.'

'Yeah, I've been assured by HR that it can be easily cleared up. So, once again, accept my congratulations and good luck in your new position. As company policy, there's a three-month probationary period.'

'Thanks.'

He left the office. He would later learn that George had only popped in to hand over some financial documents. Whatever had happened in the loo, in Andrew's opinion, was something for Osam and George to resolve among themselves.

For almost fifteen minutes, Osam sat in his locked office tearing up, holding his head in both hands, and staring down at his desk in absolute disbelief. For the first time in his life, he not only felt that he had over-achieved but also had the blessings of the gods. This was the biggest responsibility he would have to shoulder. His heart was a mixture of suppressed joy and trepidation. He couldn't believe the extent to which they were still prepared to take a chance on him in spite of the fact that he wasn't a UK resident.

Two days later, Arya was due to return to Stockholm the following day.

The sale of their house had come to a speedy conclusion. Things had happened so fast they were planning to move their possessions into a temporary storage facility at a warehouse in Reading. They still had a week to hand over the house keys to its new owners. Arya wanted them to organise an auction to get rid of cumbersome items. Osam wasn't sure.

'Do you realise you still haven't told me anything about your trip to Ghana?' Arya said as they sat on the sofa watching *EastEnders*.

'I'm not surprised. It's been a crazy time at work with all the stress involved in the handover.'

Andrew was leaving the following day, and they were due to go for a meal together. He had been so good to Osam, and Osam wanted to express his heartfelt appreciation to him.

Arya had been particularly happy for him in his newly-elevated position. He still hadn't had the nerve to tell Richard. He was in two minds as to what to do.

He realised it was an opportunity, though, whether right or otherwise, to tell Arya his story, so he told her all that had happened while he was away in Ghana - except his unfaithfulness, and his decision to return home.

'Yeah, I know. Richard said the two of you are going back home to start a business venture.'

That appeared out of the blue. He would *kill* Richard for that!

'W-W-Why did y-y-you choose to ask Richard, instead?'

'Well, it's been two days since you arrived, Osam.'

'And I was just on the verge of telling you when you interrupted.' He dashed into the bedroom and returned with copies of the land registry certificate he had brought from Accra. He felt that was the best proof that he was telling her the truth.

To his surprise, it went down easily. She seemed to have taken it so well.

'I could see it coming, Osam. I just had the hunch something happened when you told me nothing for two days.'

'So you decided the best person to talk to was Richard.'

'If you wanted me to know, you would've told me.'

'Well, that wasn't the rationale behind it. As you know, I've been so busy since I arrived. It just escaped me.'

'So, have you told your employers yet?'

'No. I felt I had to tell you first.'

'But you've just been promoted at work, Osam. You have a dream job now. That's what you always wanted, didn't you? You mean you are gonna just let go of it after so much hard work? What are you going to tell them now that everything's been made official?'

'Only Heaven knows, Arya, only heaven knows!' he responded with a hint of desperation in his usually low-pitched voice.

'Well, that's not good enough, Osam, it's just not good enough! You better start taking yourself seriously. You are a Management Accountant in a big organisation so that flimsy answer is just not good enough.'

'I'm sorry.'

'Does Richard know about your recent promotion at work?' Osam shook his head.

'Why? You know I almost brought it up? I thought he already knew. Are you flip-flopping about your planned return, or what?'

'No…Yes…Yes, I think so…ehmm…I don't know, Arya. You think it's easy to make a quick decision, huh? My uncle will kill me if I go back on my promise. And Richard. Everything's happening so quickly that I can hardly keep up, let alone make decisions. I'm stuck, stuck in the mud!' Osam said, getting angry that she was asking the right questions. She certainly knew how to give him a lot to think about.

'Well, you better start thinking fast, Osam. If you really mean what you've just told me then, you don't have time to play around with people. There are three parties involved here, you know.'

'I'll tell Richard tomorrow.'

'And work?'

'Tomorrow! Are you happy now? You're acting as if you want me out of here instantly.'

'I beg your pardon? Who's making decisions here? Or, who's actually made decisions here? Don't you try to hide from your own responsibilities and decisions, Osam. Remember, you're only telling me a day before I leave for Stockholm. I'm sure you wouldn't have told me if I hadn't pressed you to tell me what had happened in Ghana,' she said with a raised voiced.

'That's not fair, Arya. You know that's not true!'

'Yeah? And how many times have your silly lies nearly ruined our relationship? I could have walked right out on you then. It's always been me who's had to work hard to save our relationship. You kept saying you loved me, but ended up with Amelia!'

A heavy silence followed. For a long while, they sat almost motionless in their respective seats…tongue-tied. Osam was thinking about the consequences of what Arya had said.

'And what is gonna happen to all this stuff?' she asked, breaking the pronounced silence.

'Well, what do you think?'

'I don't know, Osam. You don't seem to want to go along with our home contents auction. I don't know what to think now.'

'Look, I'm not even bothered about that, Arya. To tell you the truth, the only thing that concerns me now is *us*. What's gonna happen to—'

'Well, you should have thought about that before making that decision. There is no *us*, Osam, there is no *us* anymore!'

'What about—'

'It was a mistake, Osam, We shouldn't have slept together, and you know that. Let's just say it never happened, all right?' She began weeping.

He slowly got up, walked to her seat, and cautiously hugged her. He still really loved her. But he knew he had played his cards poorly – even with all the aces he possessed. He wondered whether he had lost her - this time for good.

Chapter 43
(*Three months later – Leaving England*)

It had been a tough and a heartbreaking couple of months for Osam.

Tough, because he was leaving his dream job, something he had fought very hard for. His colleagues were sad to see him go. Even George had signed the company's send-off card. Luckily for Osam, the management was very understanding when he explained the reasons for his untimely resignation

Heart-breaking, because finally, not only was he leaving England after an almost eight-and-a-half-year stay, but Arya and he sadly agreed to end their relationship once and for all. The equity, on the insistence of Arya, equally shared. In the end, he bought out Arya's part of their home contents and opted to ship them to Ghana together with Richard's belongings. He was now temporarily renting a double room in a house near the town centre. He handed over the company car on his last day at work, so was back to using his BMW, which he was also going to ship home.

In spite of all the struggles of living in a *White man's* country, in some ways, the country had been good to him. He was returning home a better-educated and experienced person. And whether that would be enough only time would tell. He was also returning with a good financial base, due mostly to their property sale. He had enough money to last six months without having to work.

His solicitor encouraged him to wait until he had his permanent residence before leaving. He was not prepared to wait for another three years for that to go through, as it would serve as an easy way out if things went wrong when he returned to Ghana. He was prepared to burn his boats and leave with a focused and determined attitude to succeed.

Eventually, he had to leave two weeks earlier than Richard due to the sudden hospitalisation of Uncle Kojo in Accra. He had been taken ill during his recent trip to complete the land registration of Osam's grandparents' lands in Cape Coast, and to amend his will with his solicitor. Although Kuku had assured Osam that his condition wasn't serious, Osam succeeded in bringing forward his flight. He was thus expecting both of them, as well as Asante and Daddy Koo--Richard's cousins--to be at the airport to welcome him.
As he was leaving earlier than originally planned, he left in Richard's care the shipping of his personal belongings. They had agreed that Richard should hire a container to carry both their belongings.

Inside the airport terminal, Osam was pleasantly surprised to find fifteen members of the Reading Ghana Association to see him off. Apart from members of the executive, he was particularly astounded at the presence of other members. He had rarely been involved in the club's activities or attended meetings regularly, even though he was a paying member.
'It's nice to see you all,' Osam said as he shook hands with them.
'Have a safe trip,' said one.
'Regards to everyone in Ghana,' said another.
'I'll try,' Osam said complacently.
'I wish I were in your shoes,' said John, one of the recently-arrived channel tunnel stowaways.
'You miss home already?'

He nodded multiple times. He missed his wife and two young kids in Ghana. Unfortunately, he wasn't ready yet to make the return trip.

Osam thanked them - this time embracing all of them in turn, as the endless showers of best wishes filled the still Sunday afternoon air. They had played their part perfectly in this chapter of his life, but it was time for all of them to abandon the script. He wondered if he would ever see any of them again. His whole being was welling with emotion.

When the Association members left, Richard, Arya and he went up the flight of stairs to a restaurant for coffee. As usual, Charlie had not kept his word to be at the airport to see Osam off.

Richard consumed his drink rather quickly, and, perhaps sensing that Osam and Arya needed to be together alone, asked permission to leave. Osam and Richard embraced each other warmly, and Richard left them still seated at the restaurant table. Osam moved his seat round the small table closer to hers, their bodies touching.

'So, how are you getting back to Reading, now that Richard's left?'

'Ehmm...don't worry, I'll take the Railairlink coach,' she replied, shifting in her seat.

'Are you all right?' Osam asked, noticing her melancholic mood. She seemed deep in thought about something. He put his left arm around her thin shoulders and squeezed, pressing her against his side.

'I'm fine, Osam,' she replied, softly.

Osam and Arya talked at length until his mid-afternoon flight was called, ready for boarding. They chose to descend using the stairs again, instead of the lift. At the foot of the stairs, she handed Osam her M&S carrier bag while she went to the bathroom.

349

Osam dashed into the terminal's Boots shop and bought a Mars bar, her favourite, with the change he still had in his white jeans right back pocket. He removed a folded piece of paper from his left back pocket and quickly scanned his note:

My Darling Arya!
This poem, which I wrote for you last night, may reach you when I'm already airborne.
England was always a transit, whether I liked it or not.
Then I met you…
Through it all, I've always tried but failed to reach your untainted heart.
Life's about dealing with the effects of the good and the demons that it continually throws at us. I have always struggled with that precarious balancing act.
My last-ditch attempt last night at our romantic candlelit dinner failed miserably too.
I hope this will fare better.
Always…
Osam

Waiting game

Lying back in space in the starless night
Waiting patiently for my dearest one
She's gone for a while – what a lonely night!
Making me, my soul quiver with dread

Suddenly appeared in the distance a bird
Flying with rage in the chilly night
Seeking out, reaching out with a whistling tone
Calling out, crying out in the shivery night

Oh my, how I wish that I could fly
Fly high across the starless night
Like the bird seeking what I do not know
But for me, to be with my Daisy girl

Girl, oh girl, Daisy girl, how I miss you so
So much, most and sweetest of all
All night, all day – how long may I wait?
But love, oh love…that will not let go!

He looked towards the toilets, but she was still inside. He hurriedly wrapped it around the Mars bar with the aid of an elastic band. He placed it in her bag.

She returned in a little while. Osam handed her back the bag. She took it with only a wan smile.

They walked hand in hand like young lovers in absolute silence until they reached the entrance to the departure lounge. 'That's it, then,' he uttered, full of agony. They faced each other, warmly embraced and kissed. They repeated the whole action again - tighter and at length.

'You know I still and will always love you, Osam. Never forget that!' she said quietly. Her voice quivered with emotion, spearing his heart.

'Why haven't you said so? Come with me, Arya,' he said in desperation as her words sank deeper into his heart, reflecting the same feeling he had for her.

'No, Osam,' she whispered, still lost in his embrace. 'This is my home. I was born here – in Europe. I can't follow you just like that. I know very little about Africa…about Ghana. I have responsibilities here; my mum, the family business…you've made the right choice…your family needs you. You know what I mean?' She sobbed as she said those sweet but hard-to-take words. He always found it hard to express his affection in public, but for once Osam was oblivious to his surroundings.

She released herself from his embrace, gave him a peck on his left cheek, and disappeared among the large airport crowd. His eyes followed her. He realised there and then that he was doing exactly the same thing Arya had done when she decided suddenly to return home to Stockholm to be by her dying dad's side. He had never forgiven her for that. He wanted to go after Arya, but his legs felt like lead.

Though he hated to admit it, she was right. He was a prodigal son. He had to return to do his small bit for his family and country.

Accra was still shielded from the afternoon sun by the darkened rain clouds. It had been raining all day, yet life in the capital was hardly affected.

Uncle Kojo was lying on his hospital bed. He momentarily closed his eyes, opened them again, this time wide, and then shut them. His two sons who sat flanking him were telling him about the arrangements for Osam's imminent arrival. Uncle Kojo had given up the ghost. The two boys, unaware, continued talking.

It was mid-afternoon, yet England was already covered by late autumn's gloomy sky. Osam could see, through his misty aircraft window, lights beaming in the far distance. However, he couldn't tell which of the gradually fading lights were of his beloved Reading.
He would miss England; the unpredictable weather, multiculturalism, fish and chips, the rugby, the football, *Match Of The Day* TV programme, and most importantly, his *endless love*, Arya!
His heart was in shreds.
As he sat reflecting in his seat on the nearly-airborne British Airways aircraft, he remembered a song he learned as a ten-year-old boy at Sunday school:

Going home, going home
I am going home
Quiet like, some still day
I am going home

It's not far, just close by
Through an open door
Work all done, care laid by
Never fear no more

Mother's there expecting me
Father's waiting too
Lots of faces gathered there
All the friends I knew

I'm just going home

No more fear, no more pain
No more stumbling by the way
No more longing for the day
Going to run no more

Morning star light the way
Restless dreams all gone
Shadows gone, break of day
Real life has begun

There's no break, there's no end
Just living on
Wide awake, with a smile
Going on and on, going on and on

Going home, going home
I am going home
Shadows gone, break of day
Real life has begun

I'm just going home

He wasn't religious, yet tears filled his thick-lashed eyes as the song replayed in his mind.
But though the tears momentarily clouded his vision, his mind was as clear as daylight: he was truly going home.

A Glossary of Words and Phrases in alphabetical order

*

When a child is born, particularly among the Akan ethnic group of Ghana, it is named according to the day on which the birth took place.

Day	Twi	Male	Female
Sunday	Kwesiada	(A)Kwesi	Esi
Monday	Dwoada	Kwadwo	Adwoa
Tuesday	Benada	Kwabena	Abenaa
Wednesday	Wukuada	Kwaku	Akua
Thursday	Yawoada	Yaw	Yaa
Friday	Efiada	Kofi	Afua
Saturday	Memeneda	Kwame	Amma

Abrantie: The Akan name for a gentleman or guy

Agoo: *Knock – knock!* In Akan

Amee: *Come in / Enter* in Akan

Atta Kakra: The Fanti name given to the younger of twins

Atta Panyin: The Fanti name given to the older of twins

Akwaaba: The Akan word for *Hello*

Akwesi: Is the same as Kwesi, the name of a male born on Sunday

Akwesi meduru o: An Akan expression meaning I've landed or arrived, Akwesi

Ashanti/Asante: People from the Ashanti region of Ghana. Kumasi, which is Ghana's second important city, is its capital

Banku: A Ghanaian dish prepared from a combination of maize and cassava flour

Bogga: Pronounced *bogga*. Ghanaian word for someone who lives/has lived in the West

Bogga aye loose/mbre: An expression used for returnees who have run out of money

Bone shaker: A locally-made vehicle with a wooden carriage that is used for public transport

Cape Coast: The capital city of the Central region of Ghana; the former European colonial capital

Cedi: The currency of Ghana

CFA franc: CFA Franc is the currency used in fourteen countries: twelve formerly French-ruled African countries, as well as in Guinea-Bissau (a former Portuguese colony) and in Equatorial Guinea (a former Spanish colony)

CIMA: Chartered Institute of Management Accountants

Common Entrance Examination: The examination sat at the end of the six-year primary school education that enabled pupils to enter the secondary school

Connection man: These are middlemen or intermediaries who for a fee help you get things done quickly

Fanti/Fante: People of the southern coast of Ghana between Accra and Sekondi-Takoradi. They speak a dialect of Akan

Fair-complexioned skin: Ghanaians, particularly women, associate being light-skinned with affluence and beauty

Fetu Afahye: The festival of the Fantis who live in Cape Coast in the Central Region of Ghana

Fufu: West African dish of boiled and ground plantain, yam, or cassava, eaten with soups

Ga: One of the dialects spoken by the natives of Accra, a member of the Ga-Adangbe ethnic group

GBC: Ghana Broadcasting Corporation

GCE O Level: Also known as Ordinary level, the examination sat at the end of the old five-year secondary school education system that enabled students to enter the sixth form

GCE A Level: Also known as Advanced level, the university entrance examination sat at the end of the old two-year sixth form education system

Harmattan: Is a seasonal cold, dry wind which blows across Western Africa every year from November through March

Hej: *Hello* in Swedish

Hejdo: *Goodbye* in Swedish

Highlife: The style of music and dance from Ghana

Home Office: The Ministry of Interior, which is also in charge of immigration in the UK

Homowo: The annual festival of the Ga ethnic group of the Greater Accra region, which is also the Capital city of Ghana

Iced water: Chilled water measured and sold to the general public in plastic or metal cups

Jollof rice: A mix of cooked rice, tomatoes and tomato paste, onion, salt, and chillies, to which optional ingredients such as vegetables, meats, and other spices can be added

Juju: An object used in magic in West Africa, or a type of magic in West Africa

Kenkey: A Ghanaian dish made with fermented corn and cassava dough, wrapped in corn or banana leaves

Kente Cloth: A silk cloth made in Ghana by sewing together long narrow hand-woven strips

Korle-Bu Hospital: The premier health care facility in Ghana. It is the only tertiary hospital in the southern part of Ghana. It is a teaching hospital affiliated with the medical school of the University of Ghana

Kpekple/Kpokpoi: A special meal prepared and eaten during the Homowo festival

Kwame Nkrumah: Ghana's first post-colonial prime minister

Market day: The busiest day of the market week

Middle School Education: The old four-year post-primary school education system. It has since been replaced by a six-year secondary school education system

MOC: Marriage of convenience

M&S: Marks and Spencer

Nana: Name given to a leader or ruler of people or a community among the Akan ethnic group

Nkatenkwan: Soup made from peanut butter

Nkwanta: The Akan word for a junction

Obroni: The Akan word for a White person or White man

Obroni waawu: The Akan word for second-hand clothes. Literally, it means clothes of a dead white person

WAEC: West Africa Examination Council, the official examination board

Okra stew: Stew made with Okra, a tropical vegetable, that is eaten with Banku and some other Ghanaian dishes

Omo tuo: Cooked rice mashed into round forms

Opanyin: The Akan word for *elder*, a title normally used to address someone of advanced years, and also as a sign of respect for an important person

Osibisa: A Ghanaian Afro-pop band, founded in London in 1969 by four expatriate African and three Caribbean musicians

Osofo Dadzie: A Sunday night television drama

Paano hyew: Hot bread. One of many sales cries used by bread sellers

Sah: Ghanaian Pidgin English (also known as Kru English) for *Sir*

Swedish Krona: The currency of Sweden

Svenska: Swedish

Thursday Theatre: A Thursday night television drama

Trotro: These are locally-made vehicles with wooden carriage or wagons that serve as cheaper public transport. Minivans are sometimes converted for that purpose as well

Twi: One of the dialects spoken by the Akan ethnic group, who form about 47% of the Ghanaian population

Yokozuna: The highest rank in professional sumo wrestling in Japan